MW01092536

A SLIGHT PROBLEM
WITH THE

MEARA PLATT

Copyright © 2025 Myra Platt
Print Edition

Cover Design by Dar Albert

This is a work of fiction. Names, characters, places, brands, media, and incidents are either the product of the author's imagination or are used fictitiously. Any resemblance to similarly named places or to persons living or deceased is unintentional.

Without in any way limiting the author's and publisher's exclusive rights under copyright, any use of this publication to "train" generative artificial intelligence (AI) technologies to generate text is expressly prohibited. The author reserves all rights to license uses of this work for generative AI training and development of machine learning language models.

CHAPTER 1

London, England
October 1826

LORD JULIUS THORNE felt a prickle run up his spine the moment he stepped into his elegant bedchamber in the Huntsford townhouse sometime after three o'clock in the morning. He was foxed, but not so deep in his cups that he could not sense something was amiss in here. It was dark...unusually dark, even for this late hour. "Who's there?"

Someone must have closed the drapes all the way so as not allow the smallest trickle of dawn's light to steal in. Whoever that someone was, he was still in here. Julius could feel the intruder's presence in the thickness of the air.

He slowly reached into the lip of his boot to grab his pistol, but had yet to withdraw it when a soft feminine voice called to him from behind those drawn curtains. "Julius?"

His heart shot into his throat upon recognizing who had called to him. "Gory?"

Was he more foxed than he realized?

There was no chance Lady Gregoria Easton, better known as Gory to her friends, would ever be in his bedchamber. Especially not now that she had caught herself a viscount and would be married by this time next week.

He did not like to think of her married to that pompous clot, Chandler Allendale. The man was completely wrong for her, but what right did he have to judge when he had never let on about his feelings for her?

Now, he feared it was too late. "Gory, I'm drunk. Am I imagining you?"

"No, Julius. It's really me," she said, little more than a slender shadow stepping out from behind her hiding spot. Her voice was so thin and shaky, he'd never heard her sound like this before. "I did not know where else to turn."

"So you came to me?" He hurriedly lit a lamp before rushing to her side.

That he was drunk and lovesick did not help the situation. Nor had his foolish agreement to escort Gory around London all week long because her betrothed was too busy to attend to it helped in the least, either. It was hopeless to believe spending more time in each other's company might rid him of his feelings for Gory.

He was wrong.

She was stubborn, opinionated, independent, and infuriating in many ways. But she was also brilliant, warm and witty, and relentlessly determined to become the greatest forensic specialist in all of London. What other young lady would rather spend more time examining dead things than going to balls, musicales, and fashionable dinner parties?

Her quirky traits and stubborn disposition ought to have cured him of these unwanted feelings he had for her.

His stupid ploy had failed.

He was falling more deeply in love with her than ever.

He held the lamp up for a better view, and his heart immediately surged into his throat. "Dear heaven! What happened to you?"

She was wearing her wedding gown, a soft, pearl silk that he had seen when taking her to the fashionable modiste for a final fitting only yesterday. Not that he had wanted anything to do with enabling her to marry that dimwit viscount, Allendale. But she had needed a ride and he, like the clot he was, had volunteered to assist her as she went on this wedding errand.

He blinked.

And blinked again.

The blood splattered all over her gown was still there.

It wasn't a drunken delusion.

Crimson trails of it had seeped into the delicate silk, and dried splotches of crimson red stained her hands. "Never mind. You'll tell me later," he said gently, realizing she must be in shock when she did not immediately respond to his question. "Let me check you for injuries first."

He set the lamp on a nearby table, and then ran his hands along her body with aching care.

Once. Twice.

He was not surprised by the soft allure of her curves, for he'd gotten a good look at her yesterday, accidentally walking into the modiste's fitting room while she was still undressed. Why had the modiste's helper told him Gory was finished and needed assistance with her packages when she was still in there, standing in her chemise of sheerest fabric that hid nothing from his view?

Even though her back had been turned to him, there were several large mirrors in the room, so that in addition to her sweetly curved backside that was pointed at him as she bent slightly to retrieve something out of her reticule, he could make out her nicely shaped breasts in the mirror's reflection. Those ample mounds that were about to spill out of the bodice could fill the cup of his hand. He refused to dwell on what else he saw, but it was not an exaggeration to admit he would pay a king's ransom to explore her body.

He would have been sent straight to hell had he acted upon the possibilities then and there.

Instead, he had backed away before she noticed him.

But the sight of her delectable attributes was seared into his eyeballs as well as in his heart.

Gory always hid her charming figure beneath the most hideous clothes. Who knew she had the body of an angel beneath all those layers of dark muslin? Well, he had always suspected it because she was a very pretty girl.

He liked everything about her and should have said something when Allendale began to court her.

But he didn't.

By the time he realized his mistake, it was too late. Gory, the wonderfully eccentric, brilliant bluestocking who studied dead things, and was one of the foremost scholars on matters related to medical science and its advancements, was now betrothed to Viscount Allendale.

They had made the announcement three months ago.

The wedding was to take place next week.

He and his brothers had been invited, of course.

His brothers were married to Gory's best friends, Adela and Syd. The wedding reception was to be held right here at the Huntsford townhouse immediately following the ceremony. His brother, Ambrose, Duke of Huntsford, had insisted upon it when Gory's uncle cheapened out.

Her uncle was an unmitigated arse.

Had Gory accepted Allendale in order to escape the untenable situation in her own home? Julius had known she was unhappy there and ought to have done something about it, proposing to her himself.

He quickly shook off thoughts of Gory's wedding, an event he was now determined to stop if Gory gave him the slightest hint she might reciprocate his feelings. But none of it mattered now, for she was in a desperate way and trembling.

Gory never trembled.

She was afraid of nothing.

"Tell me what happened," he said, taking her cold hands into his warm ones, and having her sit in one of the cushioned chairs beside his hearth. "Let me fetch the ewer and basin. I need to clean you off while we speak. Gory, I cannot find any wounds on you. Have I missed something?"

Blessed saints, his hands had skimmed over every luscious curve and found nothing obvious.

"I don't know. I feel dizzy," she said.

He frowned. "Perhaps you were hit on the head. Hold still while I take a look at your scalp."

She pushed his hand away. "No."

"Gory, I need to–"

She pushed his hand away again. "No!"

He sighed. "All right. Maybe later. How did you get all this blood on you? Where have you been? Was someone else hurt?"

He stopped, for he was throwing too many questions at her all at once.

When she shivered again, he realized he ought to get something warm and liquid into her. But it was the middle of the night, too early for the Huntsford scullery maids to be stirring yet. In any event, he did not think it wise to alert anyone else to her presence, not until he got more information out of her.

Since he kept a bottle of brandy in his bedchamber to enjoy a glass while he read beside the fire, he now retrieved it and poured a little into a glass for Gory. "Drink," he gently coaxed, worried that she looked so pale and vulnerable.

"All right." But she handed the glass back to him after managing only a few sips. "Tastes vile, you know."

He cast her an achingly tender smile. "I know. It is an acquired taste."

The sky had been threatening rain all night and Julius now heard the first droplets striking against his window panes with sharp *pock-pocks*. He grabbed a fresh cloth from his dressing room table and dampened it in the water he had just poured from the ewer into the basin.

By the soft amber glow of the lamp, he rinsed her hands, and then washed the dabs of blood off her cheeks and off a few tendrils of hair that framed her heart-shaped face. The pins had loosened from her hair and all those glorious chestnut tresses were about to spill onto her shoulders. After cleaning her face and neck, and wiping a few droplets of blood off the swell of one breast, he took the pins out and attempted to smooth back her hair. "No," she said and stopped him.

"All right." He would try again in a moment, for he had no doubt she had been struck on the head.

Big hazel eyes framed by dark lashes stared back at him.

Her mouth was pink and lush, although tightly pursed because she was so scared. "Gory, may I help you out of those clothes? The blood has soaked through all the layers, even down to your chemise. I'll give you my robe to wrap around yourself for now. As soon as I hear the staff stirring, I'll have Adela's maid fetch you an outfit from her wardrobe."

"No!" She groaned. "No one can know I am here. I'll use your things."

Julius was not certain what to do. "You cannot walk around in my clothes. They are too big for you and will never fit your slight frame. Besides, you won't fool anyone into thinking you are a boy."

She glanced down at her breasts and sighed. "When is Adela due back?"

"You know she and Ambrose are in Oxford for the next few days. They won't be back until the day after tomorrow."

She nodded. "They've been gone all week."

"Which is why I was enlisted to escort you around town. But you needn't worry about the wedding breakfast, all is in readiness. Adela organized everything before she and Ambrose left." Although what would happen now that Gory was obviously injured? Julius set the question aside for now. The first order of business was to ensure she was comfortably settled and any wounds properly treated. "Will you allow me to help you out of your gown now?"

She nodded again.

He only meant to loosen the laces she could not reach on her own. But once he had done this, she still did not move. His brother, Octavian, now an admiral in the Royal Navy, had told him how some men, when strained to their breaking point, succumbed to battle shock. This is what Gory appeared to be suffering. "Gory, can you undress on your own?"

"No, Julius. Look at me. My hands are shaking too hard."

Dear heaven, what had scared this fearless girl so badly?

He groaned softly. "May I help you then? Would that be all right?"

The blood was so thick on her clothing, it surely had soaked through to her skin. He would need to wash everything off her as soon as possible.

"Yes, please," Gory said, obviously mimicking his thoughts. "I cannot bear to look at myself or touch anything I am wearing."

"All right." This was not how he ever dreamed of Gory shedding her clothes for him. He removed the gown and undergarments off her with painstaking care, looking his fill only for the purpose of examining her more thoroughly to determine if she had any hidden wounds. Once again, he did not even find bruises or scrapes.

Her body was sweet perfection.

But her eyes looked a bit glazed.

She must have struck her head on something…or been struck, but when he attempted to reach out again to inspect her scalp, she pushed his hand away. "No!"

And yet she made no protest when he cleaned the traces of blood off her stomach and breasts. He stifled a shudder because this girl was beyond perfect and he had lost her to another because of his own stupid procrastination.

Why did he wish to prolong his bachelor life when it was not all that enjoyable? He rarely drank to excess, although he had tonight. Of all the nights to be foxed when he needed to have his head clear! He was not one for gambling, and had not even touched another woman in months because his heart wanted only Gory.

He wrapped her in one of his robes, a black silk banyan that fell only to his knees and had shortened sleeves. He thought she would not be completely drowned in it. His fingers grazed her soft shoulders as he tried to get her arms in the sleeves. "Gory, does it hurt to raise your arm?"

"No, Julius. My arm is fine."

But *she* clearly was not.

He sighed, silently debating whether to press her about her injuries. But she was too fragile at the moment, and did not appear hurt other than a blow to her head that she still would not allow him to examine. "All right."

She was so lovely, she made his heart ache. The robe was too big for her and she ought to have looked ridiculous in it.

She didn't.

When she shivered once more, he carried her to his bed. "Get under the covers, Gory. You'll be warmer that way. I'll pull up a chair beside the bed and we can talk."

She whimpered. "My uncle is dead."

Julius feared it was something serious like this that had brought her running to him. Why had she fled here and not to her darling viscount? Well, he did not care. All that mattered was that she was here and he was going to protect her. "We had better notify the authorities. But first tell me what–"

"No!" she cried softly. "You cannot let anyone know I am here."

He raked a hand through his hair. "Why should I keep you hidden? Others will worry when they realize you are missing. Worse, the authorities might think you are the one who did him in and are now on the run because of it. And what about your viscount? You are getting married in a week's time. Do you intend to hide out here until your wedding day?"

"May I? Do you mind?"

Did he mind Gory in his bed?

If it were up to him, he would want her there permanently. "I do not mind having you here. But is it not better to report the crime to the authorities before others find your uncle's body? Where is your aunt?"

Gory sat up, and then winced. "She's visiting her sister in Windsor."

The effort of sitting up must have pained her.

She put a hand to her forehead to give it a delicate rub.

Did this not confirm she had been struck on the head?

Why would she not allow him a better look? Not that he knew the first thing about proper treatment of a head wound. But he knew just the man to summon...Dr. George Farthingale. He was the best doctor in London and could be counted upon to be discreet.

However, Julius hesitated.

He did not want to embroil anyone else in this possible murder situation until he had more facts. "Gory, when is your aunt due back?"

"Later this afternoon."

"All right, this gives us several hours to attend to the problem. Tell me everything you know."

"Julius, you haven't asked me."

"Asked you what?"

She stopped rubbing her forehead and looked up at him with her hazel eyes wide. "Whether I killed my uncle."

He arched an eyebrow. "The thought never entered my mind...but, did you?"

CHAPTER 2

"IN TRUTH, I don't know what happened," Gory said, wishing her head would stop pounding. "Julius, all I remember is hearing raised voices in the study. I was in my bedchamber and walked downstairs to see what was going on. I had no sooner walked in than I was struck over the head with some heavy object. Perhaps a candlestick because it felt thick and metallic. When I regained consciousness, my uncle was dead beside me and I was covered in blood."

"Dear heaven," Julius muttered, furrowing his brow. His steel-gray eyes met her gaze and made her melt a little inside, for behind that facade of cool steel burned hot embers that she had always wished might burn for her. "The intruder might have killed you. Thank goodness he spared your life. Let me–"

"No!" She cried out softly and shrank back when he tried once again to inspect her scalp. "It hurts too much and I don't want you to touch it."

She threw her hands protectively in front of her face.

"Gory, don't fight me on this. I need to help you."

"I know you mean well." But she still did not want him to touch the area of the wound. By the pain slicing through her, she thought the damage began just above her left ear and ended slightly behind it. "I might need stitches," she admitted, now feeling nauseated in addition to reeling from the unrelenting pounding in her head.

Being settled in his bed helped a little, for the mattress was soft and the sheets and pillow coverings smelled nice, a mix of lavender and his refreshing bay spices scent that wrapped around her like a soothing blanket.

Julius groaned as he rose to reach for the bell pull. "I am going to wake Greeves and have him send one of the footmen to fetch Dr. Farthingale immediately."

"Then your staff will know I am here!"

"They are going to find out in a matter of hours anyway. Do not get out of my bed," he warned when she started to draw aside the coverlet. "Look at you. You cannot even sit up."

"I can and I will," she said, knowing she was being foolishly stubborn, for she could hardly lift herself up without feeling like an ax had just split her head in half.

Her body began to spin out of kilter the moment she tried to stand.

But her uncle was dead and did she not have an obligation to find his killer?

"You'll fall if you try to take a step. *Blessed saints.* Just stay in bed, Gory. Why must you always be so stubborn? I won't tell Greeves the reason for summoning Dr. Farthingale. He knows better than to question me when I order him fetched at once. This is serious, your head wound cannot go untreated."

She eased back against his pillows because she was going to cast up her accounts if she attempted to rise again. "Very well," she muttered, frustrated that he was right.

Her head was still spinning and she was close to losing consciousness again. She knew Dr. Farthingale could be trusted, and how was she ever to start investigating if she did not even have the strength to get out of bed? She would be of no use at all, unable to observe the evidence and then dissect each clue without a clear head.

It was bad enough her heart was in tatters.

She was distraught, even though she and her uncle had never been close. In truth, he and his wife were odious. But he was still her blood kin and no one deserved to die in this horrible manner.

Julius left her side a moment to await Greeves, the Huntsford's reliable head butler, in the hallway.

Gory closed her eyes, but opened them when she sensed his return.

She felt disoriented, uncertain how much time had elapsed, but thought it was more than a few minutes.

Julius was silently attending to a task at the opposite end of the room, unaware she had awakened and was watching him. These Thorne brothers were big men, yet quite graceful on their feet. Julius moved with the stealth of a cat, silent and predatory, as though always on the prowl. This is what these Thorne men were, big and powerful cats. Strong. Territorial. Ready to fight for what was theirs and always protective of those taken into their fold.

She curled up more comfortably under his bedding, feeling safer than she had ever felt before as the nice male scent of him surrounded her and soothed her with each breath. Upon looking around the room, she realized she must have shut her eyes for more than a mere moment. A fire had been lit in the hearth, and Julius was now off in a corner with his back to her as he...*mercy.*

He removed his shirt, unaware she was watching, and revealed his sculpted form.

Her heart began to beat faster as she stared at his broad shoulders.

Her entire body tingled as she took in all that naked expanse of skin.

Had she died and gone to heaven?

Still unaware she was awake, he began to rinse the blood off himself. *Her uncle's blood.* He was too busy attending to his task to notice she was gawking at him. It must have gotten all over his hands and clothes while helping her out of her gown.

Her breath caught as she watched his movements by firelight.

It was as though he was performing an intimate dance just for her, each sinuous tug and flex of his muscles magnificently ethereal in their beauty. She took in every detail of his perfectly formed muscles...deltoid, trapezius...rhomboid. His dance was a waltz and Gory began to silently count in time the music in her head. *One, two, three.* He dipped a cloth into the water and then ran it languidly along his upper body.

And again.

One, two, three.

He dipped the cloth into the water and ran it over his body yet again. The droplets glistened as they trickled down his neck and slid onto his sculpted back and shoulders, a trick of the firelight illuminating him in its golden aura.

The waltz whirled in her head.

She almost moaned aloud when he turned to glance at her and she caught sight of his taut, muscled chest. He had a sprinkling of dark hair across his bronzed skin, the droplets of water also glistening as he casually rubbed the cloth along that broad expanse. Several droplets slowly wended their way downward to his lean stomach.

And lower.

Shocked by the heat of her response, she quickly closed her eyes again and dared not open them until some time later when he shook her lightly and whispered her name. "Gory," he said, his voice gentle and deeply resonant.

She sighed and turned to look up at him. "I drifted off."

"Understandable. You've been through a lot tonight." He had donned a plain, white shirt, but wore no cravat or jacket, nor even a waistcoat. Not that formality was required at this hour of the night while she was in his bed and naked beneath his robe, no less.

He settled in the chair beside the bed, his expression one of concern as he studied her intently by the dim light of the lamp on the night stand beside her and the distant glow of firelight that chased the dampness out of the room and warmed it.

His presence also warmed her and gave her comfort.

"Gory, why did you say that you did not know whether you had killed your uncle? If you were hit over the head when you walked into his study, then there was obviously another person with him who did not wish to be seen. No doubt, he wanted to remain hidden because he meant to kill your uncle...or had just killed him, and was desperate to escape before being noticed."

"Or his visitor could have been gone by the time I came downstairs, and I was the one who fought with my uncle. It is all so cloudy in my mind."

"But not in mine," Julius said, casting her an affectionate smile. "For all your spit and vinegar, you are quite soft on the inside. You may be fascinated by dead things, but you do not actually kill them."

She laughed softly and then winced, for a jolt of pain immediately shot through her temples. "We must speak to Jergins. He is our head butler. If my uncle had a caller, someone on the staff would know."

"Assuming the man had been announced. Did he show up after midnight? Was he expected?"

Gory tried to remember the details surrounding that moment, but all was still shrouded in a thick haze. It was such an odd and frustrating feeling, for her mind was usually razor-sharp and she had an excellent memory.

A chunk of that memory was lost for the moment, the blow to her head having stolen it away.

"I suppose the most important question to ask is whether your uncle was alive when you walked into his study or was he already dead on the floor?"

She pursed her lips as she tried to bring the scene to mind, then sighed in dismay. "Oh, Julius. It all happened so fast. I cannot recall."

He placed a warm hand over both of her own that were clasped before her as she began to shiver. "Gory, you are still in shock. Your hands are so cold, love. Do not fret. You will start to remember once your wound is treated and you've had time to calm down."

"But it is too important to delay," she insisted. "How are we to solve his murder if I have no clues to provide? As soon as Dr. Farthingale stitches me up, we have to return to the scene of the crime. I'm certain it will help spark my memory."

His lovely gray eyes turned dark as thunder. "You are not getting out of my bed."

"But–"

"You came to me for a reason, so let me take care of you. This also means summoning the magistrate before someone else reports the murder and you are then made a suspect. I am also going to bring in Homer Barrow. He's the best Bow Street runner in London, and I'll get him straight onto the investigation. He and his men will be able to move around without being noticed."

"Why don't you call in The Tattler's top reporter while you are at it?" she muttered, irritated by the number of people he wished to involve. "That gossip rag will delight in the story. Everybody already considers me bloodthirsty and strange because of my fascination with the workings of the human body. Can you imagine what they'll write? Earl murdered by ghoulish niece!"

"I will not allow them to write anything disparaging about you." Julius was now puffed up like a big, protective ape and scowling fiercely.

"Oh, Julius. You cannot stop them. Even *you* find me strange and barely tolerate me. Admit it. You are only being polite because I am dear friends with Adela and Syd. Now that they have married your brothers, you are required to put up with me."

"That isn't true. You know I have always been fond of you."

She ignored the comment, for he did not mean it. How could he when he spent his evenings in the arms of other women? Of course, he was discreet about it. In truth, there had been very few whispers about him lately.

She assumed this meant he had learned to hide his affairs very well.

He couldn't have stopped his rakish ways, could he?

Why would he stop when he was still unattached and free to gad about as he wished?

"You have always *tolerated* me. There's a difference between liking and tolerating. I am not even certain Allendale likes me," she admitted. "I have yet to figure out why he asked me to marry him. Perhaps he wished for a connection to my uncle. The Easton earldom is nothing to scoff at, although one would never know it by the miserly way my uncle has treated me. I expect Allendale will show his true colors now that my uncle is no longer around. I would not be surprised if he ended the betrothal. After all, why bother with me if my usefulness is at an end? Perhaps he needs my dowry. I'm not sure why he would. It isn't all that large."

Julius raked a hand through the waves of his dark hair. "If you believe his only interest is in your dowry, then why marry him? Do you love him, Gory?"

She felt her tears welling and stubbornly tamped them down. "I wanted to. I hoped I would."

"That is not an answer."

"Yes, it is." How dare Julius question her when he was the one who broke her heart by never stepping forward to court her? After Adela had married his brother, Ambrose, Duke of Huntsford, and then Syd had married his other brother, Octavian, who was now an admiral in the Royal Navy, she had allowed herself to hope she could be a match for the third brother. Him. Julius.

But he had gone on his merry way, escorting a dazzling array of *ton* diamonds to the various balls, routs, and musicales, although he was most often reported to be cavorting with ladies of questionable reputation in the later hours.

Not that she had ever seen him cavorting, but gossip about him was rampant…well, had been rampant. Nothing to connect him to anyone in particular lately. Still, he was noticed by everyone because he was wealthy and impossibly handsome. Rugged and a little dangerous with that steel glint in his eyes and the appealing cut of his gloriously firm jaw.

His hair was dark as ebony.

She ached to run her fingers through that gorgeous mane. Of course, she would never dare do anything so brazen.

Had he not made it clear he wanted nothing to do with her?

Julius was frowning. "The magistrate, the reporters, the curious onlookers, and perhaps even the killer himself will be sniffing around the Easton townhouse once your staff awakens and sounds the alarm. Homer Barrow needs to be put on the task right away. I want him to be at your house by the time others start coming around. He needs to be looking at everyone, and making note of those who look suspicious."

"What if I killed my uncle?" she asked, for the possibility was real and had to be considered. "What if he was the one who struck me and I fought back?"

"No, Gory. Not with the severity of your head wound. A blow like that would have knocked you out cold. You would not have been able to fight back. But I think you might have noticed something that could put you in danger. Did you see anything in those few precious seconds you had to look about the room?"

"Perhaps. Yes, it is entirely possible." She closed her eyes and tried to recall the scene, but her mind remained blank. However, she refused to give up hope. "Oh, Julius. My brain isn't working just yet."

"It's all right, love. Don't push yourself."

"But I must. What if the perpetrator thinks I might have seen something? Well, that could work in our favor."

He growled softly. "Are you thinking what I think you are thinking?"

"I hope so, because it is a good plan. I can be the lure to draw the villain out. Let him come to *me* instead of our having to hunt him down."

"What?"

She ignored his expression of horror. "I said, we can–"

"I heard what you said. I just could not believe how willing you are to throw yourself into the path of danger. I am going to ignore that insane idea." He was getting that apishly protective look again. "I am never going to allow that fiend near enough to hurt you."

"How are you to stop him? If he thinks I saw him, then he will be desperate to silence me before my memory returns. This is why you must take me back to the scene as soon as possible. It is vitally important for me to remember what happened."

He placed his hand over hers. "Do not force it, Gory. This is not how memory works. You must give your head time to clear on its own."

Why did he always have to be so logical?

It frustrated her that he was probably right.

He smiled when she relented with a grumble. "Rest, love. Dr. Farthingale will be here shortly."

Love.

This is what she so dearly wished to be to Julius, his one and only true love.

But he was merely referring to her in this soft way because he was concerned for her and would protect her with his life.

This is why she had run to him.

He made her feel safe.

Why could she not feel this way about her betrothed, Chandler Allendale? Theirs was best described as a friendship built on compatible interests, for he was an amateur naturalist and several members of his family, particularly one rich uncle of his, were patrons to many of London's most respected societies and charities.

Truthfully, she had been surprised by his offer of marriage but accepted him because of their mutual appreciation of these scholarly endeavors.

Would her viscount fight to the death to protect her?

Would he fight for her at all?

She was more likely to be the one defending herself were they ever accosted by brigands. Not that Allendale was feeble, but he did not have the brawn or battle abilities of these Thorne men. No, her viscount was better described as refined and elegant.

He was also scholarly and intelligent.

The only heavy lifting he was ever likely to do was lift books.

She could not see him ever rolling up his sleeves and digging into hard labor.

However, she did not think less of him because his hands were soft. Not all men had to be marvelously strong like Julius and his brothers. Allendale's refinement and love of academic pursuits were fine traits in a husband, were they not?

And yet, the dear dowagers who had sponsored her Season, Lady Dayne and Lady Withnall, had not been pleased to learn of her accepting to marry him. When pressed for a reason why they disapproved, Lady Dayne had told her, "It is not that we are disappointed, my dear. He simply does not *feel* right for you."

But what choice did she have?

Julius did not want her.

She studied him through her strained eyes, knowing she was going to cry if she stared at him too long. He was handsome enough to put women in a swoon whenever he swaggered into a ballroom or other fashionable *ton* affair.

All the Thorne brothers were handsome, and Julius was no exception. In truth, he was easily the finest looking of the three.

Even with his dark hair slightly mussed and his eyes bloodshot after a night carousing on the town, he still looked magnificent.

He even smelled delicious, which simply was not fair.

She closed her eyes and fell back against the pillows Julius had gently placed behind her head. Looking at him, knowing she could never be his, only made her heart ache worse.

Gory only meant to close them for a moment, but she must have drifted off again, this time for hours. When she awoke, the drapes were drawn aside and the sky was now a light shade of gray, signaling the approach of dawn.

Julius was once more seated beside her.

Perhaps he had remained by her side all along.

He smiled as her eyes fluttered open. "I was beginning to worry about you, Gory. But all's well now that you are awake."

He was freshly groomed and shaved.

Too magnificent for words.

He no longer wore the casual shirt he had donned after washing the blood off himself earlier – the blood from her gown and body – but the sight of him bared from the waist up was now seared into her memory. Was it not shameful that she could recall his every muscled contour but could not recall the identity of her uncle's killer?

He had on a pair of dark trousers, shirt of finest white lawn, a patterned silk waistcoat and silk cravat. He was the height of understated elegance, the colors of his waistcoat and cravat enhancing the silvery gray of his eyes.

A stirring in a corner of the room caught her attention.

She recognized the two gentlemen who were quietly speaking to each other. They turned toward her upon realizing she was awake. Dr. Farthingale was the tall, distinguished-looking fellow drying his hands beside a handsome writing desk atop which was perched the basin and ewer Julius had earlier used. The other fellow was the experienced Bow Street runner, Homer Barrow. The two men were of even height, but Mr. Barrow was the portlier one with a bulbous nose and prominent jowls.

The doctor began to put away his instruments instead of taking them out.

Gory tried to sit up, but Julius place a hand lightly on her shoulder. "Lie still, love. Dr. Farthingale just stitched your head."

"He did?" She raised a hand to the wound but dared not actually touch it. Her head felt as though laces had been tightly pulled at that spot, and the rest of her head was still throbbing.

Julius nodded. "He gave you a little something to help you sleep through it."

She did not remember that part either.

"Mr. Barrow has stationed his best men at your townhouse," Julius continued. "One is to remain at the scene along with the constables, and the other will watch the crowd that gathers on the street."

Gory liked this idea.

Julius nodded toward the Bow Street runner. "Mr. Barrow also stopped by your residence before coming here."

"For the purpose of inspecting my uncle's study?"

Mr. Barrow now stepped forwarad. "Aye, Lady Gregoria. I trust my men, but I always like to see things for myself."

"Did you find anything of note?" she asked.

Mr. Barrow tapped his forehead. "It is all churning up here at the moment. No revelations to disclose yet."

"Oh, I see."

Julius took her hand and held it gently. "He would like to ask you a few questions. Can you manage it? Or would you rather we put it off?"

"No, it must be done now. I am at your service, Mr. Barrow." She had grown to know the man from his work when assisting her friends, and liked him very much. He was intelligent and intuitive. Very little ever got past him.

"Gory, are you certain?" Julius gave her hand a light squeeze. "It is asking a lot of you."

"No, I will be all right. But I have a few questions to ask Dr. Farthingale first. Doctor, please don't leave yet. Can you tell me precisely how I was struck? I mean, the angle of the indentation. And the exact shape of my injury. Was it more of a side blow? Or was the blunt object brought down from above? Did you find shards of glass in my scalp? Wood splinters? Or porcelain? Perhaps a vase cracked over my head? Although it felt more like a candlestick or fire iron."

Julius regarded her all the while she spoke. "What does it matter how you were struck?"

"The angle of the blow might give some indication of the height of the assailant and whether we are looking for someone who favors his left hand or right hand. The object used might indicate whether it was a planned assault on my uncle...and me when I interrupted whatever was going on. Or it might have been accidental and none of it planned." She sighed. "I don't know. Perhaps none of it matters at all. But every bit of evidence is vital right now."

Mr. Barrow nodded. "Aye, I agree."

Gory continued explaining her reasoning to Julius, partly because he appeared to be genuinely interested, but mostly because he was holding her hand and she liked this very much. "Each detail might give a hint of what happened. Glass or porcelain shards lodged in my hair might indicate the killer was surprised and grabbed whatever object was close at hand. It also indicates someone untrained in violence. Someone who might have panicked and never intended to hurt me or my uncle."

"But things got out of control?" Julius mused, arching an eyebrow.

"Yes." She barely nodded her head because each slight movement sent a jolt of pain through her. "The significance of a fire iron is that it would indicate a more purposeful intent. Someone more ruthless. The fire iron would have been in his hand already when I walked into the study. Perhaps he had already struck and killed my uncle...or was about to do so when I interrupted him or her."

"Her?" Julius pursed his lips. "You think a woman was involved?"

"I don't know. But we cannot rule anyone out yet. Is that not right, Mr. Barrow?"

"Quite right, Lady Gregoria. Although I think your uncle must have already been dead or at least unconscious by the time you entered the room. Otherwise, he would have been shouting and tugging on the bell pull to rouse the staff. Your staff was only beginning to stir when I arrived with the constables and my men. It did not appear as though any of them heard anything last night."

She nodded. "Yes, that is an important point."

"I would also rule out fire implements and lean toward your being struck with a candlestick," Mr. Barrow remarked. "The room had been ransacked, so no weapon was immediately obvious."

"Nor did I notice any traces of soot when cleaning your scalp," Dr. Farthingale remarked as he closed his medical bag. "So I would also rule out the fire implements. No shards of glass or porcelain either."

Julius groaned. "I helped Lady Gregoria clean the blood off herself. I might have wiped off an important clue. It never even crossed my mind. I was more worried about checking her for injuries."

"I would not fret too much about it, Lord Thorne," Mr. Barrow said. "My man Mick is the one inspecting the scene with the constables. He will report to me shortly. Likely, they will have recovered a bloodstained weapon and put that question to rest."

He now turned to Gory as she lay in bed propped up by pillows and still wearing Julius's black robe. The fancy silk bed coverlet was drawn up almost to her neck, so she hoped these gentlemen did not realize she was completely naked beneath the robe.

But that was a foolish supposition.

Dr. Farthingale had to realize she was undressed since Julius probably asked him to examine her and make certain he had overlooked no injuries. Mr. Barrow would also know she was undressed because Julius had probably shown him the bloodstained gown and undergarments.

And here she was, naked in Julius's bed.

Dear heaven.

This looked bad.

The gossip rags would utterly destroy her if it became known she had run to Julius and was recuperating here. Never mind that she was running for her life, for that was an irrelevant detail to a lurid story that would sell their papers.

To the credit of Dr. Farthingale and Mr. Barrow, neither of them were anything but respectful and sincerely concerned for her.

There was also the obvious question of why she had run to Julius Thorne and not the viscount to whom she was betrothed. If asked this by Mr. Barrow, she could always say she was running to Adela and forgot that her best friend and Ambrose were away. Was this not plausible? Certainly less eyebrow raising than admitting she had been thinking of Julius and wanted to be in his arms.

He was big and comforting as he sat beside her.

But he now rose and gave his chair to Mr. Barrow. "Here. I'll step back while you ask your questions."

"All right, my lord." The Bow Street runner settled in the vacated chair and wasted no time in beginning his interrogation. "Lady Gregoria, just let me know if these questions are too upsetting and I shall stop the interview."

"No, Mr. Barrow. This is important. I only hope I can remember something useful."

He had to repeat the first question because her attention immediately strayed to Julius as she watched him escort Dr. Farthingale out of the room.

It upset her that he had walked out of her sight. She thought of him as her bedrock and needed his strong, steady presence beside her.

Oh, she was brash and stubborn when it came to making a place for herself in the field of forensic medicine. But she turned into an utter peahen whenever she was around this Thorne brother.

She cleared her throat. "My apologies, Mr. Barrow. Could you repeat the question?"

"Of course," he said with a kindly nod and gracious smile. "You mentioned to Lord Thorne that you were in your bedchamber and heard raised voices coming from your uncle's study. This is why you were drawn downstairs."

She nodded.

"I would like to know if you recognized who was speaking to your uncle? Did the voice sound familiar to you at all?"

She closed her eyes and tried to think back, for the knowledge was right there at the edges. "I...no, it was too indistinct. Well, indistinct in my memory for now. But I might have recognized it. Something about the voice felt familiar." She groaned. "I just don't know."

"Let it stew a while. You cannot force these things. Your memory will return in its own good time. Can you tell me anything at all about the person speaking? Was it a male voice, do you think?"

Gory tried again and frowned, for this was turning into an exercise in frustration. "Oh, dear. I cannot. Perhaps it was too muffled to make out. But I do recall my uncle exchanging heated words with whoever was in the room. And yet, I do not think he was calling out for help."

"That is important. He could have been angry but did not feel threatened."

She sighed. "Or maybe he was threatened and too afraid to speak up. And maybe I am not remembering the incident correctly at all. What I do know is that something alarmed me and drew me down to the study. It is the *feeling* something was wrong that I remember. Is it not odd?"

"Not at all, Lady Gregoria. I think feelings run deeper than mere observations. This is why they remain with us while we sometimes forget what it was that stirred them. Do you recall what your uncle was saying as he faced his assailant?"

"No. I only recall that sense of danger." She swallowed, for her throat was feeling quite parched. "Oh, Mr. Barrow. I fear I am being of no help."

"It will come back to you in time, my lady. You mustn't put this additional strain on yourself. You are fortunate to be alive. Which leads me to my next question...you were in your wedding gown. Why?"

She sighed. "I do not know. In truth, I do not recall having put it on. It is ruined now."

He nodded. "Lord Thorne showed it to me. I am so very sorry."

She ought to have been sorry, too.

In truth, she wasn't.

Of course, it was a shame the beautiful fabric had been ruined. But the damage also signified a step toward her freedom.

Was this not awful of her to think so?

Obviously, she was not thinking clearly at all. Allendale would never agree to call off the wedding because of a ruined bridal gown. Of course, the matter of her uncle turning up dead would give him cause.

"Lady Gregoria," Mr. Barrow said, regaining her attention with the sound of his gravelly voice, "were you aware of any problems your uncle might have been having with any of his business associates?"

"There were constant problems. Many of them were as oily as he was, so I expect they were always trying to cheat each other. Until last night, he always seemed able to talk his way out of a situation once his dishonesty was found out. But he was not always up to no good in his ventures. Some appeared to be legitimate."

"What makes you think so?" Mr. Barrow asked.

"A few had been profitable and returned a good income for their investors. Even Lord Allendale had invested in one of my uncle's ventures, and–"

"Allendale? Did this not worry you?" Julius had returned and was now standing at the foot of the bed, his arms crossed over his chest and his brow furrowed as he listened in. "A snake does not suddenly sprout legs and walk," he muttered. "Once a thief, always a thief."

Gory frowned at him. "Are you suggesting my uncle was a thief?"

Julius arched an eyebrow. "Wasn't he?"

"Possibly," she grumbled, and then sighed. "Probably. How was I to know Lord Allendale had decided to invest with my uncle? Gentlemen are not in the habit of discussing financial matters with ladies. But I would have stopped him had I known about it. Fortunately, the venture paid off and he was quite pleased."

"As I said, snake oil," Julius muttered. "This is how a mark is lured in."

"What do you mean?" Gory knew a lot about medical matters, but had to admit she was lacking in knowledge of general business dealings.

She only knew never to trust her uncle.

But Julius's mind was as sharp as a finely honed blade. "It is a matter of gaining one's confidence. Your uncle proposes a venture. Allendale puts in a small sum. He gets back a nice return. He invests another small sum in the next venture. Gets back another decent return. Then he is ready to invest in a big way. That's when your uncle reports the failed venture. Only there never was a venture, it was all a ruse, and your uncle has pocketed the funds."

Gory could not believe what she was hearing.

Well, she did believe it to some extent.

But her betrothed would have said something to her, surely. "Are you suggesting Allendale was fleeced, got angry, and had something to do with my uncle's murder? Julius, that is outrageous and completely off the mark."

He held up his hands. "It is just supposition, Gory. And I do not mean to single out Allendale. Your uncle probably had a dozen other lords he was looking to fleece."

"I can assure you, Lord Allendale was not one of them. Perhaps he was meant to be an eventual mark, but he was only starting out. I'm sure he reaped a handsome profit. Besides, I do not even know if he is in London. He has been very busy, which is why you were put in charge of escorting me on my errands these past few days."

"Fine, let's forget about Allendale for now," he said, raking a hand through his hair. "There's still the matter of your wedding gown. I sense it is important."

"Why?"

"Because it is such an odd thing for you to do, is it not? I saw you earlier in the evening at Lady Dunbarton's musicale and you were wearing something different. A very pretty peach silk that suited your complexion."

She regarded him in surprise. "You noticed?"

He nodded. "I'm glad Lady Dayne and Lady Withnall insisted upon a new wardrobe for you."

"They have been ridiculously kind to me." In truth, these dearest dowagers had taken on the cost of several new gowns for her, ones for every occasion, because her uncle would not part with a shilling of his own.

Julius cleared his throat. "But as I was saying about your wedding gown, why return home...it would have been late, and then change out of the peach silk into something other than your nightgown? Close your eyes and try to think back, Gory. You were in your bedchamber. Would you not have required assistance removing the gown you wore to the musicale?"

"No, I would have managed it myself. Unlacing a gown is a much simpler matter than lacing it up." As he well knew, Gory thought morosely.

Where had he gone after the musicale?

To some widow's boudoir?

"All right, so you managed the gown on your own. But then you put on your wedding gown instead of preparing for bed? Why were you wearing it? And did that not require assistance to properly lace it up? It was done up with impeccable precision. This was one of the first things I noticed when I–" He groaned and winced as Mr. Barrow eyed him. "The gown was soaked in blood. I had to get it off Lady Gregoria."

"I am not judging you, my lord. You've shown me the evidence. It is no surprise Lady Gregoria was in shock when she came to you and remains so, as one can tell by her glazed eyes."

Mr. Barrow cast her a look of genuine concern and continued. "Mick will report to me soon. We'll know if anyone on the staff was awake and might have heard something. He will have questioned them all by now."

"And the magistrate's constables will let him? Are they not in charge of this investigation now?" Gory asked.

"We have very good working relations with the constabulary. In fact, we are all Bow Street men and they often bring us in on their investigations."

"So they will allow you to see whatever evidence they gather?" Gory pursed her lips in thought. "That is a very good thing. Perhaps we shall be able to make sense of what happened if we all work together. My actions do not make any sense, do they? Why would I not prepare for bed once my uncle and I returned home from the musicale? I cannot even remember who sang or whether it was wonderful or awful."

Julius chuckled. "For the record, it was awful. The featured soprano was supposed to be a professional opera singer of some renown. Do you remember nothing of the recital, Gory?"

"No." Tears formed in her eyes. "A musical recital that I cannot recall. An argument in my uncle's study, the details of which I also cannot recall. A wedding gown that should have been carefully stowed away. Who helped me put it on? Why did I put it on? Was it connected in any way to my uncle's murder?"

She buried her face in her hands. "He was such a sneaky rat, and I loathed him. But to know he met such a violent end? Who would do such a thing to him?"

CHAPTER 3

JULIUS ESCORTED MR. Barrow downstairs because he wished to ask a few questions outside of Gory's hearing. "Is there anything you've learned so far that you did not wish to tell Lady Gregoria?"

"No, m'lord. I would not have held anything back from her. Indeed, not her. She's smart as a whip and obviously frustrated by her inability to recall what happened." He cleared his throat. "Which leads me to another very delicate matter."

"What is it, Mr. Barrow?" Julius could see the man felt extremely uncomfortable, for he was rubbing a beefy hand across the back of his neck, and his face was now as red as his bulbous nose.

"She was struck across the head, but was she accosted in any other manner? Forgive me, my lord. But the question–"

"That is why I escorted Dr. Farthingale out, to ask him this very question," Julius admitted. "He saw no indication of violence other than to her head."

The Bow Street runner released a breath. "Thank goodness."

"Indeed," Julius muttered, his heart aching over the possibility of what might have happened while she was unconscious and defenseless. This left him even more furious with himself for choosing to sow his wild oats rather than commit to Gory and settle down.

His *oats* turned out not to be all that wild in the first place because the only woman he wanted – even though he was stubbornly denying it to himself – was Gory. Once he had finally accepted his feelings, he could not bring himself to touch another woman.

He loved Gory.

"I had better get back to her," he said. "Dr. Farthingale suggested she keep to a light repast for the next day or two, some tea or broth, and soft breads to start. I'll leave her to the staff once she has finished eating because I want to check out the Easton home, too. Her bedchamber, especially. Why would she have changed into her wedding gown? This troubles me. It simply does not fit."

"Agreed, my lord. Well, I shall see you there shortly."

After escorting him out, Julius slowly climbed the stairs to return to Gory's side. He was lost in his thoughts, so he did not immediately notice that the lump in his bed was not Gory. "The little minx," he muttered, sensing something was wrong when she did not respond to his return.

She had tucked pillows under the covers to make it look as though a person was sleeping there.

He headed straight for his sister-in-law's dressing room which was the only logical place she could have gone.

"Why in blazes are you out of bed?" He growled low in his throat upon finding Gory rifling through Adela's wardrobe.

She looked achingly adorable in his robe that was too big for her slight frame. Her chestnut curls were in an unkempt tumble down her back and her big, hazel eyes glistened because she was still a little dazed.

Her cheeks were stained pink and her mouth was in a pout.

He wanted to kiss her.

Lord, how he ached to kiss her.

"I am looking for something to wear. Is it not obvious?" She stared up at him with her eyes wide in challenge and a brazen purse of her sweet mouth. He had gotten to know that look so well because Gory was always one to push boundaries and dare anyone to stop her. "I need proper clothes if I am to go out."

She had just pulled out one of Adela's gowns, a dark green wool that he knew would look spectacular on Gory. But he took it out of her hands and tossed it over a nearby chair. He shut the door to the wardrobe and gently pinned Gory against that enormous piece of furniture, purposely trapping her between his arms and leaning in with the full breadth of his body.

Her glorious eyes widened further.

Lord, she's so pretty.

"You need to get back in bed," he said with a soft growl.

Yes, that is what she needed to do and where she belonged.

In *his* bed.

She tossed him a stubborn look. "You cannot tell me what to do, Julius."

"I can and I will. You are hurt and will do yourself more harm if you start running around to hunt for clues. Look at you…"

Gad, she looked delicious.

She frowned at him. "There is nothing wrong with me."

He laughed in disbelief. "You are pale and swaying on your feet."

"Is this why you are sticking your big body too close to mine? You smell amazingly good, by the way."

He growled again, but did not move away.

She licked her soft lips. "Posture all you like, but I will not be intimidated by you. Julius, is it not right that I should be there when my aunt comes home to this frightful scene?"

"You do not even like her. She's odious. If she cannot stay with a friend for the next few days, I'll obtain a suite of rooms for her at one of the finest hotels in London. *I'll* take care of it. There is nothing you need to do."

"She has no friends. No one likes her," Gory muttered, the light pucker of her lips making him once again want to kiss her.

Gad, she was so adorably impudent.

"Fine, she has no friends and no one likes her," he repeated, tossing Gory's words back at her. "Then I shall arrange for the hotel accommodations. All shall be charged to my account. Any objections?"

"Lots. She is my odious aunt, not yours."

"But you are in my care now and that makes you mine to protect."

"But–"

"*Mine.*"

She gave a slight nod. "You are such an ape. However…thank you. I would insist on paying for her hotel room, but I have no idea what my financial situation will be or what is to happen to me now that my uncle is gone. I believe he was the last of the Easton male heirs residing in England. There is a cousin somewhere in the world. I once heard mention he resided in Virginia, although I have no idea where he might be now. Well, that is for the solicitors to determine. I must speak to Lord Allendale and make him aware of my changed circumstances."

"We'll deal with your betrothed later."

"But should I not alert him right away? He may want to jilt me."

"No," he replied more harshly than intended because the mere mention of Allendale riled him. Nor did he care that the viscount might end his betrothal to Gory since it would then leave her free to marry him.

"I would not blame him if he did abandon me at the altar," she muttered.

"We Thornes will always protect you, Gory. You will never be left alone or destitute. If Allendale begs out of the betrothal, I'll…"

Gad, could he just blurt out a proposal?

Would Gory believe he truly cared for her?

"You'll what?" she prompted.

Offer to marry her, of course.

But Gory would never believe he was offering to do so of his own free will.

She would assume he was offering out of pity.

Or duty. Obligation. Concern.

She sighed. "On the other hand, he might not beg out. There is always the possibility that my uncle's death will make me richer."

"Richer?"

She nodded. "I think so. Oh, not anything for certain, but my aunt mentioned something odd to me a few days after Allendale and I announced our betrothal."

"Do you recall what she said?"

Gory nodded. "Yes, it is only what happened last night that I cannot seem to remember at all."

"Tell me what she said," he gently prompted, still keeping her pinned between his arms, and pleased she did not mind being held against him.

In truth, she seemed to be edging closer.

"She told me Allendale only wanted me for my wealth. She sounded quite bitter about it. I thought it odd because my dowry, while adequate, is not remarkably substantial. Many debutantes come onto the marriage mart with fatter purses to lure the eligible bachelors."

"Why do you think she made the comment then?"

"I have no idea. At the time, I thought she was saying it just to be hurtful. You know, implying that no man would ever want me for myself. Perhaps I should not have dismissed the remark out of hand. I did not want to believe she was right." She trembled lightly. "But she is right, isn't she? Why should any man look at me twice? I am no prize."

Julius frowned. "You are the crown jewel. She is completely and utterly wrong."

Gory's soft laugh held such misery. "And this is why I ran to you. I think you are the only man in London who sees any worth in me. But my aunt's remark is another matter that requires investigation, don't you think? You'll have to take me to my uncle's solicitor. We need to get at the truth of my inheritance."

"Not today, Gory. You have to rest. Nor do I intend to drag you around with me while I investigate your uncle's murder." He leaned in closer, unable to stop himself because she was an irresistible force drawing him in and the attraction was too great.

What a fool he had been to let her slip away.

She ought to have been his.

His to love and protect.

Things would change from this day forward.

He did not give a fig about Gory's inheritance. Whether it was a fortune or a pittance was irrelevant to him.

He wanted her heart.

This is all he cared about.

Winning her heart.

She was still looking up at him, her tempting lips mere inches from his mouth.

Full and pouty.

"I promise to share everything I learn," he said, hardly recognizing the raw rasp in his voice. "But I need you to rest here and recover. I'll never forgive myself if harm comes to you."

"No, Julius. You mustn't ever blame yourself or I will never forgive *myself* for running to you. You do not need me complicating your carefree life. I am so sorry that I imposed on you," she said, cutting him to the quick with the remark.

"Never say that." He gave her cheek a light caress. "You had to come to me, for no one understands you as I do. No one will protect you as vigorously or faithfully as I will. I am so sorry I was not there for you last night. But I am here for you now and always. Let me take care of you, Gory."

She was still staring up at him, her lips slightly parted and quivering.

Kiss her.

Kiss her, you fool.

Tears welled in her eyes as he was about to bend his head toward hers. He paused, not wanting to press his lips to her beautifully shaped mouth unless she was willing. Were she less vulnerable, he might have pushed ahead and simply kissed her.

But not now.

"Is it not the oddest thing?" she whispered brokenly.

"What is, Gory?"

"How well you know me, almost better than I know myself. This is why it had to be you I turned to in my darkest hour."

He closed his eyes and shuddered.

Was her admission not a good thing?

She trusted him more than she trusted anyone else in her life, even her own betrothed.

"Knowing me as well as you do," she continued, her voice still shaky as she struggled not to cry, "you understand why I cannot sit back and do nothing while there is a killer on the loose."

He gave her cheek another light caress. "I'll strike a bargain with you. Rest in my bed for the remainder of the day. My staff will see to your every comfort. However, let me investigate on my own for today. We'll see how you are feeling tomorrow. But you cannot leave the house just yet. I'll report everything I find out. I'll even get you in to see your uncle's body within the next day or two, assuming you are fit enough to get out of bed."

In all his days, he had never expected to woo a young lady by offering to show her a cadaver. But Gory was like no one else. By her hopeful look, he could see that she was considering his offer.

And why not?

It was a generous offer and a great compliment to her. He was treating her as an equal, promising to include her in every facet of the investigation.

Her eyes now sparkled. "Truly, Julius?"

He nodded. "I'll make it clear to the magistrate that you are to be given full access. I'll come with you, of course."

She cast him a fragile smile. "Why? Because you are worried I might have an attack of the vapors and will need to be caught in your manly arms when I faint?"

"First of all, I am the one more likely to faint," he said with a rumbling chuckle. "But on a more practical note, I know we will need your insights if we ever hope to solve the murder. I mean it, Gory. You are the smartest person I know."

She sighed as she patted her hand over her spectacular bosom and teasingly said, "Be still my heart. Careful, or you will have me in a swoon."

Then she paled and actually did swoon.

"Right, enough of you being out of bed." He scooped her into his arms. "It's that nasty lump poking out of your skull. It must hurt something fierce. You look ashen, love. You really should not be walking around."

"I am a little dizzy," she admitted, resting her head against his shoulder as he carried her out of Adela's dressing chamber. "I'll do as you ask, but you must promise to let me see my uncle's body tomorrow, whether or not I am fit. It is too important, Julius. I'll know what to look for and will be as quick as can be."

Gory had lectured him often enough about the decomposition of bodies, going into unnecessary detail about which type of insects crawled out first. She and her bluestocking friends, Adela, Syd, and Marigold, had discussed this once over a family dinner. He and his brothers, as well as Marigold's husband, Leo, had been too queasy to continue eating afterward. Not so the ladies. They'd dug into their syllabub with unbridled enthusiasm.

Who ever claimed women were the more delicate creatures?

Julius understood why it was so important for her to inspect the body as soon as possible. But he was going to stay close to her at every step. The morgue. The solicitor's office. A visit to her aunt. "Agreed, but I am not leaving your side until we find the killer. If he thinks to harm you, he'll have to go through me first."

"Allendale might have a thing or two to say about that," she muttered, reminding him that Gory was not his to claim...not yet, anyway.

Was it too much to ask for Allendale to beg out of the betrothal?

Julius would be there to mend Gory's broken heart if it happened.

Well, he did not want her to be heartbroken.

He wanted her to be happy and ready to fall in love with *him*.

Were she in love with Allendale, Julius would have done the honorable thing and backed off. But Gory did not display any telling signs of a woman enraptured. In truth, all she was doing was trying to force herself to fall in love with that oaf.

Julius could have told her it would never happen.

Love could not be forced.

Love could not be controlled.

It was just one of those things that happened whether you were ready for it or not.

One's heart was completely in charge.

His had chosen Gory and there was no going back from it.

Gory regained his attention by putting her arms around his neck and hugging him. "Don't you dare put yourself in danger for me, Julius," she whispered as he marched back down the hall toward his bedchamber.

"Be quiet, Gory. This is not up for discussion. I am always going to protect you."

"You big ape," she muttered.

Was she now crying?

How could she think he would do anything less than guard her with his life?

Well, she had not had an easy time of it since losing her parents and put in the care of those weasels, an uncle and aunt who resented her and found their obligations to her most inconvenient. Everything this wonderful girl did was displeasing to them.

This must have been so hard for Gory.

"I'll have Adela's maid bring in that green gown you chose, along with anything else you might need once you are feeling better. But do not dress right away. In fact, do not dress at all today. Clothes will only confine you. Just stay in my bed and–"

She laughed softly. "You do realize that sounds lewd."

He chuckled. "Perhaps, but I still want you undressed and in my bed."

He also wanted to be in that bed with her, similarly unclad.

But now was not the time to declare his intentions.

It wasn't about bedding her, anyway.

It was about marrying her.

Caring for her.

Nourishing her hopes and dreams.

There was no way Allendale understood Gory as well as he did, or liked her eccentricities, intelligence, and determination as much as he did. In truth, he was worried that Allendale might break her spirit if she married him. Yes, the man and his family were great contributors to the arts and sciences, especially that rich uncle of his.

But it did not necessarily follow that Allendale would allow Gory to continue her important work at the Huntsford Academy's newly designed forensics laboratory.

Julius's brother, Ambrose, had built the museum and hall of science in honor of their father, and was now expanding it to become one of England's most prominent research centers. He and Octavian had also contributed, of course. It was a source of pride for all three Thorne brothers, and Gory's brilliant work only enhanced the academy's reputation.

Were it up to him, he would give her free rein to work there for as long as she wished.

But Allendale would not.

Few men, especially those holding titles, would ever allow their wives to work after marriage.

Members of the *ton* would view it as scandalous.

Julius knew better than to ever deprive Gory of the research she loved. To do so would steal the joy from her life and leave her heartbroken.

This is why Gory needed to marry him.

Marriage to him would never be a cage for her. She needed to remain that free bird to soar and make her mark on the world.

"I'll ask Adela's maid to bring me a nightgown and robe from Adela's wardrobe," Gory said as he set her back in his bed.

His heart tightened upon noticing a small patch of blood on the pillow from when Dr. Farthingale had stitched her wound. Julius had remained by her side while the doctor worked on her, holding her hand and caressing her cheek every time she winced in pain.

"You do that, love," he said, the endearment slipping out again.

He tucked the coverlet around her shoulders and then moved away to grab his jacket. "I won't be gone long. Just a few hours. I'll tell Greeves to permit no visitors. Not that anyone would know you are here."

"Servants talk. I would not be surprised if Lady Dayne and Lady Withnall showed up here within the hour. Marigold and Leo, too."

Julius grinned. "That's true. I'll leave word that they are allowed to see you, but no one else will be permitted. All right, Gory?"

She nodded. "I have no one else who would care to see me. Those two dowagers are like grandmothers to me. Adela, Syd, and Marigold are the sisters I never had. Now Syd and Octavian are settled in Scotland while he oversees building of the navy's new ships. And Adela and Ambrose are constantly running between Devon and London on their fossil hunts. Their lives are so much busier now."

"Marigold is still in London."

"And kept busy with fossil hunts, as well. Not to mention her wifely duties being married to a marquess." She shook her head. "I am not complaining. All of you comprise my lovely new family. I am so fortunate to have found you."

He liked that she had included him among those she considered family, and hoped their friendship would soon become something more.

He wanted to be her husband.

There was no way he would lose her to Allendale.

Once more, he shook out of the thought.

Gory had just narrowly escaped being murdered, and her uncle had not been so fortunate. Nothing mattered more than keeping her safe while they searched for his killer. Confessing his feelings might have to wait until the villain was apprehended.

"Julius, please send word to Allendale. He must be told that I am all right and recuperating or he will be mad with worry."

He clenched his jaw and nodded. "I'll send a messenger off to him now and also call on him as soon as I've finished at the Easton townhouse. But the townhouse must take priority. I want to make certain Mr. Barrow and the constables have overlooked no important clues."

"Take notes. It is easy to forget details when there are so many that will be swirling in your head. And do not forget about my aunt. She'll arrive sometime before supper and will be quite distraught. I'm sure I will be up and about by the afternoon and you can take me to–"

He growled. "You are not getting out of bed today."

"But–"

"No," he said with a lordly authority that might have sounded commanding to others, but he knew Gory would ignore him if she had a mind to disobey. And she did have a mind to do just that because being forced to lie idle while others were working on solving this mystery was the most frustrating thing imaginable to her. "Please, Gory. Trust me to take care of matters just for this one day."

She closed her eyes. "This is so irritating, Julius."

His manner softened. "I know, love. But you'll be of no use to anyone if you do not take proper care of yourself. That blow to your head was quite serious. You're fortunate it did not kill you. Promise me you'll stay in bed. I cannot be worrying about you while I am trying my best to save you."

She sighed. "I promise."

He studied her, surprised by her easy surrender.

"My head's in a spin," she admitted. "I could not even walk back here on my own. If you hadn't carried me back to bed, I would have fallen in the hallway. My body is also yelling at me and insisting I rest. It has more sense than I do, I suppose."

He donned his jacket and then strode forward to kiss her lightly on the forehead. "Thank goodness you're alive, Gory. Try to stay that way."

He marched out of his bedchamber and sought out Greeves to give his butler instructions. These included the limited list of people permitted to see Gory. "Lord Allendale, too. But have Mrs. Quinn," he said, referring to the capable Thorne family housekeeper, "remain in my bedchamber with them for the duration of Lord Allendale's visit. She is not to leave, even if Allendale orders her out. Mrs. Quinn must stand her ground and has my full authority to have him tossed out if he gives her any trouble."

Greeves nodded. "Very good, my lord."

"Mrs. Quinn also has my permission to lock Lady Gregoria in my bedchamber if the blasted girl attempts to sneak out of bed."

The butler's lips quivered at the corners in the hint of a smile. "Of course, my lord."

Did he sound like a jealous ape?

No doubt.

"It is for her protection, Greeves. There is a murderer on the loose and I will trust no one until he is caught."

"Understood, my lord. She is fortunate to be under your protection. Please believe that none of us take the matter lightly. We shall watch her like hawks."

It was a short carriage ride to Gory's home. The place was already buzzing with activity when he arrived. The constables were there, as was Mr. Barrow and his best runner, a burly fellow by the name of Mick.

The earl's body was still on the floor of the study, unmoved.

"The murder weapon is a knife," Mr. Barrow said, indicating the earl had been stabbed repeatedly through the heart. "But this candlestick is what we believe was used to knock Lady Gregoria unconscious. Just as she surmised."

"Lady Gregoria knew what weapon was used to knock her out?" a man said from behind Julius.

Julius turned and quickly took the measure of this stranger who stared back at him. "Who are you?"

"Inspector Alexander Havers, my lord." He bowed to Julius, but there was an air of arrogance in his manner. "I am the magistrate's man in charge of this investigation. At your service, Lord Thorne."

"You know who I am?" Julius nodded to acknowledge the man who appeared to be in his late twenties at most, not even thirty yet. He had hawk-sharp dark eyes, and carried himself with an authority beyond his years.

"Yes. Your family is quite well known in London."

"What did you mean by your remark concerning Lady Gregoria?" Julius asked. "She happens to be one of London's most illustrious experts in the field of forensic studies. She is in charge of the Huntsford Academy's new laboratory, as I am sure you are aware since she has already helped your constabulary solve several crimes."

Havers held his hands out wide and nodded. "I meant nothing by my comment, my lord."

"Yes, you did. Lady Gregoria is a *victim*, and I will not allow you to consider her a suspect."

Havers glanced at Mr. Barrow. "All right, for now I will rule her out."

"For now?" Julius wanted to smack the man's arrogant head against the wall, but that would serve no purpose other than to antagonize him. "I know you must consider everyone, Havers. But you will be wasting your time by fixing your attention on her. She did not do it."

"Forgive me, my lord. But that has yet to be determined." He held up his hands in supplication again when Julius scowled. "Please, Lord Thorne. I am not saying she did do it. Your high opinion of her carries great weight with me. But I am no novice to such investigations."

"He is the magistrate's top man," Mr. Barrow said. "I've worked with him on several investigations and he is very good, my lord. He'll get the job done."

"Is that so?" Julius frowned. "Make certain you get it done right, Havers. Tell me what you have learned so far."

Julius took notes as the man went over every detail. The position of the earl's body. The knife found plunged in his heart. The number of stab wounds. The bruising around his neck. The extent of the body's decomposition. "Do you think a woman could have overpowered him to stab him with such force?"

Havers nodded. "A strong woman, perhaps."

Julius arched an eyebrow. "Someone built like a man?"

"Perhaps, or someone clever and swift." He cast Julius a wry grin. "I have seen Lady Gregoria from a distance. I know she could not have done this simply by brute force. But she is very clever, is she not? And she knows the workings of the human body better than anyone else in London. She could have surprised her uncle."

"Caught him unaware? But she didn't," Julius said, his voice a lethal growl.

Was Havers purposely riling him?

Havers sighed. "Your admiration for the lady is duly noted, but her interests are best served by letting me do my job. What other questions do you have for me?"

Julius tried his best to set aside his annoyance, for nothing was more important than protecting Gory. He had promised to find out all he could and present the facts to her. If she were then able to figure out the identity of the killer based on these clues, all the better. "Was the knife angled upward or downward? Can you tell if the first knife thrust was the lethal blow? Have you drawn any conclusions as to the killer's height? Was he tall and stabbing downward? Short and stabbing upward? Or was it a direct stab?"

Havers arched an eyebrow. "Are you asking me these questions or is Lady Gregoria?"

"I am standing before you. She is recovering from her injuries in my brother's home. He happens to be the Duke of Huntsford."

"I am well aware, Lord Thorne. Lady Gregoria has a wedding coming up, does she not?" His manner turned surprisingly serious. "My job is to discover who did it. What the magistrate chooses to do about arresting that person is completely up to him. But if the clues all point to Lady Gregoria, then she had better marry Lord Allendale as soon as possible to protect herself."

Julius well understood what he meant, for Gory would need to gain the protection afforded those of the peerage in order to avoid imprisonment or hanging. Not that the privilege of peerage extended to acts of murder, but would certainly be to her benefit if the verdict was returned as manslaughter or she argued self-defense. Any tribunal would show greater deference to a viscountess. "Lady Gregoria is *not* the culprit. If the clues all point to her, then someone is setting her up to take the fall. I suggest you keep that in mind as you investigate. Who gains by getting rid of the earl *and* Lady Gregoria? That is the question you should be asking."

Having said that, he strode upstairs to Gory's bedchamber to see what else he could discover. Mr. Barrow followed him and began to report what he had learned when searching her bedchamber only moments earlier. "I spoke to her maid a few minutes ago. She confirmed this gown was the one she wore to the musicale last night."

He pointed to a pale peach confection that had bloodstains on it, too. Not as many as were found on her wedding gown that was drenched in it.

Julius knelt beside the garment. "Yes, I can also confirm this is what she wore."

She had looked delectable in that gown.

He even remembered getting an earful from Gory months ago, complaining how her dowager godmothers, Lady Dayne and Lady Withnall, had purchased clothes for her in the sunniest colors, and was it not a ridiculous waste?

Having seen her in many of her new outfits, he determined that the dowagers were quite clever in choosing these softer colors for her. They ought to have been congratulated for their efforts to turn her into a *ton* diamond and fashion a brilliant match for her.

Julius certainly had fallen under her alluring spell.

He was glad they were not allowing Gory to don her old, drab gowns that sucked all vitality from her beautiful face.

There was no prettier debutante in all of London this Season, although Gory was not happy about her transformation from caterpillar to butterfly since she had never been keen on receiving suitors. For this reason, Julius had been taken aback upon learning she had accepted Allendale's proposal.

The man had come seemingly out of nowhere and acted fast. "May I have a closer look at the gown, Mr. Barrow?"

"Yes, my lord. But carefully, please. Best not to dislodge any evidence it might hold." The Bow Street runner gave a shake of his head. "Would you care for my thoughts on the matter?"

Julius nodded, for he had formed ideas of his own and wanted Mr. Barrow's confirmation that they were of the same mind. "Indeed, I would."

Mr. Barrow cleared his throat. "I think she was wearing this peach silk gown when she walked downstairs to investigate the raised voices coming from the study. I think she was then struck from behind and knocked out cold. In fact, hit so hard that the killer believed her to be dead."

"Dear heaven," Julius muttered. "But that mistaken belief probably saved her life. Does this mean the killer was inexperienced? Perhaps his first time harming anyone?"

"Quite possible, my lord."

Julius went through the gowns in her wardrobe, noting droplets of red on many of them, as though the villain had sifted through them, heedless of the bloodstains he was leaving on these clothes.

Or perhaps each was tainted on purpose.

He then walked slowly around the room while conversing with Mr. Barrow. "The killer was probably left-handed," Julius mused, uncertain what he ought to be looking for as he attempted to reconstruct the killer's actions.

Clearly, Gory had surprised him by walking into the study as the murder was occurring or had just occurred. "She walks in...the door swings inward, so she must have made her way well into the room and was then struck behind her left ear."

He pretended to bring a candlestick down on her head in a manner that matched the trajectory of the blow. "Yes, likely with his left hand," he muttered to himself. "Otherwise, the blow would have been to her right temple."

"Very good observation, my lord. It is a possibility. Do you know if her uncle was left-handed?"

"No, but Gory...that is Lady Gregoria will know. What does it matter? He was surely already dead or dying when she entered the study."

Mr. Barrow nodded. "Aye, but it does not hurt to ask. We want to be as precise as possible, especially since Lady Gregoria seems to be worried that she and her uncle might have been the ones to do battle."

Julius shook his head. "No. Emphatically, no. She heard the argument, walked in on it, and was struck from behind by someone who favors his left hand. We must ask her if she knows of any persons within the household or among the earl's acquaintances who are left-handed. But the bigger puzzle is the matter of her wedding gown."

"Aye, that does leave one scratching one's head," Mr. Barrow agreed.

Julius walked over to the window and peered out onto the Easton garden that was not particularly well maintained. The earl and his wife were not fastidious people, but Gory was. It showed in the tidiness of her room, a surprisingly feminine room that brought a smile to his lips. For all her brazenness and bravado, there was a traditional side to her that he found endearing.

He turned back to Mr. Barrow with a puzzled frown on his face. "Why would the villain bother to change her out of the gown she wore to the musicale and put her in the one she was to wear to her wedding? Does it not strike you as particularly cruel? A cruelty perhaps aimed directly at Lady Gregoria? It also suggests to me that more than one person was involved."

"Yes, to all your conjectures, m'lord. It is not easy to undress and then dress an unconscious body. Why take the time and risk being discovered? Yet the killer was willing to do just that in order to make certain Lady Gregoria would be found this way and positioned beside her uncle's body."

"Ridiculous," Julius grumbled.

Mr. Barrow nodded. "We could easily identify the outline of her body on the bloodied carpet, so I assume this is exactly the scene they intended to set. Uncle with knife sticking out of his chest and niece with her head bashed in. However, this added touch of the wedding dress makes no sense, other than it strikes me as particularly vicious."

"Quite sickening," Julius muttered. "As is the fact they rummaged through her wardrobe and marked all these gowns with blood."

Mr. Barrow sighed in disgust. "Agreed."

"Is it possible the killer's accomplice was a woman, Mr. Barrow? Lady Gregoria's ties were perfectly laced when she came to me, and I...well, you saw her and know her condition. Would a man have done up her laces so expertly? I have never done so and I..."

Blessed saints.

He was not about to discuss his entertainments with bed partners.

"What, my lord? Were you going to say that you have done up many laces? Yes, I imagine you are quite expert at it."

Julius raked a hand through his hair. "I mean...one of the villains must have been a woman. Men simply do not bother lacing with that level of precision."

"Agreed." Mr. Barrow cleared his throat. "I have been married to my beloved for over twenty years now and have never once laced her up properly." He splayed his fingers. "Fat hands. Pudgy fingers."

Julius had gained experience in his rakehell days, but the ties he laced were usually fashioned in haste and never managed to turn out as meticulously as Gory's had been done.

"Quite strange," the Bow Street man said, frowning. "Sends a shiver through me."

They returned downstairs and shared their thoughts with Havers who listened attentively and then remarked, "Seems these culprits felt at ease within the house, as though they knew how the Easton home functioned and were comfortable moving about in it."

"Aye," Mr. Barrow said. "The perpetrator was someone familiar with this residence, I'll wager."

Julius frowned. "If you suggest Lady Gregoria again, Havers, I am going to punch you."

"No cause for that, my lord," he replied, holding out his hands in a gesture that was meant to be conciliatory but merely came across as arrogant. "Have we not made some progress? We are now looking for accomplices and possibly a left-handed killer. One of them might be a female because few men would have done up Lady Gregoria's laces so properly. Of course, nothing can be ruled out yet. The killer could have been a fastidious man."

"And yet left such a messy pool of blood?" Julius shook his head, wishing he knew more about the investigative process.

In truth, what he saw only left him more confused.

"This might have been the perpetrator's first murder," Havers said. "Yet, he could have been quite experienced with the ladies. Not his first time in a boudoir."

Julius regarded him impatiently. "What are you suggesting?"

He stared at Julius. "You and Lady Gregoria seem very close."

"Are you out of your senses?" Julius stared back at him, scowling. "Do you think she and I planned her uncle's murder? Then I struck her so hard that I almost killed her? I can assure you, I would have done a cleaner job of the earl's demise. And Lady Gregoria would have done a *smarter* job of it. In fact, so smartly done that no one would have realized his death was even a murder."

Mr. Barrow stepped between them. "My lord, might I suggest we move on to speak to the earl's solicitor? I do not think anything more will be accomplished here." He next turned to Havers. "If you dare deal this rudely with Lady Gregoria, I shall punch you myself."

"You did not need to intercede between me and that oaf," Julius said as they strode out of the townhouse and shouldered their way through the crowd that had now gathered. He recognized one of the Bow Street runners amid the throng, the man's gaze intent as he gave a curt nod to his employer and then returned to studying the onlookers. "But I meant it, Mr. Barrow. I will lay him low if he does not adjust his attitude, especially when questioning Lady Gregoria."

"He will be polite to her, my lord. He has an enormous chip on his shoulder because his grandfather was a duke."

"That man's grandfather was a duke?" This surprised Julius for Havers was built more like a prizefighter than a gentleman. He supposed the same could be said of the Thorne men, including himself, even though he was considered the more elegant of the three brothers.

"Havers happens to be the offspring of the youngest of four sons. He is the only one among all the men in that family worth a farthing. The other Havers men are all reprobates and drunkards. A constant source of embarrassment for him."

Julius climbed into his carriage along with Mr. Barrow and settled his large frame against the squabs. "That does not give him the right to take out his frustration on others."

"Understood, my lord."

They took a short detour to call upon Lord Allendale, just as Julius had promised Gory he would do. But Allendale was not at home, or so his butler advised. Grumbling, Julius climbed back in his carriage. "The wretch was not there," he muttered in response to Mr. Barrow's questioning gaze. "Hasn't been home since last night, apparently."

"His butler told you that?"

"Surprised, Mr. Barrow?"

"Yes. Most are more discreet regarding their master's whereabouts."

"I made up a story about our having an appointment concerning wedding matters. Since the wedding breakfast is to take place at the Thorne residence, he accepted the lie without question. I don't know where Allendale has been all this week, nor could his butler tell me his whereabouts this morning since he did not know either. One thing for certain, he was not at last night's musicale. Do you not think it odd for a man who is merely a week away from his own wedding to ignore his betrothed as he has done?"

"Aye, m'lord. It gives one reason to wonder."

They rode on in silence, each lost to their thoughts.

It was not long before they reached the Inns of Court. Gory's uncle used Mayfield & Sons as his solicitors. They were not of the finest character, but this better served Julius since he knew the senior Mayfields, the right honorable Harold and his younger brother, Reginald, who resembled a weasel, could be bribed to give him information that would otherwise be held in strictest confidence.

Julius was fairly well known in London's business circles as well as its elite social circles, so it came as little surprise when Reginald Mayfield rushed out of his office to greet him most solicitously. "Lord Thorne! We are honored by your presence. How can I be of service?"

Julius waited until they were seated in the solicitor's impressively large office and the door shut to afford them privacy. "The magistrate will call upon you shortly."

Mayfield paled noticeably. "May I ask what this is about?"

Julius leaned forward and eyed him intently. "The Earl of Easton was murdered last night and his niece was badly injured."

The man's expression of surprise appeared genuine.

But as facts were revealed, it could turn out that this solicitor was merely a consummate actor. Julius was not of a mind to trust anyone yet.

"Will she recover?" Mayfield asked with seeming concern...or was he seeking confirmation that Gory was not going to name him as one of the assailants?

Julius nodded. "We are hopeful."

"Thank goodness. She is an odd girl, but I would never wish her ill."

Yes, Gory was odd. Quirky. Eccentric. Independent.

Completely brilliant.

Soft and loveable.

Mayfield cleared his throat. "How may I help you, my lord?"

"I am sure you can guess, Mr. Mayfield. Her circumstances are an open secret."

He appeared surprised. "An open secret?"

Julius arched an eyebrow. "Her dowry is not the true temptation, is it? Lady Gregoria's real value is in her inheritance."

The man began to fumble with some papers on the desk before him. "I see, then you know."

"Yes. So do not play coy with me."

"My lord, may I ask who told you about her sizeable inheritance?"

"No, Mr. Mayfield, you may not. I make it a point never to reveal my sources. But the magistrate's investigator is also aware and will be asking for those documents. I suggest you allow me to have a look at them first. I may be able to deflect some of his questions."

The solicitor made a small show of appearing indignant, but Julius could see he was afraid. "Unfortunately, I am late for a client appointment and cannot show them to you at the moment. Perhaps another day?"

Julius nodded. "Tomorrow, then. But I warn you, Mayfield, you had better be ready to produce the documents, for I and the magistrate's man will be asking for them. Do not think to conveniently lose them or destroy them, for you will be charged as an accomplice to the earl's murder. Perhaps the magistrate will declare *you* the murderer."

The man gasped. "But that is absurd!"

"Is it? I do not find it so." He cast Mayfield a pointed look. "Shall we start over? Let us get serious now. No more lies or bluster, for you do not help yourself by putting me off. Confirm the details of her inheritance for me now. Let me see the relevant documents. Any evasiveness on your part will put you at the top of the investigator's suspect list…and rest assured, I'll make certain it does."

"But I did not do anything!"

Julius arched an eyebrow. "Then you need have no fear of being honest with me, should you?"

CHAPTER 4

JULIUS HAD GOTTEN a good deal of information out of Reginald Mayfield, enough of interest that he ought to have been in better humor by the time he returned home in the early afternoon. But he had also gotten enough attitude from Havers earlier in the day that he was in a bearish temper by the time he alighted from his carriage.

The clock chimed to mark the two o'clock hour just as he mounted the stairs to look in on Gory. He had hoped to find her asleep or otherwise comfortably resting in his bedchamber, and was not pleased to see Allendale seated in the chair beside her bed...*his* bed...and holding Gory's hand.

He wanted to haul the man to his feet and toss him out the window.

So what if he was behaving like an angry ape?

Allendale rose and turned toward him, appearing equally ill-tempered. "Did you not think to send word to me, Thorne? I had to hear the news from Lady Withnall."

Where had the viscount encountered that snoopy termagant?

In truth, he liked the old dowager and her constant companion, Lady Dayne, but there was no denying Lady Withnall was a meddlesome, old bat who often took amusement in stirring up trouble. "I sent a messenger to your home at the crack of dawn to advise you of what happened. I also happened to stop by there afterward to do you the courtesy of a personal visit, but you were still not at home. I suggest you not take off again because the magistrate's man is going to want answers as to your whereabouts last night."

"You condescending arse. How dare you suggest I spent the night elsewhere." He curled his hands into fists. "And what is Lady Gregoria doing in *your* bed?"

"She was almost killed last night, and this is what concerns you?" His hands were also curled into fists as he took a step toward Allendale. "If you think I am—"

Mrs. Quinn gasped to capture his attention.

Right, he'd instructed her to remain with Gory if ever Allendale came to see her.

"Please, my lords. Lady Gregoria is not well. Your raised voices can only be distressing her. She is quite fragile at the moment."

Gory?

Fragile?

He noted the blaze of fury in Gory's eyes.

She was about to climb out of bed and box them both about the ears for behaving like puffed up arses.

Julius sighed and held his hands up in a sign of surrender. He did not want her climbing out of bed. She was still too weak and he did not trust her to stand on her own. The blow had left her with a concussion, stitches in her head, and possibly vertigo since she could not walk without weaving.

"Sorry, Gory," Julius said, running a hand through his hair in consternation. "I'm finding the progress of the investigation to be quite frustrating."

"At least you are participating in it," she replied, obviously exasperated. "All I have been doing is sitting like a useless vegetable in this bed."

And yet, she looked exhausted.

Quite pale, too.

"I meant to rest," she explained when he remarked on it, "but Lady Dayne and Lady Withnall showed up shortly after you left. Then Marigold and Leo came by while they were still here. All of them had no sooner left than Lord Allendale arrived."

"Then you have not had a moment to close your eyes?" He

frowned as he turned to Allendale. "Come into the study and we shall talk. Gory desperately needs her rest. Is it not obvious she is unwell?"

Nor was she in any condition to marry that oaf within a week's time.

Nor would she ever marry him, if Julius had his way.

Had Allendale brought up the possibility of postponing the wedding? Had Gory? Or were the two determined to move ahead with their nuptials?

Allendale did not appear pleased by his request to leave Gory's side, but he gave a reluctant nod and followed Julius downstairs to the study.

"Care for a drink, Allendale?" Julius motioned to the crystal decanters of cognac, bourbon, port, and other libations perched atop a bureau in the corner of the study. This was Ambrose's domain, for he was the Duke of Huntsford and owned the townhouse, while Julius was merely a resident guest.

However, he was never made to feel like an interloper.

Ambrose had always treated him as a valued member of the Thorne family. He, Octavian, and Ambrose would give the shirt off their back for each other without ever waiting to be asked.

Since Julius was the brother who traveled most when attending to family business matters, he had never bothered to acquire his own residence in London. Why should he when Ambrose had always welcomed him with open arms, and given him and Octavian each their own suite of rooms?

Allendale settled casually in one of the plump leather chairs. "No drink for me. I won't be staying long. Nor will Lady Gregoria."

Julius moved to stand beside Ambrose's desk, his hands gripping the edge of the massive piece of furniture to keep him from grabbing Allendale and throttling the arrogant oaf.

Of course, the man had every right to be furious Gory was comfortably ensconced in Julius's bed. After all, she was Allendale's betrothed and not his. Were their positions reversed, Julius knew he would be spitting fire, angry as a hornet, and punching every wall that got in the way of his fists. "I understand your concern, Allendale. But she cannot be moved yet, not only because of her injury. There is a killer on the loose and I have already made arrangements for her constant protection. The magistrate's man will be here shortly to question her. Dr. Farthingale will also come around later today to see how she is faring."

"They can do the same at my home. We shall be married by the end of the week, so where's the scandal?"

"Not a good idea," Julius insisted because his concerns went beyond mere jealousy. This was about protecting Gory. Until Allendale could confirm where he had been last night, there was no chance Julius would ever allow him to be alone with her. "She's here because she wants to be with Adela. The two of them are as close as sisters. Adela and my brother will be home tomorrow, so there is no question she must remain here. Obviously, I have taken other quarters."

"Then I shall stay here, too," he said, eyeing Julius warily.

"No." Julius folded his arms over his chest. "No one stays here until they are ruled out as suspects."

Allendale growled. "You dare accuse me of her uncle's murder? What reason would I have to do him harm? I am marrying his niece in a matter of days!"

"Then you will not be putting off the wedding?"

"No, the arrangements are all in place, as you well know since the wedding breakfast is to take place here. I will not have the ceremony canceled or postponed. Her aunt will be in mourning, so it is understandable that she will not attend. You and I both know she is a miserable hag. If Gregoria feels we ought to retire after the ceremony and leave our guests to enjoy the wedding breakfast without us for the sake of decorum, then this is what we shall do. However, the wedding proceeds as planned. Any other questions, Thorne?"

"Yes, several more." He struggled to maintain his composure. "Where have you been all week long and especially last night? Gory has hardly seen you. Why were you not with her at the musicale? Where were you?"

"You know what, this conversation is over. I do not answer to you. In fact," he said with another growl, "I have had just about enough of you. I'm taking Lady Gregoria out of here now."

Julius shot him a lethal glower. "Over my dead body."

"That can be arranged," Allendale shot back, now starting for the door. Howeveer, he paused with his hand on the doorknob to turn back and glare at Julius. "You do not fool me for a moment, Thorne. Gregoria is mine and you will never get your hands on her."

"Do you think I would ever behave so disrespectfully toward her?" But he sure as blazes intended to woo her away from Allendale. That he had only a few days remaining in which to do it was a problem, but one that could be overcome if Gory loved him. "Answer me this, Allendale. Do you love her enough to believe in her innocence beyond any evidence put before you?"

"What are you talking about?"

"Someone is setting Gregoria up to take the blame for her uncle's murder. Maybe it is you."

"I've had enough of this, Thorne. You are fortunate I do not call you out."

Julius wished he would. Even though they were equal in height, Julius was brawnier and no stranger to battle. The man was no match for him. For this reason, he knew Allendale was merely making idle threats.

Of more serious concern were Allendale's movements last night.

Where had he been?

Until he came up with a verifiable alibi, Julius considered him a suspect. Nor did Julius overlook the fact that Allendale favored his left hand. Many still regarded that trait as a mark of the devil's work and schoolmasters often forced the use of one's right hand when writing, but it remained obvious that Allendale's stronger hand was his left one.

Was it beyond all reason to believe he might have been the villain in her uncle's study last night who knocked her out from behind when she unexpectedly walked in on him while the murder was in progress?

They were about to exchange more words when there came a

sharp rap at the study door. Allendale still had his hand on the knob and now threw the door wide open to reveal an agitated Greeves. Julius knew his butler would never have knocked so loudly unless it was something important. "What—"

He broke off and muttered under his breath when he saw Havers standing behind the distressed butler. "Forgive me, my lord. But Mr. Havers insists on seeing Lady Gregoria. However, I would not permit him upstairs without your authority."

"Quite so," Julius muttered. "Come in, Havers. Let me introduce you to Lady Gregoria's betrothed, Lord Allendale. You might ask him where he was last night."

"Arse," Allendale grumbled, drawing out his watch fob and checking on the time. "You will forgive me if I put you off for now, Havers. I have another appointment and I am already late for it."

Julius knew the man was lying. "Only a moment ago, you were insisting on packing up Lady Gregoria and moving her into your home. Did you forget about your appointment then? How convenient of you to recall it now."

"I will not stand for this. Out of my way, Havers."

"This won't take but a few minutes, my lord," Havers said, blocking the doorway. "I would appreciate your cooperation in tying up all loose ends."

"No. Get out of my way or I will file a complaint with the magistrate and have you discharged." He shoved Havers aside and stormed out of the Thorne townhouse.

"He happens to be left-handed," Julius remarked, frowning as he, Havers, and Greeves watched Gory's betrothed climb into his waiting carriage and leave with all haste. "Come into the study, Havers. Let's have a quick chat before I escort you upstairs to speak to Lady Gregoria. I must warn you, she's had visitors all morning long and was not able to rest. Allendale was here when I returned a short while ago. He needs to be watched."

"As do you, my lord."

Julius scowled at him. "You are riling me again, Havers. This is my home. I can kick you out, and I do not need to make up some blatantly false excuse."

"It is not my intention to anger you, Lord Thorne. This investigation is still in its very early stages and I cannot dismiss anyone as a suspect yet. However, if I truly thought you were involved, I can assure you, I would not be allowing you anywhere near the crime scene or permitting you access to any details of the investigation. What did you and Mr. Barrow learn from the Earl of Easton's solicitor?"

Julius motioned for him to take a seat.

Havers did so, but unlike Allendale who was all conceit and pompous swagger, he sat tensely on the edge of the chair. "You may as well tell me everything since I am going to find out anyway."

Julius was eager to relate that conversation. "Lady Gregoria stands to inherit an additional one hundred thousand pounds upon her uncle's death. Everything else goes to the next earl, some chap from Virginia. The solicitor, a little weasel of a man called Reginald Mayfield, will be sending word to him today. Of course, it could take months for a response, or longer if the heir is not at his last known address."

"And what about Easton's wife? What does she stand to inherit?"

Julius's mouth set in a grim line. "Ten thousand pounds and a small cottage in the Cotswolds. Not very generous, but…she would get that one hundred thousand pounds if Lady Gregoria dies unmarried or is somehow ruled to have forfeited her bequest."

Havers nodded. "As she would if Lady Gregoria were found guilty of murdering her uncle?"

Julius let out a breath. "Yes, for certain. But why would Lady Easton be involved in the murder of her own husband? Is she not better off maintaining her status as the current countess rather than as a mere dowager resigned to a cottage outside of London? By killing him, she loses use of their townhouse, the Easton heirloom jewelry, her comfortable allowance. The stature. The town life."

Havers arched an eyebrow. "But she stands to gain a small fortune and her freedom if she manages to dislodge that inheritance from Lady Gregoria, is it not so?"

"True, and this important detail cannot be overlooked," Julius said.

"I am overlooking nothing right now, my lord. Be patient as I continue to gather evidence. However, you would never believe some of the ridiculous motives behind cases such as these. Jealousy, anger, greed, hatred."

"Intense hatred to plot something so nefarious as to change Lady Gregoria out of the gown she wore at the musicale and dress her in her wedding attire," Julius muttered. "How does this make any sense? How could anyone manage it on their own?"

"Perhaps Lady Easton had a lover to assist her," Havers mused.

"A lover? Lady Easton?" The possibility was laughable, for the woman was a bitterly unpleasant, old crone. Still, it was not to be ruled out. "Why did she and her accomplice not kill Lady Gregoria and leave no doubt as to the widow's inheriting the hundred thousand pounds?"

Havers shook his head. "Perhaps they thought they had killed her. That was quite a wallop the young lady took to her head, if what Mr. Barrow tells me is accurate. Then again, they might not have planned to kill Lady Gregoria but merely intended to plant clues to make it appear she was guilty of the murder."

"Would this not be risky?"

Havers shrugged. "No more risky than doing her in along with her uncle. To kill Lady Gregoria would immediately place Lady Easton as the prime suspect. She might not have wanted us to look too closely. Is she not better off positioned as the heartbroken widow who stands to lose her position in society and elegant style of living while the greedy niece inherits a fortune?"

"I see," Julius muttered. "You'll need to send a man to Windsor where Lady Easton's sister resides and find out if she truly was there. If so, when did she arrive and when did she leave? Check the mail coach ledgers, too. Even though she rode to Windsor in the Easton carriage, she could have easily returned to London by public coach and then immediately returned to Windsor the same way, no one the wiser."

Havers arched an eyebrow. "My lord, I do not need instruction on how to do my job. I have already sent a man to Windsor, as it so happens."

This surprised Julius. "You have?"

He nodded. "Spouses are always a prime suspect, especially a spouse who goes to great pains to prove they were nowhere in town when the murder occurred. Makes me suspicious at once. By the way, I had Mr. Barrow put one of his men to following Lord Allendale."

"Do you consider him a suspect, too?"

"Yes," Havers said. "Lady Gregoria's dowry is ample, but nothing extraordinary. However, if you are correct about the additional one hundred thousand pounds she stands to inherit upon her uncle's demise, then this makes her quite the tempting heiress."

Julius frowned. "But I just told you about her inheritance. How would you know to have Allendale followed already?"

"Just a hunch, but now you have given me confirmation."

Julius remained frowning. "Do you think Lady Gregoria is in danger from him?"

"Hard to say. But if he is the killer, then it would not be a stretch to believe she is."

Damn.

"Never underestimate the lunacy of some of these schemes devised, my lord. Once Lady Gregoria has received her inheritance, her loving husband might plot to do her in. It has happened before. How convenient for a supposedly doting husband to return to their blissfully happy home a few months after they are married and find her dead?"

Julius growled. "Supposedly killed by the same fiend who attacked her uncle and left her for dead months earlier?"

Havers nodded. "He plays the bereaved husband while ridding himself of an unwanted wife and getting to keep all the wealth she brought into the marriage."

Julius had suspected Allendale.

In truth, it was mostly jealousy on his part that made him think ill of the man. However, was it so farfetched? His heart began to pound, for Gory truly was in danger. Whether from Lady Easton or Lord Allendale, or an as yet to be discovered villain who was afraid Gory had seen him and might identify him once her memory returned, all of them had a motive to be rid of Gory.

"The same could be said of you, Lord Thorne."

"What?" Julius shook back to attention at the accusation.

"It is obvious you want Lady Gregoria for yourself. Or is it her funds you find alluring?"

"Blast it, Havers. Shut up. Every time I start to like you, you toss off some stupid remark that reminds me what an arse you are. For the record, I am independently wealthy. Obscenely wealthy, as my bankers have no doubt informed your investigators by now. I have no need of Lady Gregoria's funds. I do not give a fig about what assets she might bring into our marriage, assuming she would ever agree to marry me."

All he wanted was Gory's heart.

"Then you are in love with her?"

"None of your business." But of course, it was this investigator's business to dig up all the information he could on every suspect.

Julius rubbed a hand along his neck and groaned. "Of course, I love her. I expect it is obvious to you. Probably to Allendale, too."

"And how does Lady Gregoria feel about you?"

"I have no idea. I hope she cares for me, although I have given her little reason to do so."

Havers regarded him in that intense way he studied every suspect. "If it turns out she does love you, then that would cause a slight problem with the wedding. Would it not?"

Julius laughed. "An understatement, Havers."

"Are you going to tell her?"

Julius shook his head. "Now? No, not while she remains among your list of suspects. If it turns out she is to be charged with her uncle's murder, then she is better off marrying a peer for protection. You've said so yourself. A viscountess is going to get every benefit of the doubt. Allendale would be her best hope, assuming he is not the killer. In truth, I do not believe he is that ruthless or conniving. Also, his family is quite wealthy. Lady

Gregoria's inheritance is substantial, but I doubt it is enough to compel an already wealthy man to commit murder. Do you, Havers?"

"I'll reserve judgement."

It tore at Julius, for he would do anything to keep Gory safe, even if it meant giving her up for good. It would wreck him, but was she not the most important thing to him?

Havers was studying him again. "You would let Allendale marry her?"

Julius nodded. "Yes, if there was no other way to protect her."

"I don't know if I would do the same for the woman I loved."

"Then you have never been in love, Havers. You would have not a single doubt if your heart had been claimed. You would sacrifice everything to keep her safe."

"My lord, why did you never tell Lady Gregoria how you felt? Were you always in love with her? If so, why did you hide it from her?"

"Because I was a fool. There. Satisfied? Does this put me back in as one of your prime suspects?"

Havers shrugged. "Maybe."

Julius frowned. "Seriously?"

"No, my lord. In truth, you are at the bottom of my list of suspects. It is also possible Lord Allendale and Lady Easton will also be ruled out."

"And Lady Gregoria?"

"I cannot rule her out yet. But we still have much to delve into. Lord Easton's business dealings are next to be explored. Perhaps this crime might turn out to have nothing to do with spouses or potential husbands...or nieces who are impatient to claim their fat inheritance."

"But you don't think this has anything to do with the earl's business connections, do you?" Julius remarked.

"In truth, I do not. It is the wedding gown, you see," Havers replied. "It simply does not fit for a business acquaintance to go to those lengths. Far too personal. Far too time consuming. Quite vindictively designed to draw attention to Lady Gregoria."

"Agreed," Julius muttered.

Havers slapped his hands to his thighs and rose. "It is time for me to speak to Lady Gregoria herself. But it must be done without you present, Lord Thorne."

Julius immediately tensed. "Why exclude me? She isn't well. I am not going to allow you to browbeat her. I'm staying."

"No." He cast Julius a hard look. "I may be inclined to eliminate you as a suspect, but I have done no such thing yet with Lady Gregoria. I will have you locked up if you attempt to interfere with my investigation."

"Blast it, Havers. She—"

"Does not need you interfering with her answers and needlessly creating suspicion about her motives. If she is innocent, I will know it."

"That remains to be determined."

"Yes, it does," Havers replied. "So let me determine it and rule her out."

Julius did not know the man well enough to trust *his* motives.

Ambition was known to corrupt men, and was Havers not one of the London magistrate's top inspectors? What if he sought to make a name for himself by using Gory as his scapegoat?

"Here is what I propose," Julius said, because he would never allow anyone to take advantage of Gory. "I remain in the room, but promise to keep my distance *and* keep my mouth shut."

"No matter how outrageous my questions?"

Julius nodded. "However, I also promise to maim you afterward if you get out of line with her. Lady Gregoria is to be treated with respect."

He thought Havers would offer more argument, but he simply laughed. "Is this what love does to a man? Turns him into a lovesick boar?"

"Unfortunately, yes. I do not care what you think of me, but I do care what happens to her. I intend to protect her at all costs, whether from the real killer or from you." Julius was not looking to start a fight with Havers. He just wanted the culprit apprehended before he could do Gory more harm.

"All right, we have a deal."

Julius led Havers upstairs.

The door to his bedchamber was open and Mrs. Quinn was plumping Gory's pillows as they entered.

Gory cast him a tired smile. "More visitors?"

Julius nodded. "This is Mr. Havers of the magistrate's office. He is leading the investigation and has some questions for you, that is…unless you are too tired to speak to him today."

She waved them both forward. "Now is as good a time as any. Have you gotten any further leads? I feel so helpless lying here, unable to do anything."

Havers took the chair beside the bed while Julius dismissed Mrs. Quinn and then moved to the other side of the room to peer out the window while Gory was interrogated.

He heard the frustration in Gory's voice as Havers asked his questions and she could not provide answers. "I'm so sorry," she said, her voice soft and gentle, "but I cannot remember anything that happened immediately before or after I was struck over the head. I cannot even remember changing out of the gown I wore to the musicale. But I must have, for I was wearing my wedding gown when I regained my wits. Why would I put it on? And who helped me lace it up?"

"We questioned your maid and she claims that she did not do it. In fact, she was already abed by the time you returned from the musicale."

"The staff retires early," Gory confirmed. "My aunt and uncle, as well as myself, have latchkeys to a side door that we use to allow ourselves in after hours."

"We questioned your head butler, as well."

"Was Jergins able to provide you with more information? Did my uncle have a late night visitor? Did he know who this visitor was?"

"No, he claimed also to be abed."

"I'm sorry the staff could not be of more help, but their sleeping quarters are too far removed from our own living quarters to hear much of anything. My uncle keeps an appointments ledger. Were you able to find it?"

"Yes, Lady Gregoria. There was no entry listed for last night."

"But there would be listings for earlier in the day and

throughout the week."

"We are going through each name written down. Was there anyone in particular you would suspect? A friend or business associate of your uncle's?"

Gory sighed. "They were all vile. Not the slightest integrity among any of his business partners, or him, for that matter. His friends were little better. As you may have gathered, he did not always keep the best company. Do you think the killer was one of them?"

"I do not know," Havers responded. "But my instincts tell me to dismiss them as likely suspects. His murder strikes me as too personal."

"Because of my wedding gown?"

He nodded. "It simply does not fit into this crime. Can you recall anything at all about how you came to be wearing it?"

Gory emitted a ragged sigh. "I'm sorry, but I cannot. It is so frustrating for me. I want to help, but I seem to be offering up nothing."

"Never say so, Lady Gregoria. You can only do your best," Havers replied, sounding surprisingly understanding. Julius wondered whether he had a soft heart, after all.

"I am trying so hard," Gory admitted.

Havers asked her a few more questions, but then stopped the interview when Gory seemed to be hit by a sudden wave of fatigue and began struggling to remain alert. "I have exhausted you. I will stop by again tomorrow," he said, rising from his chair. "Lord Thorne knows how to get a hold of me if you recall anything important in the meanwhile."

Julius remained in the background while Gory thanked him and cast him a warm smile.

Havers, this humorless investigator, actually smiled back at her.

Julius walked him out because he wanted to assess the man's impression of Gory. "Do you see now that she could not possibly have committed this heinous crime?"

Havers merely arched an eyebrow. "Let me know if you learn anything new, my lord. I understand you have made arrangements for Mr. Barrow to escort the aunt, Lady Easton, to the Wallingford Arms upon her return to London."

"Yes, if she has no place else to stay. I cannot imagine her willing to remain in their residence, especially this first night. But I intend to escort her to the hotel myself unless I am delayed elsewhere. It is only proper that I attend to the matter and not leave it to my Bow Street man."

Havers continued to regard him skeptically. "I should think Lord Allendale is the proper party to attend to the matter since he is betrothed to Lady Gregoria."

"As you know, Allendale seems to be otherwise occupied and has not given Lady Gregoria or her aunt much consideration. I find it quite odd and disturbing, which is why he must be closely watched. Where was he last night? In truth, where has he been for much of this past week?"

"Oh, I agree," Havers said. "Many unanswered questions still remain. As for questioning Lady Easton, perhaps you ought to leave the matter of escorting her to the hotel to Mr. Barrow. He knows how to engage a suspect and draw out the necessary answers."

"I would leave it to him were it not for Lady Easton's difficult temperament. She is arrogant, intolerant, condescending, and always one to put on airs."

"Ah, then you like her," Havers quipped.

Julius chuckled. "She will deem Mr. Barrow beneath her notice and never deign to speak to him. So, it must be me who does the interrogating."

"All right, but try to be subtle about it. I do not need her sensing she is a suspect. At least, not just yet." He pursed his lips in contemplation, appearing to want to say more.

When he remained silent, Julius prodded him. "You are still frowning. What else troubles you?"

"It is becoming clear to me that Lady Gregoria is very much central to this crime." He held up his hand when Julius began to protest. "Hear me out, my lord. I do not mean to suggest she is the perpetrator. Quite the opposite, I believe she may still be in great danger. How secure is this townhouse? Perhaps she ought to be moved to a safer location."

Removed from the Thorne residence and out of Julius's protection?

Not a chance.

"No. She stays right here. There is nowhere safer and…"

"And what?" Havers asked.

"I am not going to leave her side."

"Day and night?" That raised the inspector's eyebrows. "Allendale might take issue with that."

"Do you think I care?"

"I'm sure you don't," he remarked, now frowning. "But Lady Gregoria might have a thing or two to say about it. Lord Thorne, be careful."

"I always am."

"You mistake my meaning. In your zeal to protect her, you might put her in an untenable situation."

"And ruin her reputation? You know I am ready to do the honorable thing and marry her, so where's the harm?"

"The harm will occur if she is charged with the murder, as you well know. Despite your family's power and influence, nothing will protect her better than marrying Allendale."

"Or finding the real killer. This also assumes Allendale is not the killer."

Havers held up a hand again. "We can talk in circles over this. There is nothing to be done about it right now. I will admit, Lady Gregoria has fallen to the bottom of my list of suspects."

"I am pleased to hear it. What made you change your mind?"

Havers shook his head. "It was not a change of mind. I questioned her without any preconceived notions of her character. This is what any good investigator must do. All suspects must be approached with a clean and clear slate. No presumptions of guilt or innocence. If she is innocent, then–"

"She *is* innocent," Julius insisted.

"*If* she is innocent," Havers repeated, "then she may be in extreme danger. I suggest you engage Mr. Barrow's services to keep watch around the clock on your residence. I do not wish to find you and Lady Gregoria dead come morning."

Julius cast him a wry smile. "Well, that would prove us innocent. Would it not?"

Havers cast him a wry grin and winced. "That is not my preferred manner of ruling out suspects."

CHAPTER 5

GORY HAD BEEN drifting in and out of sleep all afternoon and into the evening. It was now approaching nine o'clock in the evening, for she heard the distant bonging of the clock in the hallway.

Or was it morning?

She could not tell because the drapes were tightly drawn to allow not even a ray of light into the room. Several candles were lit and there was a fire burning in the hearth. It felt like nightfall, for she sensed an evening quiet in the air rather than the bustle of morning activity. However, she was a bit disoriented and it took her a moment to realize she was not in her own bed or even in her own home.

Her breath caught.

There was someone in the room with her, a man sprawled in one of the plump chairs beside the hearth. She immediately recognized Julius, for his handsome face was bathed in a golden light that emanated from the blaze of a warming fire. His eyes were closed and his head casually rested against the cushioned seat back.

However, she did not think he was asleep.

There was too much vibrancy about him even in repose. In truth, his muscles appeared taut, his body tense and ready to spring at the slightest provocation.

She eased back against her pillows, liking the comfortable silence that filled the room.

It wasn't tomb-like, just peaceful.

There were a few familiar sounds such as the quiet whoosh of the wind outside and the hiss and crackle of burning wood in the hearth that gave the room an aura of coziness.

She took advantage of the quiet moment to study Julius in his unguarded pose.

He had the handsomest face she had ever beheld. Indeed, his facial structure was absolute perfection. Firm jaw, aquiline nose, high cheekbones, full lips that she ached to feel upon hers. Even his body structure was perfect. Broad shoulders, trim waist, long and powerful legs. Muscled arms that she yearned to have hold her.

She wiped away a stray tear that trickled down her cheek.

Would she always feel this desperate longing for him?

Gory rarely cried, but she had lost count how many times those tears had spilled forth today.

Some of those crying jags could be attributed to the laudanum she had been dosed with to stem her pain from the ugly wound now tightly stitched and pulling on her scalp. A duller pain throbbed throughout her head. Front, back, and sideways in her skull.

Some of her tears were due to this actual physical pain, but not all.

Her tears also flowed because she mourned for her uncle and the unnatural cause of his death. She also grieved for her aunt, as unlikable as the woman was. But no one should have to deal with such an abrupt and devastating change of circumstances.

Finally, Gory's tears came on at odd moments whenever she was feeling vulnerable and heartsick because of her love for Julius.

It tore her heart to pieces knowing they would never be together.

Why had she agreed to marry Chandler Allendale? All hope of building a life with Julius would be lost once she wed the viscount.

As slim a hope as that was, it existed as a possibility while she remained unmarried.

Dear heaven.

Should she not put off the wedding? No one would think twice about it if she did. Her uncle's death. Her injury. The ongoing investigation.

These were all persuasive reasons for delaying the ceremony.

Or was she merely prolonging her misery by her impractical, and somewhat desperate, wish that Julius might someday grow to love her?

"Gory?"

He must have heard her sniffles, for he was immediately on his feet and stalking toward her with the familiar grace of a big cat. "Do you need more medicine? Dr. Farthingale told me to wait until midnight before I gave you more laudanum. But…"

"I'll manage until midnight. I wasn't crying out in pain."

He grazed his knuckles across her cheek in a loving gesture. "Then why are you crying, love?"

For you.

"No specific reason. Because of everything that's happened, I think."

He sat on the edge of the mattress beside her, no doubt settling close for a better look at her. His hip touched hers, for the mattress dipped as he settled his weight on it and slid her toward him.

Not that she needed any encouragement to draw closer to this man.

This would be the closest she might ever get to being 'in bed' with him.

What a terrible pity it could never turn into something more. But why would he ever be tempted? She had to look awful, perhaps even had a few facial bruises developing, although he did not appear to be showing any signs of disgust.

"I'm sorry, love," he said gently, repeating the endearment as he caressed her cheek again. "I know it's been so hard on you. But you will be well cared for here."

"Are the wedding preparations still continuing?" She groaned as she attempted to sit up, no doubt sounding like a grunting pig rather than an enticing enchantress.

"Gory, you mustn't strain yourself. Let me help you." Julius placed his arms around her and carefully lifted her into a more comfortable upright position. The feel of his big hands on her body only made her ache worse. "About the wedding preparations...yes, they are still ongoing for now. Allendale made no mention of postponing the wedding, so I did not put a stop to anything."

She held tightly to his solid arms, absorbing their strength although she was no longer in need of clinging to him. But she pretended she was, muttering that her head was reeling. It was not a complete fabrication, but not quite true either.

She simply could not let go of Julius.

"I think I must put off the wedding," she said. "I ought to have brought it up while Allendale was here. How is it proper to continue when we are preparing for a funeral?"

"Do not say anything to Allendale just yet, Gory."

She looked up at Julius, surprised that he would disagree with her intention since he was all about traditional sensibilities and logic. "Why not?"

And why was his expression suddenly so serious?

No, not just serious but worried.

He let out a long breath. "You may need to marry him to protect yourself."

"What are you talking about? Protect myself from what?"

He wrapped her more securely in his embrace as he said, "Imprisonment. Hanging."

"Me?" She tipped her head up to stare at him, but this brought their lips scandalously close. The slightest dip of his head and his lips would be on hers.

Do it, Julius.

Kiss me.

He remained as unmoving as a monument carved of granite stone, his eyes a magnificent gray and hard as ice crystals as they remained in locked gazes.

She closed her eyes while her heart began to pound wildly and tingles shot through her body. But when she opened them again, the moment had passed.

He eased back ever so slightly, although he still held her. "Havers is investigating all possibilities. But it is clear someone wants to set you up as the murderess. However, it is also possible you are being set up as the victim who will later be found dead."

She continued to gaze at him, trying to make sense of what he was saying. "Explain it to me, Julius. Please."

He nodded and then proceeded to relate several theories as to who had killed her uncle and why. "My aunt? And you think she has a lover who is acting as her accomplice? A lover?" Gory laughed and then immediately gasped in pain. "Oh, that hurt. Don't make any more jests. You do realize this woman is an ogre. Who would find her appealing?"

"A fortune hunter, perhaps."

"Because she would have *my* fortune if she managed to have me forfeit my inheritance? This would only work if she were rid of me before I married Allendale. Otherwise, the inheritance goes to him since he would be my husband and heir. Well, I suppose she would have an argument to make in the courts that it was not mine to bring into the marriage. But that would take years to pursue and be awfully expensive, not to mention the uncertainty of the outcome."

"And if Allendale is the culprit, then you place yourself in greatest danger by marrying him. Once he has control of your funds, he can plot your demise at his leisure."

She nibbled her lip. "All the more reason not to go through with the wedding. And yet, I might be a fool not to marry him and gain whatever protection of peerage becoming a viscountess might afford me. These are my options? I suppose it is up to me to choose."

"But you are innocent, Gory. I aim to prove it."

She leaned her head against his shoulder, not quite ready to let go of him. "You have more faith in me than I do."

He growled softly. "People don't change, love. Your nature is to be soft and giving."

She laughed again and gasped once more. "Me? Soft and giving? No one has ever described me as that. I am considered odd and ghoulish. Is this not why all my friends call me Gory? Everything Havers hears about me will convince him that I am bloodthirsty and the likely culprit."

Julius kept his arms around her. "Adela, Syd, and Marigold adore you. So do Lady Dayne and Lady Withnall, who we all know is a tough, old bat who likes very few people. She is an excellent judge of character, and will not hesitate to give Havers a stern talking to if he ever dares disparage you."

"He'll need more than a stern talking to if he means to arrest me for murder." She burrowed against him. "Julius..."

"What, love?"

"What is the greater risk to me? My marrying Allendale or my *not* marrying him?"

She felt his muscles tighten. "I cannot answer this yet, Gory."

His response came as no surprise to her, but she ached so much to hear a confession of love from him. Could he not stop being logical for once? Because right now she needed his love so badly. "Is there nothing else you can say to me?"

"No, Gory. It is too early in the investigation."

He sounded pained, too.

But any pain he felt arose from his desire to protect her, and not from any wildly passionate stirring of love. Had he not made this clear to her throughout the years of their acquaintance? He'd never offered her more than a dance at any *ton* affair they both happened to be attending.

Well, every once in a while she had noticed a flicker of heat in his eyes, their cool gray irises turning hot as burning embers. But nothing had ever come of it. He must have been looking at someone else and hiding it well because rakehells knew how to be discreet when arranging assignations. Was this not the mark of an experienced rakehell, this ability to make the lady before him melt at his touch, all the while he silently engaged in a flirtation with another woman across the room?

"I escorted your aunt to the Wallingford Arms earlier this evening," he said, regaining her attention.

Gory's eyes widened in surprise.

She had not thought to ask him about her aunt even though they had been discussing her mere moments ago. "How did she respond to the news?"

"Hard to tell."

"What do you mean?"

He released her and moved off the mattress to settle in the chair that had remained beside the bed. But he then surprised her by taking her hand into his warm and comforting grip. Somehow, he always understood her thoughts and knew she needed his touch. "She assumed the role of grieving widow, but her tears sounded hollow to me." He shook his head. "I don't know, Gory. It is possible I am too close to this investigation to regard it with impartiality."

"You have good instincts, Julius. I've never known you to be wrong."

He chuckled. "Oh, I have made plenty of mistakes."

"So have I," she muttered, thinking of him and wondering if things might have been different between them if she had confessed her feelings.

Why be such a coward about this when she was brave about everything else?

"One of Mr. Barrow's runners will keep watch on her at the hotel," Julius said. "I've arranged to speak to her tomorrow afternoon on the pretext of assisting her with the funeral arrangements. Well, I do aim to help. However, it is likely that your uncle's burial will be delayed. The magistrate will not authorize the release of his body until he is satisfied all possible tests have been run and any required information has been gathered and recorded."

"How long does the magistrate think it will take?"

"A couple of days, perhaps."

"It is not their custom to hold bodies in their morgue for very long," she mused, knowing from experience when the London constabulary had brought her in on other investigations. "And we have already lost this first day. I'll need to see the body as soon as possible. Without delay, Julius. We must go first thing tomorrow morning. I should be fine by then."

Julius snorted. "You don't get out of this bed until Dr. Farthingale gives the nod."

Why did he have to be so thickheaded?

Well, was her head not just as thick? "I'll go on my own if you refuse to escort me."

"Gory, do not be stubborn about this. Your injury is serious."

"And has been properly treated, so there is no need to keep me confined. Am I to be forced to heal only to be clapped in irons when they determine I am the killer? A determination that could have been avoided had I obtained access to my uncle's body to hunt for the clues myself?"

"Gad, I forgot how irritating you can be," he muttered.

The comment was said in jest, but was there not a kernel of truth to it? This was why he would never fall in love with her. She supposed Julius wanted a traditional wife who would not question him at every turn and who knew something about running a household. Gory was better at sewing up body parts than knowing how to darn a sock or stitch a hem.

She frowned at him. "The body first, then afterward a stop at the Easton townhouse so I can return to the scene of the crime. Hopefully, it will help me remember what happened. Depending on when we finish, we can stop for a bite to eat and then head to the Wallingford Arms to interrogate my aunt. If she asks me to postpone the wedding, I will refuse. This will keep the pressure on her and force her to make a move out of desperation."

"No, Gory," he said with a sharp rasp to his voice. "You are only tell her that you will think about it. Then you and I, along with Havers and Mr. Barrow can assess the situation."

"There is nothing to assess. If she murdered my uncle, then she will have no choice but to murder me before I marry. We cannot give her time to plan another attack. I think Havers must also drop hints to her that he has ruled me out as a suspect."

"Convinced of your innocence?"

"Yes, which will only make her more desperate to be rid of me." She liked the idea and thought it was probably the best way to have her aunt tip her hand.

Of course, this assumed her aunt was guilty.

It would all come to naught if she were innocent.

But was this not worth pursuing?

Julius scowled at her.

She smiled back at him. "Of course, I will need you, the Bow

Street runners, and the entire London constabulary to keep a very close watch over me if she does come after me."

He reached over and gave her chin a light tweak. "You are not very demanding, are you?"

"Not at all. Have you not heard? I am a gem and a delight. A *ton* diamond. This is why gentlemen callers have been lining up outside my door all Season," she teased.

"You are a diamond," he said with surprising conviction. "You are also mine to look after. Do you feel up to having a little broth? Something else light for your stomach?"

"No, I'm fine." She closed her eyes a moment and leaned back against her pillows, emitting a sigh. "Julius…"

"Yes, Gory?"

"My aunt is a detestable character, but what if she is innocent? That might point to Allendale as the next likely culprit. Where do you think he has been these past few days?"

He grunted. "I don't know."

"Perhaps he is innocent, too, and was merely having an assignation with another lady. It does not bode well for our marriage if he is already off…*you know*."

"Havers is looking into his movements these past few days. So is Mr. Barrow. Your betrothed is being evasive, and I do not like this. But as you said, he could be innocent and his whereabouts have nothing to do with the murder."

"But not innocent when it comes to being faithful to me. Well, we are merely betrothed at the moment, but is it not nearly the same thing as marriage? He was out all night, and yet denied it. He blatantly lied to us."

"Perhaps he was feeling a need to sow the last of his wild oats because he means to be a faithful husband."

"Do you really believe this?" She cast him a mirthless smile. "I do not. But I have brought this on myself, haven't I? Making myself so unlikable, no other man could want me. I cannot blame them. Who wants a wife who works amid dead things all day?"

"That is only one small aspect of your forensic research," he reminded her.

"True, but you are the only one who understands what I do."

"Because of my involvement with the Huntsford Academy."

She nodded. "Who outside of you or your brothers would ever care about my research work?"

"The London constabulary is grateful to you. So are the families of victims who see the evildoers brought to justice because of your efforts. Nor should you dismiss your importance within the scientific community."

She wished more people felt the same as Julius, but he was a rare man. "When Allendale first showed interest in me, I assumed it was because of our mutual interest in science. Now, I simply do not know what to think. Should I not be able to tell if a suitor is merely courting me for my fortune?"

"Gory, did you even know you had one?"

"No, not until my aunt passed that comment. Even then, I dismissed it and never bothered to follow up on it. Stupid of me, of course. But I assumed it was all tied up in complications and I had best not rely on receiving anything, assuming there was something left to receive by the time it was distributed to me. I thought my dowry was all I could rely upon, which was true because it turns out I was entitled to nothing more until my uncle passed away. The more important question to ask is whether Allendale was aware and courted me for this reason. Do you think he was?"

"I do not know yet. But it is something to be looked into."

"What a fool I am," she muttered.

"No, Gory. Never say this. You had no reason to be on your guard. In truth, you had every reason to believe his interest was sincere."

"But I should have been more wary. Again, my fault for overlooking the obvious signs."

"What signs?" Julius asked.

Gory felt her cheeks suffuse with heat. "His reluctance to kiss me."

Julius inhaled sharply. "Has he never kissed you, Gory?"

"Oh, he has. Once or twice. He approached it with the same ardor as one might kiss one's liverish grandmother. You know, that slight purse of the lips and holding one's breath against the overpowering odor of rose water perfume."

He chuckled. "Not possible. First of all, your scent is delightful. Light and sweet as roses on warm summer's day. Second of all, you are too pretty. And your lips are...well, they are very nicely shaped. The sort of lips a man would not mind kissing."

"Ha! That is a jolly jest. Have you ever thought to kiss me, Julius?"

A log suddenly fell off the burning wood piled in the fireplace, tumbling with a pop and sizzle that surprised them and distracted their attention.

He quickly rose to attend to the fire, making certain it did not burn too low. The wind was blowing harder outside. Gory could hear its steady howl and the *pick-pock* rustle of brittle leaves being tossed around with each gust.

There was more than a hint of winter in the air, but all felt warm and heavenly while in Julius's company in his bedchamber.

Gory did not want him to ignore her question, so she asked it again when he returned to her side. "Was there ever a moment when you wanted to kiss me?"

He released a breath. "Yes, several of them."

This surprised her and she leaned forward eagerly. "Really? When? And why did you not act on that wish?"

"Many reasons. For one, your friends are married to my brothers. Complicates things, doesn't it?"

She nodded. "Yes, it would be awkward for us if we kissed and did not like it. Worse if one of us liked it and the other did not."

He shook his head and chuckled again. "We both would have liked it, Gory. But I do have a code of honor and you are an innocent. Had I ever kissed you, I would have felt obliged to marry you."

"Because my friends are married to your brothers?" She regarded him in disbelief. "And we shared a simple kiss? That is ridiculous. Why would we even tell them? No one would ever have to know."

"Are you serious? You tell Adela, Syd, and Marigold *everything*. Even if you did not, there is always the risk of our being found out. It happens often enough. How common is it to pick up a gossip rag and read about some poor girl being caught with a gentleman in a compromising position? These stories appear almost daily. However, there are more reasons why I would not kiss you."

"More?" Why was she subjecting herself to this humiliation?

"Besides being too close to my family, and also achingly and adorably innocent, you are far too curious."

Weren't all scientifically minded people curious? "Meaning?"

He cast her an appealing smile, one that ravaged her composure. "You would have wanted to explore the possibilities beyond a mere kiss."

Yes, that was true.

"Can you blame me? Your musculature is quite fascinating."

He laughed. "Gory, you cannot tell me such things. But does this not prove my point? You would have been undressing me, eager for a better look at my body, and I would not have stopped you."

More and more surprising revelations, to the point he was making her giddy. "You would have allowed me to explore you to my heart's content?"

Amusement sparkled in those devastatingly gorgeous eyes of his. "Yes, Gory."

She leaned further forward, eager to hear more. "Just how far would you have let me go?"

He arched an eyebrow. "Gad, are you really that innocent? I am a man. We are simple creatures. How far would you have wished to go? Every stitch of clothing removed?"

"Perhaps." She blushed. "For scientific curiosity, mind you."

He cast her a rakish grin. "Is that all? Merely science?"

"Well…" She cleared the sudden frog in her throat. "It would have been fun, too. I expect it would have been the most fun I've ever had in my life. You are quite finely proportioned. The breadth of your shoulders. Your muscled arms. Did you know that your body tapers perfectly from shoulders to hips?"

He remained grinning at her. "No, I did not."

"Surely, one of your paramours must have told you. Your legs are long and nicely shaped. I'll wager your organs are also in excellent condition."

He laughed. "Stop right there. I will not have you dissecting me to find out."

"I would never do such a thing!"

"Teasing you, Gory." He took her hand again and gave it a gentle squeeze. "I doubt I have ever held such a conversation with another young lady."

"Although plenty have enjoyed undressing you and kissing you."

He shook his head and emitted a softer, rumbling laugh. "Not a suitable topic for conversation, especially not with you."

"Because I am unmarried?"

"Because you are blessedly innocent when it comes to men."

"And likely to remain so," she thought morosely. "I don't think I can go through with marrying Lord Allendale. I am going to call off my wedding, Julius. I'll talk to you and Havers before I say anything to him. But how can I marry him when I no longer trust him? So, I will likely end my days a forlorn spinster because no one else will ever propose to me."

"Why are you so convinced Allendale is the only man who will ever offer to marry you?"

She shrugged. "He is the only one who has done so up to now."

"You are still young, Gory."

"Precisely my point. I am at my desirable best right now, and the only offer I have had is from a man who finds me as fetching as his liverish grandmother. What will change to suddenly make me desirable to others? Other than you, no one has danced with me more than once. They all run off screaming."

A smile twitched at the corners of his lips. "Because you purposely scare the wits out of any gentleman who dares brave a dance with you. Admit it, Gory. Conversations about cadavers and blood splatter are not going to endear you to any man partnering you."

"I do not do it all the time," she muttered. "Only to those I wish to chase away."

"Which seems to be all of them so far. Except for me. I always enjoy dancing with you."

She rolled her eyes. "You've only done so out of obligation."

"You are wrong about all of it, Gory. I have never felt obliged to dance with you."

She sniffed. "You've done it out of pity, then."

"Nor out of pity," he said with insistence. "Assuming we get through this situation, I can assure you that you will receive at least one other proposal of marriage in your lifetime."

"Care to wager on it? From whom? The only men I ever talk to are you and your brothers and the staff at the Huntsford Academy. Well, Marigold's husband, too. And her Farthingale family."

"I am not going to wager with you because I would win too easily. It would be the same as stealing from you."

"I suppose you are right. There will always be someone out there looking to marry me for my fortune, assuming I am to inherit it and not be sent to the gallows."

"I am never going to let them imprison you, Gory. In truth, I think Havers does not believe you are guilty of the crime. He's a good ally to have, for the arrests are made upon his recommendation. As for your marriage prospects, I expect they are excellent. You are intelligent, warmhearted, and beautiful."

"Do not make me laugh, Julius. It hurts my head. Not even my parents liked me all that much. Well, they were good parents and they did dutifully care for me. I truly loved them and I expect they loved me. But they did not really *like* me. They did not know what to make of me. I suppose I worried them when they realized I was more interested in taking my dolls apart than playing with them. My aunt and uncle never tolerated me, that is for certain. I could have been a perfect child and they would have despised me. Not that I was ever that good a child."

"I'm sure you were delightful."

"You are going to make me gag, if you keep spouting such compliments."

He laughed again and began asking her questions about her childhood. She found herself rambling, probably making little sense as she spoke about her past. But she appreciated his questions. No one other than her best friends and her dowager angels, Lady Dayne and Lady Withnall, ever cared enough to ask.

Her mind was suddenly awash in these recollections of her younger days. Could it be that her memory was opening up? Is this why Julius was asking her these questions?

Clever fellow.

And he did it so smoothly, appearing to be interested in her early years when all he really meant to do was jar her memory of the present.

It was a good idea, so she allowed her thoughts to wander.

Julius said nothing, just kept hold of her hand and listened to her babble about anything that came to mind. She was now blurting trivial facts about the number of bones in one's body. "Did you know that babies have more bones than adults do?"

"I did not, Gory."

"Do you not find this fascinating?"

"Yes, quite."

She laughed softly. "You do not. You are merely humoring me."

"Not at all." He arched an eyebrow, looking quite wickedly attractive as he smiled at her. "You are a font of knowledge and I am in complete and utter awe of you. What other interesting bits of knowledge do you have to impart to me?"

"My uncle has a mistress." She gasped and stared at him with her mouth gaping open. "Why ever did I say such a thing?"

Julius was also startled by the remark and seemed to be devouring her with his gaze. "Is this what the argument you overheard was about?"

Gory tried to think back to last night, but she simply could not recall. It felt more like something she had overheard weeks earlier, but it was all a fog to her. "Oh, Julius. I don't know. In truth, I do not think so. But who can tell?"

Julius remained visibly tense as he regarded her. "It came out just now for a reason. Who was he arguing with? Your aunt?"

She delicately touched her hand to her temple and rubbed it lightly, hoping to massage the thought from her brain. Losing all memory of these past hours was the most frustrating thing she had ever had to endure. "It feels more like an old argument between my aunt and uncle. Not a new revelation. How could it have been them arguing last night when my aunt was in Windsor?"

"Or so she claims. But this is something to question your staff about. If you heard them arguing, whether last night or in the past, then others in the household might have heard them, too. Perhaps it is relevant to his murder and this is why you suddenly remembered it and brought it up."

"But the voices feel different. Is it not odd that it is the *feelings* I seem to remember and not the facts? I cannot think...oh, Julius, it is all so jumbled in my head. What if I am remembering things wrong? My words might condemn an innocent person."

"Havers and Barrow are gathering clues. They'll be able to tell if something appears not to fit right. But your uncle possibly having a mistress is an important development. It adds another potential suspect. It also gives Lady Easton an added motive for murder."

"Do you think so? I would not call theirs a loving marriage. They were just as miserable to each other as they were to everyone else. Why would she care if he went into the arms of another woman, especially if the liaison was carried on discreetly? Have you ever had a mistress, Julius?"

"No, Gory."

In truth, she did not think he was the sort who ever would, even though it was not all that uncommon for bachelors or married men to do so.

"Do you recall the lady's name? His mistress, I mean."

"No. But perhaps Jergins will know it. Or my uncle's valet. Yes, they are good ones to ask. I'm sure my aunt also has that information. But it is cruel to ask her, especially now that my uncle is dead."

"It may be cruel, but it is necessary. All possibilities must be explored. If your aunt is innocent, she would want the killer apprehended and punished."

Stabs of pain shot through Gory's head as she nodded. "Julius, I am suddenly feeling so very tired. Do you mind if I close my eyes for a while?"

"Go right ahead, love." He reached over and helped her settle back into a reclining position. "Gory, your hands are so cold."

She nodded. "My insides feel cold, too. I think it must be the laudanum wearing off. Perhaps I ought to sit closer to the fire."

"Yes, you are too pale and I can feel your body trembling."

She was trembling because he was touching her and she liked it, but she was also fatigued and losing plenty of warmth, as though a window had suddenly been thrown open to allow an icy wind to blow in and surround her. However, all the windows were tightly shut and the drapes were not billowing at all. It was just her body out of kilter. "Let me curl up in one of the big chairs beside the hearth."

"All right, but I'll carry you over there." Without wasting a moment, he lifted her in his arms. He actually *swept* her into his magnificently manly arms, which would have been quite romantic were she not feeling ill and were he not worried that a killer was on the loose and coming for her.

"Julius, I can walk by myself. Although I would appreciate holding onto your arm for support because I might be a little wobbly."

"I am going to carry you, and that's an end to it." He cast her a stubborn look. "Put your arms around my neck, Gory."

She sighed. "You are being very apish about this."

"I know. Put your arms around my neck."

"Fine." He carried her closer to the fire. She could not resist giving him a kiss on the cheek as he set her down in one of the cozy chairs. "Thank you, Julius."

He tweaked her chin. "Any time, love."

A sudden thought came to her. "Why don't you get a few hours of sleep in your bed? It must be more comfortable than a chair."

"Oh, no," he said with obvious surprise. "It will not do to have anyone notice both sides of the bed rumpled."

"Are you suggesting *that* is what would compromise my reputation?"

"Yes." He moved to the bed, grabbed a blanket off it, and

tucked it around her body. She was already wearing Adela's nightgown and robe as well as a pair of Adela's woolen stockings to keep her feet warm. However, these garments were still not enough to prevent the chill surging through her bones as the laudanum wore off.

It gnawed at her.

"I am already thoroughly compromised, Julius. The two of us are alone in your bedchamber, not to mention you found me in here hours ago and undressed me." Her cheeks heated at the thought, not out of embarrassment but desire. "*Completely* undressed me."

"For medical necessity," he insisted.

"I know, but do you think anyone else will care for the reason?" She trusted Julius to the depths of her soul and knew she would always be safe with him, for he respected her and cared for her as a friend. Sighing, she continued before her feelings overwhelmed her again and she shed more tears. "The entire staff knows what has happened by now, and also knows you are spending another night – *this* night – with me."

Of course, it was merely to guard her.

But who would care about the truth when the insinuations were far more juicy?

It took only one servant to gossip and that would lead to her ruination.

Even her betrothed was aware.

Was not Allendale's reaction odd?

Despite voicing outrage earlier, he had done absolutely nothing else since. He had not even insisted on a chaperone remaining with her. Did this not prove his lack of affection for her? If Allendale insisted on going through with the wedding, it could only be because he wanted her inheritance.

Julius appeared lost in thought as he sweetly tucked the blanket around her. Was he only now realizing the potential danger to his bachelorhood?

Well, he was no fool and must have known they were compromised from the moment he found her in his bedchamber.

"I would never force you to marry me, Julius."

He place his hands on either side of the padded arms of the chair and leaned in close. "Is that supposed to absolve me of all responsibility for your ruination?"

Dear heaven.

Did his eyes have to be so gorgeous?

His hot look was melting her insides.

It was a good thing, she supposed.

Up until a moment ago, her body had been as cold as a frozen tundra.

"Yes, I wish to assure you that I will take all of the blame. If Allendale calls off the wedding, as I would expect he will if he is innocent of the murder…" She cleared her throat. "He will not get over the fact that the two of us have now spent two nights together. His own betrothed spending two nights with someone other than *him*…and mere days from the wedding, no less."

"I don't care."

"Because you are not the cuckolded bridegroom. When word gets out to the public – and it will – you might feel compelled to protect my reputation."

"And marry you because he won't?"

"Precisely. So, I wish to assure you that I would never be so cruel as to force you to marry me."

"You think this is what I am worried about? My having to take you on as my wife?"

He was making her head spin with his smoldering gaze.

Had all rakehells perfected that smoldering look?

"I know you are also worried that someone might want to kill me."

"Might? It is at the top of my list of concerns. You saw something, or heard something, and the killer cannot afford to have you remember it."

"True, but that still does not rule out the problem we are facing. If I survive, then we will have to deal with my compromised situation. I may be forced to resign my role with the Huntsford Academy. That would hurt worse than being ostracized by the *ton*. I never cared for those fancy balls and musicales anyway."

"Gory…"

"You look angry." He was still leaning close and now scowling at her.

"I am not angry."

"Then why are you frowning at me?"

"Because you are infuriating."

"I do not mean to be. I thought I was alleviating your concerns."

He shook his head and leaned in even closer so that she felt his warm breath tease her lips. "You are not alleviating anything."

"I'm not? Then why do you find me so irritating? Tell me what I am supposed to do."

"Close your eyes, for starters," he said with a raspy rawness to his voice that shot tingles through her.

"Why must I close—"

"Because this," he said and crushed his lips to hers, giving her the wildest, most insanely passionate and scorching kiss she had ever received in her entire life or would ever receive again in three lifetimes, if one believed in that sort of thing.

The kiss was endless, the pressure on her mouth sheer perfection.

She wrapped her arms around his neck and drew him closer, encouraging him to deepen the kiss because she was so desperately in need of his touch and his love. Nor was she in any hurry ever to breathe again or ever part from him, especially if she was about to die at the hands of some unknown villain or be accused of villainy herself and sentenced to the gallows.

She did not want to die before experiencing *this*.

Before experiencing Julius.

All of Julius.

Dear heaven.

Was this not a terrible complication?

But was this not also wonderful?

He had his arms around her as though he never wished to let her go. She held onto him just as urgently, clinging to his solid muscles with unabashed desperation, and offering no resistance as he deepened the divine kiss and plundered her mouth with a divinely savage intensity of his own.

She stared at him when he finally ended the kiss and drew back slightly. "Julius, does this mean you like me?"

CHAPTER 6

JULIUS HAD NEVER felt so hungry for a woman as he felt for Gory.

"Am I making too much of this?" she asked, staring up at him with starlight in her eyes. "I suppose we were only in the moment. Or did it signify something more?"

Nor had he ever met a woman so smart about everything except men.

His heart was about to explode with the realization that he was fully, deeply and irreversibly in love with her, and that wayward heart of his was torn and aching over the dangers she was facing.

Was he up to the task of keeping her safe?

Instead of thinking clearly, he was bouncing all over the place like a big, reckless ape.

"Oh, I see." She blushed and began to stammer an apology that made him feel like an utter heel because she was putting the blame on herself for believing the kiss was no more than a passing opportunity for him and he merely took advantage.

He sighed and sank in the chair beside hers with an added groan. "Not only do I like you, but...I am in love with you, Gory. How's that for a revelation?"

She stared at him. "Are you certain?"

Anyone else would have responded with an 'I love you' back at him.

It did not matter that she was about to marry that pompous sod Allendale. The obvious truth was that she had run instinctively to the man she loved, and that was *him*.

Knowing Gory as well as he did, there was not a doubt in his mind that he, not Allendale, had her complete trust and her heart.

She was now asking for clarification on whether he truly loved her because this was Gory, belittled ever since being placed under her uncle's guardianship, her brilliance and worth constantly dismissed, and now she did not understand how any man could love her for who she was. "Yes. I'm sure, Gory. I love you endlessly and desperately."

"It felt like that when you kissed me," she whispered, touching a finger to her lips. "But this is why rakehells have the reputation they do, this ability to make a young lady believe there is no one else in the world for him but her. Please do not lie to me, Julius. This is too important."

"It is only important if you love me back," he said, still savoring the taste of her soft, plump mouth that he could kiss into eternity and never tire of the sweet sensation. "That is all I care about."

"How long have you felt this way about me?"

"Always. From the moment I met you."

Her expression turned pained. "And you said nothing all the while? You were going to let me marry Allendale and..." Tears began to flow down her cheeks. "How could you?"

His heart felt raw and aching, for he had not a single excuse other than he was a stupid, selfish beast who had no appreciation for the treasure he had found until fearing he was about to lose it. Lose *her*. "Your betrothal caught me by surprise. You know how much I travel on behalf of the Thorne family business interests. It was a very busy time for me and my thoughts were on finalizing these important deals and not on romantic entanglements. Sounds lame, doesn't it? I don't know, the time simply got away from me."

"You thought there would be no rush to confess your feelings because who else would want me?"

"Never that, Gory. You are as beautiful as a fairy princess with your bright hazel eyes and tumble of dark hair. There is no one lovelier." He shook his head vehemently. "But I thought your work at the Huntsford forensic laboratory was too important to you and marriage was the last thing on your mind. Obviously, I was wrong. And suffering for it ever since I learned you and Allendale were betrothed."

She regarded him in despair. "And yet, you waited until now to say anything to me. Why did you keep silent for so long? Not even given me a hint of your feelings and let me think you did not like me."

He raked a hand through his hair, for this was getting more complicated than he wished. Of course, he had simply assumed an admission now would satisfy Gory and she would not ask any questions other than how was she to get out of her betrothal in order to marry him?

However, it seemed his admission had only given her more pain that he now needed to assuage. "I cannot make excuses for my stupidity or the mistakes that followed as I tried to figure out what to do next. First, I lied to myself and decided I could get past losing you, that I could forget you and move on. But I quickly realized it was impossible. How does one forget a fairy princess? This past week, escorting you around, has been the worst week of my life." He took a deep breath. "My second step was the decision to stop your wedding."

Her eyes widened. "How? By murdering my uncle?"

She gasped as the accusation spilled from her lips, and so did he. "You really think me capable of that, Gory?"

"No, of course I don't. It just came out because I am so angry with you at this moment."

She sounded so miserable, he wanted to take her in his arms again. But he dared not do it yet, for she was deeply hurt, a soul-deep hurt, and obviously did not like him very much just now.

But did this not also prove she was in love with him?

Well, she hadn't actually said she loved him.

But he knew it.

"You had all week to confess your feelings and ask me to stop the wedding." She stared at him as she spoke and he heard the heartbreak in her every word.

"I know. But it was such a drastic step that I wanted to wait for

Adela and Ambrose to return and talk to them about it."

"Before you said anything to me?"

"Should I not have used a little caution? I was purposely going to break up your wedding."

"And you just assumed I would accept your interference? Meanwhile, you were off carousing just as Allendale has been doing only days before our wedding."

Julius gritted his teeth in frustration. "I was never carousing. All I have been doing is playing cards with friends, as I did last night…and yes, probably drinking a little too heavily because I was so miserable over the fear of losing you. If you must know, I haven't touched another woman in months…a lot of months."

"I don't care."

"Yes, you do." He rose and went to her side to lift her into his arms.

"What are you doing, Julius?"

He settled her on his lap and sat down in the chair he had just made her vacate.

"Put me down!"

He held her firmly on his lap. "No. I want you to hear me out first."

She put her hands to her ears. "What makes you think you can toy with my heart and just kick it in any direction? You do not have the right to drop this on me and think it is all going to be fine. I almost married a man I did not love! One who might be intending to kill me, no less."

"But he won't ever get his hands on you because I am going to marry you."

"Oh, is that so? And then will you simply let me go to the gallows when Havers finds me guilty? Because you cannot protect me from going to prison. You are not a peer and Allendale is. So, I suppose I will be marked for death either way. It is now up to me to decide whether I prefer to die by public hanging or by poison, which is probably the cleanest way for Allendale to kill me. Or he might push me off a cliff while on our honeymoon. Rather messy, and I might not die right away."

He hugged her. "I am going to marry you and protect you. I

will never let anyone hurt you, Gory. I give you my sacred oath to always keep you safe from harm. I am truly sorry I botched this so badly."

She fell asleep crying in his arms.

What an arse he was to drop all this on her when she was at her most vulnerable. He ached for the turmoil he was causing her.

But he could not deny his relief in having it all come out now.

He loved her.

She knew it.

He was always going to protect her.

His valet found them in this same position early the following morning. Gory had passed a difficult night, not only for the confusion he had caused her. Her stitches had turned painful and the laudanum had not helped very much. For this reason, he had kept her cradled on his lap in the hope that his body might warm hers that had turned cold and shivering. "My lord," Robbins whispered, "shall I come back later?"

"No, give me a moment to put her back in bed. She was in a lot of pain last night."

Robbins, who was a genteel, older man with a lot of experience attending to the men in the Thorne family, was obviously at sixes and sevens when it came to dealing with ladies in the household, especially the one having taken over Julius's bedchamber and presently asleep in his arms.

He inched closer to assist Julius as he rose, but then gasped. "My lord, there is blood trickling down Lady Gregoria's ear."

"Blast, have Dr. Farthingale summoned at once." Julius frowned as he gently set Gory back in his bed. "What time is it?"

"Eight o'clock, my lord."

"That late?" But he breathed a sigh of relief. "Then the doctor will arrive fairly soon. Set out fresh clothes for me and my shaving gear. I'll take care of myself, but have Greeves send Dr. Farthingale up the moment he arrives."

"For certain, my lord."

Once his valet had shut the door behind him, Julius turned to study Gory as she lay in deep slumber in his bed. "Oh, love. I thought you were on the mend."

He wondered whether he ought to wake her, but her breathing appeared even and she seemed to be sleeping peacefully.

However, he had no medical training.

The trickle of blood along her ear appeared to be from a loosened stitch and nothing more, but did it signify something more dangerous was going on?

How could he be certain he was doing the right thing in allowing her to sleep?

He kept close watch over her even as he washed up, shaved, and then quickly dressed for the day. He had hoped she would open her eyes before the doctor arrived because they needed to discuss what had happened last night.

That kiss.

He was not certain what her response would be to him this morning.

Would she admit she loved him and agree to call off the wedding? She had mentioned that she would, confided this to him even before he had spilled his guts and told her that he loved her.

"Gory?" he whispered, hoping she was close to waking and might respond.

But she was lost in her dreams.

Although disappointed, he let her be.

Dr. Farthingale could be relied upon to keep any confidences that might be revealed once she awoke.

Julius had just finished readying himself for the day when the doctor strode in.

"I hear she bled a little," he remarked.

Julius nodded. "Yes, by her ear. I did not know whether to wake her or leave her sleeping. She does not appear to be struggling now. However, she was in a lot of pain last night. What should I have done, Dr. Farthingale?"

"My lord, there is no right or wrong answer."

That did not ease his mind, but he did not press the doctor for further explanation.

He watched tensely as Dr. Farthingale checked Gory's scalp and then woke her up. "Your eyes look clear, Lady Gregoria. That is a very good thing. How do you feel?"

She winced as she sat up. "I feel fine. I am eager to start the day. We have so much to accomplish."

The doctor frowned. "You should not be getting out of bed yet."

Gory cast him a hardheaded look. "But I must. However, I shall limit my activities to those that are vitally necessary."

Julius cleared his throat. "By this she means going to the morgue to examine her uncle's body. Then going to her home to walk through the scene of the crime in the hope something jolts her memory. Then she intends to call upon her aunt who is settled at the Wallingford Arms."

The doctor's frown deepened to mark his disapproval. "Is that all? Perhaps you might also fit in a tour of the London art galleries and theater afterward."

Gory pursed her lips in response to his sarcasm, but did not relent. "Lord Thorne has agreed to remain by my side throughout the day. He is worse than a mothering hen and will not let me overdo it."

Julius groaned. "Just letting you out of your sickbed is overdoing it."

"No, it isn't," she insisted. "I'll need one of the household maids to help me prepare for the day. Why did you let me sleep so late? We have already wasted half the morning."

"Stay put, Gory. I wasn't going to agree to any of your plans without Dr. Farthingale's permission."

"I cannot allow it, Lady Gregoria," Dr. Farthingale said, his manner quite serious.

"Why not? You said my eyes were clear and you know the trace of blood at my ear was nothing more than a loosened stitch. With all due respect, doctor…I am going to ignore your advice. So why not approach this more helpfully? Tell me what I must do if I start to feel dizzy or weak, and your advice had better be something other than advising me to go back to bed because that is something I will ignore. My life is at stake. I cannot remain here and do nothing."

The doctor glanced at Julius in dismay.

Julius was equally distressed, for he had no magical words that would make Gory see reason. "Gad, you are a bossy bit of goods."

She nodded. "I know."

"Here's what I propose," Julius said, not pleased that he was so easily giving in. "Get out of bed on your own and walk across the room toward me in a straight line."

"And if I do this?" Her hand was already on the coverlet, preparing to toss it off.

"I will take you around to the morgue and your home. We'll see how you are feeling afterward. I'll go alone to your aunt if you are too fatigued."

She snorted. "I'll be just fine."

He folded his arms across his chest. "I doubt it. The only reason I am asking you to walk across the room to me is to prove to you that you are too weak to manage it."

"Is that so, *Lord Thorne*. I am about to prove to you that I am perfectly adept." She tossed off the bed covers and cautiously stood up.

Julius wanted to rush forward, but he held his ground and waited for her to walk the length of the room toward him. In truth, she looked much better than she had last night. Her cheeks were pink and her general coloring was no longer ashen.

Her eyes appeared clear, just as Dr. Farthingale had indicated.

Julius was glad spending the night on his lap with his arms wrapped around her had helped. She had been so cold and miserable, not even the fire blazing in the hearth or the warmth of his body pressed to hers had done much to help, at first.

She looked like a stubborn fairy princess walking toward him.

Her hair was unbound and those lovely chestnut locks fell in waves upon her shoulders. Her lips were nicely pink and soft enough to kiss again. Of course, he was not about to do so while the doctor was standing there.

Nor would he dare until he and Gory had the chance to speak alone.

Blessed saints, he ached to kiss her.

There was something incredibly appealing about Gory bundled in her nightclothes and making her way toward him in her stockinged feet.

Warmth shot through him.

She reached his side and smiled up at him with loving defiance. "Well? Have I passed your test?"

Julius did not like this one bit, but he had set the task and she had accomplished it. She would never behave and stay in bed now. "You've passed," he admitted with a grunt, silently kicking himself for not setting a higher bar. "I'll have Mrs. Quinn summon one of the maids to attend you."

She let out a soft breath. "Thank you, Julius."

"I suppose it will give us the chance to talk about what happened last night," he muttered. "We can do so while riding in the carriage."

She had been smiling up at him, but her smile now faltered ever so slightly. "What happened last night?"

His heart shot into his throat.

Had she not remembered any of it? Not his kiss? Or his declaration of love?

Dr. Farthingale, who had been watching Gory and listening in on their exchange, must have realized something was wrong and frowned.

Julius silently warned him not to ask more questions in Gory's presence.

After leaving Gory to ready herself with the assistance of one of the maids, Julius led the doctor downstairs to the study and shut the door behind them for privacy.

"What has you so troubled, Lord Thorne?" the doctor asked, settling in one of chairs beside the desk.

Julius was too tense and remained standing. "She does not remember any of our conversation last night."

"Was it memorable?"

"Yes." Julius wasn't certain how much to tell him, although George Farthingale was one of the smartest men he knew and might figure out what was said even if Julius revealed nothing more. "Nor does she remember how difficult a night it was for her. I think she was suffering the effects of laudanum, and shivering so badly, I had to carry her over to the fire and cover her in blankets to keep her warm. I put her back in bed shortly before you arrived."

"And this is what concerns you?"

Julius nodded. "That and…we had a conversation that seems to have eluded her. It was not something I expected her to forget."

"Important, was it?"

"Very." Julius nodded again.

"All right." Dr. Farthingale raked a hand through his hair. "I will not deny my concern over her loss of memory. Obviously, it is worrisome. But not necessarily something that affects her physical well being. The mind and the body will not necessarily heal at the same pace. She walked across your bedchamber with surprising ease. I will admit, not even I thought she was capable of it yet."

"Nor did I, or I would have devised a more difficult task," Julius admitted with a wincing grin. "She's just so stubborn, I ought to have realized it was too easy. I'm glad she appears physically fit, but her memory has not recovered at all."

"Some of those memories are scary and painful. This is why she is suppressing them. Her stubbornness and determination are working to have her up and walking again, but they are also having the opposite effect on her recollections. She is unable to deal with them just yet, so she is suppressing everything that oversets her. My best advice to you is to keep close to her today."

"I intend to. Believe me, I do not need the reminder. I am so worried about her," Julius admitted, his emotions raw.

"I know, my lord. She is fortunate to be in your care. You are a good friend to her. Although, I expect your feelings run far deeper than that." He held up a hand. "The comment does not require a response unless it is medically relevant to Lady Gregoria's health."

Julius let out a breath. "It is relevant. As I mentioned, we spoke of something *very* important and she does not seem to recall any of it. The exact conversation is not one I would care to reveal to you just now, but it was one that ought to have been very meaningful to her."

"And she has blocked it from her mind," the doctor muttered. "Probably because it was too meaningful and she could not handle it just yet. Give her time and she will come around."

How much time?

There was only a week left until her wedding.

A few short days, seven of them, to be precise. Unless she chose to postpone it or call it off.

Last night, she had decided to call it off.

But what of this morning?

Dr. Farthingale left him a vial of laudanum to carry with him on the chance Gory might suddenly need it while they were out. "I'll look in on her again this evening on my way home. But summon me sooner if she takes an unexpected turn for the worse. I should be in my surgery for the rest of the day."

"I will, sir. Thank you for everything."

Dr. Farthingale smiled. "You Thornes certainly know how to find trouble."

Julius chuckled. "It is completely unintentional, I assure you."

After escorting the doctor out, he went into the dining room and had a cup of coffee to bide his time while awaiting Gory. He expected it would take a bit of doing before she was ready because she needed a good soak in a tub to thoroughly wash her body. She could not wash her hair because of the stitches, but the maid would do it up properly for her.

To his surprise, Gory walked downstairs on her own before he had finished his first cup. He set it down with a clatter and leaped from his seat. "Did you risk coming down the stairs on your own? Why did you not ask for help?" he muttered.

"I am not an infant." She cast him that stubborn look again. "I was careful."

He snorted.

"I held onto the railing and took the steps slowly and deliberately."

"You could have blacked out and toppled down the entire length of the staircase."

"But I didn't. I know the workings of my body, Julius. I would not have attempted it if I did not feel strong enough."

"You think you are as mighty as a lion," he grumbled, offering her the seat beside his.

She settled into it with ease and smiled at the footman who

poured her a cup of tea. "I am hardly mighty. The top of my head barely reaches your shoulders and I am half your size. Physically, you are the lion and I am but a mouse."

He laughed. "You are no mouse, either. A mongoose, perhaps."

"I resent that!" But she laughed. "All right, I never was a timid, nibbling little thing. In fact, I am starved."

This was good, he supposed.

He liked that she had regained her appetite.

Still, a mere day of healing was not enough to trust she was fit again.

He had to admit she looked beautiful though.

She wore the gown of dark green wool that she had taken out of Adela's wardrobe yesterday. The gown itself had little adornment. The only splash of color was the striking white of her fichu.

The fichu was a necessary attachment, he realized, because Gory's bosom was ample and a little too much cleavage would have spilled over had it not been properly hidden by that strip of lacy cloth.

Although meant to ensure modesty, the fichu actually drew his gaze straight to her bosom.

Now his body was out of kilter.

He grabbed her plate and went to the silver salvers on the sideboard to serve her.

"I'll have a little of everything," she called to him. "Do not stint. Pile it high."

He laughed. "All right, but do not overdo it. You'll just give yourself a bellyache and I'll have to bring you back home."

"Never!" she said as he set the plate before her. "We are not coming back here until we've made every stop."

"Stubborn chit," he muttered, watching her devour the eggs he had piled on. She then dunked a biscuit into her tea and devoured that, too.

She nodded to the footman once she had eaten her fill.

The man cleared away the remains of her meal.

Next, she turned to Julius with a winsome smile. "I am ready.

Let's be on our way."

Julius had called for his carriage earlier and it was waiting for them when they stepped outside. The Thorne family's trusted coachman, Hastings, was perched in the driver's seat and nodded to him in greeting. "Morning, m'lord."

"Good morning, Hastings. Drive slow, will you? Lady Gregoria is in delicate health."

"I am in the pink," she grumbled.

"Do not believe her, Hastings. She received a bad blow to the head and has not been right ever since."

"Not right? Well, I never!" Gory tossed him an indignant scowl, but then relented and cast him an impertinent grin. "That is very cruel of you, Julius."

"Do not chide me, you stubborn chit. Despite your claims, I know what you have been through and cannot believe you are so quickly healed. It is not possible and I am worried about you." He tucked her cloak – another item borrowed from Adela's wardrobe – more firmly around her slender shoulders and made certain the scarf he had also insisted she wear was suitably protecting her throat.

He knew he was being a mother hen, but who was to watch over the girl if not him?

"It is not winter yet," she muttered when he had finished bundling her up.

"You almost froze to death last night. Your body is still recovering from that blow to your head that knocked you out cold." He helped her into the carriage, still amazed she could do more than lift her head off his pillow.

But here she was, dressed and walking.

His heart tugged as he settled opposite her and had an unimpeded view of her lovely face. She had the most intelligent eyes that always seemed to shimmer.

He could have sworn they were sprinkled with starlight.

Of course, they were not shimmering for love of him…something she did not remember them discussing. No, they were bright and shining because the two of them were headed to the morgue to view her uncle's body and this had Gory elated.

102 | MEARA PLATT

He sighed.

Life with her was never going to be dull.

Of course, this assumed she would marry him and not Allendale.

Blast.

He could never allow her to marry that clot.

Allendale's absence was glaring, and this was an obvious warning sign that Gory could not overlook.

Julius allowed Gory to take the lead once they reached the morgue. However, he remained by her side all the while she examined her uncle's body and was impressed by how methodically she went about studying the wounds to his chest and then closely inspecting his hands and throat.

When she was done, she looked up at Julius, her expression grim.

"What have you noticed?" he asked.

"He fought off his assailant. See the broken nail on his third finger? And the traces of skin and blood beneath the other nails? He scratched his assailant. And do you see the bruising around his neck? He was held by the throat. That is why I did not hear him cry for help as he was attacked. He was being strangled. That would have taken an assailant of significant strength."

"Are you sure you did not hear him cry out? Something drew you downstairs," Julius reminded her.

"An argument, I'm sure...I think. Oh," she said, nibbling her lip. "Perhaps I did hear him cry out. Oh, Julius. I simply cannot recall."

"Anything else of note?" He really did not wish to remain in the morgue a moment longer than was necessary. The room reeked of embalming fluids, for starters. It was also cold and quite bleek.

"The condition of his body would have me rule out a woman as the killer."

"But it is likely there was a female accomplice, Gory."

"Because I was changed out of the gown I wore to the musicale and put into my wedding gown?"

"*Neatly* put into it," he reminded her.

"Is this what Havers is thinking, too? Or does he still consider me a suspect and believes you were my accomplice?"

Julius shrugged. "It is possible."

"But unlikely." She pursed her lips, a thing she did whenever thinking of something unpleasant. "He seems to trust you. Perhaps he thinks Allendale and I were the ones who colluded, and that I had him hit me over the head just to draw suspicion away from me."

"No, that blow was strong enough to kill you."

She arched an eyebrow. "Nothing says my accomplice has to have a brain. He might not have realized his own strength."

Julius sighed. "Have you seen enough? Can we go now? I feel my breakfast about to lurch into my throat."

"Oh, yes. Give me a moment to wash up. I'm so sorry you had to see this."

"Me? You are the delicate female here." He cast her a smile. "Come on, love. Let's head to the Easton townhouse. I'm hoping Mr. Barrow or Havers will be there to fill us in on what else they have learned."

She washed her hands thoroughly with the lye soap that was in a dish on a sideboard, then dried them off using a clean hand cloth plucked from among a pile beside the soap. "I'm ready."

"Good."

They climbed back in his carriage, once more making their way through the crowded London streets. Carts and pedestrians darted in all directions, slowing the horses to a walk. Still, Julius reminded Hastings to take extra care because he did not want Gory to be jounced too badly. The Thorne conveyance had elegant seats of the finest, soft leather and an undercarriage that was well sprung and sturdy.

However, Gory was a lot more fragile than she would ever admit.

Julius breathed a sigh of relief when they finally drew up in front of her former home.

"Good morning, my lord. Lady Gregoria." Mr. Barrow hurried forward to greet them, and walked them inside after Julius had helped Gory down. "I was planning to stop by to see you next.

Upon my honor, I did not expect you to be out of bed yet, m'lady. How are you feeling?"

She cast the Bow Street runner a warm smile. "Much better, only the slightest throbbing in my head. Hardly noticeable."

"Do not believe her, Mr. Barrow," Julius countered. "She only admits to a headache, but everything hurts. Her stubborn facade is in place, but she cannot hide her discomfort from me. Keep alert, for she may faint in front of us."

That earned him a frown from Gory. "I will kick you if you repeat that nonsense to anyone else."

She frowned at him once more for good measure before returning her attention to Mr. Barrow. "What else have you learned?"

They moved out of the hallway and into her uncle's study where the murder had taken place. Julius had suggested they sit in the parlor instead, but Gory shot that idea down fast. "We are here to see this very room, so why not talk in here while I have a look around?"

The study appeared to have remained untouched except for the removal of Lord Easton's body that was now laid out in the morgue. Gory repeated the question she had asked Mr. Barrow moments earlier. "Anything new to report?"

"No, m'lady." He shook his head. "Nothing yet, but we have only begun to dig around. Sometimes these things take more time than we would like. I expect to have more information by tomorrow. That's when my man returns from Windsor."

"With a report on Lady Easton's whereabouts and her movements on the day of the murder?" Gory asked.

"Yes, m'lady. And perhaps something of interest from the public coach passenger lists. I have my man working on those, too."

She nodded. "And Lord Allendale? What have you discovered about his activities on the night of the murder?"

"Nothing on him yet, either. But we shall continue to dig." He turned to Julius. "You will be pleased to hear that you have been ruled out by Mr. Havers. Your friends and the stewards at your club confirmed you were there playing cards all evening."

Gory cast him a fragile smile. "I'm glad Havers can trust you now. That ought to be very helpful. But I remain a suspect." She turned to Mr. Barrow. "Don't I?"

The Bow Street runner frowned. "Aye, m'lady. For now. I'm sure he will rule you out shortly."

Gory shook her head. "I do not see how he can when I was clearly at the scene. But I think all suspects must be brought in and checked for scratches. Do you know if the inspector has done this yet? He must attend to it right away. It is most important. I looked upon my uncle's body this morning and it is obvious he attempted to fight back. Havers must check for scratches on every suspect. Their face most obviously. But also on the neck, hands, arms, and throat. The assailant had to be tall and strong for he had one hand on my uncle's throat like this."

She reached up and held her hand to Julius's throat. "And then he used his free hand to plunge the blade into my uncle's heart. There was telltale bruising along my uncle's throat that only an imbecile could overlook. I do not know of any ladies big enough or strong enough to manage to grab their victim like this and also manage to stick a knife in him," she said, her hand still gently held against Julius's throat as she repeated the gesture of a knife being jabbed into his heart.

"See, I am not tiny. But neither am I all that tall. Lord Thorne had to bend down to allow me a good hold on his throat. I doubt my uncle would have been so accommodating to his attacker."

"That is most elucidating, Lady Gregoria," Havers said, now walking into her uncle's study where they were standing beside the very spot of his murder. "Hopefully, you will not find me to be a complete imbecile."

She stuck her chin into the air. "That has yet to be proven, Mr. Havers. Since you heard my comments, will you do as I ask? Everyone needs to be checked for scratches as soon as possible."

He nodded. "This has been done. Well, with respect to your staff. They were all looked over this morning before any of you arrived. Of course, for the sake of propriety I had one of the prison matrons come with me to search the ladies. You will be pleased to note that none of the servants were found to have fresh scratches."

Gory nodded. "I am relieved. We have good and loyal people in service here. Is the matron still here? She ought to have a look at me, too."

Havers shook his head. "Not necessary. Dr. Farthingale reported as much to me yesterday when I asked him."

"So you already knew I was not the assailant when you questioned me earlier? But I suppose that did not rule me out as the accomplice," Gory mused. "I could have easily hired someone strong enough to commit the crime."

Havers nodded. "Yes, you could have done that."

She snorted in indignation. "Do you really think I would be so stupid as to fail to provide myself with an unimpeachable alibi? Or to make such a botch of a murder?"

"Lady Gregoria, I do not know yet what to think about you. Until I am convinced of your innocence, I will consider you a suspect. But I also consider you the assailant's next target and have had you guarded for your own protection. I cannot rule out the possibility of your innocence either."

"Will you be checking my aunt for scratches?"

He nodded. "The prison matron and I were going to the Wallingford Arms next. I did not wish to disturb your aunt earlier."

"That is surprisingly considerate of you, Mr. Havers. However, she will take offense no matter what time of day you approach her. Give me a few minutes to search upstairs and then we shall accompany you to the Wallingford Arms."

Havers glanced at Julius.

"Lady Gregoria is in charge," Julius replied with a shrug. "We've finished our morning rounds faster than expected, so it is a good idea to join you in calling upon her aunt and getting that duty out of the way. By the way, I think you ought to examine Lord Easton's solicitor and his staff for scratches."

Havers arched an eyebrow. "You think so?"

Julius nodded. "Reginald Mayfield is not of the finest character and I would not be surprised if he had a hand in this somehow."

"I will. Thank you for bringing Mr. Mayfield to my attention, my lord."

Gory once again snorted in indignation. "Something you've obviously overlooked, Mr. Havers."

The man cast her an indulgent smile. "No, my lady. I have already checked him, his elder brother who is his partner, and his clerks. But it was a good observation on Lord Thorne's part and I appreciated his mentioning it."

"Oh. Gad, wipe that smug grin off your face," she said, frowning at Julius when she caught him smirking.

"I am feeling relieved, not smug," he assured her, taking her arm to escort her upstairs. "You know how worried I am for your safety. It is reassuring to know Havers is up to the task of solving the murder, and he seems to be doing fine without your interference."

She scowled at him. "My interference?"

"Yes," Julius said, his expression now stern. "You ought to have remained in bed resting, as the doctor ordered. But here you are, running all over London and wearing yourself out. That blow to your head was no jest, Gory. You woke up with blood trailing down your ear this morning."

Havers turned to her. "You were bleeding?"

Gory waved her hand in dismissal. "It was just a loose stitch that Dr. Farthingale attended to this morning."

"Still, my lady. You need to take care of yourself."

She pursed her lips, a sign that she was going to be intractable. "I am quite capable of knowing what I need to do, and that is to look around upstairs and then pay a call on my aunt. If it will help you deal with her, you can pretend I was not yet searched for scratches. It might go a little easier if she and I are both facing the same indignity of a bodily examination."

"I am fairly adept at dealing with suspects," Havers insisted.

Gory was not giving the man any ground. "You do not know my aunt. You ought to allow me to take the lead with her."

"Lady Gregoria, I am the inspector in charge here."

"And doing an execrable job if you still consider me a suspect." She did not give a fig that she perplexed Havers who was obviously not used to being defied, nor did he appreciate any interference in his investigation.

But Gory was going be a little battering ram.

Julius appreciated this about her, quite liking her fire and spirit.

Yes, she thwarted him at times. But mostly she was all heart and compassion, wanting so badly to make things right with the world.

Few men wished for a headstrong wife.

But how could he ever want someone as dull as dishwater?

Gory was also soft and loving.

Julius cleared his throat.

This was for a later discussion.

"Need a ride to the Wallingford Arms, Havers?"

"No, I have my own transport. Not quite as fancy as yours. But I'll wait for you, so we can arrive together. Does that suit you, Lady Gregoria?"

"Yes," she said, and then walked upstairs to inspect her bedchamber.

Julius excused himself and followed her up.

He remained in the doorway, quietly standing out of the way while Gory went through her things and tried to recall what had happened the other night.

She was not in her room more than five minutes before she sighed and returned to his side with a dejected look.

"Nothing?" He unfolded his arms that had been casually crossed over his chest while watching her.

"Nothing at all. Oh, Julius, why can I not remember anything?"

"It will come back to you, Gory. Do not lose faith." He took her arm and led her downstairs. "You are forcing these lost memories and this is not helping."

"I was sure that returning here would help to open the floodgates holding them back."

"Perhaps it has helped. But there is much we do not know yet about the workings of the brain. You cannot simply snap your fingers and have all you have forgotten immediately rush to mind."

"I do hate it when you are logical," she grumbled.

She kept her arm tucked in his as they took a moment to talk to the Easton staff. Julius allowed Gory to do most of the talking since the staff seemed to adore her and were heartened by her comforting words. "Please do go on with your regular duties for now. However, if you remember something, or notice anything or anyone who is out of place, please alert Mr. Havers or Mr. Barrow at once. I will try to stop by tomorrow, but Lord Thorne will come in my place if I cannot."

She glanced at Julius, realizing she ought to have asked him before telling her staff that he would. But he nodded. "Yes, you may count on me. Stay alert and report anything, no matter how trivial it appears. Do not hesitate to send word to me if you would rather speak to me before going to Mr. Havers or Mr. Barrow."

"We shall, my lord," Jergins said, stepping forward on behalf of the Easton staff. "Thank you."

He nodded and then led Gory to the carriage. "Are you ready to face your ogre of an aunt next?"

She nodded. "Yes, but stay close. She might try to bite my head off."

"I'll protect you."

She cast him a sincere smile. "I know. You've been wonderful to me, Julius."

He shrugged off the compliment. "I'm trying my best. Are you all right?"

"I'm fine. Just wondering if my aunt had a hand in her husband's murder. Do you think she did? Or could it have been his mistress seeking revenge if she was scorned? Do you know what they say about a woman scorned?"

"That she attempts to kill her benefactor and the benefactor's niece when it can gain her nothing but a death sentence?"

"Must you be so sarcastic? My point is that she might have been angry."

"I understood your point, Gory. But do you really think your uncle would have left the mistress to return to his wife? Or that the mistress would have cared enough to fly into a mad rage and commit murder had he ended their affair?"

Gory groaned. "No, I don't suppose so. Do you have any other ideas?"

CHAPTER 7

AFTER HER PARENTS died, Gory was taken into the neglectful care of her uncle, the newly installed Earl of Easton. He had ignored her for the most part, but her aunt, relishing her elevated status as Lady Easton, no longer felt the need to hide her active dislike of Gory and took every opportunity to let her know it.

In truth, Gory did not know what she had ever done to make the lady hate her so much, for she had tried to be good and obedient. Since that had not worked, she had reconsidered her plan and resolved to be whoever she was meant to be. There was no point in trying to twist herself into someone she was not when the mere fact of her existence riled this bitter woman, and nothing she did, other than disappear off the face of the earth, would ever fix that.

"Gory, how are you holding up?" Julius asked, having locked her arm in his and now feeling her tremble as they entered the elegant Wallingford Arms. He placed his hand over hers, no doubt believing she needed the added reassurance. "I am right beside you, love."

Perhaps she did need his support because she was awhirl with feelings that were fighting against each other right now and leaving her floundering with uncertainty. She wanted to be jubilant that her detestable aunt had been brought down, but how could she feel any joy when the circumstances of her downfall were so awful? The woman was a widow now and her husband's death had been brutal and shocking.

She looked up at Julius and cast him a forced smile. "I'll be all right. Just thinking of the past. Is it not odd that I remember all the years of my childhood so well? And yet, I have no memory of what happened mere days ago?"

"Not odd at all. Those old memories are embedded in here," he said, tapping on his forehead, "while the newer ones have not yet taken firm hold. They were quite literally knocked out of your head."

"I suppose you are right."

He responded with an affectionately smug grin. "I am always right."

She laughed. "Yes, and it is most irritating."

They waited in the hotel's lobby for Havers to arrive, continuing to chat in the meanwhile. Gory found it remarkable how easily she and Julius got along. They always had something of interest to say to each other, but could also be together for long periods of time in comfortable silence.

She glanced up at Julius. "You are giving me that apishly protective look again. What is on your mind?"

"Nothing, other than wishing to do just that...protect you. You are still trembling. It concerns me. I would attribute it to fatigue, but your eyes are clear and your skin has good color." He ran a knuckle lightly across her cheek. "So, I think it is the prospect of facing your aunt that has you overset."

"I am not afraid of her," Gory insisted, for she really was not. "Well, I hadn't been afraid of her until now. But murder changes everything, does it not?"

"Yes, which is why I am sticking close to you."

"As Allendale ought to be doing," she said, mostly to herself.

"No," Julius replied, now frowning. "He does not get near you until he is ruled out as a suspect."

She felt a sudden twinge dart up the side of her head to her temple, the sharp jolt awakening something in her, but what?

A lost conversation, perhaps.

Between her and Allendale? Or her and Julius?

Or neither of them.

She sighed in disgust, for she simply could not recall.

Yet, she thought it was something important, a missing conversation that she needed to remember.

Julius gave her hand a light squeeze. "Gory?"

Perhaps this lost recollection had to do with Julius.

Drat! Why could she not recall anything of the recent past?

Adding to her frustration was the fact she was also in the midst of planning her wedding. Was she forgetting something important about that upcoming event? It now felt like a great weight upon her shoulders that needed to be addressed before she made an irreversible mistake. Perhaps she was on edge because she needed to speak to Allendale about ending their farce of a betrothal and had not done so yet.

Julius continued to study her with worry.

She emitted a soft breath. "I hate this inability to remember."

"I know, but dwelling on it will not help matters. Ah, here comes Havers." He gave a mock shudder as he caught sight of the prison matron who accompanied him. "Gad, she's a scary one."

Gory giggled. "Quiet, or she might hear you. However, her dour presence is a good thing. She'll need to be fierce when dealing with Lady Easton. This could turn into a battle of dragons."

They waited while Havers walked up to the clerk at the registration desk and requested that her aunt be advised of their arrival. The man was at first dismissive of the request, then noticed Julius was among their party and immediately hopped to attention. "Lord Thorne, it is an honor to have you with us again."

Gory rolled her eyes at Julius.

Did the man know everyone in London?

Had he used this hotel for his lurid liaisons with paramours? Oddly enough, she did not think so because there were no sly, leering looks exchanged between him and this clerk. Nor was Julius the sort to mix business with illicit pleasures. He would never have settled her aunt here if this is where he brought the women he seduced.

Julius was too careful for that.

She looked on as he and the clerk exchange pleasantries, but Gory was not really listening. Her gaze was drawn to the other guests standing around the hotel's entryway.

She did not know why they drew her, for none of them looked familiar. Nor did they seem to be standing around suspiciously.

One man was seated on a plump chair reading a newspaper.

Another was lounging on one of the sofas and nursing a drink.

A couple that looked out of place in this elegant establishment appeared to be quietly quarreling with each other. The man was big and looked stern, but it was the woman who appeared to be in charge.

Gory turned away a moment to regard other guests. When she looked back, the arguing couple were nowhere to be found.

In the meanwhile, the eager clerk had scurried up the stairs. He returned a short while later, his cheeks red and his manner contrite. "Lord Thorne, my sincerest apologies. Lady Easton will not see any of you."

Gory was not surprised, for this is how the woman had treated her ever since Gory's parents had died. She was only six years old when they had passed away, fatally injured in a carriage accident. Theirs had not started out as a love match, her mother had once told her. But over the years, her parents had grown to care for each other to the point love had blossomed.

The opposite had been true for her aunt and uncle. From what she'd gathered, their marriage had started out with promise and failed soon afterward. Over the years, resentment and disappointment had replaced all traces of love and devotion they might once have felt for each other.

This is what Gory now realized would happen between her and Allendale. At best, they would develop a polite indifference to each other. At worst, misery and resentment.

Theirs was not even starting with the promise of love or devotion. Allendale was already showing his indifference in the weeks leading up to their wedding.

Where was he now?

It gnawed at her that he had been absent this entire week, especially these past few days when he ought to have been constantly by her side, or at least pretending more than superficial interest in her injury or their upcoming wedding.

Was it not odd he had spent no time with her other than a brief visit as she lay injured in Julius's bed? The argument between him and Julius over the impropriety of her recovering at the Thorne townhouse could have been more for show than any true feelings of concern.

If she and Allendale had argued over something more to cause a rift between them, someone would have told her. Wouldn't they?

Perhaps this is what was buzzing like an irritating gnat in her head.

She drew Julius aside while Havers was dealing with the clerk. "Julius," she said in a whisper, "have I said anything to Allendale about calling off the wedding?"

"No yet," he replied.

But she had to call it off unless he explained to her satisfaction where he had been the night her uncle was killed.

Dear heaven.

Had she made a deadly mistake and betrothed herself to a savage murderer?

She thought herself a good judge of character and could not bring herself to believe Allendale had it in him to kill anyone.

What if she was wrong?

"Are you certain I've had no argument with Allendale?"

Julius arched an eyebrow. "Since the murder? No, Gory. Not that I am aware. Do you recall that he came by to visit you yesterday?"

She nodded and let the matter drop.

Havers and the Bow Street men were looking into Allendale's absence and would report whatever they found out.

Havers was now frowning at the embarrassed clerk. "The lady is mistaken if she believes she has a choice in the matter. That I sent you to advise her of our arrival was merely a matter of courtesy. Run back upstairs and inform her that we will be knocking at her door in five minutes. If she does not open it, I will break it down and arrest her."

The man tore up the stairs like a rock hurled from a catapult.

Julius laughed. "That will endear you to her, Havers."

He shrugged. "I am not here to make people like me. My duty is to get at the truth. I do not like it when people avoid me. It always means they have something to hide."

"Always?" Julius asked.

Havers nodded. "Yes."

Gory had to admit Havers was smarter than he looked.

In truth, it ought to have come as a relief to her because the sooner Havers ruled her out as a suspect in her uncle's murder, the sooner she could break off her betrothal and move on from Allendale. He was moving fairly swiftly in this investigation and appeared to be quite thorough in leaving no stone unturned.

"She will see you now," the clerk reported, returning almost immediately.

"I thought she might," Havers muttered.

The four of them walked upstairs, the dour matron taking up the rear while Havers took the lead. Her aunt's maid, an unpleasant woman by the name of Flossie, stood at the open door. Her expression was haughty and unwelcoming as she watched them approach.

Julius cast Gory a reassuring glance.

"Do not fret for me. I am used to this outpouring of love and warmth," she remarked with noticeable sarcasm, smiling wryly.

Her aunt was seated on the settee in the small but elegantly appointed parlor that was part of the impressive suite of rooms Julius had obtained for her. Her chin was raised as she posed like a queen upon a royal throne. "Who are these people?" she asked Gory, her lips curled in an all too familiar sneer. "I did not realize I was to have a parade through my private quarters."

"This is Mr. Havers, the inspector in charge of the investigation. It is most important that he speaks to you," Gory said, stepping forward with respectful solemnity. "I am so sorry for–"

Her aunt turned away when she attempted to buss her cheek. "I'll have none of your false affection, Gregoria."

"You know Lord Thorne, of course," she said, trying to show a little patience now that her aunt was a widow. Indeed, she was surprised to find her aunt already clad in a gown of black bombazine silk and fully taking on the appearance of a bereaved wife. That was quite resourceful of her, considering Julius had brought her to the hotel the moment she had arrived home, and she hadn't been given the chance to retrieve any of her clothing.

Also of note was that the gown appeared to be a new acquisition and not some old thing buried in her wardrobe to be brought out only on solemn occasions.

Had Havers noted this, too?

Or was her dislike of the woman clouding her judgment? After all, it was not unreasonable to assume that an earl's wife would have a suitable attire at the ready for every eventuality. Perhaps one of the Easton footmen had delivered the gown to her last night or this morning.

She should have requested the same for herself, Gory realized. Instead, she had gone through Adela's belongings because Adela's gowns were far prettier than most of hers. Also, she could not bring herself to don any of her own gowns just yet, and might never.

The possibility that the killer had gone through them all and touched them with his evil hands left her quite sickened and ready to cast up her accounts.

"Lord Thorne acquired this suite for you," she mentioned to her aunt, struggling to make polite conversation. "I hope you are comfortably settled."

"Comfortable? After returning to London only to learn my husband has been murdered? I hardly think so, Gregoria. What a stupid thing to ask me."

She felt Julius tense beside her.

Havers stepped forward to introduce his companion. "And this is Miss Hinch, one of my able assistants."

Gory's aunt refused to acknowledge the woman. "Get her out of my sight. I do not care who she is. Gregoria, you may follow that woman out."

Julius looked ready to throttle her aunt, but Gory stopped him with a silent plea. It would not do to rile her before Havers had gotten his answers.

Rather than leave, Gory moved to the window to allow for a

small measure of privacy while the inspector questioned her aunt. Julius followed her, placing a hand to the small of her back to silently reassure her of his support.

She smiled up at him and nodded.

He kept his hand lightly at her back, his touch quite gentle and utterly divine. "Do you wish to sit, Gory? You've been on your feet for a while now."

"No, I'm all right." She stared out the window. "This suite has a lovely view of the park."

He nodded. "I thought your aunt would appreciate it more than a view of the crowded street."

"You were generous with her, providing for an entire suite. I doubt she will ever thank you for it. She—"

Her aunt's sudden screech interrupted their conversation. "I will not! How dare you! Get out, you base creature! How could you request such a thing!"

Gory turned in confusion toward Havers and her aunt, wondering what Havers had said to elicit such a response.

Julius immediately drew her closer, his protective instincts on alert as they watched her aunt leap up from her seat with her hands curled like claws and actually take a swipe at Havers. Fortunately, Havers had the foresight to take a quick step back so that her aunt struck nothing but air.

This only served to enrage her more.

She turned suddenly, her fury all on Gory now. "Did you know about this? Of course, you did, you vile creature."

Julius nudged her slightly behind him as her aunt advanced, still hurling her insults. "This is the only reason you are here, is it not? To see me humiliated. But I shall have my revenge. I'll see you hanged for what you did to your uncle."

Her aunt had taken only a step or two before Havers once again diverted her attention. "Lady Easton," he intoned in a voice that held commanding authority, "your threats will not work here. You may as well comply, for you *shall* be undressed by my matron."

"I refuse!"

"Enough, Lady Easton," Julius said calmly, but with no less

authority as he nudged Gory securely behind him while he stepped forward. "How else is Mr. Havers to rule you out as a suspect?"

Her eyes widened. "A suspect? How is it possible when I was with my sister in Windsor and only returned to London after my husband's murder? The impertinence! Who do you think you are? You have no right to speak to me in this highhanded manner. You are nothing more than a *third* son."

"I have never pretended to be anything other," Julius replied evenly. "However, allow me to point out that your situation is not what it once was. You have lost your status in the eyes of the *ton* now that your husband has passed on."

"I am still Lady Easton! A *countess* while you are no better than a commoner, for all your pretentious airs."

"Not *the* countess for long." Julius spoke with an icy frankness that surprised Gory because she had never seen Julius appear other than mild-mannered. But he was seething now, and showing a bit of the steel determination he usually kept hidden beneath his veneer of calm. "If the new earl is married, you are merely the dowager countess, wholly dependent upon his largesse and that of his wife. Even if he is not yet married, you are still at his mercy because he controls the purse strings."

"I will not be spoken to in this crude fashion!"

Julius eyed her coldly. "Nor will I, Lady Easton. Forgive my crassness in pointing out the obvious, but your fancy airs will get you nowhere. I understand you have received a great shock. However, you only draw more attention to yourself by refusing to cooperate with the magistrate's man. Mr. Havers is his *top* investigator and will not be turned away, especially if you continue to behave as though you have something you wish to hide."

Gory's aunt turned her rage back on Havers. "Is this how a grieving widow is to be treated? Dare to lay a hand on me and you shall rue the day you were ever born!"

Havers called over Miss Hinch who dutifully approached. "Check Lady Easton's maid first."

"Aye, sir."

The matron dragged a terrified Flossie into the adjoining bedchamber and shut the door. They heard a few screams, then all was quiet.

"She isn't strangling the maid, is she?" Julius asked.

"No, my lord." Havers stood with his arms casually draped across his chest, but Gory could see he was keenly observing her aunt. "It is not our habit to harm those we interrogate. Lady Easton, it will be your turn next. We can either attend to it in the respectful privacy of your finely appointed quarters or at the ladies prison. Your choice."

The door to the bedchamber opened and Flossie scurried out in tears, her demeanor no longer smug or scornful.

The matron remained standing at the threshold of the bedchamber. "No marks, Mr. Havers."

He grunted in acknowledgment and turned to Gory's aunt. "What is it to be Lady Easton? Lady Gregoria has also agreed to be inspected for scratches. Perhaps it will feel a little less odious if you go through the procedure together."

"I do not want Gregoria anywhere near me," her aunt shot back. "Why are you bothering with me when she is clearly the guilty party? *She's* the one who stands to gain by my husband's passing. *She's* the one who was home with him. *She's*—"

"How do you know she was home with him at the time?" Havers asked.

The question obviously caught her aunt by surprise, but she quickly recovered and cast Havers a disdainful look. "Where else would she be?"

Havers said nothing, merely continued to stare at her in silence.

Dear heaven, this man was wily.

Her aunt was shifting nervously and fumbling for her handkerchief as a means of distraction while she came up with a plausible response. "Was she not at home? Then how was she injured?"

Havers still had his gaze pinned on her aunt. "How do you know Lady Gregoria was injured?"

She waved her hand in the air, her handkerchief fluttering as she once again strained to come up with an answer. "Everyone gossips. I'm sure I heard it somewhere. From one of the servants, likely. Were you not injured, Gregoria?"

Havers shot her a glance that warned her to remain silent.

She pursed her lips tightly and stepped closer to Julius's side, watching as Havers continued to interrogate her aunt. "Lady Easton," he said with a disquieting calmness to his voice, "why did you claim just now that Lady Gregoria is the one to gain by his lordship's passing?"

She tipped her chin up. "My husband told me what she stood to inherit."

"And when did he tell you this?"

His tone remained calm and unhurried, but there was no denying how sharply focused he was on getting his answers.

"I do not recall. How am I expected to remember such a trivial thing?"

"Oh, I doubt it is trivial, Lady Easton. This was the first thing out of your mouth, so I would wager it was quite important to you."

Her aunt became flustered once again. "It was not important to me at all, but I felt compelled to point it out to you since you are determined to get at the truth. She stood to gain the most, and this is something you ought to know."

"Indeed, it is. Thank you for pointing it out. Anything else you would care to tell me about your niece?"

She shot Gory a malicious look that had Julius once again drawing her closer to him. "Gregoria has never liked us. Do not be fooled by her innocent look. She is a bloodthirsty ghoul who is fascinated by dead things. She ought to be your main suspect. Look to her, for she is the one who stands to inherit a fortune. I cannot think of a better motive for murder than greed."

"Yes, it is quite a tempting one."

It saddened Gory to see how much hatred was reflected in her aunt's eyes.

What had she ever done to the woman to deserve such vicious spite?

"Gregoria also had the wherewithal to kill him since they were alone together in the main quarters of the townhouse," her aunt accused, continuing to spew her bile.

"What makes you think she was alone?"

Gory's aunt grew flustered once again. "What do you mean?"

"She could have returned home with a party of her friends. Those friends might have provided her with a solid alibi."

Her aunt snorted in disdain. "My niece is reviled by all who know her. She has no friends other than a handful of ladies who are equally strange and ghoulish. I would not be surprised if they all conspired to murder my husband. They are a coven of witches."

"Are you accusing a duchess, a marchioness, and an admiral's wife of abetting a murder?" Havers asked.

Her aunt must have realized she had overstepped by drawing suspicion upon Adela, Marigold, and Syd. "I will not listen to any more of this nonsense! Get out. All of you. Get out!"

Gory cast Julius a pleading look.

He nodded. "Havers, we'll await you in the lobby."

Taking Gory firmly by the elbow, he led her out and did not let go of her arm until they reached the lobby. "What a waste of time," he muttered.

"How was it wasteful? Havers now has an understanding of the workings of our miserable family. My aunt did not take long to toss me into the fire, did she? I knew she would accuse me. She would have done so whether I stood to inherit a fortune or not a single farthing because she hates me that much. Am I so unlikeable, Julius? I know I am odd, but…"

She was going to upset herself if she thought too hard about it.

Especially about being strange and unlikeable, which she was if those in the *ton* were to be believed. But this was also the reason why Julius would never fall in love with her, was it not? He tolerated her and protected her because of her ties to his family. From time to time these past few days he had referred to her as 'love' instead of merely calling her Gory. But he used the endearment mostly out of pity. She would never hear serious words of affection escape his lips or ever receive a marriage proposal from him.

Not that it should matter to her because she was betrothed to Allendale and everyone believed she would marry him in a few days.

But how could she bind herself to him now? That he was a viscount was of no importance to her. She did not care about his title. This was not the reason she had agreed to marry him.

A sharp pang suddenly shot through her head. "Oh, ow!"

Julius grabbed her as she faltered. "Gory! What's wrong?"

"I don't know. *Ow*."

"Again? That does it, I'm taking you home."

"But–"

"No. Your body is warning you that it is about to give out."

"It is doing no such thing. I think it is a memory trying to surface."

"Do not force it, Gory. Let me get you safely home and back in bed."

"But the memory is right there. If only...I... It's about my wedding, and– Ow! There it is again."

"Blast it, Gory. I'm taking you home. Not a word of protest." He lifted her in his arms, drawing everyone's attention as he carried her to their waiting carriage and deposited her gently on the seat bench.

"Why did you do that? I could have walked to carriage on my own. Now, everyone in the *ton* will be gossiping about us."

"So what?" He dismissed her concerns with a shrug and turned to the driver. "Hastings, do not allow Lady Gregoria to move from this spot. I'll be right back."

After tossing her a warning glower, he marched back inside to leave word for Havers that he had taken her home.

Well, not to *her* home.

They were returning to the Thorne residence.

Another pang shot into her temples, almost blinding her with its sharpness.

Julius returned at the very moment she cried out and doubled over.

Drat.

What miserable timing.

Now he was going to fuss over her like a mothering hen.

"Bloody hell," he muttered, jumping in beside her and rapping on the roof to signal Hastings to drive off. "Do not dare tell me you are fine."

"But–"

He hauled her onto his lap and wrapped his arms around her as the carriage lurched forward. "So help me, Gory," he said between clenched teeth, "do not even think to get out of my bed for another week."

"You are being ridiculous."

"Me? Yes, I suppose I must be. After all, I am the one who foolishly allowed you to traipse around London when I should have known better than to agree."

"It was important. I'm glad you did." She closed her eyes and rested her head against his shoulder. It was such a lovely, broad shoulder. His scent was divine, too, an aromatic blend of maleness and bay spices that soothed her as she breathed him in. "We accomplished a lot today and it is only noon. Plenty still to do, but–"

"But nothing. I am putting you back to bed."

"Stop saying that. What is the point of leaving me stuck in your bedchamber alone, bored and languishing?"

"Keeping you alive and healing is the entire point of it. You won't be bored or stuck alone for long. Adela and Ambrose are due to arrive home today. Adela will not leave your side for a moment. Syd and Octavian ought to arrive tomorrow or the day after. Marigold is always around and will hop in her carriage to join you any time you ask. No doubt Lady Withnall and Lady Dayne will do the same. You'll have your ghoul club back together and that ought to keep you occupied."

"It is an explorer's club, not a ghoul club," she muttered. "Adela and Marigold have made some of the most exciting fossil discoveries ever heard of in England. And if Syd were a man, she would have been allowed to attend medical school and become as brilliant a doctor as George Farthingale."

He groaned. "I know, Gory. Do not lecture me. I am merely speaking out of turn because I am so worried about you."

She snuggled against Julius because being wrapped in his arms was simply divine. "You are forgiven. Even I will admit our stopping everywhere was not my brightest idea. But these first few days are so important to solving crimes because the clues are still fresh."

"And Havers is doggedly pursuing each and every one of them. Nor should you forget that the solution to who did it and why may be in your head. You need to rest in order to allow those memories to flood back."

"I hate it when you are right," she grumbled.

She felt his gentle rumble of laughter against her cheek that was resting on his chest as he said, "I am *always* right."

"You are such a clot, Julius."

He kissed the top of her head. "I know."

As the pain began to ease, Gory sat up.

Julius settled her on the seat bench beside him, but kept hold of her hand as she gazed out the window. The sky was beginning to fill with rain clouds, she noted as the carriage rolled along the busy London streets. They skirted along the park and drove through some of the most fashionable squares in London to reach the Thorne townhouse.

Julius helped her down once the carriage had drawn to a halt in front of his home. His expression remained stern and his eyes were the ominous gray of those gathering storm clouds.

Despite being annoyed with her, his touch remained as gentle as ever.

Why could it not be him that she was marrying?

Mistaking her lovesick woe for nausea or fatigue, he scooped her in his arms again and carried her into the house. "Greeves, let Mrs. Quinn know that we shall be dining in my bedchamber."

Gory frowned at him. "We?"

"Yes, I am not leaving your side." He turned back to Greeves. "Only light broth and soft bread for Lady Gregoria. And she'll require a fresh nightgown. She needs to get out of these street clothes."

"All I need is a short nap," she insisted. "I am not taking off my clothes."

"You are taking off every stitch," he shot back with a growl. "I will attend to it myself if you refuse."

She gasped. "Don't you dare!"

Gory could not believe what he was saying.

Nor could Greeves whose face had turned crimson.

Was Julius truly a great ape reincarnated?

"Greeves, summon Dr. Farthingale, too," Julius commanded, setting her down but a moment to assist her out of her cloak and remove her hat. He handed them over to the butler, and then scooped her into his arms again. "The doctor is to be summoned without delay."

"I do not need a doctor," Gory protested. "You are insufferably overbearing."

"And you are insufferably delusional if you think that blow to the head you received was not serious."

"I know it was. But I also know my own body. All I need is a few minutes of rest. The doctor will be stopping by later. There is no need to bother him now."

"No need? You almost fainted in the carriage from the pain shooting through your head." He turned to Greeves. "Send for him right away."

"Yes, my lord." Greeves motioned to a nearby footman and sent him off on the errand.

Satisfied, Julius turned his gaze back on her. "As for you...clothes off. Bed."

"Gad, you dolt!" she cried as he started to march up the stairs with her still in his arms. "I am going to kick your shin raw if you do not stop this outrageous behavior at once. Poor Greeves is having an apoplexy." Which he was because the poor butler had turned red as a beet and was emitting strangled coughs.

Julius did not seem to care what anyone thought of his actions.

But she did. Was she not in enough of a fix? Injured, left for dead, and still considered a suspect. Not to mention the real killer had to be plotting to silence her before she could remember who he was. "Put me down, this instant, Julius!"

"No. Stop squirming or we will both tumble down the stairs."

He continued the march to his bedchamber without a care for

what anyone on the Thorne staff thought of his beastly behavior. He was still behaving like a great ape when he shoved open his bedroom door that had been left ajar while his valet was putting his belongings in order. "Robbins, get out. I need to put Lady Gregoria in my bed."

"Gad, Julius!"

"No argument, Gory. You are to stay in my bed."

"Stop calling it *your* bed. For this purpose it is just a bed. *A* bed. Anyone's bed. Not possessively yours."

He cast her a melting smile. "But it is *my* bed...and you are going in it."

"You are such a dolt." Her head was once again aching quite badly, and if she were less stubborn, she would not have put up any fuss at all. In truth, she could hardly see straight, not to mention she was feeling nauseated again. "In fact, stop talking altogether. I am going to kick you if you say another word."

"And I will kiss you if *you* say another word."

His valet gasped.

"Ignore him, Robbins. He is insane and highly irritating," Gory grumbled, seeking to assure the man whose face had also turned crimson.

Was Julius on a mission to embarrass his entire staff?

"Summon Adela's maid," Julius insisted, settling her on the bed. "Lady Gregoria is getting undressed whether she likes it or not."

Gory did not know what had gotten into Julius.

His gentlemanly reserve was gone and all that was left was this brutishly protective beast.

She did not like his behavior at all.

Well, she might not have minded so much if he intended to join her. But that was a lost cause, wasn't it? She was so desperately in love and aching for him that she had even dreamed he'd kissed her and proposed to her last night.

Truly pathetic.

And now her head felt ready to explode.

To admit she was in pain meant she would be removed from the investigation.

This was so frustrating and galling.

Julius had taken gentle care when removing her hat and cloak, and now did the same in removing her gloves.

Also galling were the tingles coursing through her body every time he touched her. "I will declare myself ruined and insist you marry me, if you do not stop fussing over me."

"Is that supposed to scare me?" Julius knelt in front of her to remove her walking boots. "I'll obtain the special license this very day and marry you tomorrow."

"Lord Thorne!" Robbins was gaping at his master for Julius had taken improper hold of her leg, his hand wrapped around her calf to stop her from kicking him. "Lord Thorne…"

"What?" Julius asked with marked impatience, no doubt aimed at her since the poor valet had done nothing to irritate him.

Robbins raked a hand through his thinning hair as he cleared his throat. "Is this not…unseemly? Lady Gregoria is scheduled to wed Lord Allendale in a matter of days."

"I am well aware. Have I not been taking her around on wedding errands all week long? Has this house not been turned upside down with *her* wedding preparations? Go polish some boots, Robbins. I do not need you taking her side."

Gory meant to toss back a snide retort, but she suddenly couldn't seem to form the words. Her head felt as though it was splitting in two. "Ow. Ow. *Ow*."

"Robbins, wait! Apologies for my rudeness." He caught Gory up in his arms as she started to fall forward off the bed. "Run downstairs and fetch Mrs. Quinn right away. Have her bring smelling salts and clean cloths. *Hurry*. Gory, stop fighting me. Your head is bleeding again."

She stopped resisting because he sounded genuinely worried.

In truth, so was she.

The light had suddenly gone out of the room, which made no sense because it had been broad daylight only moments ago. Perhaps it was those gathering storm clouds causing the darkness. Yes, it had to be.

The possibility that she had just lost her sight was too horrific to contemplate.

"Just lie still, Gory. Dear heaven. What was I thinking to let you out of my bed?"

"It wasn't your choice," she said weakly, offering no resistance when he began to undress her. "Julius, what's happening to me?"

"I don't know, love. Please lie quietly. Let me get you comfortable."

"I'm glad it's you beside me," she whispered.

"So am I, love," he replied, his voice rasping. "I won't leave you."

"Why do you call me that? *Love*. It's nice, you know. No one has ever called me by an endearment, not even Allendale."

He said nothing as he loosened her laces and left her only in her chemise. "Gory, do you remember anything of what we said to each other last night?"

"No." Perhaps this is what was giving her the pounding headache. "What did we say? Was it something important?"

CHAPTER 8

JULIUS PACED IN front of his bed while Gory slept peacefully under the covers.

Dr. Farthingale had come and gone, giving him assurances that Gory would be all right and that all she needed was a solid night's rest. However, she was to remain in bed for the next two days at a minimum and that was a firm order, one that Julius was not going to allow her to ignore.

Even though her sight had returned almost immediately, she had scared the blazes out of him and there was no point in taking chances that she might incur permanent damage next time.

"I will make certain she behaves like a proper patient," Julius had assured him.

It was now close to eight o'clock in the evening.

The sky had darkened and a night's chill had set in, but all was warm within his bedchamber because he had lit a fire and made certain it remained stoked.

Adela and Ambrose had not arrived home yet.

In truth, Julius was in no hurry to have them return because Adela would take over Gory's care and he would then be shut out. He was not ready to give Gory into anyone else's care, not even Adela's.

Certainly never to Allendale's care.

Where was the man?

He had not stopped by at all today.

This sat so ill with Julius.

How could any bridegroom ignore his bride when their wedding was mere days away? Just under a week away, to be precise. Not to mention his bride was injured and might have been killed. What was Allendale doing?

Julius could not tear himself away from Gory for a moment.

Shouldn't Allendale be feeling the same concern?

A soft knock at his door distracted him from his thoughts.

He stopped pacing and hurried to open it. "What is it, Robbins?"

"Mr. Havers and Mr. Barrow are here to see you, my lord."

The bed sheets rustled as Gory struggled to sit up. "Send them up here, Robbins."

"No, put them in the study. I'll be right down." Julius turned back to her with a frown. "I thought you were sleeping."

"I was merely resting my strained eyes. Do not leave yet, Robbins. This discussion is not settled."

"It is settled. Leave us, Robbins." He continued to stare at Gory. "Strained? Is this how you would describe losing your vision?"

"It was merely blurred, not completely lost."

"Merely?" He let out a sound of disgust. "You were blinded for a few minutes."

"Not that long, and I feel much better now. Robbins! Do not dare take another step from this room unless it is to escort Mr. Havers and Mr. Barrow up here. I need to hear what they have to say."

Julius threw his hands into the air. "Blast it, Gory. Why must you always be so contrary?"

"How is it wrong of me to want to know what they've found out? I was the one almost killed, not you."

"Precisely, and you are still healing."

"Under your excellent care. You are to be commended, for no one could have done a better job of nursing me back to health than you."

He groaned. "Your attempt to flatter me into doing your bidding will not work."

She cast him a fragile smile that was his undoing.

"Oh, hell," he muttered, for there was something in the way the firelight reflected in her eyes that made them sparkle. How could he resist her when she looked so beautiful? There was a delicacy to her face that had his heart beating faster and crumbled his resistance. "Fine."

"Then we are agreed you will let them up here?"

"Yes, you little nuisance. I suppose you would have followed me downstairs if I attempted to meet them without you." Julius sighed as he turned to his valet. "Robbins, show them up here. The empress has spoken."

Gory cast him a hurt look. "I am not trying to be difficult. Do I not have a right to know what is going on? The killer failed to silence me the first time, so is there any doubt he will try again? Should I not be doing everything I can to avoid being his next victim?"

This was also his greatest worry.

Gory remained in danger until her memory returned and she could identify the killer or his accomplice.

Julius waited until Robbins went off to fetch their visitors before addressing Gory's comments. "I am the one who needs to be doing everything possible to stop the killer from reaching you. That's why I am taking every precaution. This is not about hiding information from you, but all about keeping you safe."

He raked a hand through his hair and began to pace in front of her bed. "You were in such a bad way only a few hours ago. You cannot dismiss how dangerous it was for you to have lost your vision, even if it was only for a moment or two."

She sighed. "It frightened me, too."

"Just give your body time to heal, all right? You are too vulnerable in the condition you are in right now."

She nodded.

They said no more as Havers and the Bow Street runner entered the room.

There was one chair already placed beside the bed, and Julius now brought over a second chair. He offered them to their visitors while he remained standing since he was too agitated to sit. "What news, Havers?"

"My man found three names in the public coach ledgers for the Windsor to London route the day of Lord Easton's murder. Two women and a man. Now, it could be mere coincidence that all three bought return tickets for the first coach to Windsor out of London at break of dawn the following morning. We are having the clerk who sold them their tickets and the coach drivers on the London/Windsor route describe these three to an artist who often assists us in our investigations. We'll see if he comes up with some recognizable portraits."

Gory pursed her lips. "Do you believe my aunt and her sister were the women?"

"It is a possibility," Havers said with a nod. "It is also possible the sister's husband was the male accomplice. However, I am ruling out nothing yet. It is just something to note as we continue to gather all the clues. My men are on the task. They will also be checking Lady Easton's sister and her husband for scratches."

"What about Lady Easton herself? Did she finally consent to being searched?" Gory asked.

He cast her a wry smile. "I would not call it consent, but she was searched. Not a mark found on her."

Gory pursed her lips in thought. "Because it was likely the sister's husband who was the one struggling with Lord Easton. I've met him. He is a big man and certainly strong enough to keep him in a choke hold while sticking a blade into his heart. Oh…"

Julius felt a lurch to his own heart as she gasped and suddenly began to rub her forehead. "Gory, what is it?"

"Nothing…I'm all right."

"You don't look all right. Gory, please. You are hurt. Stop pretending you are in the pink of health."

She looked up at him through pained eyes. "It was just another memory trying to come forward. I don't understand why they are stubbornly refusing to do so."

"Because whatever you saw was frightening to you," Julius said gently.

"I am not a coward," she grumbled.

Julius wanted to gather her up in his arms again, but her frown as he started toward her put him off. She did not want him coddling her in front of these two investigators. He understood her point, so he kept his distance since she now appeared to have gotten over the worst of these latest throes.

"Not a coward," she muttered again.

He rested a shoulder against the bedpost and folded his arms across his chest. "I never said you were. In fact, you are the bravest lady I know. But this is why I am so worried about you. There is something shocking to you that is lurking on the edges of your memory. You are afraid to face whatever it is."

She snorted, but then gave a reluctant shrug. "Maybe."

Julius turned to Homer Barrow. "Anything to report yet?"

Mr. Barrow nodded. "My lord, this is something I would rather discuss with you in private. It is a most delicate matter."

Gory immediately perked. "Does it concern Lord Allendale?"

"Aye, m'lady." He cast her an apologetic look that boded bad news.

She sat forward and clasped her hands around her knees that were drawn up under the covers. "Then I need to be included in the discussion, Mr. Barrow. He is my husband-to-be. I must be told what is going on. Do not spare me any of the details. I deal with dead bodies regularly in my research work. I doubt anything could be worse than that."

"But this is about the living, m'lady," Mr. Barrow gently remarked. "It is the living who have the capacity to give the greatest hurt."

"All the more reason why I must be told. I am already imagining the worst about him. He has not been around to see me all week, other than a brief visit yesterday. He has not come by at all today. I assume he has not called on my aunt, either. I am not even certain he will show up on our wedding day. Not that there ought to be a wedding under these circumstances. But he has not even bothered to present himself in order for us to discuss postponement of the ceremony. What has he been doing, Mr. Barrow?"

"I am truly, truly sorry, Lady Gregoria," the Bow Street runner said, emitting an anguished breath. "But he has been attending to another young lady. She is about your age and…she has just given birth. There is a child involved. A little girl."

Gory regarded Mr. Barrow, too stunned to speak for the obvious pain it was causing her.

"Was he was with her the night Lady Gregoria's uncle was killed?" Julius asked, for Gory was in no condition to ask the question herself.

"I do not have an answer for you yet. I have a man looking into the matter as we speak."

Julius nodded. "Thank you, Mr. Barrow. Please let us know as soon as you have the information."

Allendale's downfall ought to have pleased him.

Surprisingly, it did not.

This is not how he ever wanted to win Gory's hand in marriage.

She looked heartbroken and humiliated.

"I knew he did not love me," she said in a raw whisper. "It all felt so wrong from the very start."

"You do not appear to have loved him either," Havers stated matter-of-factly, showing utter disregard for Gory's feelings.

Julius immediately leaped to her defense. "Shut up, Havers. You are out of line."

Gory shook her head. "No, he isn't. I suppose it has become rather obvious ours was not a love match. But I thought Allendale and I had enough mutual interests to sustain a good partnership. I did not really think it through, did I? He must have known of this young lady being with child when he proposed to me."

"Gory…" Julius did not know what to say to make this revelation less painful to her. Nor could he understand what Allendale was thinking to propose marriage to Gory while involved with another woman.

Well, men had children out of wedlock often enough. It was not all that uncommon. But to not even wait a heartbeat before proposing to another woman? That seemed extremely callous to Julius.

Did this not add to his suspicions about Allendale?

Was he plotting to marry Gory, secure her inheritance, and then dispose of her so he could be with this other woman?

Havers must have noticed his mounting fury, for he cast Julius a warning glance. "Lord Thorne, there is no point in speculating. But I do apologize to you, Lady Gregoria, if I have inadvertently caused you more hurt. We will have our answers shortly. There could be an innocent explanation for his actions."

"Such as what?" Julius shot back.

"I do not know, my lord. But leaping to conclusions does not help this investigation. No matter how low the opinion you have of Lord Allendale, his actions could be wholly unrelated to the crime."

"But is it not most suspicious?" Julius asked.

"Yes, it is. As is Lady Easton's refusal to be searched. But when we did finally search her, she had no scratches. Need I remind you that we have yet to interrogate Lord Easton's business associates. I have not ruled any of them out, either. It is quite possible a disgruntled investor or business partner could have perpetrated this crime."

"And what do you make of Lady Gregoria being found in her wedding dress?" Julius asked.

"It has not slipped my mind for a moment," Havers replied. "This is why I have taken it upon myself to investigate the personal connections first and foremost. However, I have not ignored any other potential connections. My best men have been assigned to interview Lord Easton's business acquaintances. We shall know more once I receive their reports, but that gown being put on Lady Gregoria points to the solution being closer to home."

"Home," Gory muttered with a grunt. "I thought my returning there would stir my brain, but I felt nothing as I stood in the study and stared at the very spot where my uncle had been murdered. Complete and utter blank."

"Sleep on it tonight and let's see what the morning brings." Havers rose and motioned discreetly for Mr. Barrow to do the same. "Lady Gregoria, we will bid you farewell for now. Lord Thorne knows to summon me if you remember anything important. But you serve us best by resting and allowing your memory to heal."

Julius walked the two men out. "Stop by if you discover

something else of interest. I do not care the hour. It is vital that I be kept fully apprised. Lady Gregoria will not stop fretting until the killer is caught. Nor will I, truth be told."

"Nor I," Havers assured him. "If she was not involved in her uncle's murder, then she knows who was. She saw the killer and he saw her. This is why Mr. Barrow has placed his men to watch your townhouse. Unfortunately, I do not have the resources to put my constables on round the clock watch, but you are in good hands with Mr. Barrow's runners. I'll see what I can do about assigning a man or two from my constabulary onto the task as a supplement."

Julius nodded.

"I'll be stopping next to question the lady with whom Lord Easton was having an affair. Thank you for sending word to me about her. The Easton head butler knew of her and gave us the information we needed. This is yet another path for me to explore, although I doubt she has any involvement. The lady is a widow and was left well settled by her late husband. She and Lord Easton were childhood acquaintances who...er, resumed their acquaintance upon her husband's passing. The arrangement seemed to work for all involved, and nothing had changed to upset that smoothly sailing boat."

"So, you have ruled out the widow?" Julius asked.

Havers nodded. "She was sincerely bereaved to learn of his passing. Seems fitting, for we all should have one person in the world who cares if we live or die."

Once the two investigators had departed, Julius returned to his bedchamber.

Gory regarded him eagerly when he entered. "Did they say anything more to you?"

"Havers found out the name of the lady with whom your uncle was dallying. Although I would not call it dallying, for I think the two sincerely cared for each other."

"They did?"

Julius nodded. "Who knows? Your uncle might have turned out decent had he married this lady instead of the dragon he chose."

"Unfortunately, he didn't," Gory said in a whisper, no doubt thinking of her own situation with Allendale.

Yes, he was stopping that wedding.

There was no way in blazes he would allow Gory to commit herself to a life of unhappiness.

He cleared his throat. "I told Havers and Barrow to call on me at any time of the day or night if they learn anything new. Meanwhile, Mr. Barrow's men are guarding the property and I am going to stay beside you again tonight to guard you. I'll remain with you for as long as it takes until the killer is caught."

"Adela and Ambrose are scheduled to return tonight. They might not be so keen on having us share your quarters."

"Adela will understand the need and support me. Ambrose might make token protest, but he would do no less for Adela. He won't interfere. But I do not really care what anyone thinks. You ran to me for help and that makes you *mine* to care for."

She arched an eyebrow. "Yours?"

He nodded. "That's right. Mine, and mine alone."

She cast him an achingly sweet smile. "Do all men have this protect-the-little-lady instinct? Even Havers was treading delicately around me toward the end of his visit, and he is one of the most indelicate men I have ever met."

Julius laughed. "Yes, he's quite abrasive. But I think it is a necessary trait in his line of work, a requirement if he is to get anything accomplished."

"Yes, I suppose. What time is it now, Julius? The hour is getting late and Adela and Ambrose should have arrived by now."

"Are you going to fret about them, too? I expect they are close to London by now. One of the carriage horses might have thrown a shoe and delayed their return. They'll be here first thing in the morning, if not tonight."

He settled in the chair Mr. Barrow had vacated moments earlier. "Do you mind terribly being alone with me for another night?"

She shook her head and laughed lightly. "Oh, it is far too late for me to have any regrets. No, of course not. You are the only one

I trust to keep me safe. Julius, I am so grateful to you for all you have done for me. You've never once complained about my imposing on you."

"Because you are not an imposition at all. I would be mad with worry if you were anywhere else or with anyone else."

She leaned against the pillows piled high at her back and closed her eyes a moment. "The woman who wins your heart is going to be the luckiest woman in the world. I do not know how I am ever going to repay your kindness."

"No repayment necessary. Can I get you anything, Gory?"

"Yes, I would love a betrothed who does not cheat on me." She sighed. "Only jesting."

He leaned forward and gave her cheek a light caress. "You deserve better than Allendale. You know you will have my full support if you choose to end the betrothal."

She nodded. "Yes, yours and that of all my friends. Adela, Syd, and Marigold were not pleased when they learned I had accepted Allendale. Nor were Lady Dayne and Lady Withnall who were sponsoring me for the purpose of getting me married off. In truth, I was more than a little surprised when they claimed I would never be happy if I were to wed Allendale and urged me to hold out for a love match."

"But you didn't. Why did you give up on love, Gory?"

"Isn't it obvious?"

He shook his head. "No, not to me."

"Oh, Julius. No one is ever going to love me," she said, her lips now trembling.

Was she going to cry?

"You are wrong, Gory." He gave her cheek another caress, liking how warm and soft her skin was to his touch. "There is someone in the offing who loves you very much."

"Hah! That is a jolly jest."

He considered declaring himself here and now, but he had done it already last night and she had completely forgotten their conversation and – more telling – forgotten their kiss.

Adding to the weight of all she was carrying on her slight shoudlers, today she had momentarily lost her vision because she had climbed out of bed too soon and exhausted herself. He was not certain how she would respond if he declared his love again.

She had enough turmoil in her life and already too many feelings that she was suppressing.

"I wished so hard for that perfect, romantic match," Gory admitted. "Truly, I did. But in my heart, I knew it would never happen for me. So, I took the leap and accepted Allendale. That has all fallen apart now, obviously. I will tell him I am ending the betrothal when he shows up here next, assuming he ever deigns to put in an appearance any time soon. Who knows? He might not show up on our wedding day, either. Do you think he means to jilt me at the altar?"

Julius arched an eyebrow. "Would you care?"

"No, it would be a relief. Facing a life alone is far better than being shackled to a liar and a cheat. Perhaps he is even a murderer. I did not think he had it in him to kill anyone. But he has deceived me in every other regard. Is it much of a stretch to believe I was wrong and he is capable of the most heinous, basest crimes?"

"We will deal with Allendale tomorrow, Gory. There is nothing you can do about him now."

"All right, but can we talk about my uncle's business acquaintances?"

"Why them? Well, all right. What have you not already told Havers?"

"I don't know. But I think it will help if we keep going over the possible culprits. My brain needs to keep working, and running through their names again might help me remember something."

"If you think so." Julius did not really believe it served a purpose, but he was no experienced investigator. Nor was he a doctor who might know how to treat a patient with memory loss. If Gory thought talking things through with him might help her recover, then he did not mind going along with her wishes. He would put a stop to their discussion if it proved too fatiguing or frightening for her. "If we are going to discuss these business connections, then let's include the solicitor, Reginald Mayfield, as well."

"You did not like him," she commented.

"No, he's oily. You think so, too."

She nodded. "What else about him troubled you?"

"He knew of your inheritance."

"Why is this of any concern? Julius, he was the draftsman of those documents. Is it surprising that he would know every detail of what I am to receive and when? Why should he wait until now to do something about it when this bequest was likely established at the time of my father's death? In truth, this had to be my father's doing because my uncle would not leave me a ha'penny, if it were up to him. We should pay a call on Mr. Mayfield tomorrow and ask to read the testamentary documents."

"We? I have already seen them and given them a brief perusal. I want to get them out of his hands before he does something to damage them."

"Excellent idea. I'll go with you. When? First thing tomorrow morning?"

"Gad, do you have to fall flat on your face before you agree to stay in bed and rest? Do not give me a hard time about this, Gory. No running around for you tomorrow or the day after."

"I am not an invalid," she grumbled.

"Actually, you are."

He could hear her teeth grinding in response to his remark. "I am not nearly as bad off as I might appear."

He tweaked her chin. "Said the girl with stitches poking out of her head and who almost went blind. You know, there is not another young lady in London who would make a fuss over being in my bed. Most would leap at the opportunity."

"I happen to like your bed very much," she retorted. "It is soft and quite comfortable. I would not mind being in it quite so much were I not required to remain in it *all* the time."

Julius was contemplating bringing up the subject of her doing just that, of marrying him and sharing not only a bedchamber but a lifetime with him. Why not just tell her again? Why not get those words out again and deal with the consequences as they arose?

After all, she had run to him for a reason.

He knew what the reason was, too.

She loved him.

Him.

He was about to say something when he heard a flurry of activity in the downstairs hallway.

Blast.

Had Ambrose and Adela returned?

"Gory, there is something you need to know."

She sighed. "Yes, Julius. You want me to stop being difficult and recuperate. I suppose it is also easier for Mr. Barrow's runners to guard me if I am not waltzing around town."

"Right, but that isn't my point. I...oh, hell..."

"What, Julius? Please, I do not require more lectures from you."

"I do not lecture you."

"Well, you are highly opinionated."

"And you are not?" he grumbled. "No, forget I said that. You have every right to express an opinion. In truth, you are often very clever and I value everything you have to say."

"But?"

"But nothing." He leaned in closer, so that their lips were mere inches from each other and their breaths mingled. "This is what I am trying to tell you...and hopefully you will remember this time."

"Remember what?"

"This." He crushed his lips to hers, kissing her with scorching abandon and all the love in his heart, for there was no time to properly explain his feelings for her any other way.

Her lips were plump and sweet, and he wished to savor them endlessly. But he heard footsteps on the stairs and knew the door would burst open at any moment.

He tore his mouth off hers. "*This*, Gory. Can you find it in your heart to wish for *me*? To want *me*. To love *me*."

Adela rushed in before she could respond.

"I cannot believe you were almost killed!" she cried, and raced to Gory's bedside. "Greeves just told us what happened to you."

Ambrose hurried in just after her and tossed Julius a questioning look. "Is it true?"

"Yes." He glanced at Gory who was staring back at him with her eyes wide and mouth slightly parted while she ran her fingers lightly across her lips.

Lord, he was going to nibble that deliciously fleshy bottom lip the next chance he got.

He raked a hand through his hair and cast her a tender smile, one he hoped conveyed how deeply he cared for her.

She responded with a look of utter confusion.

What had he expected when kissing a girl who believed it was impossible for anyone to love her?

"Gory, you and I will talk later. All right?"

She nodded numbly.

"Good." He decided to leave the ladies to catch up, but motioned for Ambrose to follow him out. "Let's talk in your study."

An icy draft blew into the house as they marched downstairs because the front door was wide open while the footmen unloaded the bags and supplies his brother and Adela had brought home with them.

One would think they had been gone a month and traveled to far off lands, but they had been gone no more than a few days and only to Oxford. But Ambrose was a devoted husband and father now, so traveling with Adela – since she would never leave their baby at home – required a nanny and a wagonload of infant supplies.

Now all of them were back and the house was a lively din.

Julius shut the study door behind them to avoid the noise, and then crossed to the sideboard to pour his brother a glass of port. "Here you go, Ambrose."

He needed one, as well.

"Thanks, little brother."

Julius chuckled as he poured his own drink. "I'll be eighty and you'll still be calling me that just to irk me."

"Probably, assuming I am around that long to irk you."

"Oh, you will be. Vexing me shall keep you thriving," he teased.

"Well, I would not want to depart this life too early and miss all the excitement. Adela and I leave you to watch over Gory for a few days and look what happens." They settled in matching leather chairs beside the hearth and Ambrose began to pepper him with questions.

Julius gave him a full account.

"That's everything up to now, Ambrose. We're hoping Havers and Barrow will have more answers for us tomorrow."

His brother, always too astute, regarded him closely. "Is it really everything? I think you have left out something quite important."

"Such as what?" Julius studied the remains of the port in his glass, noting how the firelight from hearth's blaze caught the delicate crystal and enhanced the deep crimson of the wine. It brought to mind the caked blood he had washed off Gory that first night which was more of a brownish-red because it had dried on her skin.

"Does Gory know you are in love with her?"

Julius laughed. "Am I that obvious?"

"Yes, to me," his brother said with a nod. "You haven't let her out of your sight for a moment since the murder occurred. Nor have you allowed Mrs. Quinn to move her out of your bedchamber. You do understand the consequences of her spending these nights in your bed, the two of you together without a chaperone."

"I was guarding her. Nothing untoward happened between us."

Ambrose arched an eyebrow. "But you would like it to happen."

"Desperately," he said with a bitter laugh. "However, she is betrothed."

Ambrose drained the last of his wine and set the glass down on the small table beside his chair. "Betrothed to the very man who might have killed her uncle. It doesn't count. You are going to do all you can to prevent that wedding from ever happening, aren't you?"

He nodded. "Yes, but only because she does not love him. I would never interfere with her happiness if she truly cared for

Allendale. Of course, this assumes he isn't the killer."

Ambrose shrugged. "I don't suppose it matters now. After all that has happened, you know she is going to call off the wedding without need of prompting from you."

"Yes, but she has not done it yet."

"But she wants to."

Julius nodded. "However, Havers does not want her inciting any suspects just yet. Gory, on the other hand, wants to hurl those cannonballs and lure the killer straight to her."

Ambrose frowned. "Sounds like something she would do."

"She is fearless. Usually. However, she saw something on the night of the murder that scared her. She wants to remember what it was, but at the same time, she is fighting to suppress it."

"Understandable," his brother said, pursing his lips in thought, "especially if it was Allendale she saw committing the crime. Well, she will end it with him whether he turns out to be innocent or not. What are you going to do once she breaks free of the betrothal?"

"Propose to her, of course." He began to shift uncomfortably. "I told her last night how I felt about her, but she did not remember any of our conversation."

Ambrose frowned. "Has she suppressed that, too?"

"Apparently, but I know she loves me. I haven't a doubt. She would not have run to me otherwise. I started to bring it up again when you returned."

"And we interrupted you?"

He nodded. "So, I will try again in a few days and hope this time it sticks. I kissed her just before you and Adela burst in. I have no idea what is going through her mind right now. But she is mine, as I am hers. No one is going to come between us."

"Is this how I sound when I speak of Adela?" Ambrose grinned. "Egad, I have never seen a more possessive look on any man's face than yours right now. No wonder women think of us as baboons. I assume this means Allendale is never going to get near her again, even if it turns out he is innocent."

"Bloody right," Julius muttered, draining the last of his wine. "Well, Gory insists on seeing him in order to end the betrothal. I'll be right by her side. If he is the murderer, he will not take kindly to her ruining his plans. Anyway, their meeting won't happen tomorrow unless he surprises us and shows up here. But I doubt he will. His attention is caught up with that young lady and her newborn."

"Adela and I will do all we can to help you." Ambrose rubbed a hand over his face that appeared strained and quite weary from his journey. Julius had not meant to add to his brother's concerns. Being the Duke of Huntsford, Ambrose had a full plate of responsibilities that he attended to dutifully.

Julius only meant to alert him to what had happened.

Protecting Gory was Julius's responsibility, one that he was not about to shirk. "Much appreciated, but there is nothing for you to do. Gory is mine to look after. Homer Barrow and his runners are assisting me with her protection. Havers is on the investigation and peering under every rock. He'll soon figure out who committed the crime."

"Well, the preparations for a wedding are all in place," Ambrose said. "All that needs to be done is switch the bridegroom. I wonder how Allendale will react to the news?"

Julius shrugged. "We'll soon find out, won't we?"

CHAPTER 9

GORY SPENT THE next two days in bed, ready to scream with boredom, but not ready to put up a fuss because the weather had been so horrendous. Two days of a continuously howling rain mixed with an unusually wintery blast of cold air had left the London streets dangerously slick with a coating of sleet covering the roadways.

But the clouds were now burning away under the force of the sun and the air was warming to a more accommodating temperature for this time of year. When Gory arose and drew open the drapes to peer out the window, she smiled upon seeing those clearing skies and bursts of sunshine attempting to break through the layers of gray.

"Excellent," she muttered to herself and padded over to the fireplace and the chairs beside it.

A few embers still glowed red within the fireplace grate. The fire had mostly died out, but Gory took a moment to place more logs atop the ashen pile in the hope of getting the flames rekindled.

Julius was uncomfortably sprawled across the chairs, his big body partly spilling over the seat back of one chair and his long legs resting atop the other as he remained fast asleep.

He did not respond to her presence as she fussed with the dying blaze.

Once finished, she shook him gently. "Julius..."

She shook him again when he remained unresponsive. "Julius,

are you awake?"

"I am now," he grumbled, opening one eye and groaning as he struggled to sit up from his awkward position. "What time is it?"

"Seven o'clock. Did you not hear the clock just chime?"

His eyes were now open and those gorgeous gray orbs stared back at her with a mix of heat and irritation. "No, I did not. You seem awfully chirpy this morning."

She nodded. "Because this is going to be a day that will change the course of my life for the better. I am going to break it off with Allendale today. No more delays. Word must go out to our guests at once that there is to be no wedding. I expect most of them will not be surprised since word of my uncle's death will have spread beyond London by now."

She held up a hand when he sought to respond. "No, do not try to talk me out of it."

"Why would I talk you out of it? I kissed you, Gory."

"I have not forgotten that scorching kiss," she said softly. "I have been thinking of little else for the past two days. Did you mean it?"

He nodded. "Yes, love. I did."

She let out a breath. "I kissed you back. I meant it, too. Havers has had enough time to discover more about Allendale. Where was he on the night of the murder? Not that his guilt or innocence will change my opinion. We are only three days away from my wedding now and something must be done. Many things, actually. Not only the wedding guests must be told, but the orchestra must be notified. The bakers. Wine merchants. Adela's staff is going to start baking today and this must be stopped."

"Gory, we need to talk."

She regarded him with confusion. "Is this not what we are doing? I did not want to wake you earlier, but I have been up since before dawn making lists of everything that must be attended to over these next few days."

He sighed and stretched his muscled body. "Leave it all just as it is."

"Why?" She frowned at him, although he did look marvelously rumpled and handsome enough to melt hearts. The bristles of his day's growth of beard felt rough against her palm as she now laid it against his cheek. His hair had a boyish cowlick at the top and the ends curled becomingly at the nape of his neck. "How can I possibly leave this disaster of a wedding as it is? I need to confront Allendale and end it. Now. Today. Not a moment longer."

"Got it, Gory."

"And it has nothing to do with the fact that you kissed me the other day. By the way, we have to talk about that, too."

"I know." He yawned and stretched once more as he rose. "Let me wash up and get dressed, then we can discuss everything."

"Well, there is nothing much left to say about Allendale. I am resolved to end it with him. Neither you nor Havers ought to stop me. Just be ready to protect me if he gets angry and attempts to lash out at me."

"I would kill him if he ever set a hand on you."

"Marvelously apish of you, Julius. And much appreciated, I would add."

He grunted.

"I also intend to find out more about the young lady and her newborn. It is not right that the child should be given up to a foundling home. In fact, it is quite heinous of Allendale to do something so cruel to his own offspring."

"Assuming the child is his," Julius remarked.

"Who else's would it be?"

"I don't know, but Mr. Barrow should have more information for us today. And who is to say he has any intention of giving up the young lady or the child? Just be patient. We'll get at the truth."

Gory rolled her eyes. "I am trying. It is not easy."

"I know, love." He gave her chin a light tweak.

These Thorne brothers were marvelous specimens of manhood. Gory always enjoyed standing beside Julius, especially. The two of them seemed to fit just right despite the difference in their height. Perhaps it was the muscled breadth of him that made him perfect to snuggle against.

No doubt, this is why her heart fluttered whenever she stood beside him.

He had given her a breathtaking kiss two days ago, but she

had also had recurring dreams of an earlier kiss. That dream kiss had felt so real, too. She could still feel the warmth of his mouth on hers.

It was ridiculous, of course.

She had yet to figure out what it all meant.

She understood Julius was wonderfully protective of her, but was it only protective urges he was feeling toward her? With Adela and Ambrose now returned, it seemed Julius had withdrawn a little. He had not brought up the subject of their kisses despite having had several chances to do so on the nights they were alone.

Was he reconsidering?

She did not want to be a mere passing fancy for him.

She wanted to be his one and only.

But how could she ever be that to any man, especially one as handsome, intelligent, and appealing as Julius?

"Gory, you are frowning."

She shook her head. "No, just thinking."

He tweaked her chin. "You do too much of it. Can you relax that sharp brain of yours and stop trying to force the memories to return?"

"Why? All I need to do is remember what happened and this murder will be solved."

"Havers and Barrow will be along shortly to give us updates. Let's see what they have to say before we make our plans."

"I hate it when you do that," she grumbled.

"Do what?"

"Spout common sense and logic."

His smile was affectionate as he said, "I'll leave you to wash up and dress. Meet you downstairs for breakfast?"

She nodded, for she was feeling much better than she had been these past few days. Enforced bed rest did that to a person, she supposed. This was why Dr. Farthingale had prescribed it for her in the first place. "Julius…"

"Yes?"

She took a deep breath. "Why did you kiss me the other day? Adela and Ambrose burst in just afterward and we had no chance to speak about it. Was it just a momentary urge and does not merit discussion?"

"What do you think I meant by it?"

She laughed. "Oh, no. I am the wrong person to ask. I know nothing about men, other than dead ones whose stories are told by the physical clues found on their unresponsive bodies. I have never been involved romantically with anyone, not even Allendale. Do not expect me to understand what your steamy kiss signified. I have a *hope* as to what it means, but that is all."

He gave her cheek a light caress. "All right, then I will simplify it for you. It means that I am in love with you. Fully committed, crazy in love."

Her eyes rounded and her mouth gaped open because of all the answers she had expected in response to her question, this was not one of them.

"I have always loved you," he said, drawing her into his arms. "There was never a moment since meeting you that I did not love you."

He had said the same in her dream.

"Clear enough?" he asked with the whisper of a smile upon his lips.

She nodded numbly.

Had it been a dream? That first kiss? And then he'd kissed her again shortly before Adela and Ambrose returned.

A second kiss?

Or was it only the first and the other had been a dream?

Was she dreaming now?

Her head began to throb.

She put her hands to her temples and began to rub them gently. "Why did you never tell me this before? How could you let me attach myself to Allendale?"

He sighed as he continued to hold her in his embrace. "Gory, we had this conversation the night after your uncle was killed. But you were in no condition to hear it, so you've forgotten what I told you then. Has any of it come back to you?"

"I don't know. I can no longer tell what is real and what is not. It is this detestable laudanum I need to stop taking."

She found herself struggling as her memories were getting all jumbled in her head.

"Gory, hush." Julius stroked her hair, running his fingers gently through her unbound mane. "I see that merely thinking about it...thinking about *us*, is distressing you."

She looked up at him, searching his face as though all the answers were within his eyes. "Us? As in a permanent *us*? Do you want me beyond a kiss?"

"Yes, Gory. Have I not made that evident? I want you for always. If I ask you again to marry me, will you remember it? Will you accept me?"

The pounding in her head grew stronger. "You've asked me before?"

He nodded. "The same night I gave you that first kiss. To be clear, the kiss I gave you the day my brother and Adela returned was our second."

Tears formed in her eyes. "I did remember, but I could not believe it was true."

"I'm so sorry I was not honest with you from the start," he said with an aching depth of feeling. "I was not honest with myself either, thinking I was not ready to commit to any woman, not even one I knew that I loved. Nor could I believe we three brothers could fall in love with three bluestocking friends who were as close as sisters. As the youngest, was I merely going along with my older brothers? I was so determined to stand on my own that I almost lost you because of my stupid hesitation. And it was stupid because I really hadn't a doubt about my feelings for you."

"I had no idea. I wish I had known."

"And I wish I had said something to you. I was torn apart with agony when I learned of your betrothal. But I thought you were happy, that this match with Allendale was what you wanted. I would not have interfered with your happiness for the world."

"But I was miserable, Julius."

"You hid it well. I did not realize it until last week when I was taking you around London on your wedding errands how badly you were hurting. The moment I understood yours was not a love match, I resolved to break up your wedding."

"You did?" She had no idea this had been on his mind.

Dear heaven.

"Then, your uncle was murdered and you..." His voice hitched. "You almost died. I have been in torment ever since, blaming myself for not speaking up sooner."

"All the more reason why I must confront Allendale today."

"Agreed, but not before we hear from Havers and Barrow. I will feel much better about allowing you to see Allendale if he is ruled out as a suspect in the murder."

"*Allowing* me?"

He sighed. "All right, bad choice of words. I am not going to be a tyrant and demand your unquestioned obedience. Blessed saints, I do not think that word – obedience – exists in your vocabulary. But neither will I stand by and do nothing while you run straight into danger. Do I not have an obligation to protect you?"

She arched an eyebrow. "Well, for the moment the obligation should belong to Allendale. But he has been an abject failure. Not that I am usually in need of anyone to protect me, although I would not mind having you behave apishly when coming to my rescue from time to time."

"From time to time?" He groaned. "I hope you will *never* need rescuing from a dangerous situation again. You are too stubborn and fearless for your own good, Gory."

"I am not foolish."

"I never said you were. But you do overestimate your cleverness at times. There are some situations when nothing can save you but brute strength, and that is something you do not have. Are we going to argue over this now?"

"No," she grumbled. "But are we in agreement that Allendale must be told there will be no wedding?"

He raked a hand through his disheveled hair, somehow still looking magnificent despite the unruly mop and his day's growth of beard. "Yes, agreed."

"Julius... thank you."

"I do not need to be thanked for encouraging you to break off your betrothal to Allendale. It is purely selfish on my part, as you well understand by now."

"That is not why I said it."

He regarded her quizzically. "Oh, then why?"

"Because when I lost my parents, I lost the only two people who ever loved me...and even they were not quite certain about it, at times. But I know they cared. They simply did not understand me. But you do. You know me better than I know myself."

He smiled.

"No one has ever loved me truly and deeply. But now, I have that possibility with you. It is a very odd feeling, but also very nice."

He caressed her cheek. "Then it is a good thing I have a lot of love to heap on you. I do, Gory. Never doubt it."

Gory's heart felt lighter than it ever had before.

She smiled back at him. "I knew I ran to you for a reason."

"Your heart knew I was madly in love with you, even if you did not realize it yet," he said.

When one of the maids arrived to assist her, Julius marched out to afford her privacy. His valet had taken to setting out his belongings in one of the guest rooms, and this is where Julius prepared himself for the day.

Gory hummed a lively tune as she washed and dressed in his quarters that she had now taken over and hopefully would always remain because he had declared his love for her. Getting herself ready for the day took longer than usual because the poor maid was terrified of accidentally touching her wound that was healing nicely but had not yet fully mended.

Dr. Farthingale would remove the stitches in a couple of days, but until then, they would remain poking out from behind her ear. The maid carefully styled her hair so that it fell in a soft wave to cover the area of the injury.

The stitches would not be visible unless one looked closely.

Now presentable, Gory hurried down the grand staircase to join Julius in the dining room. She smiled brightly upon seeing him seated at the table with his brother and Adela, all of them chatting as they ate their breakfast.

"You look lovely, Gory," Julius said, rising to escort her to the seat beside his.

She glanced down at the violet gown of softest wool she had worn. "This is another of Adela's that I've borrowed. Thank you, Adela."

"Not a problem. Take whatever you like from my wardrobe. I have so many beautiful gowns, it really is ridiculous."

Ambrose shrugged. "You are my duchess now. It is necessary."

"I think you just like to spoil me," Adela retorted, leaning over to kiss him on the cheek.

Gory was so happy for her friend. In truth, she was happy for her band of friends who had all made love matches. First Adela, then Marigold, and most recently, Syd. Was it possible she would find her happiness next?

Julius had always been the man of her dreams.

"I'll have a few of my gowns sent over here," she said, knowing it was not right to impose on Adela when she had an entire wardrobe of her own at the Easton residence. "That is...I hope you will allow me to stay here a little while longer. I cannot go back home yet. The thought of returning to that place curls my stomach. It has not felt like home for a very long time."

"You needn't," Julius assured her, giving her a meaningful stare. "And you look beautiful, even if the gown is not your own."

"Thank you, Julius." No one had ever complimented her like this before. It was not merely his words, but the way he brightened whenever he looked at her.

Was she not doing the same whenever she gazed at him?

Love was a wonderful thing.

Adela and Ambrose were smirking.

She tried not to beam like a lighthouse beacon, but it was impossible to suppress when she was so happy. "I have missed all this week at the forensics laboratory," Gory said, turning to Ambrose with a look of apology. "But I think I will be fit enough to return next week."

Ambrose shook his head. "Gory, your absence was already planned due to your...ah, um...you know, the wedding."

She glanced at Julius.

That mere glance confirmed Ambrose and Adela had been told everything. Well, perhaps not about their kisses. But she understood by the looks on their faces that Julius had confessed that he loved her.

Adela had always known of her feelings for Julius.

Gory smiled, for her dear friend was beaming almost as brightly as she was now that she knew Julius loved her back.

"I think it is best if Julius and I go by ourselves to speak to Allendale on your behalf," Ambrose said, biting into a chunk of freshly baked bread he had slathered with marmalade.

"No, it isn't necessary." Gory set her teacup aside to let the piping hot tea cool. "Julius and I will handle the matter. We are going to see him today."

"Assuming we find him at home," Julius muttered.

"We will track him down wherever he might be." Gory spared a nod for the footman who set the sugar cone beside her because she liked to take her tea very sweet, and then continued. "Not only must I break off our betrothal, something I doubt he will fight me on because of the risk of exposing his scandal, but–"

"The heel," Adela muttered.

Gory agreed. "But I also want to be sure he is properly taking care of the young lady and her child."

"And if he is not going to take proper care of her?" Ambrose asked.

"I'm not sure." Gory sighed in dismay. "I will find a way to help the mother somehow."

She was not certain how she would accomplish it because her own financial situation was uncertain. With her uncle now deceased, what would happen to her dowry? And would there be a battle over her large inheritance, assuming there was anything left to inherit. It was quite possible her uncle had squandered it all.

Nor did she forget that Havers, despite presently relegating her to the bottom of his suspect list, still had her on that list. It would take no more than a bit of planted evidence to shoot her straight to the top again. Was it fair to impose on the Thorne brothers to help Allendale's mistress, or sweetheart, or whatever she was, if she could not?

Well, she had not even met the woman or spoken to Allendale about her, so there was no sense in speculating.

The four of them spent the rest of their mealtime speaking of Ambrose and Adela's trip to Oxford and the lecture series the two of them had given at the university. "It was extremely well received," Adela said. "They would like us back again soon."

Ambrose nodded. "But it won't be for some time yet. Our schedules are too busy, nor can we ask Marigold to take up the laboring oar."

Gory understood because Adela and Marigold were both new mothers and loathe to part from their babies even for a few hours.

Syd had recently joined them in that league.

Gory hoped to catch up to them.

In truth, motherhood and all things domestic had not been on her list of priorities until recently. But with all her friends married and starting families, she feared they might drift apart from her. But it was not only motherhood that had them poised to go their separate ways. Her friends had all made love matches.

She did not think it was possible for her until Julius had revealed his feelings.

Was this real or was she still dreaming?

Did Julius truly love her and want to marry her?

In all her imaginings, she had never expected to be breaking off one wedding merely days before the ceremony was to take place, and holding onto hope of another with the man she truly loved.

How would Allendale take the news?

Surely, he had to know their upcoming wedding was an impossibility.

Julius took her hand and gave it a light squeeze, no doubt understanding what was going through her mind. "I think Havers and Barrow have arrived."

He had just uttered the remark when Greeves stepped into the dining room to announce their presence.

Ambrose rose. "Have them join us here, Greeves. I'm sure they must be hungry."

This is what Gory liked most about these Thorne men. They all had wealth, good looks, and wielded substantial authority, but they were not at all prideful or puffed up. They carried themselves with humility toward those beneath their station. Yet, there was no mistaking their commanding aura.

In Gory's opinion, their innate kindness and consideration of others was the true source of their strength. It was the reason they were so much respected and admired.

Ambrose dismissed the footmen after they had served their guests coffee. "Shut the doors behind you," he added so they could now speak privately to the investigators. "Anything new to report?" he asked Havers.

"Yes, Your Grace. We have ruled out Lord Allendale as a suspect."

"Because he was with the young lady on the night of the murder?" Gory asked.

Havers blushed. "Yes. I am truly sorry, Lady Gregoria. It has now been confirmed by several sources."

"Do not be sorry, Mr. Havers," she replied. "I am glad he is not to blame. But this does not change my decision. I will not be marrying him. I plan to advise him of this today."

"Understandable," Havers said with a nod. "But you cannot go alone. You are not out of danger yet."

"I am well aware," Gory assured him.

"I will escort Lady Gregoria to Lord Allendale's and anywhere else she insists on going," Julius said. "Allendale may not have had anything to do with Lord Easton's death, but that does not mean he will behave reasonably when informed the wedding is to be called off."

Gory nodded. "You should not worry about me, Mr. Havers. I have no intention of going anywhere without Lord Thorne."

Despite what they all thought, she was not reckless. Well, not very reckless. She certainly was not going to do anything foolish while a killer was still on the prowl and she was his prime target. In any event, Allendale might not have harmed her uncle, but she agreed with Julius. Her betrothed would be irate when she broke off their betrothal. Also, she meant to press him about the young woman and her child and that was a topic that might infuriate him.

"What news about Lady Easton?" Julius asked, his comment reminding her that she had not given her aunt any thought.

That was rather shameful of her.

Yes, her aunt was an ogre.

But even ogres deserved some sympathy when grieving.

Of course, this assumed her aunt was not the murderess, a fact which had yet to be determined.

Havers frowned. "The coach driver and clerk who sold the tickets on the Windsor to London route and return to Windsor could not identify the man and two women with any certainty. However, they were quite certain that the man was not Lady Easton's brother-in-law. They did not recognize him at all. Nor did he or Lady Easton's sister have fresh scratches."

"They didn't?" Gory was frankly surprised. "So all three of them are now ruled out? I was sure…well, it is not right of me to accuse my aunt or her family. Being unlikable does not mean any of them are capable of committing heinous crimes."

"Oh, I think Lady Easton is capable of anything," Adela said. "She treated you so badly growing up, Gory. Even now, she refuses to see you and had the gall to suggest you not attend your uncle's funeral. Then she tried to plant false stories in the gossip rags, hoping to make it appear you are the guilty party. It is a good thing Julius and Ambrose were able to stop those lies from getting into print."

"She tried to do this?" She turned to Julius in surprise. "Why did you not tell me?"

He groaned. "You were still recovering from your injuries and already distressed over the way she was trying to shut you out. When the Tattler's editor contacted us last night to advise us of this juicy story he had been handed, Ambrose and I told him it was a lie and he should not run it."

Gory's eyes narrowed. "You threatened him?"

Julius shook his head. "No, we merely told him it was not true. He would not have reached out to us unless he believed as much. I did not think it necessary to mention it to you and add to your concerns. You already knew your aunt would try something underhanded."

"I suppose," she said, although she did not like finding out about this latest bit of mischief in this manner. Julius could have told her. Yes, she was trying to heal and this might have interfered with her recovery. She would have been riled and unable to sleep, for certain.

But was it not important for her to be kept advised of all that went on? "Is it awful of me to be sorry that my aunt will now be struck off the suspect list?"

Havers arched an eyebrow. "Oh, she is still at the top of my list. Nor have I dismissed her sister as one of her confederates, although it is fairly certain now that the sister's husband was not involved."

"Why excuse him?" Adela asked.

"Because he was the one most likely to have received the scratches when my uncle fought back," Gory explained. "And Mr. Havers said none were found on him."

Havers nodded. "That's right."

"And what of Lord Easton's business partners?" Ambrose asked. "Have you ruled them out, too?"

"Not yet, but Mr. Barrow can better address your question since his runners have been assisting my constables in keeping an eye on these gentlemen as we confirm their alibis."

Mr. Barrow cleared his throat. "Most have been ruled out, surprising as this might be. Less than a handful left now, including the solicitor, Reginald Mayfield and his elder brother, Harold."

"Truly?" Gory was not really surprised that her father's oily solicitors would betray the family's trust so brazenly. They might have been willing to do anything shady to hold on to the new earl as a client.

"Nothing solid to go on just yet," Mr. Barrow said, touching his nose. "In following both Mayfields, we have seen them engaged in several unsavory activities."

"For this reason, I am having a closer look at them," Havers said. "I know they did not have fresh scratches either, but this does not absolve them of any involvement."

Havers now set down his coffee cup and rose. "Well, we still have much work to do. The murder of an earl, whether he was liked or not, still has the royal family deeply concerned. We are all eager to have this investigation quickly resolved."

"Aye," said Mr. Barrow, rising as well. "Lady Gregoria, I'll have a man keeping watch on you when you ride to Lord Allendale's residence. It cannot hurt to have someone backing up Lord Thorne. All you need to do is let my runner know where else you intend to go. He must be kept apprised so he can guard you at all times."

"We will give him all our details," Julius assured.

Mr. Barrow cast Gory a warm, grandfatherly smile. "Mr. Havers may still have his suspicions about you, but I never doubted your innocence for a moment. I've had my men watching this townhouse for several days now, but they haven't spotted anyone lurking. This does not mean the danger has passed. Indeed, I fear it is increasing with every day that goes by. Someone knows you saw them with your uncle on the night of the murder. That someone is going to come after you to silence you before your memory returns. Please be as careful as you can, m'lady. Do not stay out too long. Return here as soon as your business with Lord Allendale is concluded."

Julius took her hand again.

She smiled at him. "I am not afraid."

He frowned. "But that is entirely Mr. Barrow's point. You should be, Gory."

"Indeed, Lady Gregoria," Havers said, now also frowning at her. "I would rather we solve this crime *before* the killer has the opportunity to harm you."

"I am well protected," she insisted. "You are all watching over me. And I will keep my outings to a minimum. But let us be practical about this, Mr. Havers. You are unlikely to solve the mystery of who committed the crime unless the killer tips his hand by coming after me. How else is he to be caught?"

"By my superior investigation skills," he replied.

Gory arched an eyebrow. "How has that worked out so far?"

CHAPTER 10

THE ALLENDALE FAMILY was quite prominent in Society and also fairly wealthy, if gossip proved true. Not that Gory ever listened to gossip, but she had done some investigating before agreeing to marry the viscount. Lady Dayne and Lady Withnall had also confirmed he came from an honorable family and he himself had a good reputation. Their displeasure came not from any lack in him, but from the fact they did not view theirs as a love match.

But to Gory, Allendale and his family had seemed perfect, and she liked that many of them were men of science.

However, any respect she held for Allendale himself was gone now.

She took a deep breath as she and Julius stood at the door of his Belgravia townhouse awaiting his butler to let them in. Julius, having come here just a few days ago to inform her betrothed of her uncle's murder, was immediately recognized by the butler. "Lord Thorne. Oh, dear, I am afraid his lordship is not here."

"Is he with the young lady?" Gory asked, no longer caring that Allendale's actions had humiliated her. "Please, Hartley. This is of dire importance. Where is he?"

The man appeared dismayed, no doubt worried he would lose his position if he told them.

"No matter," Julius said amiably, taking Gory by the elbow to lead her away. "Just let him know we stopped by and that he must come see me as soon as possible."

The butler emitted a breath of relief and nodded. "Rest assured, my lord. I will."

Gory frowned at Julius as he led her away. "Why did you not press him?"

"Because I know where he has housed the young lady and her child."

Gory came to a halt as they were about to step into the carriage. "You do?"

"Yes, Mr. Barrow told me yesterday."

"And this is another thing you did not think necessary to report to me?"

"I am telling you now. And no, talking about the other woman to you last night would have had you irate and leaping out of bed to pace in anger."

"I am not angry with the woman. Or the child. How can I ever be?"

"I know you would not think cruelly of them. But you do get righteously indignant and I did not need you running off to see her or confront Allendale while you were prescribed bed rest by Dr. Farthingale. Do not pretend for a moment you would have obeyed the doctor's orders."

He was right.

Still, it rankled. "Anything else you haven't bothered to tell me?"

"No, that's everything." He helped her into the carriage, his warm hands at her waist to lift her in. "We're heading to Bayswater. The young lady is settled in a private house there."

He took a moment to give their driver the direction, and then climbed in and settled opposite her. "All right, Gory. Ask your questions. I know you are bursting to do so."

Gad, it irked her that he knew her so well. But it was also a bit of wonderful that he understood her as well as he did. She did not think the same could be said of her in regard to him because she spent so much time with her nose buried in her research at the Huntsford Academy that it occupied most of her brain.

Also, Julius often kept his thoughts to himself and his actions were often subtle, so one had to be looking closely to understand what he was doing or feeling. Indeed, she'd had no idea he was in love with her because he had kept so tight-lipped. "Do you know the young lady's name?"

"No."

There he was, being tight-lipped again, the answer direct and without embellishment. "Have you seen the house? Is it a nice place?"

Julius shook his head. "I haven't seen it. But Mr. Barrow reports that it is on a pleasant square and the house is well maintained."

Gory knew there were several institutions of higher learning in the area. For this reason, one would find many students and academics residing there along with many taverns and coffee houses that stayed open late to cater to their scholarly patrons. "Do you have any more information to impart to me?"

He shook his head. "That's all I know."

It took them a while to wend their way through the busy streets and reach the house. Gory was surprised Julius had not made a move to sit closer to her or attempt to kiss her again while they were in the privacy of the carriage.

He appeared distracted.

"Why the glum face? Are you not pleased that I am breaking it off with Allendale?" she asked, hoping to end the prolonged silence between them and shift attention to a more personal topic.

"I am, Gory. It is our being out here on the London streets that has me preoccupied. I'm worried that someone will toss open the door whenever we stop, and shoot you. The streets are a crowded tangle and we are moving slower than a turtle."

She ought to have realized his mind would never remain inactive. "Mr. Barrow's man is following us. And your driver, Hastings, knows to keep careful watch."

"Yes, but it takes no more than the blink of an eye for something disastrous to happen."

She nodded. "I'm sorry I am giving you such a hard time."

"You aren't to blame."

But her lost memory was the problem.

She had rested for two days straight since her last outing, as dutifully required, and nothing of her memory had come back. It was almost a week since the murder and they had made no progress in finding out who had done it.

Julius stepped out first and looked around before allowing her to step out of the carriage. "Come on, love. Let's get this over and done."

She placed her arm in his and held her breath as they marched to the door and Julius gave it a commanding knock. They soon heard footsteps, and a plump, older woman opened the door. "May I help you?" she asked, her eyes widening as she stared at them.

It was obvious she was not expecting anyone, and certainly not anyone so finely dressed.

"We are here to see Lord Allendale," Gory responded.

"You needn't be alarmed," Julius said, his voice gentle as he spoke to the woman who appeared about to panic and slam the door shut in their faces. "We know Lord Allendale is here, as well as the young lady."

The woman regarded them uncertainly, but Julius's calm demeanor followed by an engaging smile had worked its magic. She gave a curt nod and stepped aside to allow them in. "Who may I say is calling?"

"His betrothed," Gory blurted because she was angry and not about to hold back.

Julius sighed and once again spoke gently to the woman. "Lady Gregoria Easton and Lord Thorne."

She led them to a small but well appointed parlor. "I'll let him know you are here, m'lord. Would you care for tea? It is cold outside."

"No, we are fine," Julius said. "We know he is preoccupied, so we will not take up too much of his time."

"That's right," Gory muttered the moment the woman left to summon Allendale, "I'll just punch him in the nose and perhaps break a vase over his head for good measure, and then we can leave."

"Sounds like a solid plan," Julius said, casting her an indulgent smile. "Never mind that you don't love him or that we will never get answers out of him after you assault him physically."

She sighed. "I was just mouthing off. I am not really going to do anything to him, not until we have our answers. Do not forget that he proposed to me while this other woman was carrying his child. What he did to me was heinous."

He arched an eyebrow. "If he was the one who got her in the family way, then what he did to *her* was just as heinous. But we are here to get answers, not to pass moral judgment. After all, do not forget that you ran to me, and then uttered not a word of protest when I undressed you completely."

"But I was injured and in shock. I ran to you for help, not for seduction."

"Nor have you uttered a word of protest about my remaining with you in my bedchamber every night since."

"That is also different," she retorted, ignoring the flush of heat to her cheeks. "You insisted on protecting me. It was all completely innocent."

"As his behavior might be. That is all I am pointing out."

Gory had not counted to thirty before Allendale tore down the stairs and stormed into the parlor where they had both just taken seats. Julius rose and stepped in front of her, partly to greet Allendale, but mostly to block her betrothed from approaching her.

Allendale peered around Julius's broad shoulders to stare at her. "What are you doing here?"

Gory had leaped to her feet the moment he strode in and now curled her hands into fists. "I might ask the same of you. What is going on here?"

Julius place a protective arm around her, though Gory sensed it was more to protect Allendale from her wrath rather than the other way around. Oh, she dearly wanted to poke the bounder in the nose.

She knew just the spot to strike, too.

The delicate cartilage along the bridge of his nose ought to get that blood gushing effectively.

"It is not what you think," Allendale said in a rush, emitting a deflated breath.

"Then clarify it for us." Julius was still hovering protectively close to her and now placed a possessive arm around her waist, once again likely protecting Allendale rather than the other way around.

"Why did you not tell me about the child?" Gory wanted to grab the nearest heavy object and hurl it at Allendale's head. "Or the young lady?"

"Because it is none of your business," he said.

Gory gasped. "I was to be your wife! Did you not think I had a right to know?"

Allendale stared at her a long moment. "Was?"

"That's right, past tense." Gory felt no pleasure nor vindication now that the moment of confrontation had arrived. "I cannot marry you. How can you think I would ever agree to exchange vows with you after you've fathered a child with another woman? You had to have known of her condition when you proposed to me. How could you demean me in this fashion? How could you treat *her* so abysmally? And what do you plan to do with the child? You cannot place it in a foundling home. I will never forgive you if you do this to your own daughter."

His eyes widened. "You think she is mine?"

The comment took Gory aback. "Whose is she, if not yours?"

Allendale's lips were in a thin, taut line as he said, "I cannot tell you that."

"And you think I will simply accept this and pretend all is well between us? That will never happen. The wedding is off. Our betrothal is off. I hope never to see you again. It is for the best, isn't it? Ours was never going to be a love match."

"Love?" He laughed harshly. "No, Gregoria. Ours was never going to be that. Do you know why?" He pointed upstairs. "Because *that* disaster is what love gets you, ruin and an unwanted child. And again, not my child."

"And you would have me believe this? Then what are you doing here?"

"Helping me out," a young lady said from the doorway.

Gory's heart went out to her, for she looked so fragile and her skin was so pale. "Miss...I'm sorry if our shouts disturbed you.

Lord Thorne and I came here to make certain you were all right. We did not mean to frighten you."

The vulnerable girl glanced at Allendale. "Tell Lady Gregoria who I am. She deserves to know."

Allendale walked over to the frail thing and led her to the settee. Once she was comfortably settled, he turned to Gory. "This is my uncle's ward, Sarah Martin."

"The blame for my situation," Sarah said, "lies squarely with me. Marriage to the father is impossible. He is a married man. The Allendale family has disowned me, as I feared would happen. But it still did not stop me from behaving recklessly. Only Lord Allendale took pity on me and has come to my aid. If his uncle finds out he has helped me, he will be furious and take it out on him. For this reason, we've had to maintain utmost secrecy."

"Oh." Gory glanced in dismay at Julius.

"He is quietly trying to find someone honorable and kind to marry me. That chore has taken up much of his time. And now I've ruined your wedding plans, too."

"No," Gory said immediately, "this changes nothing. I'm so sorry, Allendale. As things are...it can never work between us."

Allendale looked exhausted and defeated.

This made Gory feel worse.

How could she hate him when he was risking so much to protect Sarah and her daughter? "You need have no fear that Lord Thorne or I will ever break your confidence. Do what you must for Miss Martin. Let me know if I can help in any way."

She now turned to his uncle's ward. "My own uncle was murdered several days ago and the killer is still unknown. Our wedding must be put off because it is inappropriate for a celebration to go ahead as planned under the circumstances. You see, my uncle was my guardian. Our household is in mourning."

She grimaced and continued. "Not that my aunt considers me a part of the household any longer. She despises me and does not even want me to attend the funeral. I would not be surprised if she has already tossed all my belongings onto the street. It is nothing new. She has always despised me."

Allendale expressed surprise. "Gregoria, I am so sorry. I

168 I MEARA PLATT

should have...well, there are many things I should have done. I did not think... Is this why you turned to Lord Thorne and not to me?"

He did not appear at all enraged, another confirmation that theirs would have been a distant and loveless marriage.

She nodded.

"So is this it then? Perhaps we can merely postpone until a more suitable time. Please, I do not want to lose you."

"Oh, I do not think you will really care," she said, now speaking gently but with certainty. "We both deserve better than what we were about to settle for. The breakup can be done discreetly. No one will question our ending the betrothal. They'll blame the murder as the reason. They'll also understand my circumstances have changed for the worse and I may not be quite the prize you expected. The new earl is a distant relation I have never met. I no longer have any significant standing in Society. Nor would anyone blame you if you doubted my innocence regarding my uncle's murder."

"I never doubted your innocence," he assured her.

She was glad he felt this way, but it would not stop the gossips from spreading malicious lies. "The point is, no one will question your reasons when we break it off. The whispers will spread that you came to your senses before marrying that ghoulish Easton chit."

He cast her a wry smile. "You did play it up quite a bit, scaring most of the young men who sought to court you."

She winced to acknowledge the truth of his words. "In piling the blame on me, no one will bother to dig further about *you* and your reasons. This means Sarah and her daughter will safely remain a secret."

"So I am to be saved while all the ill will falls upon you, Lady Gregoria?" Sarah remarked, looking dismayed.

Gory nodded. "They think the worst of me anyway. It is nothing new for me. However, Lord Thorne and his family will protect me. Do not worry, for I will be fine. Just do what you must to protect yourself and your daughter."

Julius cleared his throat. "Allendale, there will be formalities to ending the betrothal. I'll have my solicitor draw up the proper release papers this very day. I'll let you know when they are ready."

Allendale set his lips in a thin line. "What if I refuse?"

Gory's heart beat faster in dismay, but Julius was the one to immediately respond. "You'll lose everything. Lady Gregoria may be softhearted, but I am not."

"Is that a threat, Thorne?" her betroth shot back with a growl.

"Take it any way you wish, but you will never get your hands on Lady Gregoria or her funds. It is *all* out of your reach now. Must I say more? You do not fool me for a moment. What's it to be? An amicable parting...or must I have a chat with your uncle?"

Allendale's expression was one of resignation. "I'll sign whatever is put before me."

Gory breathed a sigh of relief.

He now turned to her. "But in exchange for my cooperation, I ask that we merely tell everyone the wedding has been postponed due to Lord Easton's death. Then in a few weeks we can declare the betrothal ended. We are less likely to draw less attention upon us if we proceed in this manner. I am only thinking of protecting your good name, Gregoria."

"All right." Gory was hoping it would end sooner, but could not complain about achieving the desired outcome. What did it matter if it took a week or two longer to be fully free of him? In truth, she was saddened it had to end this way.

Julius did not look pleased, but Sarah chose the moment to burst into tears and this ended their conversation.

Gory had never thought of Allendale as particularly tender or caring, but he was quite attentive to Sarah. Perhaps she was the one he secretly loved. Perhaps he and Sarah were in love with each other, and she had foolishly given herself to another man.

Dear heaven.

Gory had come so close to making this same mistake by agreeing to marry Allendale when her heart had always belonged to Julius.

As for Allendale, he had proposed to her because he purposely did *not* want to fall in love. He'd chosen her because he thought she would keep her distance, bury herself in her work at the Huntsford Academy, and leave him in peace to do whatever he wished to do with his life. He would not give a fig about her plans because he had no romantic feelings toward her.

All quite logically reasoned out and so pitifully sad.

Sarah needed to rest and Gory suddenly felt fatigued, as well.

Her head was starting to throb.

Julius noticed the subtle change in her demeanor immediately. "No need to take up more of your time, Allendale. I think we've said all that needs to be said. I'll be in touch with you shortly."

He escorted Gory out and helped her into the carriage.

He climbed in next and gave the driver the command to move on as he settled beside her. "Home, Hastings."

"Aye, m'lord."

Julius took her hand in his as the carriage got underway. "That was rough for you, wasn't it?"

She nodded. "Not what I expected."

He gave a mirthless laugh. "Nor I. I'll drop you back home and then head to my solicitor's to get him working on the betrothal releases."

"But Allendale asked us to wait a few weeks before formalizing anything."

"I will not wait to have those documents drawn up. He can sign them whenever he is ready, but I want them in front of him as soon as possible."

She nodded in understanding. "You do not want him changing his mind and refusing to end the betrothal. Oh, Julius, he won't. He really does not like me. Was it not obvious?"

"But he may like your inheritance."

"The one hundred thousand pounds? Are you suggesting he knew of it? After seeing him with Sarah, I really do not think his motives went beyond securing my dowry, and then leaving me to my research work while he spent his time with Sarah."

"Gory, do not be naive. He knew about the inheritance for certain. Did you not notice the calling card on the silver tray upon the table in the entryway?"

Gory blushed. "No, I was too incensed to pay attention. Whose card was it?"

"Your uncle's solicitor, Reginald Mayfield."

She stared at him incredulously, then gasped as she realized the importance of what he had just told her. "Oh! That obsequious little weasel seems to turn up everywhere, doesn't he? Then Allendale is exactly the fortune-hunting fiend you believed he was. Yes, let's go to *your* solicitor right now and have him start on those release papers. It is not out of the way. Why return home when you are only going to turn around and ride straight back here? I'll wait in the carriage while you speak to him."

"Very well, we'll go straight there instead of home. But I'll have you come in with me. I dare not leave you unprotected even for a moment." He thumped on the carriage roof. "Change of plans, Hastings. We're to call on my solicitor first."

Gory did not mind remaining by his side as they ran this second errand, for she loved the way Julius always stood by her, as though reminding her that she would never be alone or needing to fight on her own while he was there to support her.

Julius cleared his throat. "It is practical to have you with me for another reason."

"Oh, what is that?"

"So we can discuss the terms of *our* betrothal agreement. That is…if you will have me as your husband, Gory. I know this is not the best time to toss this at you, but I've botched this badly once already and refuse to make the same mistake again. I was concerned you might need the protection of privileges afforded a peer such as Allendale, but there is little danger of Havers arresting you for your uncle's murder now that he has gotten to know you. With that concern addressed and minimized, I would like to bring you under *my* protection as soon as possible…for always."

Her heart began to beat excitedly. "You are asking me to marry you?"

"Seems so, doesn't it?" He cast her a dazzlingly affectionate smile. "Yes, I am. Is this not the natural progression when a couple is in love?"

So many feelings surged through her and engulfed her.

She felt the urge to laugh and cry at the same time, to rejoice and also to worry. Would she make him happy? Could she manage a household and remain active at the Huntsford forensics laboratory? "Few consider love important, but you Thorne men are obviously different."

He surprised her by nudging her onto his lap and regarding her with heartfelt sincerity. "Will you, Gory?"

She hugged him fiercely. "Yes! With all my heart. I never thought I could be this happy."

Suddenly, she drew back and stared at him in dismay. "But what if Allendale has a change of heart and does not sign the papers to end the betrothal? What are the legal consequences?"

"He will sign them," Julius responded with a lethal calm that any opponent would find rattling to their senses. "I am not giving you up, Gory. There will be a wedding, I promise you. But it won't be you and Allendale standing at the church altar. It will be you and me. Just when it will be, I cannot tell you for certain. But it will not be more than another few days. I will marry you the moment he signs those papers."

She rested her head against his shoulder and sighed. "I have created such problems for you."

"No, love. I created the problem in not revealing my heart sooner."

"Perhaps if I spoke to Allendale again and–"

"No, I do not want you anywhere near him or that girl," he said with surprising vehemence.

She looked up him, confused by his tone. "Why not? And why are you referring to Sarah as *that girl* as though she is not as much a victim as I was? Why, Julius? Did you notice something else?"

He nodded. "Yes, but I'll tell you later. We're here."

Gory scooted off his lap as the carriage drew to a halt in front of his solicitor's building. "What did you notice?"

"I'll tell you once we are home." He cast her a soft look as he helped her down. "And it is *our* home…well, it is Ambrose's to be accurate about it. But my point is that you belong with me now. The only way I give you up is if you truly do not love me. The choice is yours and only ever yours, Gory. No one else can break us up, for I will always fight for you."

"I would do the same for you," she acknowledged. "Your happiness matters most to me."

He nodded. "I'll only be happy if I have you as my wife."

"Oh, Julius, do stop saying such wonderful things to me." She placed a hand to her cheek because she was blushing again.

"I see you are awful at accepting compliments." He shook his head. "Get used to it, Gory. I have lots more to heap on you."

"I must be dreaming," she muttered. "You do realize I am getting the better part of this bargain."

"No, love. I am the fortunate one." He tweaked her nose.

She laughed and then cast him a wincing smile. "Do not be so quick to admire me when I continue to be foolish. I was so incensed, I missed every obvious clue and jumped to the wrong conclusions. But it is a good thing my heart has sense, for I've loved you from the moment I set eyes on you, and that love never wavered, even as I made a terribly wrong decision in agreeing to marry Allendale."

"That won't be happening now. For many reasons, I'm glad your wedding to him will never go forward," he said with a noticeable furrow of his brow.

A shiver ran through her as she stared back at him. "What reasons? What else did you notice that you haven't told me?"

CHAPTER 11

JULIUS HAD HINTED at something about Allendale and Sarah.

Gory was now keen on pursuing his reasons for disliking them beyond Allendale's keeping his attentions toward Sarah a secret from her. He was obviously troubled by the pair, or perhaps something one of them had said. But had not Havers ruled them out as suspects? And how could Sarah be in any way involved in the heinous crime when she was giving birth that night? A woman in the midst of labor pains does not blithely hop out of bed to ride across town and do someone in.

"What did you see that felt wrong, Julius? Besides Mayfield's card on the salver, of course."

"I'll tell you later."

She sighed and held him back. "Can you not give me a hint?"

"Let's deal with my solicitor first, and then I'll tell you once we are home. Do not press me, Gory. My answer will remain the same."

"Really? You are going to make me wait? How can you dangle that lure in front of me and then leave me wriggling on the hook when I take the bait?"

"First of all, you are not a fish, and have you never heard the adage that patience is a virtue?"

She rolled her eyes.

He laughed. "Gad, you are a curious, little thing. Will you be as curious to learn about…never mind, it is not an appropriate topic to be discussing now."

She blushed again. "Are you referring to the bedchamber?"

He looked wickedly handsome as he arched an eyebrow and nodded. "Yes, and do not get irate about my being eager for it."

"Me? Irate? I cannot wait for that moment to happen. I want to learn *everything* with you. But I should not let on how much I am looking forward to it because this will swell your head." She wrapped her arm in his as they walked inside the building and made their way to the cabinet of Deacon & Mosley, the solicitors Julius used to manage his affairs.

"Julius, that first night I came to you," Gory said in a ragged whisper as they walked down the hallway toward their chambers, "I know I was in shock, but your every touch soothed me. I was not even embarrassed when you removed my bloodied clothing. It just felt right. I want you to know this is how much I trust you. You have always made me feel safe."

"And I shall always keep you safe," he said with a rasp to his voice.

Gory released a breath as they walked into the impressive Deacon & Mosley offices. The floors were richly carpeted and the desks and bookshelves were of the finest rosewood cabinetry. Mr. Deacon immediately hurried forward to greet them. "Lord Thorne, a most pleasant surprise. What brings you here?"

Julius introduced Gory to the gentleman. "A delight, Lady Gregoria."

He led them into his private office, a large chamber decorated as richly as the common areas. Gory took a seat in one of the soft leather chairs and Julius settled beside her. She winced as Julius explained the situation to Mr. Deacon, for it sounded to her ears as though she were a flighty debutante who had changed her mind about marrying one man mere days before their wedding and immediately managed to sink her claws into another, namely Julius.

Not that he explained it that way, of course.

But what else could Mr. Deacon think?

However, his expression remained stoic as Julius related his intentions and provided details about their situation. If the solicitor held any doubts about her, or the wisdom of Julius attaching himself to a woman the likes of her, he did not show it.

Perhaps she was being too hard on herself, but having been used to people thinking the worst of her, it was not easy to believe anyone could possibly admire her as sincerely as Julius did.

"The betrothal agreement between Allendale and Lady Gregoria is held by Lord Easton's solicitors, Mayfield & Sons," Julius advised.

The distinguished looking man arched an eyebrow. "The Mayfields? No worries, my lord. I shall send one of my clerks to them to collect the necessary information. We'll prepare the termination of betrothal and settlements right away. Since Lady Gregoria is of age, her signature ought to be sufficient."

"Good," Julius said. "Now for the next matter."

"Another matter?" Gory frowned lightly. "Is there more needed to end my betrothal to Allendale?"

"No, but I want to draw up our own betrothal agreement now, too."

Gory was surprised but did not protest. "Oh, I see. But we do not know yet for certain what I shall bring to the marriage."

"I do not care. This is about my protecting *you*. It does not matter what the new Earl of Easton, whenever he appears, decides to do about your dowry."

"Or the matter of my inheritance." She turned to Mr. Deacon. "I believe I am to inherit one hundred thousand pounds, but I expect Lady Easton will contest it."

"None of it matters to me," Julius insisted. "Whatever Lady Gregoria brings into our marriage shall remain hers to do with as she wishes. Make certain this is clearly stated in the terms."

"But I would share everything with you." She meant it, too. There was no finer man than Julius, nor was there anyone she trusted more. "Is it not *our* marriage? Should we not look out for each other? Besides, the law gives it all to you anyway."

He chuckled. "Yes, and this is why I am contractually committing to giving it back to you."

Mr. Deacon cleared his throat. "My lord, this all seems quite rushed. Perhaps you ought to give more thought to what you are willing to provide for Lady Gregoria. Shall we leave that discussion for a later time?"

This was an obvious hint by his solicitor to have Julius seal his lips and not give away everything to her because he was besotted by love. Gory thought this was quite humorous. Julius was too sharp a businessman ever to act rashly in any investment, be it securing a property or a wife.

However, she agreed with his solicitor. "Yes, Lord Thorne. This is something that ought to be discussed outside of my presence."

Julius cast her a stubborn look. "No, have I not been clear about my desire to protect you?"

She wanted to kiss him even though he was being obstinate. "But you can be clear between you and your solicitor. I should not be involved in the discussion."

Julius turned serious. "I want you to be involved. You are already so much a part of the Huntsford Academy and our family. Your forensic research has added to the academy's acclaim. What do you need me to provide you in order to continue your work? And we'll need to decide on what to provide for our children."

The thought of a life and children with Julius had her heart in flutters and filling her with warmth. It seemed miraculous that this unexpected love should flourish out of the ashes of tragedy. Julius mentioned he had intended to reveal his feelings for her and stop her wedding to Allendale. But what if he had never found the right moment to speak to her? What if she had inadvertently said something to change his mind?

He had kept quiet for months believing she and Allendale were a love match. Were it not for the fact he had been roped into escorting her around London this past week, he might never have spoken up.

She would never have known his true feelings and married the wrong man.

They had come so close to disaster.

But here they were now, a true miracle in the making as they discussed plans for their children and their future. "Yes, do what you must, not only for our sons but our daughters, as well. They all need to be secure. As for me, my needs are not lavish."

Julius nodded. "I will not have you lacking in anything. You need to have independent means to maintain your style of living *and* conduct your research work."

But he laughed at his own words. "However, I want your promise that you will not run amok around London at all hours and barrel into places you should not be patronizing on your own."

"Rest assured," she said with a smile, knowing she'd had more than one or two hoyden moments during their acquaintance, "I shall not be found starting fistfights in taverns or lurking around graveyards once our children are born."

"Good, I'll want that in writing," he said with such fluid charm, she thought at first he was in jest.

But he was serious!

Did he not trust her to keep out of those indelicate places?

Well, he had good reason.

She tipped her chin up, but her chuckle as she spoke gave away she was not really angry. "I take that as an insult to my integrity."

He grinned. "Take it anyway you like, but I'll have your promise. No after hours visits to graveyards, Gory."

"As if I would ever dig around a cemetery like a thief in the night," she said with a huff. "But you cannot restrict my morgue activities."

Mr. Deacon's eyes widened. "Lady Gregoria, surely you jest!"

No, not really.

"Please do not fret, sir. Lord Thorne knows I will be a dutiful wife and do nothing rash."

Julius coughed. "Well, work on the termination of Lady Gregoria's betrothal first. I'll send along more details of the terms we would like in our betrothal agreement later."

Mr. Deacon had a bemused look on his face as he escorted them out and bid them a good day.

Julius laughed softly as he assisted Gory into the carriage. "I think we shocked the poor man."

She *tsked* as he settled beside her. "You really did not have to scare him. I have never actually dug up a body. But I think that for all your proper manners and cool demeanor, you like the idea of a wife who can challenge you and might be a little daring. Just a little, mind you. Because you are also apish and do not want anything bad to happen to anyone under your care."

"Is that so?" But he was grinning once again, and looked irresistibly appealing as he did so. "You think you know me so well?"

She shook her head. "Not nearly as well as you apparently know me. But I must not be as awful as the *ton* makes out if you are able tolerate me."

He raked a hand through his hair and sighed. "I love you to pieces, Gory. I think that's a bit more than merely tolerating you."

"Same here," she said in all sincerity. "You take my breath away. Would you kiss me now, Julius? My reputation is already in ruins because I have been sleeping in your bed and we have likely been seen riding together without a chaperone, and me betrothed to another man, although not for long."

"With pleasure, love."

She closed her eyes as he leaned toward her, expecting a moment of magic and eager for his warm, commanding lips to press down on hers. But she was instead shoved to the ground and had the breath forced out of her lungs as he crushed her with the weight of his big body atop hers.

At the same moment, a shot rang out that echoed off the carriage walls. "Julius!"

Was he hit?

She had felt his body move reflexively against hers in that moment.

"I'm fine. Do not move," he ordered, grabbing his pistol from the lip of his boot and managing to fire off a shot, although she did not think he struck the assailant. "Damn it, he's getting away."

He told her to stay on the floor, and then ordered Hastings to take her straight home. Before she had the chance to protest, he was out of the carriage and had slammed the door shut. She fell back as Hastings spurred the team to a reckless speed that had other drivers cursing him as he cut them off. He also had her jouncing and bouncing, unable to regain her footing sufficiently to even attempt to climb back into her seat, much less manage to jump out to chase after Julius.

One would think she was in a runaway cart barreling down a cliff.

But it was not long before Hastings, shouting for Greeves, drew the team to an abrupt halt in front of the Thorne townhouse.

He had jerked on the reins so hard, Gory had tumbled onto the floor again. "Botheration!"

She was still sprawled on the floor, desperately trying to fix her gown that had entangled in her legs, when the door flew open and Greeves, along with a small army of footmen, lifted her out. "Quickly, m'lady," Greeves said as he and the footmen formed a protective wall around her while hurrying her into the house.

"But Lord Thorne—"

"Knows how to take care of himself," Greeves assured her.

No doubt this was true, but she was also afraid he had been struck. There was a spot of blood on the sleeve of her gown and she knew it was not her blood.

Adela, Marigold, and her two dowager angels, Lady Withnall and Lady Dayne, came rushing out of the ladies parlor where they must have been enjoying a morning's conversation. "What happened?" they asked and began to hurl questions at her that she could not possibly answer.

Ambrose and Leo, Marigold's husband, hurried out of Ambrose's study and asked the same questions.

Gory, her heart racing for worry over Julius, quickly related the details of the incident as calmly as she could manage. The men listened intently, both of them seeming to be of the same mind as they told the women to stay away from the windows while they searched the grounds.

"You think the killer ran here?" Gory asked in surprise. "But he was on Regent Street and Julius chased after him."

"It is fairly certain the killer had at least one accomplice," Ambrose said, for he had been kept apprised of all the details of the murder and knew as much as Gory herself. "Who is to say that only one of them was capable of murder? This second person might be lying in wait right near here," Ambrose said. "In fact, this is what I would do if I were the killer and desperate to silence you. I'll stake my dukedom there is someone positioned close by."

He had no sooner said the words than they heard one of the Bow Street runners shout a warning and saw an agile figure clad in black leaping over the stone wall at the rear of the garden that divided the grounds from the mews.

Ambrose and Leo took off after him.

As Gory and her friends stared at each other in dumbfounded silence, they heard the distant clopping of hooves, no doubt the assailant taking off on horseback.

She did not know if Homer Barrow's runners also had horses at the ready and could chase after him.

Unfortunately, she did not think they had.

The house was well guarded, so how was it possible for anyone to climb over the wall without being seen?

This troubled Gory.

It was one thing for her to have entered the house unnoticed and slipped into Julius's bedchamber on the night of her uncle's murder. Ambrose and Adela were away, so the staff was not quite as vigilant as they might have been. Of course, the house had been properly closed up and secured before the last of the staff retired for the night.

This was a well run household and no one shirked in their duties.

But it had taken little effort on her part to jiggle the latch on a side door until it unlocked, for she was very good at breaking into places for purposes of medical research. She would have been quite adept had she ever decided to steal anything...which she would never do.

She was no thief.

Julius had made the matter of turning the Thorne townhouse into a fortress a priority. Everyone was on heightened alert because there was a killer, possibly two, on the loose who were desperate to silence her.

She stared at Adela and Marigold, both of them new mothers, and her heart sank. "I cannot stay here."

"What? Why?" Adela muttered.

"How could I have been so thoughtless?" Gory berated herself for not sooner realizing the danger she posed to her dearest friends.

What if this villain had gotten into Adela's home? Or harmed Adela's family and guests while trying to silence her? Gory knew she had to go into hiding elsewhere. But where? And would this be enough to protect these friends she considered her beloved family? "I am putting you all in peril. You and Marigold have your children to think about."

"But what about you?" Adela insisted. "Now that Ambrose and I are back from Oxford, our staff is once more on full alert. Not to mention, there are teams of constables and Bow Street runners also in place to guard you from anyone who approaches this house. They are already on the task."

Marigold and her dowager angels nodded.

But Gory was not convinced. "If it is so safe, then how did that assailant get over the wall unseen?"

"Ambrose will give us the details when he returns," Adela said with unwarranted confidence. "Need I point out he did not remain unseen. One of the Bow Street runners spotted him and sounded the alert."

"Because the villain was on the move," Gory countered. "He might never have been noticed had he remained in his hiding spot. Then, all he would have had to do was wait until nightfall and then sneak into the house unnoticed."

"And shoot you?" Marigold muttered, obviously doubting such a thing could happen.

But Gory knew this had been too close a call to dismiss. "He probably would have stabbed me in order not to wake anyone."

"Well, he's jumped back over the wall and must have had a horse tethered near the mews," Lady Withnall remarked.

Gory shook her head in dismay. "Yes, we heard him gallop off, did we not? How does one hide a gigantic beast and not raise anyone's suspicions? Is this not proof enough that we are not as safe as we believe? All the more reason for me to find another hiding place."

"Then I'm going with you," Julius said, walking in with Leo

and Ambrose.

"Julius!" Gory ran to him and slid her hands up and down his arms and chest. "Were you hurt? Did he shoot you?"

She gasped as her hand came away with blood.

"Gory, it is just a scratch," he insisted, attempting to dismiss her concern.

"A scratch?" She stared at the crimson blotches on her fingers.

"Greeves!" Ambrose called to his butler. "Have Dr. Farthingale summoned straight away."

"At once," the harried butler muttered and scrambled off.

Julius, the dolt, cast her a sloppy smile. "Worried about me, Gory?"

"Someone has to, since you obviously are ridiculously careless in taking care of yourself. He might have killed you!"

"But he didn't," Julius pointed out.

Gory was ready to say more, but he did not appear to be in serious pain or particularly weakened. Perhaps the shot had only grazed him. Even so, he was being impossibly casual about it. This truly irked her, but had she not been just as stubborn in dismissing her own injury?

She hoped his would turn out to be no more than a scratch.

That it could have been so much more damaging had her rattled. She put a hand to her stomach because the realization of just how close she had come to losing Julius made her ill.

"We lost the fiend in the crowd on Regent Street," Julius said, watching her with obvious concern, "but Barrow's man got a decent look at him. He thinks he will be able to recognize him if he sees him again."

"Good," Leo said, frowning. "This is just the break this investigation has needed."

"What about the man who scaled the townhouse wall?" Lady Dayne asked.

"No one got a good look at him," Ambrose said with a grunt of frustration. "He must have avoided the Bow Street runners positioned at the rear of this house by climbing over Lord Greene's wall."

Gory's head was spinning as they spoke. "Ambrose, who is

184 | MEARA PLATT

Lord Greene?"

"Our elderly neighbor. The villain probably waited until no one was in sight, then scaled my neighbor's wall and sidled along his property to sneak onto mine."

"Intending to remain hidden until nightfall," Leo remarked. "Your shrubbery is lush enough to offer him ample cover."

Ambrose growled. "I'm tearing it all out today."

"You will not," Gory insisted. "You have a beautiful garden and must not ruin it."

"Do you think I care about a few bushes and flowers over the safety of my loved ones?"

"Ambrose, you are getting bent out of shape," Adela said calmly. "The garden will be mostly bare by the end of the month and will remain that way until spring."

"But it is not bare now and clearly provides cover for a killer." Ambrose cast his wife a fiercely protective look. "I'm not taking any chances. Am I not responsible for the safety of my family?"

Adela sighed. "We could get a guard dog. That would be just as effective, if not more so. Do not harm those lovely flowers. I forbid you to rip them out."

Ambrose turned to Leo. "Can you believe this?"

Leo shrugged. "Well, Adela has a point. A guard dog is a good idea. Even a little, yipping thing will do the trick. It does not have to be a monster of a hound. Marigold has her Mallow. He's mostly spoiled and useless, but he'll bark loudly whenever there is danger."

Marigold grinned. "Yes, whenever a squirrel approaches."

The moment of levity quickly passed because the fact remained that two assailants had gone after Gory today and they hadn't caught either one of them.

Gory shuttled Julius upstairs and meant to take him to his bedchamber, but he held her back as they were about to start down the hallway. "No, I'll wait for Dr. Farthingale in one of the guest bedrooms."

"Absolutely not. You will be tended in your bedchamber, and I have no intention of waiting until he arrives to start treating that injury. I will hear no argument about it. Robbins does not need to be darting back and forth to fetch you a change of clothes or help you wash up. And should you not be comfortably settled, especially if the doctor prescribes bed rest for you? You must be in your own bed."

"With you?" he asked, amusement glinting in his eyes.

She frowned, but inwardly little butterflies flitted in her stomach. She dreamed of the moment she might sleep in his arms. "We'll switch. I'll take the big chair and you'll have the bed."

He gave her cheek a light caress and whispered, "We'll see. I just want you near me, Gory."

"Always." She emitted a ragged breath, willing to agree to anything so long as he took care of himself.

Ambrose soon followed her upstairs because this was his younger brother and he was worried about him even though he tried not to show it. Protective instincts and family affection ran strong in these Thornes. "How can I help? We cannot leave my brother dripping blood on my elegant carpets while waiting for the doctor to arrive."

"First thing is to get his shirt off so I can assess the damage." She nudged a reluctant Julius into his bedchamber and ordered him to sit on one of the wooden chairs that Ambrose now moved in front of the hearth.

"What next?" Ambrose knew she was the most trained among them in medical matters, so he voiced no objections when she took the lead in giving orders.

"Help me remove his jacket." This was followed by their removing his cravat and waistcoat.

Gory stared at his shirt that was a bloody mess.

"I can do it myself," Julius grumbled, wincing as he stubbornly took over the task and attempted to pull his injured arm out of the shirt sleeve.

Gory put a gentle hand on his shoulder, trying not to notice that his shirt was half off and his chest was on display. She was surprised by the warmth of his skin, somehow thinking it would feel cold to the touch.

But he was alive and vibrant.

Thank goodness.

"Stop, Julius. You will only make things worse. I am responsible for taking care of you until Dr. Farthingale arrives. You are bleeding and must be feeling a little lightheaded."

"I am fine."

But Gory could see the strain on his handsome face and knew he had to be in more pain than he was letting on. "Right, and I am the Queen of Sheba," she muttered. "Do not dare move, you stubborn man."

"Says the worst patient in the world now giving me orders," he muttered. "Have you done a single thing the doctor has asked you?"

"I stayed in bed for an eternity, rotting like a vegetable."

He laughed. "You hopped out of bed a day after you were almost killed, and refused to remain resting until your vision became so blurred, you could not count the fingers in front of your face."

"And then I dutifully did nothing for two entire days. Our situations are completely different. I had to get out of bed in order to solve the crime before those killers came after me, as they did today."

"You are both miserable patients," Ambrose said, putting an end to their discussion. "But the fact remains you are still bleeding, Julius. Stop grumbling and let Gory tend you."

She asked Ambrose to fetch the basin and ewer off his bureau.

Julius frowned as he watched her dip a clean cloth into the basin she had partially filled with water and began to gently wipe the blood off his arm.

He continued to frown as she gingerly poked around the area of his torn flesh. "This is ridiculous," he muttered as Ambrose looked on.

Gory sighed and turned once again to Ambrose. "Oh, and I'll need a bottle of brandy. And more fresh cloths."

"Robbins can attend to me," Julius said. "I do not need my *duke* brother acting as my servant. Go back downstairs and see to your guests. I'll be fine with Gory and my valet. In fact, I'll be fine with just Gory to minister to my needs."

He turned to her with a naughty grin and puffed out his chest.

"You have the softest hands."

"And you have a nasty gash where the shot tore through your arm. Be quiet and stop ogling me like a naughty boy."

Ambrose, after casting him a warning glance, hurried off to do her bidding. The warning did no good, for Julius still had a naughty grin on his face. "Stop fussing and give me a kiss, Gory. That is the best medicine for me."

She needed to make certain no metal fragments had lodged in his arm. The ball had gone clean through, but bits of it might have detached, and this was a danger. She tried to explain this, but he wasn't listening.

Instead, he placed his hand to the back of her head and gently drew her toward him. "Gory," he said, his expression raw and intense, "I'm glad it was me they shot. I would have turned into a mad, wild ape if they harmed you."

He gave her the softest kiss, his lips barely pressing down on hers. Still, she felt the heat behind it and blushed when he released her.

"Behave yourself," she said in a ragged whisper, trying to remain calm. That he had been hurt defending her had her stomach in knots and her heart in a twist.

She would never recover if she lost him.

"Oh, Julius," She whispered, stifling the urge to cry.

"What is it, love? I did not mean to overset you, but I needed to kiss you. I needed to feel your soft lips against my mouth and feel your heartbeat against my own."

"I liked your kiss. But I came so close to losing you. Julius, you were *shot*."

"And *lived*." He shook his head. "Come closer, Gory. I also need to hug you." He held out his good arm to take her into his embrace.

She melted into his arms and hugged him as fiercely as she dared. "It should have been me, not you."

"Never, love. Don't you know by now that I'll never let anyone hurt you?" He gave her another soft kiss on the lips. "No tears, Gory. Look at the good that came out of this incident."

"What good? There is nothing good about your getting hurt."

"Other than I now have my shirt off…and we are alone, and you have the chance to explore my musculature."

"Your musculature?" She laughed and hugged him again. "Yes, this is a scientific opportunity I dare not pass up."

She let out a breath, for he was so beautifully built. Firm. Muscled. There was something shockingly primal about her response to him. She had wanted to run her hands all over him when first seeing him without his shirt, the streaks of blood trailing down his arm.

She had never experienced womanly urges as powerful as these before.

Julius smiled, knowing exactly what she was feeling because he understood her so well.

She eased away when Robbins strode in with the bottle of brandy. "His Grace asked me to take over for him," he muttered, sounding a little indignant at the thought of anyone, even Ambrose, thinking to take on his responsibilities.

"Pour me a glass, will you?" Julius asked his valet while watching Gory apply the brandy to a dry cloth. "I need a light refresher before Lady Gregoria gets her wicked hands on me and burns me by applying the brandy to the wound. A terrible waste of perfectly good spirits."

"I'll be as gentle as I can. Thank goodness it is merely a graze. However, even a graze is a serious matter since infection can set in unless the wound is promptly and thoroughly cleaned. Robbins, I'll need bandages."

"At once, m'lady." The dutiful valet ran off to do her bidding.

While Robbins was off on the errand, she continued to check for any fragments that might have lodged in his flesh. "Your arm will require stitching."

"I gathered as much. How are you holding up, Gory?"

"Me?" She laughed softly. "I should be asking this of you."

"No, I'm fine."

She let out a breath and set aside the bloodied cloth. "Now, it is just a matter of waiting for the doctor to arrive."

"Give me another hug, love."

"Oh, because I hurt you? I'm so sorry, Julius. I tried to be as gentle as I could."

"You were. I am feeling no pain. I just want to hold you in my arms."

She nodded and wrapped her arms around his neck. "I wished so hard to be in your arms. You have no idea how badly I ached for this."

Dr. Farthingale arrived within the hour to tend to Julius.

Gory insisted on remaining with him, something no other doctor would have permitted since she and Julius were not even betrothed. But Dr. Farthingale was never one to judge, so if Ambrose had no objections to her presence beside Julius, he had none either. Besides, he knew she was not the sort to be squeamish. "You did a fine job, Gory. I'll stitch him up now. Are you sure you want to watch?"

She nodded.

Julius regarded her thoughtfully. "Give me your hand, Gory. It won't feel as painful if I hold onto you while the doctor works on me."

He was thinking of *her* pain, not his.

She nodded and held out her hand.

He entwined his fingers in hers, his grip light, yet solid and comforting.

It was a powerful gesture.

All these years on her own and never having been shown love had left her scarred. But Julius was determined to heal her, to let her know that he would always be her anchor, her protector throughout their lives.

She watched the doctor work on him, hardly breathing as he applied needle and thread to Julius's damaged flesh.

"Done," Dr. Farthingale said a few minutes later.

"Gory, you can breathe again," Julius remarked, casting her an indulgent smile.

She laughed. "You noticed."

"Hard to miss." He gave her hand a light squeeze. "Thank you for staying by my side."

She cleared her throat, hoping she would not turn into a watering pot again. Julius was being so kind and caring, she felt overwhelmed.

No one had ever shown her this amount of love or consideration.

How could she ever, ever have accepted to marry anyone but him?

Later that evening, Mr. Barrow called on them as their subdued group was having an early supper together. Gory had been frustrated by today's events, bursting to know what else Julius had noticed during their visit to Allendale this afternoon, and now eager to know what Mr. Barrow was about to tell them.

Between the turmoil of the carriage attack, the intruder chased away from the townhouse, and Julius being injured, her mind had gone numb and she had not given Allendale or her aunt or the investigation more than passing thought. "What news, Mr. Barrow?"

"We've gotten a break in the case."

Everyone leaped to their feet.

Lady Withnall's nose was twitching like a rabbit's. "Do not leave us in suspense, Mr. Barrow. What has happened?"

"We caught the fellow who shot Lord Thorne." He made the announcement with obvious pride and a good dose of relief.

"That is excellent news," Ambrose said.

Gory's heart stuck in her throat like a big, ungainly lump, so that she sounded hoarse when she spoke. "Where is he? Who is he? Did he say who hired him? I'll grab my cloak. Where are you holding him?"

Julius was standing beside her and now grabbed her wrist to hold her back. "You are going nowhere."

Her eyes widened. "Did you not hear what Mr. Barrow just said? This is the breakthrough we have been hoping for."

He cast her that man-protecting-his-woman look again. "I'll go. You need to stay here and let Ambrose's staff and the Bow Street men do their job and guard you."

"But–"

"Gory, only one of them has been caught. Obviously, this means the other culprit is still on the loose." He turned to Mr. Barrow. "Has the man you caught given up any names, or even disclosed his own?"

"No, m'lord. He hadn't said a word before I left him to report to you. Mr. Havers is interrogating him as we speak. That inspector's a clever fellow and will get something out of him, mark my words."

"But if he does not? All the more reason for me to come with you," Gory insisted. "I might recognize this person, especially if he was doing business with my uncle and had come to our house before."

Julius stared at her in disbelief. "If that is so, then your head butler can identify him just as surely as you can. Stay here and keep away from the windows. We do not need a repeat of what happened this afternoon."

To emphasize his point, he glanced at his arm that had been neatly stitched and bandaged, and was now covered by his shirt and jacket.

"There is little chance of another attack," she said, trying to stem her impatience. "His accomplices won't try anything now that Havers has their companion under interrogation. If anything, everyone involved in the crime must be fleeing London for fear of being caught. Mr. Barrow, is there anything new at all about the person who leaped over the townhouse wall this afternoon?"

He shook his head. "Still nothing, I am sad to report."

Gory let out a breath of frustration. "Do you think this trespasser could be a woman? Is this what Mr. Havers might be questioning the man about? You told us the coach registers showed a man and two women who took a coach from Windsor to London and immediately back the next morning."

"Gory, do not get distracted by the sex of the villains," Lady Withnall said. "First, we do not know yet whether the coach registers are significant at all. Although the trespasser lurking in the garden appeared as slender and agile as a woman when leaping over the townhouse wall, it takes a lot of upper body strength to accomplish this, something few women have. Nor is it likely a woman would wear men's clothing or ride astride a horse and not be noticed."

"All good points, Lady Withnall," Julius remarked, turning to

Gory with an arch of his eyebrow. "We already know there had to be at least two people involved in the murder of your uncle. Who is to say there are not a dozen people involved? Let's hear what Havers has to say."

"Based on my experience," Leo remarked, "it is just as likely the pair you encountered today are wastrels hired out of one of the dockside taverns and paid to silence you, Gory. They probably had nothing to do with the murder of your uncle and were only hired now because the real culprits are worried they are being closely watched."

"But why attack in broad daylight on a busy street outside of their known territory?" Marigold asked her husband.

"I don't know," Leo replied. "These are not the brightest men, are they? Greed is their motivation."

"This idle chatter is getting us nowhere," Gory said with marked impatience. "I am coming with you, Mr. Barrow. And Julius has something more to tell us about what he noticed today during our visit with Lord Allendale."

Ambrose shot his brother a questioning glance. "What else happened besides the attack on your carriage?"

Julius growled and hauled Gory out of the room with him. "You did that on purpose, you little minx."

"I am a mongoose, not a minx. I wasn't going to reveal Allendale and Sarah's secret, just get you to take me along with you. It worked, didn't it?"

"Do you think I care if the world knows what Allendale did?" He sighed. "All right, come with me."

She grabbed her cloak and stuck close to Julius to make certain he would not change his mind, then breathed a sigh of relief once he helped her into his carriage.

Since Mr. Barrow had arrived on horseback, he chose to ride behind them rather than join them in the conveyance.

Gory was glad for the chance of a private word with Julius.

They could have spoken earlier, but she had been too overset by his injury to think about anything but him.

"Do not be angry with me," she said, since he would not stop frowning at her. "You know it is important for me to confront this man. Perhaps having a look at him will stir something in my memory and help us solve the crime. Did you think of that?"

"Of course, I did. But the risk to you is greater because you are out on the London streets again," he grumbled. "Did you think of that?"

"Yes, and I would not have insisted on my joining you if I agreed with your assessment of the risk. Nor would you have agreed to bring me along if you really thought it was a significant peril. Now, will you tell me what else you noticed while we were confronting Allendale?"

CHAPTER 12

JULIUS SAT OPPOSITE Gory in the carriage as they made their way to Bow Street in the fading light. The sun was setting, and its vibrant rays shone upon Gory's dark hair and reflected in her eyes, giving them that familiar incandescent glow.

His heartbeat quickened, another familiar occurrence whenever he was around her.

She was not only beautiful, but had an ethereal quality about her that should have seemed odd because she was so scientifically minded. But there was just something charming in the vibrancy of her eyes and the openhearted sincerity in her smile.

Yes, she was a magical, lovely thing.

But she also gave him fits and headaches because she refused to remain safely in hiding. This was Gory, and she was not about to cower in fear. It was a good thing, he supposed. That she was lively and alert meant she was on the mend and returning to her normal self.

Of course, this also meant she was back to being a stubborn handful.

Was this not better than worrying about her ever recovering from the vicious blow that would have killed her except for the miraculous grace of good fortune?

Yes, Gory was someone very special.

He needed to marry her.

"Julius, tell me what you noticed."

He cleared his throat. "I am not saying that Allendale and

Sarah had anything to do with your uncle's murder, mind you. But they were definitely planning something unsavory that had to do with you."

"Because you noticed Mayfield's card in the salver when we walked in?"

He nodded. "It immediately put me on my guard, and confirmed my suspicion that Allendale knew of your potential inheritance beyond the dowry *before* he proposed to you. Do you want to hear more of what I think?"

"Of course. Go on," she urged, taking a deep breath in anticipation.

"All right, here's what I think happened. Allendale either paid Reginald Mayfield for information about you, or might have overheard something by accident and learned there was more coming to you than the ten thousand pounds you were to receive upon your marriage."

"But he would also realize that nothing more was to come to me before my uncle passed away."

"True, but he may not have been in any particular hurry. Your dowry was adequate to maintain Sarah and their daughter in relative comfort while the two of them waited for your uncle to die of natural causes. Of course, I do not know that he would have waited all that long before deciding to help your uncle along to his demise."

"I cannot believe Allendale is so depraved."

"Why? Because he outwardly appears to be a gentleman?"

Gory nodded. "And you referred to the baby as *their* daughter. But Allendale insisted the child was not his. You really do not like him, do you? Why do you believe he is so underhanded?"

He regarded her steadily. "Because Sarah is not who they claim she is."

Gory's eyes widened. "How do you know this?"

"I have seen her upon the stage. She is an actress. I mean, she is a *real* actress."

Gory gasped and leaned forward, practically tumbling out of her seat in her eagerness to hear more. "You saw her on a Covent Garden stage? Are you certain?"

He nodded. "Not a doubt."

In truth, he had seen her much closer up than on a stage. Not that he had ever been intimate with her, but he had been to a few *demi-monde* parties and recognized her as one of the scantily clad courtesans who had made advances toward him and his companions. "I have no idea if Martin is truly her family surname, but I can assure you that she is no ward to anyone in the Allendale family. That nonsense spouted by Allendale about his having to keep his assistance a secret has more to do with his family's outrage when they discover he is consorting with an actress and has fathered a child with her."

He realized the discussion had to be humiliating for Gory, but the truth needed to come out.

"So," she said quietly, "I was merely the camouflage to hide his true purpose."

"And it was not necessarily a harmless purpose, I fear. As I said, once you were securely wed, I do not know that Allendale would have waited so patiently for your uncle's demise."

Her eyes widened as she stared at him. "That is too cold and calculating. I cannot believe Allendale would purposely hurt my uncle."

"What makes you believe he wouldn't? And what of you? What plans did he have for you once that inheritance was securely in your bank account?"

"No!"

"Gory, do not be naive." The truth was going to hurt her badly, but it had to be told. "Is this not a distinct possibility? I am not saying that he would have harmed you for certain. All he needed to do was get his hands on your money. As your husband, he could have spent it however he wished, even if it left you destitute. You could not have stopped him because the law is on his side. But neither can I rule out the chance of his deciding to be rid of you, as well."

"Leaving him free to marry Sarah after a suitable period of mourning?"

Julius sighed. "Ten thousand pounds is a goodly sum, but one hundred thousand would have made him a very wealthy man and freed him forever from the constraints of his family."

Tears formed in Gory's eyes, but she quickly wiped them away. "So, I was completely disposable to him."

"Yes, Gory. I think so." He understood how severely his words must have stung. "Blast," he muttered softly, "I'm sorry."

"Don't be. I always prefer honesty, even if it is painful to hear." She shook her head and cast him a wan smile to reassure him, but she was shivering lightly and tears were forming once again to cloud her lovely eyes. "Why should a man of independent means like Allendale bother with such an evil plot? He is the viscount, so why should he worry what his friends, family, or Society think?"

Julius shrugged. "Perhaps Allendale is not as independent as he likes to let on. His holdings might not produce sufficient income to maintain his style of living. If this is so, then he would need to remain in his family's good graces, especially in the favor of his rich uncle who probably provides him an allowance but also keeps tight rein over all the Allendale family members, whether viscount or commoner. So, what better way to remain in his uncle's favor than to marry *you*, someone I am sure his philanthropic uncle admires? Allendale gets control of your dowry which would keep Sarah comfortably supported for the next few years."

"And he would not have to give his uncle an account since the funds did not come from his uncle's coffers," Gory mused.

Julius nodded. "Correct. He also acquires you, a wife who will be so involved with her forensics research that she will not bother to question him about his daily activities or particularly care where he spends his evenings."

"That is awful." She sighed. "But this is me, is it not? Always with my nose in a book."

He gave her cheek a light caress. "Or poking about in the entrails of dead things."

"Not always," she said in lame protest, then winced. "Sometimes."

"That you do it at all is shocking to the *ton*. The point is, that dastardly pair counted on you to remain oblivious and unsuspecting when your uncle suddenly died, whether by poison, natural causes, or in a tragic accident, and left you inheriting one hundred thousand pounds."

"You are very cynical, Julius. First of all, Allendale could have married an heiress who came with a vast sum upon their wedding day. Second, just because he wanted my money does not mean he would have done anything to speed the inheritance along. He might have been willing to wait for my uncle to die of natural causes."

"First of all, no father able to provide a dowry of over thirty thousand pounds would have settled on a viscount of questionable wealth as husband material for his daughter. That size of a dowry would have landed his precious darling an earl at a minimum, but more likely a duke or a marquess if the reward was one hundred thousand pounds."

Gory harrumphed.

"You were chosen because your family was shockingly inattentive toward you. The added bonus was that you were *you*, a bluestocking who cared for your forensics research more than matters romantic. Any other new bride would have expected Allendale to be a devoted husband and would have made a fuss had he gone off to Sarah instead of attending to his blushing bride. He did not need that sort of problem to draw unfavorable attention upon himself."

"This is conjecture about the future, but my uncle's murder has already occurred."

He nodded. "Which is why I do not believe Allendale killed him, although he may have planned to do it in the coming years. That someone beat him to it must have upended his schemes."

"So, Allendale is firmly ruled out despite his reprehensible conduct?"

"That's right. And he is reprehensible, Gory. Do not soften toward him. He lied to you and continues to lie even now that you've found out his secret. Sarah looks sweet and innocent, but I assure you that she is not. She is a better liar than Allendale."

"All right, Julius. I get the point."

"Sorry, love. But they are a dangerous pair and I do not want you to lose sight of this fact. As for your uncle's murder, my wager is on your aunt. She stands to lose any chance at that one hundred thousand pounds upon your marriage. Indeed, your marriage has always been the key to this crime. It is why they took the time to put you in your wedding gown."

"It was a foolish statement to make. Had they taken the time to make it look as though a robbery had taken place, Mr. Havers would have started his investigation in an entirely different direction."

"Possibly, but he's quite clever. I don't know that he would have been fooled for long. Your aunt would have been at the top of his list of suspects no matter what clues were left for him to find. That wedding gown stunt was a sheer act of hubris on her part."

"Sloppy work, thank goodness. They were so busy making certain my laces were straight, they forgot to check that I was still breathing." Gory rubbed her head lightly. "Dr. Farthingale plans to take my stitches out the day after tomorrow. That was to be my wedding day."

"I cannot say I am sorry your wedding has been called off."

"Nor am I," she admitted, clasping her hands together to keep them from shaking. "I was at risk from all sides, and completely oblivious. Allendale. My aunt. I continue to be at risk until Havers arrests all who conspired to kill my uncle. However, I still would rather believe Allendale only intended to take my money and was willing to wait patiently for it to come to me."

"Is this not despicable enough?"

"Yes, Julius. It is."

He reached out and drew her onto his seat bench because he wanted her close. The danger surrounding her these past few months had left him feeling ill, especially since he was partly responsible for not stepping up and admitting he loved her.

Yet, she would have been in danger no matter the intended bridegroom. Whether him or Allendale, the risk to her was the same.

Lady Easton needed Gory to remain unmarried or the one hundred thousand pounds would slip through her fingers. That haughty lady was the one with all the motivation to be rid of Gory and Lord Easton, especially if Easton was about to humiliate her by going public with his own mistress. Perhaps he was even planning to move the woman into his home while sending his wife off to one of his country estates.

Well, it was all mere supposition on his part.

The fact remained, the inheritance was the lure...and Gory stood in the way.

The realization that she had been walking around all these months with a big target on her back made him shudder. That she had walked in on the killers before they were ready to come for her is what likely saved her.

He did not think she was ever meant to survive the night.

She burrowed against him.

He wrapped an arm around her waist to draw her even closer. "Shall we change the conversation to something lighter?"

"No, keep going. I think we are close to the end now. Keep tossing out ideas about that night."

"Well, I do not think there is much more to say. The culprits must have been shocked to learn you had survived, and this meant they had to quickly adjust their plans. Their best option was to try to make you out to be the murderess."

"Or try again to dispose of me, as they tried today. Havers still has me on his list of suspects," she reminded him, although he hardly needed any reminder of her precarious position.

"No longer, Gory. He is as worried for your safety as I am. He fully appreciates how narrowly you escaped death that night."

She shivered. "I hope this second attempt concerns him just as much."

"Because I was hurt? You know it is but a scratch." He shrugged it off. "I'm sure Havers has taken serious note of this incident and will get as much information as he can out of the man now in his custody."

"What if the man refuses to talk? What is our next step then? Perhaps you and I ought to attend my uncle's funeral and–"

"No," he said decisively. "I will not have you walk into enemy territory."

"It is a funeral, not a battle."

He arched an eyebrow. "Do you not understand that your aunt is in a panic and afraid you might remember something if you spend more time in her company? This is why she does not want you visiting her or attending your uncle's funeral. She is pushing you away, not only because she despises you, but because she is afraid you might recognize one of your assailants. She cannot afford to have that happen, especially in the midst of the funeral service."

Gory looked up at him. "You've given this quite some thought."

"I've had nothing but you on my mind for months now. I need to keep you safe, Gory. I need to marry you and keep you out of your aunt's clutches."

He leaned his head out the window as their carriage approached the magistrate's office. "Bundle up, love. It's just a light mist right now, but the skies are about to open up."

They hurried inside the nondescript building situated amid a row of similar buildings constructed of gray stone. Mr. Barrow followed immediately behind them and was recognized by the guard at the entrance who gave him a cheerful greeting. "Mr. Havers is still occupied with the man what got brought in," the guard told them.

Mr. Barrow thanked him and took the lead as they made their way through the dank, dimly lit halls. "Let's hope Havers got some information out of that shady cove," he muttered.

Gory pursed her lips. "What if he did not?"

"Never you worry, m'lady. That Havers is a clever fellow. He will have the man tripped up and admitting something by now."

"Where was he found?" Julius asked.

"Hiding out in one of the dockside taverns, m'lord. This is what these villains often do, run back to familiar places. But this means others who frequent these shady places will know who he is and can tell us more about him. So, it does not matter very much if he refuses to talk. We have ways of getting the information we need by questioning other tavern regulars. I've left two of my men there to question the owner, his serving maids, and patrons. Someone will know who he is and who he's been keeping company with lately."

Julius and Gory waited outside the door while the Bow Street runner went in to see how Havers was progressing.

Julius felt particularly protective of Gory right now, perhaps because they were about to confront one of the perpetrators of the crime. "Are you all right, love?"

She nodded. "Just furious with myself."

He tucked a finger under her chin and raised her gaze to his. "Why?"

"How can you ask this after all we spoke about in the carriage? I pride myself on my cleverness, and yet, I was completely taken in by my aunt. Not to mention Allendale, too. And Mayfield, although I never trusted that oily solicitor. How did I never notice the trouble brewing? Or make the connection between Allendale and Mayfield? How did I not spot Mayfield's calling card staring back at us from the salver in the Bayswater house?"

"Killers are not in the habit of announcing their intentions. You could not have known any of it. Nor should you ever blame yourself for being unaware. You've been through a lot, Gory." He raked a hand through his hair. "Do you realize how close a call you had that night?"

She nodded. "Yes, I do realize. Had they been professionals, they would have noticed I was not dead yet and finished the job."

Mr. Barrow popped his head out the door. "Are you certain about confronting this man, Lady Gregoria?"

She did not hesitate in her reply. "Yes, Mr. Barrow. It must be done."

Julius escorted her into the windowless room that was bare except for a table and several chairs. A lantern hanging on a peg embedded in the wall shone a harsh light upon the captured man and made him appear quite big and ominous. The light also shone upon Havers, revealing his glint of determination to get the murder resolved. Two of his constables were positioned behind their prisoner. They stood half in shadow and appeared just as resolute as Havers.

Julius was glad for the extra protection, and never more so when the man they had been interrogating suddenly leaped to his feet and tried to lunge at Gory. Julius immediately planted himself in front of her, forming a protective wall between the pair while the two constables struggled to subdue this hulk of a fellow.

They finally managed to get him back in his seat, but not before he had pointed his stubby finger at Gory and began shouting, "That's her! That's who paid me! She's the one who told me to go after her uncle! She did!"

Gory was immediately incensed. "Is that so? Did I also tell you to kill me, too? And when you failed the first time, did I insist on your attempting to kill me again today?"

Julius held her back because this man was twice her size and capable of hurting her if she got too close to him.

He nudged Gory behind him and kept her firmly in place while he spoke to the villain. "Try again and this time tell us who really paid you."

Julius knew he had to remain calm even though he was furious and wanted to pound his fists into the man's ruddy face.

Havers, appearing completely unaffected, rose and ordered his constables to put the man back in his prison cell.

"Ye can't hold me! I told ye all I know. Wasn't that our deal?"

Havers folded his arms across his chest. "Our deal was for you to tell me the truth. Take him away," he said, repeating his order to the waiting constables.

Once they had carried the protesting man out, Havers offered Gory the vacated seat.

She shook her head, visibly shaken as she said, "I would rather remain standing."

"As you wish, my lady," Havers said, studying her intently. "Let me assure you, I did not believe him."

Gory let out a breath of relief. "Upon my honor, I have never seen him before. Did you find scratches on him?"

Havers nodded. "Yes, he had fading scratches along his cheek and neck. But did you notice his hands? Gnarled and pudgy. There isn't a chance he laced you into your wedding gown."

Gory glanced at Julius before returning her attention to Havers. "Then who did?"

Havers rubbed his hands across his face a moment, a sign of

his obvious fatigue. The man was dogged, to be sure. Julius wondered whether he had gotten any sleep at all since assigned the murder investigation.

"Havers," Julius prompted, "I can see you have your suspicions. Care to share them with us? I also have ideas I wish to share with you. But you go first."

He thought Havers would insist on first learning what Julius had to impart, but he did not and proceeded to recount his findings. "We've ruled out Allendale. His alibi holds. We have also ruled out the Earl of Easton's business acquaintances. They can all substantiate where they were at the time the murder was committed."

"Have you ruled out my aunt because she was in Windsor at the time?" Gory asked.

"She would like us to do so, but no. She has been at the top of my suspect list all along and remains so despite her apparent alibi. Most murders are committed by people who knew their victim. A disenchanted husband or wife is often the culprit. Divorce is out of the question, so that leaves few options for getting rid of an unwanted spouse."

"Or a niece who stands in the way of a large inheritance," Julius muttered.

Havers nodded.

"Has Mayfield been helping Lady Easton out?" Julius asked. "He seems to have his hand in every pie. Gory and I noticed his calling card on a salver when we called upon Lady Gregoria's betrothed earlier today...former betrothed."

"Your Bayswater visit." He turned to Gory. "Yes, I know about it. I'm glad you've called the wedding off. Keep away from Allendale. He's a questionable sort."

"Questionable?" She stared at Havers in confusion.

"He has a weak moral compass. Outwardly a gentleman, and that outward appearance is very important to him, especially since it keeps him in good standing with his rich uncle. But he is also one who believes the world owes him more and he has every right to claim his spoils. His frustration in not getting what he wants runs deep. He did not have a hand in your uncle's murder, but I think it is only because someone else got to him first."

Gory cast Julius a meaningful glance before returning her attention to Havers. "Lord Thorne came to the same conclusion. Consider me warned. I will have nothing to do with him from now on, but I do feel quite foolish to have been so taken in by him."

"No, my lady," Havers said, his tone quite gentle. "You have been kind and trusting. That is a strength in you and not a fault, as I am sure Lord Thorne will agree."

She blushed to acknowledge the compliment. "Where does this leave us now, Mr. Havers?"

"Well, we will have to do a bit more investigative work to draw in all the bad players."

"Can you dupe the solicitor, Reginald Mayfield, into providing the proof needed to arrest Lady Gregoria's aunt?" Julius asked.

"Doubtful. The man is greedy and would betray his own grandmother to save himself. But he's also wily and no fool. He will never admit to being an accomplice to murder. This also assumes he was involved in the murder. I am not convinced of it yet. He considers himself more of a factotum, a middleman who facilitates exchanges of funds without asking any questions."

Gory frowned. "Even if he was not at the scene when the crime was committed, he must have suspected what was about to happen. And I think we are now running out of time because my aunt and her accomplices are becoming more desperate to silence me. This is the second attempt on my life that has been thwarted. A third cannot be far behind. And if that big man your constables just hauled out of here was not the one who expertly laced me into my wedding gown, then who did? We must take action to draw out the remaining culprits."

"Oh, Gory. I do not like that look in your eyes." Julius's heart began to race. "Do not even think to put yourself out as a lure."

"But—"

"No, you need to stay hidden and close to me."

Havers agreed with him. "We will track down the others and take them into custody. Once we have them here, we can easily play one against the other, offering clemency to the one who

206 | MEARA PLATT

confesses first. You will be amazed how quickly they will betray each other."

"You think there is more than one accomplice? But finding them could take days," Gory insisted. "If they have run off, you may never find them. Meanwhile, my uncle's funeral is to be held the day after tomorrow. Is it not ironic? What was to be my wedding day is now a day of mourning. I suppose it is apt. Let me go to the funeral and stir things up."

Julius growled softly. "You were purposely *dis*invited. Your aunt does not want you there."

"I was merely encouraged not to attend," she insisted.

"*Strongly* encouraged to keep away," Julius reminded her.

"And you think this will stop me? She won't dare make a scene if you are with me, especially if we pull up in Ambrose's carriage with the Huntsford ducal crest emblazoned on it."

"And then what? I walk away and give your aunt's accomplices the opportunity to harm you?"

She was giving him a stubborn look again.

"I would not really be alone because Mr. Barrow and Mr. Havers will have their best men close by to guard me."

Julius growled again. "Out of the question, Gory. Do you realize how easy it is for someone to slip up behind you and stick a knife into your ribs?"

She pursed her lips, a sign she was not happy about the situation. Nor was he, but he was not going to relent and allow her to place herself in the path of danger. "Then how are we to lure my aunt into making a mistake?"

Havers stepped forward. "There is no need. Does this man not look familiar to you at all?"

Gory now stared at Havers. "What do you mean? Should I know him?"

"Perhaps not." Havers frowned. "It does not matter. I am certain your aunt knows him, and I will get her confession in time."

"You will get it *in time*?" Gory said, repeating his words. "What if we run out of time? Are we not better served by dangling bait in front of her?"

"Stop referring to yourself as bait," Julius said between clenched teeth. "Put the idea out of your head at once."

Havers regarded him a long moment. "What if I came up with a plan?"

"Do you have one in mind?" Gory was all in before Havers responded to her question. Smiling, she stepped forward. "Excellent. What do you need me to do?"

CHAPTER 13

JULIUS KNEW ALL eyes were on him as Gory, Havers, and Barrow awaited his consent to Gory's attending her uncle's funeral. He frowned at Gory. "You'd probably knock me out and tie me up, leave me trussed in a cupboard if I refused."

"I would be very gentle with you," she teased. "But I am going and you mustn't stop me. I'll never be free of the danger if we don't take this opportunity to force them into making mistakes."

"I still do not like it." He held up a hand when she thought to protest. "I'll go along, but I have terms."

"And what might those be?" Havers asked.

"I remain beside Gory at all times. No one replaces me as her last wall of protection."

Havers grinned and arched an eyebrow. "That is acceptable to me, although the magistrate might not take kindly to hearing the Duke of Huntsford's brother was stabbed during the melee that erupted at the Earl of Easton's funeral. Try not to get hurt, will you?"

Julius cast him a wry smile. "Do your job and get the assailant before he reaches me."

Havers nodded. "I will do my best."

Julius saw that Gory was already beginning to fret for his safety. *His.* What about hers?

She nibbled her lip and then looked up at him. "Perhaps you ought to let–"

His eyes were a fierce smolder as he said, "No one stands next to you but me, Gory. That is my first requirement and not negotiable."

"Ape," she muttered, but cast him a loving look. "And what is your second requirement?"

He cleared his throat. "That you marry me tomorrow. You do not attend the funeral unless you are already married to me. We'll make the announcement that we are husband and wife at the funeral. I do not care about the scandal of it. I want Lady Easton and her associates caught by surprise and at odds with each other over their next steps. They are more likely to make their mistakes if caught off guard."

"But how can I marry you when I am still betrothed to Allendale?"

"You won't be bound to him for long," Julius assured. "I'll have Allendale sign off on the termination of your betrothal tonight. Mr. Barrow will assist me in ensuring it is done."

"No, I'll go with you to confront Lord Allendale," Havers said. "It is more official that way. Besides, Mr. Barrow and his men are more capable than my constables when it comes to taking on guard duties, I regret to say. They will do a better job of protecting Lady Gregoria while we are off on this errand."

"Mr. Havers, why are you suddenly so certain of my innocence?" Gory asked. "You did not even toss me a doubting glance when that man leaped up and began shouting that I was the one who paid him off."

"Because I already know who was paying him. One of my men saw the exchange and reported it to me."

"But how would they know where it was to take place? Or who the parties involved were to be?" Julius was amazed and now eager to hear more.

"The Wallingford Arms," Havers replied. "I am good at what I do because I notice the smallest details. Your attention was fixed on Lady Easton, but any investigator worth his salt will know it is pointless to concentrate on her. She is not one to ever get her hands dirty. She is not one to ever go down to the docks herself to pay off an accomplice, or ever demean herself by performing maid's work."

"Maid's work?" Gory regarded him, confused.

Havers nodded. "Your aunt might have come up with the spiteful idea of having you found in your wedding gown, but she was not the one who laced it up so perfectly."

"Then who did?" Gory asked, and then immediately gasped. "Her maid! Oh, how stupid of me not to think of it. How obvious! Her devoted maid, Flossie, had to be the one. Mr. Havers, you have my sincerest apologies for ever doubting your competence. When did you catch on to her?"

Julius was curious, too.

Havers cleared his throat. "From the first day…um, within an hour of my arrival at the scene of the crime. We conducted interviews with the Easton staff, but I already knew I had to look closely at the maids rather than the footmen or butlers because no man was going to dress you so meticulously in your wedding gown. That was the key to all of this, wasn't it?"

Julius laughed mirthlessly. "Yes, I thought so. But I did not know how to make the connection between that gown and Lady Easton's guilt."

"Well, it was right there all along," Havers said. "Once I had interviewed and dismissed all the staff sleeping under your roof on the night of the murder, I knew it had to be Lady Easton's maid who had done the job. She was the only one sufficiently familiar with your home and who would have had a latchkey available to her – Lady Easton's key – to let herself and her accomplices in that night."

Julius frowned. "But she had gone to Windsor with Lady Easton."

"And quietly returned to London by public coach to commit the murder while Lady Easton remained in Windsor and covered up her disappearance," Havers said.

"However, there was another woman involved," Gory added. "Because the coachman reported two women and a man traveling together. And you are now certain the other woman was not Lady Easton?"

"That's right," Havers acknowledged. "I have my suspicions as to the identity of the other female, but I am waiting for confirmation on that."

"Do you think it was Lady Easton's sister?" Gory asked. "After all, Lady Easton was visiting her in Windsor when the murder happened. Was she complicit?"

"No." Havers frowned as he shook his head. "In fact, Lady Easton's own sister and her husband are quite innocent in this affair. I will admit, that possibility threw me off the scent for several days because I allowed my preconceived notions to get the better of me."

"I'm glad they were not involved," Gory said softly. "They were always decent to me."

"So, who was the second woman?" Julius asked. "You've said you have your suspicions. Can you tell us who you think she is?"

"I believe the two women in the coach were Lady Easton's maid and the maid's sister."

Gory gasped. "Flossie has a sister?"

Havers nodded. "Who also happens to live in Windsor with her husband. I believe the husband is the very man we are holding in custody. I'm awaiting confirmation on their identities, so I cannot say for certain yet."

Julius felt his heartbeat quicken, for it seemed as though all the pieces were rapidly falling into place. Once Flossie and her sister were brought in for questioning, how long would they hold out before pointing fingers at Lady Easton?

Mr. Barrow had expressed his concern about convicting the wrongdoers if none of them confessed. But even if they never confessed, surely there would be enough circumstantial evidence to bring them all to justice.

Perhaps Lady Easton would never be arrested if her underlings refused to name her, but what harm could she do without them to assist her?

It was quite possible Lady Easton might simply accept her fate and slink away.

"Gad, I am so dense," Gory muttered.

"Me, too," Julius said with a sigh, truly vexed with himself for not figuring it out sooner. "As you said, the wedding gown held the solution all along. Gory's maid adored her and would never have betrayed her or harmed her in any way. So, who was the next most obvious person to lace her gown so perfectly? The only other lady's maid in the house, of course."

Havers nodded again. "Yes."

"And you immediately put that together along with the fact there was no evidence of the house being broken into." Julius shook his head. "You seem to have all the answers, Havers. And we now have solid leads on all the conspirators, do we not? Have you sent constables out to bring the rest of them in?"

"No, that I will not do until I have them reliably identified. I have my men watching Lady Easton and her maid closely. Unfortunately, we do not know where the maid's sister is at the moment." Havers sighed as he ran a hand across the nape of his neck. "But rest assured, we are looking for her. We can only hope she will turn up at the Wallingford Arms at some point in order to get her next instructions."

"Do you think the woman would be so foolish as to show up at the hotel now that her husband is in your custody?" Julius asked. "She has to be worried constables are posted there. Unless she is a fool, she has to know their plot is beginning to unravel."

"If she dares not approach Lady Easton at the Wallingford Arms, then she is most likely to risk approaching her amid the crowd at the funeral," Gory suggested. "All the more reason for me to attend. She must be desperate to collect whatever reward she was promised and somehow get her husband out of custody."

"If he is her husband," Havers clarified. "I'll await solid proof before making any pronouncements."

Gory smiled at him. "All right, you have earned my respect, Mr. Havers. What matters is that he poses no threat for now. Lady Easton has lost this man who was her 'muscle'. But will she come up with another plan to get at me during the funeral? Flossie is completely devoted to her and will not hesitate to do her bidding."

"What's her incentive to do anything once you are married to me?" Julius asked.

"The fear that I will remember what happened and be able to identify whoever was there that night. By identifying them, I would be able to link them to her. That danger will never go away so long as I am alive. Julius, I have already agreed to serve as the bait. We must not falter now that we are so close to the end." Gory winced as a stabbing pain suddenly shot through her temples.

Julius immediately placed his arms around her. "Gory, let me take you back home. You're not well, and we've accomplished more than enough tonight."

She took a deep breath and then another. "No, I... Oh! Oh, heavens. *Ouch!*"

"Blast it, Gory. Never mind home, I'm taking you straight to Dr. Farthingale."

"No, I'm not in pain."

He cursed softly. "Really? Has *ouch* suddenly developed a new meaning?"

"Don't be smart, Julius." She winced again and then released a defeated breath. "It was there, the memory of that night. But it's gone again. Gad, why won't it come out?"

Julius growled. "Because it was terrifying and painful, to you. But that memory need never return. Keep it lost and buried forever. As you said, we are almost at the finish line. Havers will do the rest and get us across it."

"And he will cross that finish line, but with my help," she insisted.

Julius understood her desire to bring the investigation to a rapid close. Did he not feel quite miserable about the continuing danger to her? Her life would remain in peril while the perpetrators believed Gory had seen them and would eventually remember.

His heart was in a painful twist because he knew that he could not talk Gory out of going to her uncle's funeral and purposely provoking her aunt. That she would have an army of constables and Bow Street runners on guard around her while she prodded that sleeping bear did not allay his concerns.

Was all their vigilance enough to guarantee her safety?

But he also understood why Gory was so insistent. The rumors swirling around her being the guilty party would persist unless Havers definitively solved this murder. It was not enough to put the man he had in custody on trial, and would it not be disastrous if the wretch chose to lie and accuse Gory in open court of being the one to pay him?

Gory the ghoul.

Everyone would believe she was responsible for her uncle's murder.

Lady Easton, unless proven guilty with a certainty, would stir up more trouble by also spreading rumors and blaming Gory. The malicious woman could play the innocent victim to the hilt. Long suffering widow. Left impoverished while her cruel and spiteful niece got a hefty inheritance.

Of course, he and his brothers would defend Gory's honor. But the consequences would be dire, especially to Ambrose. That sort of scandal could destroy the Huntsford Academy's reputation. Everything Ambrose had sought to build in honor of their father would be brought down because he had the audacity to place Gory in charge of their forensics laboratory. It had already stirred controversy when she was first appointed to the role. To now have her implicated in the death of her uncle...no, the Huntsford Academy would never recover.

Gory was voicing similar concerns as she spoke to Havers to assure him of her desire to cooperate. "I will have damaged not only my reputation, but that of the very people I consider my closest family."

Dread coursed through Julius. "All right, Havers. What do you need us to do?"

Havers did not look happy, no doubt also having concerns about involving Gory, but he set out his proposal. "All you have to do is arrive shortly before the funeral service is about to start and make certain Lady Easton sets her eyes on you. My men as well as the Bow Street runners will already be there watching her and her maid. We'll see who Lady Easton whispers to and who scrambles away to do her bidding."

Julius gnashed his teeth as he listened. "Let's discuss the perimeter. How close am I to allow that person to approach Lady Gregoria before I stop them?"

"That is our role, not yours, m'lord. We'll stop anyone before they get too close," Mr. Barrow assured.

Gory turned to Julius. "See? It is all under control."

"Assuming they are watching the right people," he grumbled.

"But I'll have you near me to keep me safe if something goes wrong. Are you serious about marrying me tomorrow?"

He nodded. "Absolutely."

She reached up and kissed him on the cheek.

Havers cleared his throat. "I suggest we take Lady Gregoria back to your home now, Lord Thorne. Then you and I shall pay a call on Lord Allendale."

Julius agreed. "Time to let that scoundrel know we are onto him."

Gory put a hand on his arm. "You will make certain the baby comes to no harm, won't you?"

This is why Julius knew he loved Gory.

She was the oddest mix of fearless and compassionate.

But how was he to protect her when the fearless part of her would have her running straight toward danger?

CHAPTER 14

JULIUS WAS RELIEVED to return to the townhouse he shared with his brothers because he did not think there was any place safer for Gory in all of London. Havers had hopped in the carriage with him and Gory, for the two of them planned to drop Gory back here, and then move on to his solicitor's office to pick up the betrothal papers.

Julius looked forward to confronting Allendale.

That man needed to be out of Gory's life forever.

Greeves hurried out as Julius assisted Gory down from the carriage. "Admiral Thorne and Lady Syd have arrived, my lord."

Gory smiled. "They're here?"

She ran into the house to greet them.

Julius sighed as he exchanged glances with Havers. "Come in a moment, Havers. I'll introduce you to my brother and his wife. If you think Lady Gregoria is a handful, just wait until you meet Lady Syd."

Havers chuckled. "Can't wait. Obviously, you Thornes are not attracted to docile ladies."

"Nor do I think you will be when your time comes," Julius remarked. "It will take someone quite clever and spirited to keep up with you."

"Was that a compliment, Lord Thorne?"

Julius laughed. "Dear heaven, it might have been. Careful, Havers. Once this investigation is over, I might consider you a friend."

"I would be honored if you did," he said with surprising humility, for Havers was not a particularly humble man.

It was not surprising to Julius that Leo and Marigold, Lady Withnall, and Lady Dayne had remained and were present along with his brothers and their wives when he walked into the parlor with Havers. Gory was as happy as he had ever seen her, for she and Syd were the closest among their circle of friends. Adela and Marigold were unquestionably dear to her, but Syd held a special place in Gory's heart because they had both been raised in troubled homes and understood what the other must have felt growing up unloved.

Julius made quick introductions, although everyone had met Havers by now except for Octavian and Syd.

Once pleasantries were exchanged, Julius took Octavian aside. "Glad you made it home, you big ox."

His brother laughed. "Syd insisted on heading down here with days to spare in order to ensure our timely arrival. But it seems we needn't have rushed. I'm told there's been a slight problem with the wedding."

Julius nodded. "That is an understatement."

"So, it is all true? There is to be a switch in bridegrooms?"

Since Octavian was grinning at him, Julius assumed he approved. Octavian was a hulking beast of a man who rarely smiled and generally scared people away. But he was perhaps the softest of the three brothers, and he certainly doted on Syd.

Syd doted on him, as well.

This is what Julius hoped to achieve with Gory, this complete sense of belonging to each other and knowing their union was right and perfect.

"Yes, a bridegroom switch. I hope to marry Gory tomorrow morning." Julius then turned to address everyone since they probably had been listening in anyway. "You are all invited to our wedding."

Cheers rang out.

Lady Withnall stamped her cane in approval. "About time, dear boy. I was beginning to despair."

"Indeed," Lady Dayne, said with a shake of her head. "We

were so worried you were going to allow the wrong bridegroom to claim our lovely Gory."

"That would have been a disaster," Octavian remarked. "Glad you came to your senses, you dolt."

Julius spared a loving glance at Gory. "I will admit that I was unpardonably slow to act. But never doubt I was going to be the one to marry Gory."

"Thank goodness," Syd murmured.

"However, there is still much to do if anything is to happen tomorrow," he cautioned. "First, the matter of Gory's betrothal needs to be undone. Next, I must obtain the marriage license. If you will excuse me and Mr. Havers, we must get on the task."

He walked out with Havers, but his brothers followed after them.

Ambrose was frowning. "Do you really think Allendale will release Gory from the betrothal? Perhaps he will see reason if Octavian and I join you."

Octavian nodded.

Julius sighed. "I do not need my big brothers protecting me. Havers and I have it all under control. Just watch over Gory while I am gone."

Ambrose arched an eyebrow. "That's it?"

"And show up at the church tomorrow morning. That's all I need you both to do. Do not forget. Ten o'clock sharp."

Octavian gave him a light smack on the head. "We all still live together. Do you think our wives are ever going to allow us to oversleep? They'll be up at the crack of dawn to attend to Gory. We'll be tossed to the dogs if we dare show up a minute late."

"Better get on your way now," Ambrose advised. "However, I'll be waiting for you at the parish church. See you there in about an hour. Is that enough time for you? Well, no matter. I'm going to wait there no matter how late you are. I'll make certain they have the license ready for your signature. They won't dare turn a duke away."

"Or an admiral," Octavian added. "I'll be waiting there with Ambrose."

Julius released a breath once he had climbed in the carriage and settled on the bench opposite Havers.

Havers chuckled as the conveyance rolled away. "So, this is what having a loving family looks like."

Julius arched an eyebrow. "You mean me and my brothers?"

He nodded. "Every male in my family line is a complete and utter arse. The woman are no prizes, either. When I was younger, I was convinced I was a changeling. Who were these people, I would often ask myself as I watched them make the stupidest mistakes imaginable? But as I grew older, there was no mistaking I was a Havers. I have the uncanniest resemblance to my father. Fortunately, it is only a physical resemblance."

"All the brains and common sense were concentrated on you?"

Havers shrugged. "I am observant, for certain. Not sure how smart I am."

"You did not get to be the magistrate's top investigator by sheer luck or good connections. You earned your status." Julius was serious about this, for he had not met a man more sensible or with more solid instincts than Havers.

"For all the good it does me," he muttered, shrugging again. "I did not wish to say anything to Lady Gregoria, but it is possible Lady Easton will get away with her husband's murder."

Julius shook his head. "No, she won't. If you understood Gory, you would know she will never let the matter rest until all the responsible parties are brought to justice. She needs to have the matter resolved for all the reasons she mentioned. Vindication. Preserving her good name and that of the Huntsford Academy. Certainty in the outcome, which is the only way to dispel rumors of her guilt."

Havers arched an eyebrow. "Why did you express reluctance when you obviously agree with her concerns?"

"Because I still want to protect her. If there is any way to bring this matter to an end without involving her, I am all for it."

"So am I," Havers admitted. "What good are all my efforts if I cannot ensure her safety?"

"What you do is invaluable," Julius insisted. "You've rid London of many evildoers. You've saved countless lives. Do not shrug off your importance, even if you are momentarily stymied in putting this case to rest. Lady Gregoria and I, for all our wisdom, had not figured out who murdered her uncle. We had our suspicions, of course. But you were onto Lady Easton from the start. She had planned it all out so carefully, but you were not fooled."

"Just working the probabilities," Havers said as the carriage rolled smoothly along the London streets toward the solicitor's office. "That is all it is. Probabilities."

The hour was growing late by the time they arrived at the offices of Deacon & Mosley, but theirs was a busy practice and there were always solicitors and clerks working late into the night. Julius went in on his own to retrieve the document to be signed by Allendale.

He was not surprised to find Deacon still there, for the man was as dogged a fellow as Havers. Assign him a task, and he was going to stick to it until it was done.

"Lord Thorne, I did not expect you until tomorrow morning."

"I know. My apologies for imposing on you at this late hour, but the matter of ending this betrothal has become quite urgent."

His solicitor frowned, but did not probe further as to the reason. "We have prepared it in duplicate so that each of you will receive a fully executed version once all parties have signed."

"Very thoughtful of you," Julius muttered, not caring what Allendale did with his copy after it was inked. What worried him presently was Allendale panicking and running off with Sarah in order to hide out until the matter of Lord Easton's murder had been settled.

How was he to obtain his signature then?

Well, Havers had put a man onto the task of watching that pair and would have reported if they were trying to run off.

It was not long before they reached Bayswater and the neatly maintained house where Sarah and her child had been settled. The older woman who had opened the door to him the first time recognized him and allowed him and Havers entry without question.

The woman stared at Havers.

He gave a polite nod. "Mr. Havers, ma'am. The viscount is

acquainted with me."

"Acquainted, indeed," Julius muttered once the woman lumbered upstairs to advise Allendale of their arrival. "I hope he does not leap out a window to avoid you. Perhaps I ought to have left you in the carriage."

"No, it is better for Lady Gregoria's sake if he knows I have my eyes on him. Not only for her sake, but for that of the next heiress that bounder decides to court."

Allendale hurried down the stairs and stalked into the parlor where they had been left to wait.

"What do you want now, Thorne? And why did you bring *him* here?" He nodded disdainfully in the direction of Havers. "I thought we had a deal."

"We do. I am only here to get your signature on this formal acknowledgment ending your betrothal. Sign both copies, and then we shall leave. Nothing more will be required of you. And nothing will be mentioned to your family."

"So long as you do not break the law," Havers added.

Allendale snorted, shot them both a dark look, but then strode to his writing desk and hastily scrawled his name on both sets. "Satisfied?"

Julius nodded. "Take care of your child, Allendale. If you do one thing right in your life, make it that."

"Save your righteous breath, Thorne. I will never acknowledge her as mine."

"Never?" said a soft voice from behind them.

The three of them turned to see Sarah Martin standing in the doorway. She appeared frail and overset as she stared at Allendale. "But she is yours. I gave up everything for you. Lord Thorne, I am so sorry I lied to you and Lady Gregoria. I was afraid of what she would do if she knew Lord Allendale was the father of my child. But then, she spoke so kindly to me…"

Allendale rushed to her side. "Sarah, you know I will take care of you both. I gave you my word of honor."

Julius and Havers left them to work out whatever their situation was to be going forward. Havers grunted the moment they were once again settled in the Thorne carriage. "What do you think he will do, Thorne? Does he have any honor?"

"I doubt it. Who knows? I may have been harsh in my first impression of Miss Martin because of her prior employment. I think she sincerely cares for Allendale."

"He seems to care for her, too," Havers remarked.

"For her sake, I hope he does. I don't know if he will ever have the courage to marry her, though. He enjoys being a gentleman, and that also means not working hard, if at all. He was counting on Gory's dowry to pay for Miss Martin and the child. And now that he knows you are watching him, he will have to think twice before preying on some other heiress. He may have to connive his uncle into lending him funds until things quiet down. I'm sure he'll make up some excuse to soak the old goat."

"So long as he does not decide to gain inspiration from Lady Easton's actions and plot to murder his uncle," Havers remarked with a wry smile. "Perhaps I'll have another visit with Lord Allendale, just to be neighborly."

"An excellent idea." Julius hoped he was wrong about Allendale's weak character.

Lots of people were greedy, but rarely did any of them turn to murder. Nor did Sarah appear to be particularly grasping or evil, just a mother trying her best to protect her child. That she apologized for her deception spoke better of her morals, but did not completely absolve her of wrongdoing. She and Allendale had no qualms about using Gory's money for their own purposes.

Well, hopefully a visit from Havers would keep both of them from doing something foolish.

They next stopped at St. Michael's parish office to obtain the marriage license. Ambrose and Octavian were waiting for him when he arrived. Their presence had smoothed matters over, and the vicar – despite having been awakened from his slumber – issued the license without delay or complaint.

Once that was done, his brothers took the license and betrothal document into their safekeeping, and then hopped into Ambrose's carriage to return to their wives.

Julius had his own transportation and now offered to drop Havers off at his home. "Where do you live?"

A Slight Problem With The Wedding | 223

Havers laughed. "Lord Thorne, I live, eat, and breathe at the magistrate's office on Bow Street. I rarely ever go home. However, I would appreciate your delivering me to the Wallingford Arms since Lady Easton is still settled there and it would not hurt to see who pays a call on her tonight."

"Very well, but do not forget to show up at my wedding tomorrow."

Havers arched an eyebrow. "You are serious?"

"Yes, of course. I would not invite you if I did not want you there. I speak for Gory, as well."

"I am honored, but do not take offense if I fail to show up. My efforts are better spent watching Lady Easton and her maid."

"Do you think they will hatch another plot to silence Lady Gregoria before the funeral?"

Havers nodded. "I know they will. They are as frantic as cornered beasts."

"I hope they turn on each other," Julius muttered. "Do you think there is any honor among murderers?"

"Oh, I expect they will betray each other in time."

"But when?" Julius muttered, aching for Gory's ordeal to be over, one that he had brought on because of keeping silent as to his feelings.

"My lord, you have such a look on your face. Are you blaming yourself for what happened to Lady Gregoria?" Havers leaned forward as the carriage rolled along the streets of London that were starting to quiet for the night. "What if you had been the one to propose to Lady Gregoria first? No Allendale, no other suitors. Just you. The attempt on her life would still have occurred. Only, it might have been successful. Changed circumstances, changed outcome. Did you ever think of that?"

Julius raked a hand through his hair. "Do not be logical *or* philosophical about this, Havers. I just wish to be married to her already. I won't sleep a wink tonight, for I'll be too worried about what Lady Easton plans next."

"Let me and Mr. Barrow worry about her and that sour-faced maid of hers." He cast Julius a wry grin. "You'll need to be at your best on your wedding day...and especially on your wedding night, if I may be so crude as to point out the obvious. Wouldn't want Lady Gregoria thinking she ought to have stuck with Allendale."

Julius laughed.

They drew up in front of the Wallingford Arms a short while later and Havers hopped down from the carriage. "Until tomorrow, my lord."

Julius leaned back against the squabs and let out a breath as the carriage moved on, this time headed for home.

All was falling into place, and yet he was still worried.

What had he and Havers overlooked?

CHAPTER 15

GORY HAD WANTED to remain downstairs with her friends to await the return of Julius and his brothers. They were a sight, all of them pacing except for her two dowagers godmothers who were as serene as ever seated in their grand chairs and calmly sipping tea. "Wearing a hole in the carpet will not make any of the Thorne boys return faster," Lady Withnall remarked. "Why are you so tense, my dear? Is there a doubt Julius will succeed? You ought to know by now he is quite fierce when he needs to be."

"They're back," Adela said, suddenly grabbing Gory's hand.

Ambrose and Octavian marched into the parlor a moment later, smiling in triumph as they showed them the marriage license and betrothal document successfully obtained.

"Thank goodness," Gory whispered, much of the tension flowing out of her.

Leo strode to the men and took a moment to peruse the papers. "Well done, my friends." He turned to his wife and winked. "Looks like we'll be attending a wedding tomorrow."

Marigold clapped her hands and hopped up and down in delight. "The best news ever. Oh, Gory! I am so happy for you."

Everyone clustered around Gory to congratulate her.

She hugged them all, including the dowagers who had so kindly taken her under their wing when her aunt and uncle had refused to spend so much as a shilling on her. What a charming way to grow up, always being made to feel she was a waste of time and no one could possibly wish to marry her.

Indeed, no one could never accuse her aunt or uncle of doting on her.

For this reason, she found the kindness of these dowagers all the sweeter and almost came to tears as she embraced them.

Once all her friends had taken a turn congratulating her, she begged to be excused. The hour was not so late by *ton* standards, but it had been a day filled with turmoil that had left her feeling weary. Warmth curled in her belly as she hurried upstairs to the bedchamber she had taken over from Julius. She would have the lawful right to share it with him by this time tomorrow.

Would all truly go as planned?

Adela followed her up to assist her out of her gown, but Gory knew it was really a pretext to assure herself Gory was fine. "Only someone as stubborn as you would be hopping out of bed and running around town after being so badly injured," Adela gently chided, noting the fatigue in Gory's eyes. "You really ought to have let Julius handle matters while you recovered. And do not dare pretend you are in the pink of health when we can all see how each excursion drains you."

"Would you have done anything differently if it was your life at stake?" Gory asked, slipping out of her gown as they spoke. "I trust Julius, of course. I know I am in the best of hands with him. I also know that Mr. Havers and Mr. Barrow are on the task and very capable. But it is still *my* life and *my* reputation poised to be destroyed, not to mention the damage I might do to the Thorne family merely because you are all standing in support of me."

Adela sighed. "I understand. I suppose I would have been just as determined."

Gory laughed. "Would have been? You behaved exactly as I did, or have you conveniently forgotten flattening Ambrose while chasing after that thief who purloined the valuable book from the Huntsford Academy library?"

"Poor Ambrose," she muttered with a mirthful giggle, handing Gory a nightgown and then staring at it for a long moment. "You are still borrowing my clothes. Not that I mind in the least, but is there a reason you have not brought yours over yet?"

Gory released a heavy breath. "Most were ruined the night my uncle was murdered. A few were not, but I cannot bring myself to wear them ever again. The thought of holding any of my gowns or undergarments against my skin sends shivers through me. Those fiends put their hands on everything, purposely putting their blood taint on all I own."

"Oh, Gory. I am so sorry."

She nodded. "It makes me ill just thinking of it."

"How awful!" Adela hugged her fiercely. "And how stupid of me not to realize the reason. Yes, give all your clothes away or burn them. Julius will provide you with whatever you need. In the meanwhile, take anything of mine that you want."

Gory hugged her back. "I promise to stop scavenging your wardrobe soon, but give me a few more days. I need to get through the funeral first, and then I will impose on Julius to take me to my modiste for new gowns."

"Impose? He's a Thorne and will give you the moon if you asked it of him. Honestly, Gory. Did you ever believe this happy outcome was possible? All four of us making love matches…and now you, Syd, and I can call each other sisters. Having married the Thorne brothers, this is what we shall be in actuality and not merely in friendship."

Gory nodded. "It is all wonderful. However, I am not married yet. I'll be holding my breath until we exchange vows. The morning cannot come soon enough for me. I love him so much, Adela."

"I wonder if our dowager godmothers knew it all along. Do you think Lady Withnall and Lady Dayne understood this would happen for all of us?"

Gory nodded. "Quite likely, for they are all-knowing, aren't they? I only wish they had bound and gagged me before I accepted Allendale's proposal. Lady Withnall might have done it had she caught me in time."

"Oh, yes," Adela said with a light laugh. "That little termagant can be quite daunting when she wants to be."

"Well, this betrothal mess has righted itself now. All that is left to do is bring the villains to justice. I don't know that Julius and I can ever move forward until that happens."

"It will happen, Gory. Havers is quite a clever fellow and has managed to stay a step ahead of everyone, even you and Julius. That is quite impressive, isn't it? I don't know anyone smarter than the pair of you...and do not tell Ambrose I just said that," she added with a light gasp and chuckled.

Gory climbed under the covers once Adela left.

She did not know whether Julius would join her in this bed tonight, but hoped he would consider it. She longed to be held in his arms and feel the heat of his body beside her. What was the point in waiting for tomorrow night when she already felt bonded to him?

Perhaps it was only a bond of stitches, for they both had been injured due to her uncle's murder.

Did these incidents not stitch their hearts together, as well?

She was about to drift off to sleep when she heard him enter the bedchamber. "Julius?"

"Right here, love," he said with a deep resonance to his voice that she found so familiar and comforting.

How deeply she had ached for him from the moment they'd met.

She heard the quiet click of the door as he closed it.

"Ambrose showed me the marriage license. Is it really happening?" She sat up, smiling as she watched him approach the bed, a golden aura settling about him as he stood strong and proud, illuminated by firelight.

"Without a doubt, love. Marriage. Tomorrow." He gave her a soft kiss on the lips that was nevertheless filled with heat and yearning, and then moved away to sit on one of the big chairs by the hearth while he took off his jacket and boots.

He did not appear to be having difficulty moving his arm, which was a good thing. He had shielded her and taken the bullet meant for her. Her heart would have been forever in torment had he been seriously hurt.

But he made the injury seem like nothing, hardly more than a scratch.

Perhaps this was all it was to him, for he was much more stoic than she was and nothing seemed to daunt him.

Had she not been there to see Dr. Farthingale stitch his wound, she would never have known he was hurt.

Her own recovery had not gone quite as smoothly.

Even now, her head was throbbing and the dull pain was constant because a few days of lying quietly was not enough to heal any person receiving such a brutal blow. Hopefully, she was on the mend despite pushing her endurance, and a good night's rest would see her restored. "Julius…"

"What, love?"

"You are not thinking of passing another uncomfortable night in that big chair, are you?"

He smiled as he removed his cravat and waistcoat. "I expect so. Do you have any other suggestions?"

"Yes…must I say it?"

He cast her a knowing grin as he walked toward her again, looking quite irresistible while unbuttoning his shirt.

She was suddenly very much aware of him.

There was something so beautifully appealing and masculine about his standing before her with his shirt casually open to reveal the golden glaze of his skin and the dusting of dark hair across the expanse of his broad chest.

His gaze turned hot, his eyes now fiery embers as he studied her in return.

She knew what was running through his mind, for she was having the same improper thoughts about him. Did he dare touch her yet? She hoped he would, and was it not obvious she wanted him to?

He seemed hesitant despite his obvious desire.

"Julius…" She understood his hesitation, for he had a highly developed sense of honor and would need considerable coaxing before agreeing to 'despoil' her before their wedding night.

But was it not more important to seize whatever happiness was offered to them in this moment? Nothing was certain in life. If Lady Easton's third attempt to silence her succeeded, she did not want to die without ever having experienced a night in his arms.

"I feel as though we have just run a gauntlet," Julius muttered, now settling in the chair beside the bed as he contemplated what to do.

Honestly, why was he thinking so hard about this?

"We are still running that gauntlet," Gory reminded him. "Which is why I hope you will understand what I am going to say next." She licked her lips and then cleared her throat. "I want us to share your bed. Now. Tonight. With all the implications I am sure are now rushing through your mind. Everyone believes we must have already done...*you know*. And we will be married in a matter of hours anyway."

"My brothers know I would not touch you before we are wed."

"Oh?" She tried not to look too disappointed.

He must have found her dismay amusing, for he reached over and gave her another light kiss on the lips. "Lord, you taste sweet."

She sighed. "I do not need to wait until we are married to know you respect me. Honestly, Julius. Isn't respect highly overrated?"

"No, it is not," he said, laughing as he removed his shirt, displaying the rippling muscles kept hidden beneath the fine, lawn fabric. "But are you sure, Gory?"

She stared at the unsightly row of stitches now visible on his arm. The area along the seam of those stitches was inflamed and red, and patches of discolored yellowish-purple bruising were visible around the outer edges. "I'm sure. But I suppose I will understand if you are not feeling well enough to–"

"Me? I'm fine."

Was this not Julius?

He would never admit to feeling anything other than *fine*.

Indeed, this had to be his favorite word. I am *fine*. All will be *fine*. Ignore the blood dripping down my arm.

Fortunately, no blood was dripping now.

But it had been at the time.

"And you, Gory?"

"What? Me? I am in the pink of health."

He snorted.

"I am," she insisted.

She had earlier unpinned her hair that now fell down her back in a tumble. She carefully ran her fingers through the curls, trying her best to avoid her own stitches as she put order to them. Dr. Farthingale had planned to take them out tomorrow, but she was going to insist on waiting another few days so that nothing interfered with tomorrow's wedding or her uncle's funeral the following day.

She cast him a come hither look. "I want this, Julius."

A slow smile swept across his face. "Lady Gregoria, are you seducing me?"

She chuckled. "I would if I knew how. I am hardly a temptress. But I do not see the point in waiting when I am willing and this big bed is right in front of you with me already in it. It is crying out to be used." She playfully put a hand to her ear. "Can you not hear it calling out to you?"

"Loud and clear, love." He set aside the chair and climbed into bed beside her, gathering her in his arms. He had kept his trousers on, no doubt on purpose, which meant he was not going to claim her tonight. But any disappointment she might have felt quickly melted away as he next positioned himself over her, propping on his elbows as he looked upon her with enough heat to melt her bones.

"How about a compromise," he offered.

She nodded. "What sort of compromise?"

"This." He proceeded to show her what she had been missing while ignoring all the marriage mart affairs, all the elegant balls and routs, and instead keeping her nose buried in books and research these past few years.

His kisses were slow and delicious, the soft grind of his mouth on hers deep and utterly decadent, as sinful as a Viennese dessert. Her heartbeat immediately quickened and hot tingles coursed through her veins. But it was the ache that came along with the delight that surprised her, this overwhelming need to share intimate moments such as this one over a lifetime together. Was this not exactly what he was offering? Each kiss and each loving caress represented his promise to love her, to build a life with her and protect her.

She melted completely when he said it aloud, his words a

match to his actions. "I love you, Gory."

Once, and then twice he put voice to his feelings and trailed searing kisses down her body. She echoed the same back to him, for after all these years of guarding her heart, pretending she could manage on her own and fooling herself into believing she never needed to find love, here was Julius offering this very gift of himself to her.

How could she not love him back with all the fullness of her heart?

She held onto him as his every touch scorched her and marked her as his, as his love brought goodness and trust, hope and dreams, and scrubbed away the evil taint of that dreadful night and the unhappiness of her past.

Julius was offering a new leaf, a new chapter, a new book of her life.

She was ready and eager when he untied the bow at the front of her nightgown and slipped his hand inside to cup her breast.

She cooed when he began to gently knead it.

She actually *cooed* like a little bird.

He cast her a wickedly affectionate smile and then ran his thumb across the taut bud of her breast in a light, swirling motion. "Make that sound for me again, love."

Her eyes widened. "No, it is appalling."

"It is beautiful," he insisted, taking the bud into his mouth and…

Oh, sweet heaven.

She was going to bill and coo and squawk like a magpie if he did not stop. But he knew what he was doing to her, knew those slow, languid circles he was making with his tongue would leave her hot and mindless. "Julius," she cried with a soft, wrenching moan.

Then his hands…oh, those beautiful, rough hands, slid down her body and one came to rest between her legs. He gave her no more than a moment to absorb the intimacy of the gesture before his sensual fingers began to stroke her *there.*

She clutched his head, not wanting him to stop whatever he was doing because these sensations he aroused in her felt so good and right, even though she did not think she was doing anything right herself. She purred and moaned, wrapped her fingers in his hair and tugged his head, pushed and wriggled against his hand as he continued his bold but gentle onslaught.

An unbearably hot, sweet pressure mounted within her. "Julius, what's happening to me?"

"I have you, love. Let yourself go. You'll always be safe with me."

She knew this, had always felt it was true, and this allowed her to give herself over to these sensations because she trusted him so completely. Starlight and sparkles burst all around her as she lost control and tumbled into a splendid oblivion. How else was she to describe this incredible feeling? Perhaps not so much tumbling as floating, because now that he had her wrapped in his arms, she was gently being carried upward toward the heavens. Nor was it oblivion so much as a newly discovered place within her own body, a place that was beautiful and freeing.

In trusting him, she felt the long existing tangles of her heart unravel.

And she was making those *cooing* sounds again.

Julius kissed her, his manner gently soothing the rampant beats of her heart. "Better now, love?" he asked, his expression smug and conquering as her breathing calmed.

He stared at her with mirth in his eyes.

Had she just made a fool of herself? "Julius, I am so sorry."

"Whatever for?"

"This…this ridiculous, wildly out of control response. I didn't know what I was doing, or what I was supposed to do."

"Gad, Gory. You were perfect." He propped on his elbows, for he was still atop her and trying to keep his full weight off her. "So beautiful and perfect. I'm glad you enjoyed yourself."

She could not resist laughing. "That is an understatement. It was thrilling."

"For me, too."

"But I did not touch you."

"Love," he said, kissing the tip of her nose, "you touched my heart as no one else ever could."

"Well, that is all right then," she murmured, nestling against him and resting her head on his chest when he eased off her and rolled onto his back.

After a moment, he tucked a finger under her chin and tipped her face up so that their gazes met. "It was the best. Never doubt it."

He then cast her another conquering smile.

Perhaps she had done something right, after all.

He seemed quite pleased.

"Yes, the very, very best," she agreed, falling asleep with his arms wrapped around her.

Sometime nearing dawn, a movement startled Gory.

She realized it was Julius shifting closer to rest a hand atop her hip, as though feeling the need to hold onto her even in sleep.

His touch felt wonderful and warmed her.

She did not care that the fire had died out in the grate or that there was a slight chill to the night air.

Julius was beside her and it was paradise.

She turned slowly toward him, wanting to study his handsome face in repose. The graying light of approaching morn filtered in through the windows, allowing her to make out more than mere shadows.

As her eyes adjusted to the dim threads cast upon their cozy bed, she could see the outline of his firm jaw and patrician nose.

She ran her hand lightly along the muscled length of his arm, the good one that was uninjured, and held her breath as she trailed her fingers along the breadth of his chest.

This elicited a soft growl from him. "Is it morning already?"

"Almost, I think. I have no idea, but I cannot sleep. Are you not too excited to sleep?"

He chuckled as he stretched his fine body and gave her a glimpse of his splendidly rippling muscles while he flexed them. "Big day for us."

She nodded and smiled.

"You look so pretty by the dawn's light, Gory." He sat up and took her hand, raising it to his lips to kiss it before he rolled out of bed and strode toward the window to fully draw aside the curtains and allow the hazy streaks of sunlight in. "The staff will be stirring soon."

He glanced at his side of the bed and shook his head. "We ought to make up that half of the bed so that–"

"It isn't necessary, Julius. They'll never believe you slept anywhere but beside me."

He shrugged and attempted to make it up anyway.

She helped him, only because she realized this troubled him more than it did her. This was his nature, this need to protect her not only from physical harm but from any disgrace. He did a remarkable job, and she had to admit one would have to look closely to see that his side had been slept in. Of course, a well trained maid would know. One only had to feel the warmth of the sheets.

She was not going to point this out to him.

Instead, she smiled up at him. "Job well done."

He kissed her lightly on the lips. "I'll gather my things and get out of here. Syd and Adela are going to come knocking on our door any moment now."

"But it's still early."

He laughed. "Get used to having a family that actually cares about you. I'm sure they have been awake for an hour already, pacing in their rooms while waiting for the sun to peek above the horizon before bursting in here."

"They wouldn't dare just walk in, not while you are in here with me."

"Are you serious? Since when do you or they ever respect proper boundaries?"

She cleared her throat. "We would for something like this."

He laughed again and planted another kiss on her lips. "Doubtful, but enjoy your morning because those two army generals are going to wage a campaign to pamper you relentlessly."

"Sounds nice."

He kissed her yet again, and then gave her neck a light nuzzle, careful not to leave a mark on her skin from the scratchy stubble of his night's growth of beard. "Enjoy their onslaught."

Gory smiled as he strode out.

All she needed to do was take a quick bath and wash her hair. Once her hair dried, she would ask Adela's maid to style it with a little added flair to mark this special day. Nothing too drastic, but perhaps a few flowers in her curls or some glittery clasps.

Julius turned out to be right.

One would think her friends were preparing her for the queen's visit for all the fuss they made over the simple chore of preparing her for her wedding. A tub was rolled in, much as she expected. Then Syd and Adela poured fragrant oils in it.

Oh, dear.

She hoped Julius would find these fragrances to his liking because they were going to soak into her skin and not be her usual scent at all. They were pleasant enough, tones of vanilla and honey, and left her skin silky smooth. But would Julius be put off because these were something new?

Or was she thinking too hard about this?

After all, her friends had been through their own wedding day and night, so should she not rely on their experience?

"Gown next," Syd said. "I would have you borrow one of mine but Adela's are much prettier. Mine are mostly sturdy woolens meant for the colder Scottish weather."

"I'll be right back," Adela said and sprinted out of the bedchamber.

She returned with an armful of gowns and two maids in tow who carried in shoes and undergarments. "These are new and have not yet been worn," she said, pointing to some silk camisoles and an assortment of chemises. "And these three gowns are new, as well. Take your pick. Or I can bring in more."

One would think a maelstrom had torn through the bedchamber by the time Gory's outfit was chosen. She and her friends agreed upon a lovely, tea rose silk that suited her complexion and seemed to brighten her eyes.

In truth, Julius was the one who put the pink in her cheeks and the sparkle in her eyes because she could not think of what he had done to her last night without blushing or smiling.

On a more serious note, Syd and Adela also helped her select a gown for tomorrow's funeral. Adela's maid brought in several that were of more somber colors, and Gory chose a violet silk that was so dark in shade, it appeared to be indigo. She thought it was a perfect choice, not quite black and not at all frivolous.

She felt relief in getting that unhappy chore out of the way.

As the ten o'clock hour approached, they all climbed into their carriages. Julius insisted on riding with her since he was serious about protecting her at all times and had no intention of ceding the task to anyone else, not even his brothers.

Before Gory knew it, they were standing together in front of the altar and exchanging vows. As Julius looked into her eyes and promised to always love and protect her, a physical change came over her. It was as though a heavy spirit weighing her down for years had suddenly lifted off her and disappeared. Gone. Done. Defeated. Her heart felt lighter and she was suddenly imbued with a hope and happiness she had never felt before.

When the vicar pronounced them husband and wife, she threw her arms around Julius's neck and struggled not to sob as she said, "Thank you."

He closed his arms around her waist and lifted her to him, holding tight as he whispered back, "I have you, Gory. Always. You're mine to love and protect forever now."

The handful of friends and family present were about to come forward to congratulate them when the chapel doors suddenly burst open and a pistol-wielding harridan came charging at Gory, shrieking, "You've ruined everything!"

Julius flung himself over her at the same time two shots rang out, or was it merely the echo of only one?

No, it had to be two.

The shrieking woman suddenly went quiet...and so did Julius.

Gory's heart shattered, for she had felt the jerk of his body atop hers as she fell backward against the stone altar that broke her fall.

But she knew...oh, she knew... Julius had been hit.

"No, no!" Her voice was barely above a whisper and strangled with agonizing sorrow. "Julius, no! Tell me you are all right. Julius!"

There was a flurry of activity around her.

She ignored the chaotic whirl, all her attention on Julius and how to keep him alive. "Julius! Speak to me, please. *Please*," she begged, willing to strike any bargain to exchange her life for his.

After a moment that felt like an eternity, he groaned and struggled to sit up. "Bloody blazes. Gory, are you hurt?"

"You're talking!" She squeezed out from under him, daring not to feel elated until she had managed to inspect his body.

After ordering him to stay down, she searched for signs of blood on his light gray morning coat.

A red stain was beginning to spread along the meaty muscle of his uninjured arm.

Was it just his upper arm the mad woman had struck?

She dared not feel any relief yet, for the mere fact of his being shot was serious. And *twice* in a matter of days, no less. Was it another graze? Or had the bullet lodged deep and needed to be dug out? "We must get him to Dr. Farthingale's surgery at once."

She had no sooner said the words than Ambrose and Octavian fashioned their arms together to form a stretcher and carried a protesting Julius out his carriage.

"I can walk!" Julius bellowed.

"Shut up, little brother," Octavian and Ambrose replied at the same moment.

Leo had tossed his arms protectively around Marigold, but now released her and stepped forward to take charge of the ladies as well as the vicar who was pale and trembling. The saintly man was the one who required all the help because Gory and her friends, the dowagers included, were quicker to regain their wits and now wanted to leap into action. "Take care of your brother," Leo called out to the Thorne men. "I'll take care of matters here."

"I'm going with Julius," Gory insisted.

As she hurried after them, she realized the crazed woman had likely been killed. She was lying so motionless on the chapel's cold, stone floor. Kneeling beside her was Havers and two of his constables who must have been hard on her heels and shot the shrieking woman at the same time she got off her shot and hit Julius.

Havers glanced up at her, his expression pained. "Lady

Gregoria, I'm so sorry. I was mere seconds behind her. I…"

"This isn't your fault," Gory assured him, and then rushed out to climb into the carriage with Julius.

Ambrose insisted on joining them while Octavian agreed to return to the others. "Take care of him, Ambrose. You can count on Leo and me to deal with everything else." He cast Gory a feeble smile. "I would send Syd with you, but I think you are as adept as she is in treating wounds. Keep the little squirt alive, will you?"

She nodded.

"Little squirt? I'm going to punch you, Octavian. I swear, I will," Julius said with a pained laugh.

Octavian nodded. "I look forward to the day you have the strength to manage it."

No more was said as their carriage rolled away at a breakneck clip. Gory insisted on removing his jacket, and then Ambrose helped her slice open his shirt sleeve because Julius refused to walk out onto the street shirtless, even if it was merely to walk into Dr. Farthingale's surgery. "Others might be in his waiting room."

She did not argue the point since removing the sleeve was all she needed to do in order to examine the damage. Unlike the first time, this shot had lodged in his arm, just as she feared. She had worn a silk shawl that matched the lovely tea rose gown she was wearing and now slipped it off her shoulders to use as a tourniquet of a sort because she had to stem his bleeding. "This is all my fault," she started to say, but was immediately silenced by both Thornes.

"You cannot be blamed for the cruelty of your aunt," Julius insisted. "She's the one with the wicked plots. She's the one who tried to have you and your uncle murdered, and when that failed, tried to have the blame for his murder put on you."

"Is it over yet, do you think?" Gory let out a shaky breath, for the red stain was spreading quickly on the shawl and she did not like this at all.

Bleeding out was the greatest danger at the moment.

Nor did it help that they were bouncing around the carriage while it careened toward the doctor's surgery. She dared not slow the driver because getting Julius promptly treated was of the greatest urgency.

Julius gave her a light kiss on the cheek. "Don't worry about me, love. I'll be fine. I promise you."

Ah, yes.

There was that word again. *Fine*. I'll be *fine*.

She prayed it would be so.

Dr. Farthingale had just finished with a patient when they hurried in. There were others seated in the waiting room, but he took Julius first. "Gory, come in with him. I'll need you to assist me. Your Grace, might I suggest you wait in my office. You'll find it more comfortable."

Ambrose nodded. "Do not worry about me. See to my brother."

"Scrub your hands thoroughly, Gory," the doctor told her once he and Ambrose had assisted Julius into the examination room and onto the table.

He ordered Julius to lie quietly, and then left his side to wash up, as well. "I boil my instruments after each use," he began to explain. "I also insist on keeping this surgery spotless. Dirtiness is what leads to infection. The ancient civilizations seemed to understand this, but so much of their knowledge has been lost over the centuries."

He continued to speak as he now moved on to swab the area of Julius's arm and clean away the blood. "You were not as lucky this time, my lord. The bullet is lodged in the muscle. I'll give you a sedative, but it is not going to be strong enough to have you feel no pain."

Julius nodded. "Gory, if this scares you, I–"

"I'm staying. Do not feel the need to be stoic for me. Cry like a baby, if you must. I know you are the bravest, most wonderful man alive, and nothing you say or do in here will ever change my opinion of you. So, all you have to do is stay *alive*. That is all I need you to do for me."

She held his hand while the doctor dug into his arm and dislodged the hot ball of lead. The pain had to be unbearable, but Julius seemed to handle it, for he hardly cried out. However, he did squeeze her hand awfully hard more than a time or two.

She did not mind, for it was more important to provide any comfort she could.

Seeing him suffer was so much worse than having to suffer a wound herself. Since he did not need her falling apart over him, she held herself together and followed Dr. Farthingale's instructions as he stitched Julius's arm.

"There," Dr. Farthingale said upon finishing his handiwork. He studied this new row of stitches that matched the smaller row Julius sported on his other arm.

Gory let out the breath she had been holding.

"This is awful," she said when the doctor left the room for a moment to report to Ambrose.

"What?" Julius asked groggily, too weak to sit up yet. "My arm?"

"No, Dr. Farthingale did a perfect job on that. I was referring to the situation, this ongoing danger to you now that you are shackled to me. Julius, you mustn't keep trying to save me."

He snorted.

"I'm serious."

"All right, next time I shall grab your little body and plant it in front of me to use as a shield," he said with obvious sarcasm. "Sure, let me break my sacred vows to honor and protect you. No problem."

She sighed. "I think Havers or one of his constables shot the woman. She wasn't moving, so I think she might be dead."

"Too bad he couldn't stop her *before* she managed to get off her shot. Did you see who it was? The maid, Flossie? Or her sister?"

"I couldn't tell. I'm sure we will hear the entire story once we get home." She smiled at the remark because the Thorne townhouse was now her home, although she expected Julius would insist on their acquiring a residence of their own in the coming months.

Dr. Farthingale gave Julius some apple cider to drink, had him rest for a little while longer because he had lost quite a bit of blood, and then put his arm in a sling to keep it from getting knocked about for the next few days.

Only then did he allow Julius to be taken home.

"Gad, we look a mess." Julius cast her a pained grin as they settle together on the seat bench opposite Ambrose.

Ambrose groaned. "An understatement. Well, it makes for exciting storytelling, something to tell your grandchildren in later years. Although, I would not encourage them to have such wild adventures when their turn comes to court and marry."

"I've ruined Adela's gown." Gory sighed as she glanced at the bloodstains on it, for it was one thing to ruin her own gowns, but to also destroy Adela's? And this tea rose silk was so lovely and delicate.

"I'll buy her a dozen more," Ambrose said, shrugging it off. "She'll chide me and insist she doesn't need any. But this is what makes the three of you – Adela, Syd, and you – so perfect for us. It is our hearts you treasure, and that is something priceless."

"Gory also treasures the Huntsford forensics laboratory," Julius teased. "Stop her if she pulls out a scalpel and tries to dissect me."

"Julius!" But she knew he was starting to feel better if he had the wherewithal to tease her and toss jests. "I think you have been cut up enough for a lifetime."

He laughed but soon sobered. "Gory, let me take you away from London. We needn't attend your uncle's funeral. Ambrose and Adela can represent us there."

She pursed her lips, wanting to agree with him.

It was an impossible situation, but she had to attend the funeral and allow the last of this ordeal to play out. Also, she wanted to pay proper respect to her uncle. They were both meant to die that night, and this formed a sort of bond that had never existed between them while he was alive. "Do you think Havers will arrest my aunt and her cohorts now? Will this latest incident provide the proof to bring his investigation to a close?"

Julius released a breath. "I hope so. Three attempts on your life are more than enough. Besides, I have no more arms to give to their wayward aim."

Gory's eyes began to tear.

She had held herself together in Dr. Farthingale's surgery, but it all suddenly felt too much for her.

Julius leaned over and gave her a kiss on the cheek. "Stay strong for me, love. Do not falter now that we are almost at the end."

Almost.

But not ended yet.

"Havers might be waiting for us at home, ready to give us a full report," Ambrose said.

Julius nodded. "Let's hope so."

They rode on through the busy streets, the three of them now silent and lost to their thoughts.

Gory listened to the din of pedestrians and carriages converging on each other, of drivers shouting to each other to watch where they were going, and bystanders dodging out of the way. Hawkers could also be heard on occasion selling their wares.

The ride along the park was quieter, and Gory was relieved when they finally turned onto the pretty square where they resided and Ambrose's magnificent townhouse came into view.

Julius insisted on stepping down from the carriage on his own, scowling at Octavian when he rushed out of the house to help him. Wisely, Octavian backed away and allowed his brother to manage on his own. "Stubborn arse," Octavian muttered with a sigh of sufferance before turning to Gory and helping her down. "Are you all right?"

She nodded. "Yes, just a bit shaken."

"Everyone was worried about you. My brother, too, of course. But they like you better."

Julius chuckled. "Shut up, Octavian. Have you heard anything more from Havers?"

"He's here and has news, but he refused to tell us anything before you returned."

Ambrose overheard the remark as he stepped down. "I'll have Greeves set out tea for all of us while we listen to what he has to say."

Gory wanted to hold onto Julius's arm as they strolled in, but she did not know which arm to take since both were injured. Julius addressed the matter by taking hold of her hand with the one not in a sling and entwining his fingers with hers as they walked in.

He kept hold of her hand even as they settled on the settee in the parlor to hear what Havers had to say. They both looked a mess, but no one dared point it out since they were all eager to hear what the magistrate's top man would reveal.

"As Lord Thorne is aware," Havers said, nodding toward the door as Mr. Barrow hurriedly walked in to join them, "I spent the night at the Wallingford Arms to keep watch on Lady Easton and her maid. We have enough to arrest them both."

This was met with murmurs of relief from all of them.

"I think her maid will now give us the confession we need because her sister is dead, her brother-in-law is in custody, and there have been too many attempts on Lady Gregoria's life to pretend she was the one who devised the plot to kill Lord Easton."

"Thank goodness," Lady Dayne muttered.

Havers turned to Gory. "My constable was not trying to kill the sister, but one's aim cannot always be counted on to be accurate under these circumstances. The woman ought to have known better than to draw her weapon, and she got what she deserved. It was pure evil intent on her part since she knew we were moments behind her and she could not escape capture."

"Then it was Flossie's sister who shot Julius?" Gory asked.

Havers nodded. "Yes. Unfortunately, she managed to elude us last night. I still have no idea where she hid out. Hopefully, the man we have in custody will be able to tell us. It is now confirmed he is her husband. With each bit of information, the net tightens around Lady Easton."

"If you did not know where Flossie's sister was hiding out, then how were you able to follow her?" Syd asked. "When did you pick up her trail?"

"Never did pick up her trail," Havers admitted. "However, we knew that if she had somehow managed to learn Lady Gregoria and Lord Thorne were to marry this morning, she would go to the church to stop them."

Julius frowned. "How could she know we were to marry?"

"She may have been watching this townhouse, or heard the

news from a servant who heard it from another servant...and so on. Who knows? All that matters is we knew this is where she had to go to stop your marriage from taking place."

"Yet, you were not at the church to grab her the moment she arrived. What happened?" Ambrose asked.

Havers cast him a pained look. "Alas, Your Grace. To my great dismay, I was called into the magistrate's office as we were about to leave, and this delayed us a precious few moments. The magistrate wanted to tell me that the husband we still have in custody offered to give us his full confession. I will get to that man next. I'm sure he will not play coy with us once he learns his wife is dead. There'll be no loyalty among thieves now."

"What is to happen at tomorrow's funeral?" Gory asked. "Should Julius and I go? This is what we had planned on doing. I would still like to attend, but let me hear your reasons if you think we should not."

Havers shrugged. "I think there is little danger now. We have just one more loose end to tie up and then I believe we are done."

"And what is that loose end?" Julius asked.

Mr. Barrow now stepped forward. "It is the matter of the Easton solicitor, Reginald Mayfield."

"I knew he was involved," Gory muttered. "Such a wretchedly oily man."

"He and Lady Easton have been carrying on an affair for well over a year now," Mr. Barrow said.

"Ew!" Marigold blurted, her eyes wide as she stared aghast at her husband. "You suspected as much. I thought you were being too cynical."

Leo sighed. "I'm sorry I was proved right."

Gory's thoughts were becoming a jumble. "Julius saw Mayfield's calling card on the salver in Lord Allendale's entry hall. Wasn't Mr. Mayfield helping him?"

"No," Havers said.

"Then what was he doing with Allendale?" Syd asked.

Lady Withnall was first with the answer. "Attempting to blackmail him, of course."

Havers arched an eyebrow. "That is exactly right. Well done,

Lady Withnall."

Lady Dayne set down her teacup and regarded her friend in surprise. "How did you guess the truth, Phoebe?"

"Logic," she replied.

Octavian shook his head. "I would not have guessed this, and I pride myself on being logical."

"I do not think you are as logical as you believe you are," Syd said to her husband. "You must admit, falling in love with me was about as far from logical as a man could get and still be considered sane. Thank goodness you were not thinking clearly at the time…well, one could even say you were not thinking at all. I was nothing but trouble for you."

Adela laughed. "All true, but may we move on? How did you figure out Mayfield's involvement? And how exactly was he involved in the murder of Lord Easton?"

"Yes, do tell," Gory said, listening intently as Havers proceeded.

"We believe Allendale overheard Mayfield and Lady Easton furtively discussing your inheritance at one of the Society affairs they attended several months ago."

She nodded. "That would explain Allendale's sudden interest in me."

"When Mayfield realized Lord Allendale was actively courting you, he knew the man had to be stopped before he got you to the altar."

"Does this mean they intended to murder Allendale, too?" Gory asked.

"Perhaps it was a passing thought, but you were the one standing between Lady Easton and the inheritance, so I think you were always their primary target. Mayfield must have found out about Allendale's secret relation with…well, you know what I am getting at," he said, referring to Sarah Martin. "He reasoned that Allendale could be extorted into breaking off the betrothal. He had left his calling card as a warning. Lord Allendale is fortunate they chose to take this less violent approach to ridding themselves of him."

Julius snorted. "One rat taking care of another rat."

Havers paused to take the cup of tea offered as Greeves rolled in a teacart. "You and your uncle were always the targets, Lady Gregoria. It became obvious your uncle had to go as soon as possible because he had taken up with that widow, you see. He was quite serious about her. Perhaps divorce was never an option, but Lady Easton could not risk it. Both of you had to die."

Mr. Barrow now chimed in. "Lord Allendale is very fortunate they did not add him to their list of murder victims. It was a close thing, to be sure. But when Mayfield realized the viscount could be persuaded by blackmail into breaking off the betrothal, this is what he set about doing. This would gain them time to get at you again, Lady Gregoria, in addition to making Mayfield a little profit on the side by demanding payment from the viscount for his silence."

"But all their plans were falling apart because Lord Thorne was in love with Gory and determined to marry her," Lady Dayne remarked.

"Exactly, m'lady." Mr. Barrow shook his head. "I have come across many disreputable characters in my line of work, but these...sometimes I think I am getting too old to be in this business."

"You save lives and stop crimes," Julius said, "and this is invaluable."

"What happens next?" Gory asked.

"We now arrest Mayfield and your aunt's maid," Havers said.

"And what about my aunt?"

"She will be taken into custody, as well. For now, we shall hold her at the Wallingford Arms. It is up to the magistrate to decide where to confine her, but she will be charged with the murder of her husband and not be permitted to attend his funeral. After all, what is the point when she is the one who killed him?"

CHAPTER 16

AS JULIUS ESCORTED Gory to their bedchamber at the end of the evening, he realized that attending to his husbandly duties would take quite a bit of strategy since he had one arm in a sling and hurting like blazes while the other arm was not in a sling but also hurt like blazes.

Of course, he had no intention of letting Gory know he was feeling any discomfort because this was their wedding night and he did not want her treating him like a delicate patient. He wanted her hot and eager because he meant to claim her tonight.

It came as no surprise to him when Gory began to fuss over him the moment they entered their quarters. She assisted him out of his clothes and into his black silk banyan that was easy enough to slip off when the time was right.

In turn, he unlaced Gory's gown and smiled as she took it off, leaving her only in her chemise, a lovely gossamer garment that hid nothing of her body. His heart pumped a little faster as he watched her set aside her shoes and watched while she slid the stockings off her legs.

Beautiful legs.

He would take over this task for her next time.

She looked so exquisitely delicious.

Nor did she appear shy about shedding her clothes and remaining in nothing but her chemise, even though she was shy by nature. However, he knew she already felt immeasurably bonded to him.

He liked that she trusted him so completely.

Did he not feel the same about her?

Was he not happiest whenever she was with him?

"We do not have to do anything other than sleep tonight, Julius. I do not understand how you can possibly be feeling up to–"

"I am fine."

"You always say this, but you are clearly not in any position to–"

He cut her off again. "That is entirely the point."

She looked up at him in confusion, her expression adorable as she stared at him with big, bright eyes and a tumble of curls framing her sweet face. "What exactly is the point?"

"Our positioning." He cleared his throat, for he wasn't certain Gory was adventurous enough yet to go along with his suggestion. "I want to claim you. You wish to be claimed, do you not?"

She nodded. "Very much."

"Good," he said, trying not to grin because she looked so earnest. "There is a way to accomplish it."

"How? You winced the entire time I helped you off with your shirt. You'll rip your stitches if you put any weight on your arms."

"Precisely why I am not going to do that." He took the small wooden chair beside the bed and carried it closer to the hearth. If they were both going to strip naked, they might as well be warmed by the fire blazing nicely now that he had tossed several more pieces of wood into the flames.

Gory watched him as he strove to position the chair properly. "What are you doing?"

"I do not have to claim you in a bed," he explained, motioning to the chair.

"Are you suggesting you can do this in...*that*?" Her eyes widened as she walked a slow circle around the chair. "A little, wooden thing? How?"

He settled onto it and held out his arms to her. "You need to sit on my lap."

But he stopped her when she was about to simply sit down. "Um, not quite like that. You need to face me and straddle me, as a man does when on a saddle."

She coughed. "Are you serious?"

He cast her a wicked grin. "Yes, Gory. Do you trust me?"

"You know I do." She smiled and tentatively complied. "This feels quite naughty."

His blood immediately heated as she straddled him.

Sweet heaven.

"It is naughty." His grin widened. "Are you willing, love?"

She wrapped her arms around his neck and pressed her body to his. "Eager and willing with you."

"Good," he said in a raspy murmur, "because I think you're going to like this."

He certainly planned to enjoy himself.

It was not long before they had shed the last of their clothing.

Gory looked spectacular by firelight, her body pink and smooth, and the rosy tips of her breasts tasting like honey and a hint of vanilla as he closed his mouth over one ample mound and gave a lick of his tongue. At the same time, he stroked her between her thighs to ready her for his entrance, and was not surprised when it did not take long to accomplish the desired result because their bodies seemed to have been made for each other.

They both knew it.

They both felt the perfection of it.

He had removed his arm from its sling, but it hurt like a demon so he merely wrapped that arm around her waist to hold her steady while the less injured one did most of the work. She closed her eyes and gave herself over to him, to his fingers stroking her intimately and readying her for his entrance.

All manner of feelings overcame him as he entered her and filled her. The mindless, primal craving, of course. That heat and hunger could not be denied as his fingers traced the outline of her beautiful form.

But there was also a sense of oneness of their hearts, of the peace in knowing this was the woman who would share a lifetime with him. Hers was the lovely face he would see each morning when he awoke, and her smile was the smile that would brighten each day.

She had closed her eyes, and this allowed him to watch her expression as her own primal needs surfaced. He saw her awareness and a moment of embarrassment as these new sensations washed over her, and felt her trust in him as she gave herself over to his touch and guidance. They were wrapped together in a bubble, only the two of them existing in this moment.

He tasted her as they fell into an easy rhythm of their bodies, and he inhaled the sweet, hot scent of her.

She tasted of warm honey and he could not get enough, for she aroused all his senses.

Her soft *coos* and purrs of pleasure drove him wild.

He buried his hand in her hair, his fingers plunging and sliding along the lush, silken strands. "Gory, my sweet, sweet wife. I love you."

"Julius, I'm…"

"I have you, love," he said, kissing her and knowing she was nearing her release. Lord help him, he was going to burst at any moment, too. But he wanted her to be pleasured first and silently praised heaven when she tumbled over that glorious edge.

He held her and kissed her deeply, kissed her on the mouth to absorb her cries, and followed soon after with his own explosive release that was as forceful as a cannon burst. Grunting and growling, he spilled all he had inside of him as he reached his heights of pleasure. But this was his own fault for not touching – or ever desiring to touch – anyone other than Gory for too long to count.

She was all he ever wanted.

He knew it the moment he first set eyes on her.

She still had her arms wrapped around him, holding onto him tightly as she recovered her composure, her breaths steadying and her heart no longer rampant but falling into an easy beat.

He gave her cheek a light caress as he recovered from the heights of his own release. "That was nice, love."

She laughed. "That was scandalous."

"But felt so good, right?" The arm he had taken out of the sling was a fiery burn along the length of it, so he dropped it limply to his side and held her close with just the one less injured arm that also ached, but it was a manageably dull pain and easily ignored.

Mostly, he just felt a great satisfaction. "Truly, Gory. How do you feel? Did I hurt you?"

"No, it all felt wonderful. There is a lot to be said for proper positioning." She cast him an impish but affectionate smirk. "You know I am never going to look at a chair the same way again."

He chuckled. "Nor will I."

He gently lifted her off him and then rose to pour some water onto a dry cloth. After dampening it, he returned to her side and began to wipe the mess of his discharge from her thighs and intimate spot. The cloth came away with a spot of blood on it, too, since this had been Gory's first time.

He set aside the cloth, feeling a moment of regret that this experience was not more romantic for her. But she did not seem to mind or appear disappointed at all. He was glad for it because her happiness was important to him.

He showed her how much she meant to him by taking her into his arms again and pouring every measure of his love and his heart into a scorching, searing kiss.

She was his now.

His.

And he would always be grateful to the Fates that brought them together.

The kiss might have been a touch too rough, a bit too conquering, but her lips were soft and irresistible, and he had tried his best to keep it gentle.

She smiled up at him when he eased his mouth off hers. "That felt wonderful, too."

"I'm glad. You might be a little sore by morning."

She shook her head. "I won't mind."

He took her hand in his. "Come to bed now, love."

He wanted to make love to her all night, but resolved not to touch her again tonight. They had a funeral to attend tomorrow and she needed to be alert and at her best. The danger may have passed, but her feelings of turmoil and sorrow were still fresh.

He drew her close as they settled in bed together. "Sweet

dreams, love."

She sighed. "A funeral tomorrow, and I still cannot remember what happened that night."

"I hope you never do," he said, his body immediately tensing and his heart aching for what she might find out once she remembered. "There is a reason you suppressed it. Let those memories stay buried forever."

He hoped time would allow any terror of that night to disappear for good. "Think of this day forward as the first chapter of a new book we are going to write for ourselves as husband and wife."

"Out with the old and in with the new?" she remarked.

"Yes." He smiled when she snuggled against him, for this is how she was meant to be, curled up contentedly beside him and happy as a kitten lapping up cream.

"Still, I think it is important for me to remember."

"Don't, love. It can only bring you pain."

She nodded. "I am not afraid of a little pain. Besides, you will be there to take me in your arms and assure me that I am now safe because you will always protect me. However, I think you will have your wish about my never remembering. It is quite possible that the little piece of memory was knocked out of my brain forever."

He quietly rejoiced.

He hoped she was right.

He also wanted her thinking of happier thoughts as she drifted off to sleep. "Gory, where would you like to go on our honeymoon?"

"I see straight through your ploy." She reached up and kissed him on the cheek.

"Not a ploy. I want to take you away to someplace you have always dreamed of going. Someplace the two of us can be together with no responsibilities or cares to interfere with our getting to know each other better."

"The only place I've ever wanted to be was in your arms and I am here right now."

"Charmingly said, but I really want you to give it some

thought."

"All right, I will. However, I want you to know that I am the happiest and most content I have ever been in all my days. There is nothing better than this, although I am going to need an entire new wardrobe because I cannot keep borrowing Adela's clothes."

"Ah, yes. That shall be our first stop after tomorrow's business."

"Julius, you can call it what it is…a funeral. My uncle's." She sighed. "I cannot believe my aunt and that horrid weasel, Reginald Mayfield, were lovers. What could they possibly see in each other?"

"Greed, mostly. A mutual love of wealth and comforts. She needed him to act as the go-between and he needed her in order to have any chance of accessing a share of the inheritance for himself. But this is not what I want you thinking about as you fall asleep."

"I won't. I shall dream of your magnificent body."

He laughed. "Scars and all."

"Very manly scars." She kissed him again. "Hopefully, the last ones you will ever acquire because of me."

He expected there would be more, for Gory was not the sort to shirk from danger. Perhaps acquiring a husband and having children in the near future would temper her adventurous nature. The Huntsford Academy forensics laboratory would also keep her out of trouble since her investigatory work would be confined to there, working behind the scenes in solving any crimes.

He wished her sweet dreams again.

It took him a while longer to fall asleep because he had declined taking any laudanum to ease the pain of his fresh stitches. But he was soon lulled by the comfort of Gory's warm body curled against him.

He awoke to sunshine and the sound of the household stirring.

Gory looked achingly adorable while asleep beside him.

He smiled as he took a moment to study her in repose. Her cheeks were a soft pink, her hair was a beautiful, dark tumble against the pillow, and her lips were full and rosy.

Soft, plump, kissable lips.

The blanket shifted, revealing more of her body.

A deep ache stirred in him.

He did not mean to fix his gaze on her full breasts in their creamy splendor, but how could he not admire their sweet perfection? However, he did not allow his gaze to linger because the sun was well above the horizon, and this meant they were running late for the funeral service.

It could not start without them.

Still, it was bad form to be late on such an occasion.

"Good morning, my little mongoose," he said in a whisper, shaking Gory gently awake.

Her smile as she opened her eyes and caught sight of him stole his breath away.

She put a hand to his cheek, her palm scraping against his stubble. "Good morning, Julius. What time is it?"

"Not sure, but I think we need to start getting ready." He handed her his banyan. "Here, put this on. Looks much better on you than on me. I'm going to ring for my valet and would rather he not get an eyeful of you."

"What about you?"

He shrugged. "I'll toss on a pair of trousers and get ready in one of the spare bedchambers. Adela's maid can take care of you in here. That's another thing we'll need to sort out, these dressing room arrangements. But not today, no rush for it."

Being generally efficient, it took Julius little time to wash, shave, and dress for the somber occasion. The sun was bright against a cloudless blue sky, ironically beautiful for such a somber day. Also beautiful was Gory, who once again stole his breath when he walked back into their bedchamber to escort her downstairs. "Love, you look wonderful."

"Suitably dignified?"

Suitably delicious, but he could not say this while her maid and his valet were present. "Perfection."

"Oh, you mustn't forget your sling," Gory said, taking a moment to put it on him over his protest.

She won that small battle of wills.

Not that he minded having her fuss over him.

"There will be a crowd and I do not want them bumping into

you and recklessly jostling your arm," she said, taking another moment to straighten out the sling so that his arm rested comfortably in it.

They rode out all together, with brothers and their wives, after a light breakfast.

Indeed, the meal was a very light one since no one was hungry.

Leo and Marigold, as well as the two dowagers, arrived at the church shortly after them. The crowd was larger than Julius expected, but it was not really a surprise. Everyone wanted a glimpse of the earl in his coffin and the niece first rumored to have done him in.

But gossip was now rampant about Lady Easton being charged with the murder of her husband. Her absence had been duly noticed and this drew even more speculation among the onlookers.

Julius did not like crowds.

Especially not here and now when the conclusion of the investigation was still too fresh. Perhaps he was being obsessive and overly cautious, but what if someone had been overlooked?

How did Havers know he had all the players in custody?

He realized Havers was worried about the same thing, for Julius spotted him amid the crowd, studying everyone who passed through the church doors.

Nor did Havers give more than a curt nod to acknowledge their arrival when he and Gory walked in, a sign that he was on the job.

Julius took a moment to scan the crowd, as well.

People from all walks of life were ambling in. Finest nobility, well-heeled gentry, commoners and those of the servant class took seats in the pews after greeting Gory.

Lady Easton's sister and her husband made an appearance.

This did not sit well with Julius, for he still had his doubts about them. But Gory greeted them politely and did not appear to resent their presence.

Instead of having them removed, Julius remained on heightened watch while they asked after her, expressed their remorse over what Lady Easton had tried to do to her, and then moved on to take their seats. "I can order them tossed out," he whispered in Gory's ear.

"No, they've always treated me fairly. Have they not been shamed enough by my aunt? They'll go to see her next, assuming the magistrate will allow their visit."

"You are kinder than I would be."

"Havers is convinced they were not involved and that is good enough for me. Besides, I've been treated badly most of my life and refuse to do the same to others."

The Easton head butler, Jergins, walked in with a contingent of family servants.

Gory noticed them and waved them forward with a welcoming smile.

Mr. Barrow was also in the crowd, his gaze on the receiving line, especially on those who were inching closer to Gory.

Julius felt a chill run up his spine.

Was something going on?

He glanced at Gory who appeared regal as she graciously offered a gloved hand to each person passing on the queue.

Octavian and Leo, must have sensed something was off, as well. While their wives spoke with Farthingale relations, Huntsford Academy staff, and generally mingled, Leo took up a position near the head of the queue while Octavian planted his large frame immediately to the right of Gory.

Julius was standing immediately to the left of her, so that those on the queue passed by him first. His attention was on people's hands rather than their faces. He intended to flatten anyone brandishing anything that glinted metal.

Octavian leaned over Gory's head to speak to him. "Switch places with me."

"No." He knew Octavian meant to be the one standing in front of Gory and able to stop anyone suspicious from grabbing her, but he was not about to give up that role.

Octavian emitted a soft growl. "Your arm is in a sling."

"It is fine. Gory made me wear it."

She glanced up at him in surprise. "I *made* you wear it?"

"I *wanted* to wear it because it was important to you. We'll

258 | MEARA PLATT

discuss it later. I'm busy right now."

Her eyes widened as she stared up at him again. "*You* are busy? What is it that you are doing other than standing beside me?"

"Protecting you, which is what Octavian wants to do, but I am not conceding my spot to anyone, not even to my brother."

She pursed her lips and frowned at him. "What are you not telling me? Is there something more I should be worried about?"

He raked a hand through his hair. "No...that is, I don't know. Havers and Barrow are here, but not for friendly reasons. Look at them. They are obviously on the lookout for someone."

"Who?"

"I don't know, love. Octavian and Leo noticed it, too."

"Odd," she said, emitting a shaky breath. "All morning long, I've had this feeling we were overlooking something. I thought it was just my foolish imagination, but apparently not. I'm glad you are all looking out for me."

"Perhaps it is nothing," Octavian sought to assure her. "We could all be wrong about this."

"Doubtful. You Thornes have excellent instincts when it comes to danger. If only I could remember..."

"Don't, love." Julius did not want her dredging up that fateful night, and he certainly did not want her to have any sudden revelations here and now in front of all these strangers who did not care for her.

Most were here in the hope of seeing a lurid spectacle.

He did not want Gory providing it.

However, he noticed the furrow of her brow and knew she was now trying to break through to those bad memories.

Blast.

He turned his attention to those seated in the pews and noticed Harold Mayfield several rows back, his head bowed as though in prayer. Why was he here and not in front of the magistrate trying to talk him into freeing his weasel of a brother?

Of the two, Harold was the more respected, and actually had a decent reputation. However, Julius had never thought much of either Mayfield. Was he here in an attempt to salvage some of his reputation?

The man suddenly glance up and stared at Gory with a look of such pure hatred, it momentarily stunned Julius. But he quickly recovered his senses and nudged Gory behind Octavian, knowing an ox team could not drive through his brother. "Keep her behind you."

He then tossed off his sling and leaped across the first few pews just as that villainous solicitor noticed him and withdrew something gleaming from the pocket of his jacket. Ignoring the gasps and cries of those he had shoved aside, Julius landed atop the heavyset man quite clumsily, but with sufficient force to momentarily knock the breath out of him.

Julius gasped in pain as his freshly stitched arm struck the man squarely in the chest.

Ow.

That hurt like a bloody demon.

Ignoring those agonizing jolts shooting up his arm, he grabbed the man's hand and forced it back almost to the point of breaking. "Drop it," he growled.

"Do as he says, Mayfield," Havers commanded, pulling a metallic object out of the man's stubborn grip. "It is over."

He then turned to Julius and cast him a look of surprise. "When did you figure out both Mayfields were involved?"

Julius let out a pained laugh. "I didn't. I saw him look upon Gory with hatred in his eyes, and then he reached into his pocket as I approached. He may have been pulling out his fob or a pair of spectacles, for all I know. What was it?"

"A pistol."

"Bastard," Julius muttered, still wincing in pain as he clambered to his feet.

Havers regarded him with a glint of amusement in his eyes. "Your theatrics weren't necessary, Thorne. I was about to grab him when you suddenly pounced on him and squashed him like a bug. Your arm must be giving you agony right now."

"It is fine," Julius grumbled.

Havers arched his eyebrow. "I would argue the point, but there's a little more work to be done."

"Here? Now? What else—"

"Got 'im," Mr. Barrow's most experienced Bow Street runner called out, dragging a young fellow toward them. Julius recognized him as Harold Mayfield's son who was a junior solicitor in the family firm, the *son* in Mayfield & Sons. "Caught the little whelp about to set a blaze in the clerestory, no doubt to create a distraction while his father made an attempt on Lady Gregoria's life."

Mr. Barrow had now joined them, too. "Nice work, Mick."

A crowd had gathered around them, the onlookers buzzing with excitement over the spectacle this funeral had just provided. Havers ordered them all to stand back. Above the din of the crowd, Julius heard Gory calling out to him. "Tell your big ox of a brother to let me through!"

He realized Octavian still held Gory behind him. "Octavian, let her go before she hits you with something hard."

Gory flew into Julius's arms the moment his brother stepped aside. "Are you hurt? You wonderful idiot, I saw you land hard on your arm."

"I am fine. I landed on Mayfield's soft belly." He was feeling a bit dizzy and his arm burned whenever he tried to move it, but he was never going to admit this to Gory. "What matters most is that you are safe."

Her eyes were as big as the moon in full glow as she studied him.

He cast her a sloppy grin.

She picked up his sling and lovingly formed a cradle in which to place his injured arm. "Do not dare tell me you are fine," she gently chided. "You are breathing hard and you wince every time I put a hand on you."

"What matters is that *you* are fine."

She nodded. "Not a scratch on me."

They said nothing more as they watched Havers, his constables, and the Bow Street runners haul the assailants into a prison wagon. Many in the crowd followed these men out while others still buzzed around him and Gory.

Everyone was eager to know what had just happened.

Octavian and Leo held back anyone who got too close.

The vicar, quite shaken himself, ordered those who remained to take their seats. He commenced the funeral service ten minutes later.

Julius took hold of Gory's hand as they took seats in the front pew, and kept hold throughout the sermon. His thoughts strayed as the vicar droned on about the earl and the nobility of his life, which was an utter joke. The man was a miserable wretch and had mostly ignored Gory all these years. Perhaps the widow he had taken up with shortly before his death might have made a better man of him, but who was ever to know?

The woman was discreetly seated in one of the rear pews and was perhaps the only person in the church who genuinely grieved his passing.

And what of the Mayfields?

How stupid of him not suspect all of them had been involved, including the elder Mayfield's son whose life was now ruined because his oily father and uncle had involved him in their crimes.

Julius would not be surprised if it turned out this youngest Mayfield had been the assailant who hopped over Lord Greene's wall and then made his narrow escape by riding off on horseback the other day.

Because of their greed, they were all going to spend the rest of their lives imprisoned.

Gory emitted a soft breath when the sermon finally came to a close. "My uncle must be enjoying this send off. He always wanted to be the talk of the *ton*."

Julius nodded. "He'll have all of London talking about him for years."

"Julius," she said, walking out of the church with him once the vicar's sermon was over.

"What, my love?" He helped her into their carriage and settled beside her with a grunt. They were next to head to the graveyard for her uncle's interment.

Then home.

This is all he wanted to do, take Gory home and start making plans for their life together. Their happiness.

"Julius," she repeated, casting him a loving smile, "I think I am ready for our honeymoon."

CHAPTER 17

JULIUS WAS RELIEVED when Dr. Farthingale arrived early in the evening to take out Gory's stitches and then examine him. She went first and returned downstairs to their merry band of friends and family about ten minutes later. "Your turn, Julius," she said with surprising cheer, taking the chair beside Lady Dayne that he had just vacated, and then proceeding to show them all the fine job the doctor had done healing that nasty gash behind her ear.

Julius stalked upstairs to their bedchamber, knowing he was going to receive a lecture from the doctor about his rash behavior today.

But was not saving Gory's life worth any harm to himself?

Dr. Farthingale chuckled lightly as he strode in. "Your wife tells me you engaged in circus acrobatics at the funeral service this morning. Let me have a look at the damage you've done to yourself."

"No damage, I am fine." But he winced as he removed his shirt, unable to ignore the jolts of pain still stubbornly searing through his arms.

Bloody blazes.

"See, I am perfectly fine," he insisted, only to be met with the doctor's doubtful stare.

"Your wife also warned this is what you would tell me. You are fortunate the stitches held and there was no bleeding. Your arm is not broken, either. Another fortunate circumstance, since I understand you landed hard on it. The pain must be blistering."

Julius grunted. "I'll survive."

"Yes, you will…thanks to my good care." He grinned. "Need I tell you to take is easy for the next few days?"

"You can tell me." But Julius was making him no promises.

The doctor had just finished examining him when Havers arrived to give their group the latest news. He was accompanied by Mr. Barrow who had been working hand in hand with the London constabulary to close this investigation.

Havers took the lead since he was the magistrate's man. "It turns out all the Mayfields were involved in this sordid affair from start to finish. Both of the elder Mayfields set about wooing Lady Easton, but it was the little weasel brother, Reginald, that she fell for and they had a rather torrid affair."

"Ew," Marigold said, staring at Havers in dismay. "Did you have to tell us that? It is revolting, no matter which brother she chose for her dalliance."

Havers arched an eyebrow. "More so than murder? I should think having an affair is the least of their crimes."

Julius nodded. "Go on, tell us more."

"We now have them all in custody, all the conspirators. The Mayfields, Flossie, and Flossie's brother-in-law have all suddenly developed diarrhea of the mouth. Each of them is desperate to sell out the others in the hope we will show leniency in their punishment."

"And Lady Easton?" Ambrose asked. "Has she said anything?"

"No, that woman is an iceberg. She's holding firm despite everyone pointing fingers at her." He raked a hand through his hair and turned to Gory. "You are completely absolved of any wrongdoing. I hope this pleases you."

She nodded. "It does, but what a shameful tragedy. All she ever had to do was ask me for a share of my inheritance and I would have given it to her."

Havers appeared surprised by her remark. "Why would you ever agree to such a thing? She treated you abysmally over the years. You owe her nothing. Nor would she have given you so much as a table scrap had the situations been reversed."

"I know. But to deny her would have been petty and cruel of

me. This is what *she* was, but that is not and has never been my character. I would have given her enough to maintain her respectful position as dowager countess. The new earl might have done the same, but I don't think she ever considered this possibility."

"Because she was a pig at the trough and would have kept everything for herself, as Havers said," Octavian remarked with a grunt. "She got what she deserved. Same for her fellow conspirators."

"I'll pull my men off guard duty," Mr. Barrow said, now addressing Ambrose and Julius, "unless you see a reason to keep them on the task."

Ambrose exchanged glances with Julius. "Your call, Julius."

He nodded. "Keep them on for another week. The threat from Lady Easton is over, but gossip is rampant. There will be newspaper men hoping to dig up more lurid stories about the Easton family, or scavengers hoping to turn a profit over some trifle of Gory's they might steal. Your guards will dissuade anyone from approaching us."

"Very good, my lord." Mr. Barrow expressed his good wishes to Gory and left.

Havers did the same soon afterward.

Julius let out a breath. "It's over, Gory. How do you feel?"

"Relieved," she said, but Julius knew she considered her memory loss as unfinished business.

He really needed to take her away from London and put physical distance between her and the events of that awful night.

He turned to the two dowagers. "Do you have any recommendations for us? I want to take Gory on a honeymoon trip."

"We cannot go anywhere until I have new clothes," Gory insisted. "And I've ruined several gowns of Adela's as well. Those will need to be replaced."

"I know, love. We've spoken about it and we'll take care of all of it tomorrow." He would pay a king's ransom to get her an entirely new wardrobe within a week's time, and sail off with her to the ends of earth, if necessary.

When they retired to their bedchamber later that evening, Julius felt something was wrong because Gory was too quiet.

Perhaps the finality of it all had gotten to her.

She sat on their bed watching while Robbins assisted him in taking off his clothing. He had not intended to have anyone other than Gory help him, but she seemed to be elsewhere in her thoughts and his arms were hurting too much. Pain coursed through his fingers and interfered with his finer movements such as undoing buttons.

"Will that be all, my lord?" his valet asked, helping him into his banyan.

"Yes. Thank you, Robbins." At Julius's nod, he quietly left the room.

Now alone with Gory, Julius walked over to the bed and sat beside her. "Care to tell me what is wrong?"

She nodded. "I've been having flashes of memory since shortly after supper."

He inhaled sharply. "What are you seeing?"

"Nothing that makes sense yet. Perhaps more will come out in my dreams tonight."

He hoped not.

This was not good news to him because he knew it could only bring anguish.

She rubbed her temples and muttered something about having a pounding headache.

"I'll help you undress, and then I am going to hold you in my arms all night."

"Even though your arms are sore? Why won't you take some of the laudanum Dr. Farthingale left to get you through the night?"

"I don't need it. I am fine."

She laughed softly. "You are so predictable."

"All I need is you, Gory. You are the best medicine for me." He assisted her out of her gown and the two of them climbed into bed.

She had no sooner rested her head against his chest than she began to cry.

Julius turned to her in alarm. "Gory?"

"Oh, I've been so stupid. Ow. *Ow.*"

Julius eyed her intently. "What is it, love?"

She closed her eyes as he wrapped his arms around her. "Flossie and her sister were who I saw standing over my uncle's body when I entered the study. Our gazes locked for an instant, and then I was hit over the head...really hard."

"And lost consciousness," Julius muttered, his heartbeat quickening as he listened.

She took several deep breaths. "We had returned from the musicale, my uncle and I. Something felt *off* but I could not put my finger on what it was. My uncle said something about having a drink before he retired to bed. He went into his study while I went upstairs to my bedchamber."

Julius kissed her lightly on the cheek as she began to tremble.

"I walked into my room. The fire was dying, so I tossed another log into the hearth and took a moment to stoke the flames. My maid had laid out my nightgown on the bed, but I was feeling a little cold and wanted stockings for my feet." She eased out of his arms in order to indicate her movements about the room. "I was about to close my door when I heard voices coming from my uncle's study. I heard Flossie talking, perhaps giving orders to someone. I could not hear clearly what she said, only that my uncle sounded angry and I heard him tell her to get out."

She looked up at Julius, casting him a vulnerable smile in response to his reassuring gaze. "But how could it be my aunt's maid when she was in Windsor? This was my first thought."

"So you decided to return downstairs and investigate?"

"Yes, but I was not really concerned. I assumed my aunt had returned unexpectedly and sent the woman down to my uncle, perhaps to demand something of him. I was still dressed in the gown I had worn to the musicale."

"The peach silk?" Julius took her hands in his to warm them.

"Yes, I am certain of it. I...I..."

"Gory, you do not have to do this. It does not matter any more, love. Havers has gathered enough evidence to convict them all."

"Oh, Julius, let me tell you the rest of it. The dam has been unblocked and it is all coming out in a flood of memories now."

"All right, but I want you to stop if it gets too much for you to bear." However, he could tell by her expression that she was going to plough on to the end.

"As I started downstairs," she continued with determination, "I heard my uncle commanding them *all* to leave. That's when I realized there were others besides Flossie in the study with him."

"Did you turn and run then?" He immediately shook his head, realizing she probably had been more curious than worried. "No, you walked straight into the lion's den, didn't you?"

"I had recognized Flossie's voice and did not think there was anything dangerous going on. After all, he and my aunt often exchanged unpleasant words. I just assumed this was more of the same, except that my aunt had sent Flossie to do her dirty work for her this time."

"I'm not blaming you, love. How could you have known what you were walking into?"

"I should have realized. Do I not pride myself on my forensic knowledge? As I neared the study, I heard my uncle's muffled cry and then he made an odd gurgling sound that I should have recognized as strangulation had I been paying closer attention. It was quickly followed by a thud, as though something had fallen onto the carpet."

She released a ragged breath and groaned. "I thought he might have knocked over a book on his desk and nothing more. So, I stupidly walked in, still not realizing anything was seriously wrong. But I had taken no more than a few steps into the room when I saw my uncle bleeding on the floor. So much blood. And there was Flossie and a woman who resembled her standing over his body and quietly bickering over how messily it was done. Flossie had the knife in her hand, red and dripping. Both suddenly went silent when they saw me."

Julius kissed her on the forehead. "Oh, love."

"Flossie looked beyond me to whoever was standing behind the door and said, *kill her*."

"Merciful heavens, Gory."

"Then I was struck over the head. I never saw who hit me."

"It doesn't matter. Havers has that man in custody and he will never be set free," Julius insisted. "Gory, I'm so sorry. I should have been there for you."

"Don't you dare shoulder any blame. How could any of us have expected something so monstrous? I must have passed out for the longest time, long enough for them to change me out of the peach silk and into my wedding gown. I'm glad I did not feel their vile hands on me."

"Dear heaven, so am I," he said with an ache to his voice. "It would have taken nothing for them to notice you were still breathing. Even the slightest moan from your lips and they would have hit you again. Only by the grace of heaven were you spared."

She nodded. "My uncle's body was motionless beside me when I awoke. All I could think to do was get out of that house. I didn't know who to trust. Was Jergins involved? Was my maid? Of course, no one else in that household would have ever betrayed us. But at the time, I was so scared and functioning on raw instinct."

"And you ran to me."

"All I could think of was finding you. I wanted you to hold me in your arms and protect me. This is what my heart knew you would do. I had to seek you out because I loved you and you were the only one I could ever trust to help me."

"I have you now and always will, love. I'll never let anyone hurt you."

"It is over now, but I can only ever identify Flossie and her sister as the two who were present that night."

"It does not matter. They have all turned on each other like a pack of jackals. Nor should you forget that the sister's husband had the requisite scratches, so he can be tied to the murder, too."

"But my aunt has not confessed yet."

"She does not need to ever say a word when the others are all talking like trained parrots. It will all come out, every sordid detail. Havers will get their confessions down from start to finish. We know your aunt gave Flossie the latchkey to the townhouse and then covered for Flossie's absence while in Windsor. The mail coach agents will confirm they saw Flossie, along with Flossie's sister and husband, on the coach to London and on their return just a few hours later. You can now give Havers your statement about who was in the study when you walked in and saw your uncle on the floor."

"What about the Mayfields? I do not think they were in my uncle's study that night."

"Doesn't matter. Jergins or others in your household can attest to the affair Lady Easton was carrying on with Reginald Mayfield. Mr. Barrow's man caught the Mayfield son attempting to set a fire in the church just before the funeral service was to start, and I caught the elder Mayfield trying to shoot you. They are not going to get away with anything. In truth, I expect the Mayfields will be the first to sing like nightingales if promised a more lenient sentence. Damn cowards."

The clock chimed the midnight hour.

Julius gave Gory a lingering kiss.

She cast him another vulnerable smile. "I came to you with so much blood on my hands and on my gown, but all I felt was relief when you undressed me and washed me. Yours were the healing hands I needed on me. Yours was the gentle touch that soothed me. I don't know what I would have done if I hadn't found you."

"But you did find me, love."

She nodded. "I would have searched the moon and stars for you. Then you walked into your bedchamber, and I knew in that moment I was safe. I was with the right person and I needed to be with you for the rest of my life. I had you to help me deal with the murder and...then I intended to ask you for help in dealing with my wedding."

He grinned. "That slight problem with the wedding...namely, the wrong bridegroom."

"Julius, in my heart, I knew I could never marry anyone but you."

"Same here, love."

"I'm so glad it was you. It was always meant to be you," she whispered as they both drifted off to sleep.

EPILOGUE

London, England
April, 1827

NIGHT HAD FALLEN and a chill lingered in the spring air as Julius strode into the Fullerton townhouse where another of Lady Fullerton's ever popular routs was taking place. The ballroom was a crush, but Julius had no problem finding Gory, who was in attendance along with most of his family and friends, except for Octavian and Syd who were back in Scotland now.

Julius had been away himself on Thorne family business for an entire month that felt like an eternity because he missed his wife terribly. For this reason, he had come directly here, hastily dropping his bags at home, and then washing up and donning his evening attire before hurrying over to seek out Gory rather than wait for her to come home.

As expected, she was seated in what he termed the wallflower corner, which is where he used to find her when approaching her for a dance before they were married. She sat with Adela and Marigold, and another young lady who resembled Marigold. The four of them were hovered over something in Gory's hand, no doubt some hideous glob that had yet to be identified but would turn out to be some groundbreaking discovery of hers.

"Mind if I intrude?" he asked, interrupting them.

Gory looked up at him with a big smile on her entrancing face and the light of love in her eyes. "Julius!"

She melted into his open arms.

"Sweetheart, you are sight for sore eyes," he said, hugging her fiercely as he momentarily drew her away from her friends.

She laughed and kissed him. "So are you. I missed you so much. We did not expect you back until tomorrow. How was your trip?"

"Productive. I'll give Ambrose my full report tomorrow." He had no desire to talk about dull business affairs tonight when she stood before him looking radiant. "How are you feeling, my love?"

"Never better." She patted her stomach to show him the smallest bulge now starting to form, and then took his hand so that he might feel this latest change in her body.

He drew in a breath, amazed by the wonder of it all. "Gad, Gory. Are we really going to be parents?"

"I've made it past four months now, but there is still quite a way to go." She studied his expression. "Oh, now you are giving me that apishly protective look. I love that look, but do not dare think to confine me to bed rest. That time will come soon enough."

He sighed. "I just want to keep you safe."

"You have done that, kept me safe and *happy*," she stressed because it had taken some doing for her to get beyond her memories of the fateful night that had changed her life so starkly. The trials, all leading to convictions for her aunt and her cohorts, had captured everyone's attention for months.

It was still all the talk.

He worried that having to deal with the incident day in and day out was going to be too much of an ordeal for Gory, but she was proving to be quite resilient. She had not even been resentful of losing most of the inheritance she was to receive when it turned out her uncle had squandered the bulk of it.

How ironic, that all the misery Lady Easton had caused would have yielded her no more than five thousand pounds because Gory's uncle had faked the ledgers and embezzled the funds down to almost nothing.

Perhaps the new earl would restore it in time, assuming he was a man of honor and able to return the earldom to profitability. But Julius never wanted Gory to worry about this, for she was his to care for and protect.

When he remarked on it, she responded by crediting him for what mattered most to her, and this was her healing.

Perhaps he had played a small part.

But Gory's true strength came from within.

"Let me introduce you to Marigold's cousin," Gory said, shaking him out of his straying thoughts. "Her name is Tulip, and she has just arrived from Burnham, a charming village in Somerset."

He chuckled. "Tulip? Yet another Farthingale flower? I pity the poor bachelor who's about to become embroiled with her."

She playfully frowned at him. "No comment necessary. You do not hear Leo complaining about his marrying Marigold, do you? Or any husband complaining about a Farthingale they married? She's lovely. Come meet her."

"All right, love," he said, allowing Gory to drag him back to her circle of friends.

Tulip greeted him with a cheery smile.

"Are you here for your come-out?" Julius asked politely once introductions had been made, for she appeared about the right age. Indeed, perfect fodder for those two dowagers, Lady Dayne and Lady Withnall, who did have uncanny instincts when it came to matchmaking.

Tulip nodded. "I would have preferred to wait another year, but…" She shook her head and sighed. "I am glad to be here now and staying with my father's cousin, John Farthingale, and his wife, Sophie. I expect you know them quite well. Their home on Chipping Way seems to be a hub of activity."

"A lovely madhouse," Marigold interjected.

Tulip smiled. "I was afraid London would overwhelm me, but it helps to have Marigold residing just across the street from me. Our mutual cousin, Violet, lives right next door. Not to mention the lovely Lady Dayne is on the other side of us. Her grandson is married to John and Sophie's daughter, Daisy. I suppose you've met all five of their daughters."

Julius nodded. "All but Lily, since she resides in Scotland with her husband."

"I haven't seen Lily in years," Tulip admitted. "She and I are kindred spirits when it comes to love of science, although I am no match for her brilliance. I thought I would be dissuaded from any scholarly pursuits while here, but everyone has been quite wonderful to me and encouraged my interests."

She smiled at Gory, Marigold, and Adela, then continued. "Marigold introduced me to your wife and sister-in-law, and I now consider them dear friends. I have already attended two of Gory's lectures at the Huntsford Academy, and cannot wait to attend my first meeting of their explorer's club."

Julius winked at Gory, knowing how much she enjoyed the club that she and her friends had formed. "I expect you have also been bombarded with invitations from your Farthingale cousins. Quite a few of them reside in London."

Tulip laughed. "Yes, and *bombarded* is an excellent description, isn't it? We are more of an advancing army than a family. We travel in hordes. We are everywhere and no one can escape us."

Julius thought her description humorous and exceedingly accurate. "Well, I am glad to make your acquaintance."

The girl seemed to fit right in with this circle of bluestockings, if her excitement over the object Gory still held in her hand was any indication.

Julius now took a closer look at this curious thing trapped in amber. "What is it, Gory?"

She giggled. "Well, the British Museum's expert inaccurately identified it as a fossilized finger bone."

Her three companions broke into guffaws and titters.

He sighed. "But you know what it is, don't you? Dare I ask?"

Gory nodded. "It is actually a fossilized…protrusion of the male persuasion. You know, the thing that protrudes on men but not on–"

"Got it." He winced. "A human male?"

"No, monkey male. And most certainly not a finger bone."

Her friends laughed again.

He took the amber object out of Gory's hand and gave it over to Adela. "You are the duchess and ought not be condoning my wife's wicked behavior."

But he laughed and shook his head as he took Gory's hand.

"Come dance with me, sweetheart."

He led her onto the dance floor as a waltz commenced, marveling at how dazzling she looked. Truly, a fairy princess. Or an imp. A beautiful imp. This was Gory, brilliant, eccentric, and completely loveable with her big eyes and tumble of dark curls.

"By the way, the new Earl of Easton has been located by your solicitors," she told him as he led her in a twirl.

He was enjoying the feel of her body beneath his hands, a slightly fuller body but no less beautiful, for she was carrying his child. "Have you met him?"

"Not yet. He won't arrive for several months. He wants to sell his farm in Virginia and wrap up all his affairs before coming to England. But here's the juiciest bit of gossip I doubt you've heard."

"Another scandal?" He twirled her toward the doors leading onto the terrace because he wanted to get his wife alone in the moonlight and kiss her thoroughly.

"The magistrate's top investigator, Alexander Havers, is now a *duke*. Can you believe it?"

Julius laughed. "Havers? Seriously?"

She nodded. "He is the new Duke of Davenport. Coincidentally, his seat is in Somerset, but Tulip has never met him or any of his family. Not that she would, since the Farthingales are tradesmen and not considered quality by *ton* standards."

"I don't think Havers gives a fig what the *ton* thinks. Well, that is an interesting turn of events. He confided in me about his family situation when we were dealing with Allendale. He made it sound as though the possibility of his ever acquiring the title was remote."

"Remote or not, it happened," Gory insisted.

"All within the span of a month? How did each heir die off so suddenly?"

"That is a mystery for him to handle. The deaths were all ruled as accidents. However, the fact that they occurred in such short succession has drawn attention from the authorities. You'll have to ask him, if you want to know more about it. Shall I invite him to supper one night so you can quiz him on it?"

"I wouldn't intrude on his privacy like that."

"Well, I would," Gory replied. "I cannot believe the tripe that is being written in the gossip rags about him and his Davenport relatives. Completely unreliable when it comes to the truth. But he'll confide in you because he considers you a good and trustworthy friend."

"I hope so. Still, I would not be so quick to dismiss the gossip about his relatives. He considered them a dismal lot."

"Tulip has a low opinion of them, as well. In fact, she purposely avoids Havers because she does not trust he will be any better. She mentioned the Davenports were much disliked in the area, but there was little anyone could do to curb them because they were too powerful."

"And must have made powerful enemies, I'll wager," Julius muttered.

"Do you think Havers needs your help, Julius? He seems quite uncomfortable with his new status."

"Not surprising. He has had a difficult upbringing and will not be keen to take on the social burdens of a dukedom. I'll wager the abuse he experienced in his childhood turned him inward, and this is how he best protects himself. To suddenly be thrust into the social whirl as one of the *ton's* most sought after bachelors will be quite an adjustment for him. It will probably send him into hiding," he jested, although there was a kernel of truth in his remark.

"He won't be able to hide from those eager mamas seeking a match for their daughters," Gory remarked. "Well, that should be interesting."

Speaking of Havers and his difficult upbringing made Julius think of Gory's and how unloved she had been. Yet, here she was, a beautiful soul who cared for others and maintained an optimistic outlook on the future.

Forged in strength.

This is what she was.

And yet, she also maintained an exquisite softness.

"And here's another bit of news you'll never believe," she said, smiling up at him while still wrapped in his arms as they stepped and twirled to the music. "Allendale has married Sarah Martin."

"What?" He shook his head and laughed in disbelief. "Are you serious? One would think I had been gone ten years and not a mere month for all the changes occurring in my absence."

"Having you gone felt like an eternity to me," she said with a wealth of feeling. "At least Allendale and Sarah's scandal took a little attention off my uncle's murder. I'm glad Allendale truly loved her all along."

Julius frowned. "And would have used you to further his aims, stealing your money to set *her* up in style and comfort. I did not think he had the spine to openly declare his affections, especially knowing the risk he took of being disinherited by his rich uncle."

"No one did, except perhaps Sarah. She believed in him. I think she has been a good influence on him."

"That is an understatement. The man is a rat, and I still think he was just as dangerous to you as Havers and I originally feared."

"Then he is all the better for being guided by Sarah. Lady Withnall agreed with your assessment of him, too. She is never wrong about anything."

Julius chuckled. "I am certain that old bat is a top agent for the Home Office. That cane she uses, pretending she needs it for support, probably contains an arsenal of hidden weapons."

"I've often wondered about that myself." She grinned. "I wonder if she would let me examine it. I'd love to get my hands on it."

Julius kissed her on the nose. "Here's an idea, how about you get your hands on me?"

She laughed and eagerly agreed. "That is also an intriguing proposition. You've steered me toward the terrace. Are you planning on getting me alone in the dark? Having your wicked way with me?"

"Yes, in fact. I was. Do you mind?"

"Not in the least, but I think we are not the only couple with this idea. How about we return home instead? I'm feeling a terrible headache coming on," she remarked with obvious theatricality. "But before we make our excuses and leave, I have one more thing to tell you."

"Only one?" he teased. "What is it, love?"

"Lord Ashborn is selling his townhouse."

"How did we get from my claiming your luscious body to talking about houses?"

"Because it has all merged into one in my head. You. Bed. Our privacy, which is something we have little of while living under your brother's roof. Not that I ever wish to sound ungrateful. He and Adela have been exceedingly kind and generous to us. Me, particularly. But they must be feeling this same lack of privacy in their own home. I think it is time we settled into a place of our own, especially with a child on the way."

"Well, that's all right then. I will speak to Ashborn first thing tomorrow morning."

"Thank you, Julius." She nodded. "Isn't it perfect? We would still be close to Ambrose and Adela, just a few doors down from their home."

They bid their friends a hasty goodnight, apologized to Lady Fullerton for the sudden headache Gory developed, and hurried home, probably fooling no one as to their true intent.

Upon their arrival home, they marched straight upstairs.

Julius wasted no time in stripping down to his trousers the moment they were in their bedchamber and he'd shut the door.

His eyes were on Gory as she changed out of her gown, but he stopped her as she was about to don her robe. "Give me a moment to look at you, love."

She was shy, but never with him.

She smiled when he began to trace his fingers with reverence along the changes to her body. "You are so beautiful, Gory."

She blushed. "I am soon going to be very ungainly."

"Never. You have the sweetest body. It was all I could do to keep from devouring you at Lady Fullerton's rout. You have me falling more deeply in love with you each day. I did not think it was possible to feel something more than I already do. But the passage of time forges a stronger bond between us whether we are together or not. This month apart from you was sheer agony for me. I ached to have you curled up beside me again."

"I missed you, too. I hugged your pillow every night."

"And now, I hope you will hug me." He smiled wickedly. "I

hope you will do more than merely hug me."

Her smile was dazzling. "What do you suggest?"

He lifted her in his arms and carried her to bed.

She ran her hands along the scars on his arms. The stitches had long since been taken out but the scarring was there permanently. "Do these ever pain you, Julius?"

"Do yours?"

She put a hand to the tender spot behind her ear. "Sometimes, but not too often now. What about you?"

"No, love. No pain. I am fine."

She laughed. "Fine? You always say this."

"Because this is how you make me feel. I'm even more than fine. Shall I prove it to you?"

She nodded.

So he did, several times that night, in fact.

But he was always gentle with her, and always aware of the precious bundle she carried inside of her. He fell into the best sleep he'd had in a long while because she was beside him and he breathed in the familiar, honey scent of her skin that he adored.

He had botched everything up to their wedding.

No proper courtship.

A wrong betrothal.

A hasty ceremony.

But their marriage was a different matter altogether. He was determined there would never be a problem with the marriage.

None.

Ever.

For nothing mattered more to him than Gory.

"I love you, sweetheart," he whispered as he drifted off to sleep.

She snuggled closer to him. "Love you back, my wonderfully apish husband. Love you forever."

He smiled as she shifted her warm, little body even closer to his.

All was right with the world now, wasn't it?

Not a single problem with this marriage at all.

THE END

Dear Reader

Thank you for reading *A Slight Problem With The Wedding*. Julius Thorne, the very capable and confident youngest of the Thorne brothers certainly had his hands full keeping Lady Gregoria Easton safe from the villains who killed her uncle, the Earl of Easton, and getting her out of her betrothal to the wrong man. Yes, realizing Gregoria was meant to be his and no one else's just a week before the wedding was cutting it a little close. But none of the Thorne men had an easy transition from bachelor to husband. In *The Make-Believe Marriage*, Julius's handsome brother, Captain Octavian Thorne, vowed to protect Lady Sydney Harcourt even if it killed him, which sometimes was a close thing because the hoyden did not know how to stay out of trouble. In *A Duke For Adela*, their eldest brother, Ambrose, Duke of Huntsford, had his hands full keeping the lovely Adela Swift safe after she was determined to find the thief who stole a rare manuscript out of her hands while she was engaged in scientific research in the Huntsford Academy library. I hope you have been enjoying these latest in the Farthingale series, including *The Viscount And The Vicar's Daughter, A Duke For Adela, Marigold And The Marquess, The Make-Believe Marriage, A Slight Problem With The Wedding*. Coming up next is the romance for Marigold's cousin, Tulip Farthingale. In *One Night With Tulip*, she'll find her match with Alexander Havers, the brilliant investigator you met working for the London magistrate in *A Slight Problem With The Wedding*. Alexander has inherited a dukedom and his seat is in Somerset, which is where Tulip was born and raised. He's headed back there not only to restore the estate but to figure out whether the deaths of his father and brothers in rapid succession were accidental or planned. But while still in London, seems he has just compromised the lusciously adorable Tulip, so his life is never going to be the same. Read on for a sneak peek of *One Night With Tulip*.

I welcome you to all the stories (including several novellas) in the FARTHINGALE SERIES, and if you are in need of even more Farthingales, then please try my BOOK OF LOVE SERIES where you will meet a host of Farthingale cousins, all of them sweet and innocent young ladies who cannot seem to keep out of trouble. In fact, they attract trouble wherever they turn, especially when it involves some very steamy, alpha heroes and that mysterious, red-leather bound Book of Love.

SNEAK PEEK OF THE UPCOMING BOOK: ONE NIGHT WITH TULIP CHAPTER 1

London, England
August 1827

"MISS FARTHINGALE, WHAT is the matter?" Alexander Havers, the new Duke of Davenport, had not expected to run into Tulip Farthingale when he stepped into Lady Fullerton's garden on this hot summer evening, hoping to get away from the crush of revelers in the ballroom at one of her famous routs.

The night was steamy, threatening rain, if the heavy scent of grass and damp leaves was any indication, although not a drop had fallen yet. But a light haze had settled over the trees and lush shrubbery, dimming the rows of lanterns gaily strung along measured intervals and giving the impression of a fairy garden.

A church clock *bonged* in the distance to mark the midnight hour.

This also marked his last night in London before he returned to Somerset and the Davenport estate his predecessors to the title had left in shambles. He thought he had been alone out here until the lovely Tulip had run straight into him and bounced off his chest, for she had been moving very fast.

He caught her in his arms to steady her, wrapping her lithe body securely in his embrace as wispy tendrils of haze circled around them.

Blessed saints.

She felt surprisingly good in his arms.

"Oh, dear!" She looked up at him, her big blue eyes reflecting the firelight from one of the garden lanterns. "I've done a dreadful thing, Your Grace."

"You have?" He struggled not to grin at the earnest expression on the face of this charming bluestocking he would have liked to know better. "What have you done? You know I am no longer working for the London magistrate, an impossibility now that I have inherited a dukedom, so I will not report you to the authorities. Your secret is quite safe with me."

Until a few months ago, he had been simply Mr. Havers, and had yet to get used to being addressed with the deference accorded his new title. While he had not changed who he always was in essence, most around him had suddenly turned into fawning toadies. Those who had ignored him in the past now fussed over him, pretending they had always admired and adored him.

Young ladies went to great lengths to throw themselves at him since he had also become London's most sought after bachelor.

Not Tulip, however.

She avoided him as much as she could because she was wary of the Davenport reputation. Only recently had she started to thaw toward him, hopefully understanding he was nothing like the dishonorable Davenport dukes who had come before him.

He kept hold of her, rather liking the soft feel of her body against his palms.

She was draped in pale blue silk, a hue that matched the color of her striking eyes, and he thought her the prettiest thing he had seen in an age.

"Lord Finley Caruthers took me for a stroll in the garden," she said, clearing her throat as though it pained her to make the announcement.

"That is a serious crime," he intoned, taking care not to laugh.

"Please do not be smug about it. He wanted to kiss me and–"

"You let him?" He frowned, knowing exactly what a dishonorable hound like Caruthers meant to do once alone with Tulip and it was not restricted to a single kiss.

"No!" Her eyes rounded in horror, then her expression turned sheepish. "But I almost let him do it."

"Almost?"

She nodded. "You see, I wanted to be kissed."

Dear heaven.

Alex would have obliged her, and been a far safer partner than that lout, Caruthers.

"But then I realized that I did not wish *him* to be the one to kiss me. Especially not for my first time."

"Your first?" His heart lurched, and then suddenly began to pound erratically.

Why was his heart pounding?

This was his last night in London. One night. Only one night and he would be off to Somerset for as long as it took him to get his dukedom back in order.

You fool, just let this evening pass quietly.

But he ignored the warning.

He ignored the simple and effective rules that had kept him out of compromising situations all summer long. Do not engage a girl in conversation – especially not this girl and not while you are holding her in your arms. Do not look at a girl's lips – especially not this girl's lips that he had ached to kiss since meeting her.

She was now giving the fleshy lower lip a soft nibble.

He could go on with more rules that he was obviously abandoning because this was Tulip and he did not understand why he could not get enough of her.

To his chagrin, she seemed quite comfortably nestled in his arms and was making no attempt to move away when she could have easily done so.

She should have done so.

He would never be so boorish as to prevent her.

"Yes, my very first kiss." She nodded again, the dark curls surrounding her lovely face bobbing delightfully. "Because I have never been kissed before."

"That is usually what a *first* indicates," he said, then quietly cursed himself for his snide response. He blamed it on the heat coursing through him. "So, never?"

"Not once in all my life," she continued, giving him a slight frown for his impertinence. "And I thought it was time to take the leap. But as his lips drew closer to mine…"

"What happened?"

Her face scrunched in distaste. "I panicked and ran off. How could I kiss anyone who did not have my heart? Should it not be splendid and meaningful, a kiss to cherish all the days of my life?"

Oh, gad.

This is why he stayed away from innocents.

They were so…innocent.

"All right, I'll keep an eye on you as you head back into the ballroom. Just promise me you will stay close to your family for the rest of the night."

Tears now formed in her eyes as she solemnly promised. "I feel so ashamed."

"Why? It was just a harmless kiss that never took place, although it might have led to something far more compromising."

"I know. I think this is what scared me into running away from him. He was not looking at me in any nice way."

Alex glanced around the garden, wondering where Caruthers had gotten to. Should he not have caught up to Tulip by now? "Um, did you by any chance hit him before you ran off? With a heavy object, perhaps?"

"No," she said with a sniffle. "I simply ran off when he attempted to stick his face close to mine. And then he stuck his tongue out from between his pudgy lips and…*ew*. But, oh. I see. He should have walked right past us to return to the ballroom, but he hasn't yet. I promise you, I did not touch him. And the garden paths are sufficiently lit so that he should not have lost his way or tripped over a tree root."

Alex let out a breath as he repeated his earlier instruction. "Go back inside the ballroom. I'll stay out here but watch you walk in."

"And then you'll go in search of Lord Caruthers? Should I not go with you?"

"That entirely defeats the purpose of getting you safely away from him."

"But I am with you, so he would never dare anything. Besides, I know exactly where I left him and you do not."

He ignored the stubborn expression on her face. "This is not a large garden. Just point me in the general direction and I will find him. *Without* your assistance. I do not want you within reach of him again."

"All right, I–"

Several lanterns close by began to sway and pebbles crunched as Caruthers trod heavily toward them, looking ferociously angry. "There you are, you little... Ack!"

Alex did not wait for the curse to come out before he tossed Tulip behind him and in the same motion grabbed the angry lord by the throat. "The lady refused. It is over, Caruthers. Do not make more of it than it is."

"She's a damn tease," he growled when Alex released him a moment later, for he wasn't trying to strangle the lout.

"She is young and innocent, and you ought to have known better than to lure her away from the ballroom."

"You mustn't blame him, Your Grace," Tulip said, but had the good sense to remain behind him as she spoke. "I am the one who suggested it. I give you my sincere apology, Lord Caruthers. It was wrong of me, quite foolish and wrongheaded. I beg your forgiveness for any embarrassment it may have caused you."

"Your turn now, Caruthers," Alex prompted when the oafish lordling said nothing in response. "Accept her apology and move on."

"I'll show you acceptance," he muttered, appearing ready to take a swing at Alex, then remembered he was now a duke, and thought better of challenging him. Not to mention Alex was bigger and stronger, and a more ruthless fighter.

"You'll regret this, Davenport! And so will your pretty pigeon!"

"Not as much as you will if you dare trouble her again tonight," he said while making certain Tulip remained safely behind him.

Obviously frustrated by the impenetrable barrier Alex presented, Caruthers repeated his threat and stormed off toward the ballroom.

Tulip watched with trepidation as her spurned suitor stomped up the terrace steps. "What do you think he means to do?"

Alex did not know, but he doubted the man was going to stay quiet.

He glanced up at the sky that was covered in a layer of clouds, as though the heavens had slammed their door against him, refusing to listen to his silent appeal for this little altercation to resolve without further problem.

But he knew it would not.

An entitled lord like Caruthers was not going to take rejection lightly.

Sighing, he placed Tulip's hand in the crook of his arm. "Come back inside with me."

Tulip held him back a moment. "But is it safe for you? I mean, people might think I went into the garden to kiss *you*. Is it not better for me to walk in alone as you first suggested?"

"No. That was before Caruthers leveled his threat." He was not going to risk that angry lord deciding to stake a claim on her and alleging he – and not Alex – had compromised her.

If any false accusations were to be leveled, better they be leveled against him because he would always protect Tulip.

She held him back again. "But it is certain to cause you more trouble if we walk in together."

He arched an eyebrow. "Why are you so concerned about me, Tulip?"

"Should I not be? Haven't I caused you enough of a headache for one night?"

"Aren't you Farthingales notorious for this very thing?" he

teased. "Do not alarm yourself. This is nothing I cannot handle."

But Alex knew trouble was afoot when he saw Caruthers march out of the ballroom with John Farthingale in tow. John was the Farthingale family patriarch entrusted with Tulip's care, and Caruthers was obviously giving him an earful of lies. On their heels came a small army of ladies and gentlemen, several of whom he recognized as indiscriminate gossips.

The snake had wasted no time in spewing his venom.

"There! I told you! There's your precious ward, Farthingale. See how cozy she looks beside Davenport? Did I not tell you he had ruined her?"

Tulip gasped and curled her hands into fists. "How dare you spout those abominable falsehoods! And to think, I–"

Alex held her back. "Be quiet, Tulip."

"But he is a lout," she said in a whisper, knowing they had to get their stories straight. "I apologized to him and he took it with utter lack of grace. Well, I'll show him."

"No, you'll be quiet and let me handle the matter," he said with quiet authority.

She was only going to dig herself into a deeper hole than she had already dug for herself if she told the onlookers it was Caruthers she had lured into the garden. Did she not realize she might be forced to marry the wretch?

Alex would never allow this to happen. "Tulip, close your eyes."

She widened them. "What? Why?"

"Because I am going to kiss you. Do you or do you not want a first kiss? Would you mind terribly if it was with me?"

"Why would *you* ever want to kiss *me*? And why now when everyone is watching?" She gasped, suddenly realizing the implications.

"Quickly now, yes or no. They are marching down the stairs toward us."

"Are you mad? It will ruin you."

"To be precise, it will ruin *you*. It has already ruined you."

"And you are determined to save me?"

He nodded. "It is me or Caruthers. Do you mind becoming my

duchess?"

"Yours? But–"

"*Choose*, Tulip."

"You."

He drew her into his arms and kissed her with all the heartfelt sincerity he could muster, which was surprisingly a lot because he actually liked her.

In addition to her obvious physical charms, she had shown moral rectitude. What other young lady would have apologized to him and Caruthers? What other young lady would have felt any remorse for her mistake and not blamed anyone but herself for her lapse in judgment?

What other young lady would have sought to protect *him*?

But was it not up to him to protect her?

"Wise choice," he murmured, pressing his lips deeper onto her slightly open mouth that was open because she was still trying to talk sense into him, but he was beyond listening. Nor would anyone else among the approaching throng ever listen to what she had to say in her own defense.

They had seen her standing beside him in the shadows of Lady Fullerton's garden and were already poisoned by Caruthers' lies into believing the worst had taken place.

That beast was determined to destroy the sweet innocent forever.

Alex counted to three before removing his mouth from hers, already regretting the end of their kiss because she had the prettiest lips, soft and plump, and they tasted of mint and champagne.

He stared down at her.

She appeared distraught as she returned his gaze. "Why did you do this? Don't you realize what this means?"

He nodded. "You've just received your first kiss...and your first marriage proposal."

GET ONE NIGHT WITH TULIP NOW!

Interested in learning more about the Farthingale series? You can subscribe to my newsletter and also connect with me on Facebook and other social media. You can find links to do all of this at my website: mearaplatt.com.

If you enjoyed this book, I would really appreciate it if you could post a review on the site where you purchased it. Also feel free to write one on Goodreads or other reader sites that you peruse. Even a few sentences on what you thought about the book would be most helpful! If you do leave a review, send me a message on Facebook because I would love to thank you personally. Please also consider telling your friends about the FARTHINGALE SERIES and recommending it to your book clubs.

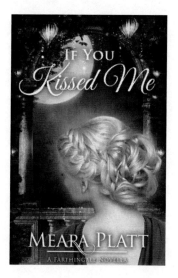

**Sign up for Meara Platt's newsletter
and you'll receive a free, exclusive copy**
of her Farthingale novella,
If You Kissed Me.

Visit her website
to grab your free copy:
mearaplatt.com

ALSO BY MEARA PLATT

The Moonstone Hero
The Moonstone Pirate
Moonstone Landing (novella)
Moonstone Angel (novella)

BOOK OF LOVE SERIES
The Look of Love
The Touch of Love
The Taste of Love
The Song of Love
The Scent of Love
The Kiss of Love
The Chance of Love
The Gift of Love
The Heart of Love
The Hope of Love (novella)
The Promise of Love
The Wonder of Love
The Journey of Love
The Treasure of Love
The Dance of Love
The Miracle of Love
The Dream of Love (novella)
The Remembrance of Love (novella)

BOOK OF LOVE CONNECTED NOVELLAS
All I Want For Christmas (novella)
Tempting Taffy (novella)

DARK GARDENS SERIES
Garden of Shadows
Garden of Light
Garden of Dragons

Garden of Destiny
Garden of Angels

THE BRAYDENS
A Match Made In Duty
Earl of Westcliff
Fortune's Dragon
Earl of Kinross
Pearls of Fire
Aislin
Genalynn
A Rescued Heart
Earl of Alnwick

THE LYON'S DEN SERIES
The Lyon's Surprise
Kiss of the Lyon
Lyon in the Rough

DeWOLFE PACK ANGELS SERIES
Nobody's Angel
Kiss An Angel
Bhrodi's Angel

ABOUT THE AUTHOR

Meara Platt is an award winning, USA TODAY bestselling author and an Amazon UK All-Star. Her favorite place in all the world is England's Lake District, which may not come as a surprise since many of her stories are set in that idyllic landscape, including her epic fantasy romance (romantasy) Dark Gardens series. Learn more about the Dark Gardens and Meara's lighthearted and humorous Regency romances in her Farthingale series, Book of Love series, and Silver Dukes series, or her warmhearted Regency romances in her Moonstone Landing series or Braydens series by visiting her website at www.mearaplatt.com.

Made in United States
Cleveland, OH
23 March 2025

15462155R00173